THE STEEP
APPROACH TO
GARBADALE

IAIN
BANKS

THE STEEP
APPROACH TO
GARBADALE

MACADAM CAGE

MacAdam/Cage
155 Sansome Street, Suite 550
San Francisco, CA 94104
www.MacAdamCage.com

First published in Great Britain in 2007 by Little, Brown

Library of Congress Cataloging-in-Publication Data

Banks, Iain, 1954-
   The steep approach to Garbadale / Iain Banks.
      p. cm.
   ISBN 978-1-59692-271-6
   1. Children of the rich—Fiction. 2. Family—Fiction. 3. Family
secrets—Fiction. 4. Scotland—Fiction. 5. Domestic fiction. I. Title.
PR6052.A485S74 2007
823'.914—dc22
                                                                    2007019569
Paperback edition: October 2005
ISBN 978-1-59692-303-4

Printed in the United States of America.

10 9 8 7 6 5 4 3 2 1

FOR LOST LOVES

WITH THANKS TO:
YVONNE FRATER, PATRICK GREENOUGH, ADÈLE HARTLEY,
LAURA HEHIR, SIMON KAVANAGH, GARY LLOYD,
EILIDH AND LES MCFARLANE, AND CAROLE SIMPSON

1

His name is Fielding Wopuld. Of those Wopulds, the games family, the people with their name plastered all over the board of *Empire!* (still the UK's best-selling board game, by some margin). They're behind a heap of other stuff, too, of course, but that's the famous one, the one people tend to have heard of, whether it's the original snail-play version featuring cardboard, paper and plastic or its slick, attractively rendered and award-winning electronic successor, currently riding high in the computer games charts.

Vice-President, Sales. That's his position in the family firm: in charge of a multimillion-pound budget promoting their various wares around the world, persuading wholesalers, online concerns, retail chains and big store groups to stock and sell their product. Doing well at it, too – hefty bonus last year.

Henry Wopuld, the guy who first dreamed up *Empire!* back in Victorian times, was his great-grandfather, so for whatever it's worth he's kind of direct in line. Fielding is still just thirty and keeps himself in pretty good shape with a variety of sports. He drives a Mercedes S-class, has a whole bunch of friends, a very beautiful and sexy partner and generally lives the kind of successful life most people can only dream of.

All of which does kind of raise the question in Fielding's mind,

What the hell am I doing here? as he drives into this scummy-looking housing estate in Perth. This is Perth, Scotland, we're talking about here, not Perth, Australia. Perth, Australia, is a beautiful, bright, sunny kind of place sprawling between the desert and the ocean – lots of surf and sizzling barbies and gleaming bronzed bodies. Perth, Scotland, is smaller and a lot less high-rise, sitting surrounded by low hills, forests and farmland. It boasts a variety of nice buildings and some very attractive detached properties facing the river, but not a lot of bronzed bodies that Fielding can see. He knows Scotland a bit – various family members have chosen to reside here for reasons best known to themselves and the Wopulds still, for now, have one of those vast huntin', shootin' 'n' fishin' estates in the far north of the place – but this is the first time he's been to Perth, he's fairly sure. The Fair City they call it, apparently. And it's okay, he supposes, if you like old stuff and history and that sort of thing. He always had the impression that it was pretty posh and full of people wearing corduroy, tweeds and Barbour jackets, but this housing scheme on the outskirts looks like Chav City, Ned Central – a sink estate at the bottom of the U-bend.

He's driving down Skye Crescent – the whole scheme is nothing but islands – between long blocks of three- and four-storey flats covered in patchy pebble-dash spotted with poor-quality graffiti. The tiny gardens at the front of the flats are just plain unkempt. He's used to kempt.

There's a lot of litter about, some of it flying about in the breeze coming funnelling down the street from the bright September clouds. He hasn't seen any bottles of Buckfast lying in the gutters – or any people lying in the gutter for that matter – and the kerb is lined with cars rather than wrecks, but – well – still.

Okay, some shops here, doors open but windows covered in metal grilles even now, during the day. Couple of thin, pimply youths standing outside something called Costcutter, sharing a bottle and watching the car slide past. *Yeah, it's an S-class 500 AMG, boyz. Look upon it and weep. See what you might get if you do your homework*

2

and work hard. Whatever. Just keep your fucking hands off it. The delicate art of not making eye-contact while looking hard and supremely confident.

Uh-uh: there's a bottle, there in the gutter. Just a little green beer bottle. Beck's, possibly. Not so bad.

He finds number 58 by a process of elimination. The sat-nav gave up at the start of the street and there's no sign where the number should be, by the security grille at the side of the door; however, the entrance before was number 56 and the one after is 60, so he's pretty confident. Check for broken glass, park carefully, nice and tight by the kerb. Swing the wing mirrors up into their parked position, just to be on the safe side. Deep breath and prepare to go out into the mild air. First, though, into the glove box and administer a few quick squirts of Versace, up each sleeve and on the back of the neck. At least something around here isn't going to smell of shit.

He stands on the uneven pavement, watching from the corner of one eye as the car alarm flashes the indicators once. Smells like somebody is cooking tinned Irish stew for a late breakfast or an early lunch. What does he feel like? He feels like a shark out of water, that's what he feels like.

He knows this is how a lot of people live, and he's sure they're not all druggies and nutters, but, Christ, what a soul-destroying spot, what a place to basically get the hell out of as soon as you can.

Shit, I forgot the fucking briefcase. Now he was going to look like a dickhead, getting out of the car, locking it and standing here, then having to unlock it again almost immediately and getting the case out. Maybe he should leave the briefcase in the car. There's only mail in it, anyway. A bunch of letters and bills and junk his dingbat cousin probably never wanted in the first place. Mail your man abandoned months ago, on another job, in another country.

Nope, can't leave the case in the car because it's sitting on the back seat, in full view. A Zero Halliburton aluminium case like you see in the movies, which in this kind of neighbourhood – well, in almost any kind of neighbourhood, to be fair – just shouts *Steal me!*

3

at a zillion fucking decibels. He can't see anybody watching him, but it feels like the whole street is. He unalarms and reopens the car, takes the case, re-alarms casually (but still makes sure the hazards flash) and strides purposefully up the short path to the security door, kicking the gaudy wreck of a broken toy gun out of the way as he goes.

The block's glass-and-metal door looks like people have thrown up on it and then tried to rinse off the mess by pissing all over it. This obviously didn't work because apparently then they tried setting it on fire. The button by the scarred plastic name-plate for flat E just sort of sinks into its housing. No buzzer sounds anywhere.

He pushes on the door and it scrapes open. Inside there are shiny concrete steps and a suspicious smell of disinfectant.

Well, Fielding, he tells himself, *the only way is up.*

'Hey, Al? Al? Al, ya dozy cunt, fucken wake up. Al! Come on, big man. Wakey fucken wakey.'

He opened his eyes one at a time, to allow for anything unforeseen. The world converged into focus, as though the effort was all its. The thin, pointy, slightly chipped-looking face of Mr Daniel Gow – Tango all the rest of the time when he wasn't wearing a suit and trying to look sincere while somebody more privileged pleaded his case – looked down at him.

'Tango,' he said, croaking a little. He rubbed his face, then shifted in the sleeping bag, feeling its nylon covering snag on some carpet tacks left exposed on the bare wooden boards of the small room. He looked up at the light coming through the thin sheet nailed over the window. 'What, late afternoon already?'

'No even eleven yet, pal. But ye've got a visitor.'

He blinked, rubbed his eyes and coughed, twisting and sitting up, his back against the bare, magnolia-painted wall. He scratched his chin through a fairly full brown beard. 'Official kind of visitor?' he asked. His voice was slightly slurred. 'Kind of visitor a person might associate with manila envelopes and threats regarding non-compliance, or

4

failure to attend an appointment arranged by an institution of a govern-mental nature?'

'Naw, dude. Posh. A suit.'

'A suit?'

'Aye, a suit. He's no wearin a suit, but he's a suit all the same. Teeth like Tom fucken Cruise. Smells like a expensive hoorhoose; the dugs took one sniff of his shoes and started sneezin. They've retreated to the kitchen. Surprised ye hauvnae caught a whiff of him already. Currently standin near the windae in the livin room, watchin nae bugger fucks with his motor. Briefcase like the kind that always has drugs or bings a money in it, in the fillums. Says he's yer cousin.'

'Ah.' Alban McGill rubbed his face, smoothed his beard down as best he could and scratched fingers through thick, curly, light brown hair. His face and lower arms were the kind of deep tanned red that fair-skinned people get when they spend a lot of time outside, though his upper arms and torso, which were thickly muscled, remained pale. Part of the small finger on his left hand was missing. 'A cousin,' he said, sighing. He blinked at Tango, who was squatting, watching him. 'Give a name?'

Tango's pinched-looking face, stalagtital beneath the grey dome of a shaved head, wrinkled. 'Fielding?' he offered.

'Fielding?' Alban said, obviously surprised. Then his brows furrowed. 'Oh, yeah; the teeth like Tom Cruise. Okay, fair enough.' He scratched his chest, looked round the room at his boots, back-pack and clothes. There was an open bottle of red wine on the floor near his watch, the top lying nearby. Further along the skirting board lay a shadeless bedside lamp. 'Fielding Wubble-you,' he pronounced. He reached out towards the wine bottle, then seemed to think the better of it, frowning.

'Cup a tea?' Tango suggested.

Alban nodded. 'Cup of tea,' he agreed.

My names Tango, this is my house. Technically it belongs to the council, but you know what I mean. Al is my guest, welcome to crash here any time. Met the big guy in a pub year or two ago with the guy's he was working with. Foresters, chopping down trees and the like. Been doing just that somewhere nearby, living in caravans in the mighty forests of Perth and Kinross. Serious drinker's. The ones he was with, anyway. Few games of pool, few rounds of drink. Him and one of his pals came back to mine for a couple of cans and a smoke. Also, Al was getting on very well with a girl we were with. Sheen, I think it was. Maybe Shone. Either way. Think him and the lassie went off together late on.

No, wait, Sheen/Shone (delete as applicable) went off with Big Al's tree-chopping compadre, not him. Al seemed keenish for a bit but then got all that dead quiet way he gets when he gets stoned and drunk and doesn't say much and all he seems to want to do is drink some more and stare into corners or at blank walls at maybe something nobody else can see, so Shone/Sheen turned her attentions to his mate. Fair play to the girl. Must have thought she was doing all right with Al – he's not bad looking and he's nice and got a soft, well-speaking kind of voice – and I think Al's pal said Was it OK? even if it was said just with the eyebrows and a sideways nod kind a thing, and Al just grinned and nodded, so, like I say, fair do's.

Well, I think so. Truth be told I was a bit out of it by then.

Anyway, he's been back a few times since and he's spent the last couple of weeks here at the abode of yours truly since he got invalided out of the forestry service for growing insensitivity. Which sounds a bit daft I know but apparently is true. He looks about my age (I was born in November 1975, so I've got the Three-Oh coming up in a couple of months – fucking hell!!!) but he's actually five years older than me. Probably look even younger if he ditched the face-fungus.

Anyways, here we go with the making of the tea. While I'm doing this, tripping over the dogs and checking in the fridge on the milk situation the door goes again and I let in Sunny and Di and they go in and nod to the Fielding guy – who is still standing at the window so he can see his car – and they sit on the couch and spark up a couple of Camel Lights, On Which Duty Has Not Been Paid. Their both trying to give up so only smoking Lights and so find they have to smoke more for to get the full effect. They'd both be about ten years the younger of me. Sunny's full name is Sunny D and his even fuller name is Sunny Daniel, to distinguish him from me, as I'm a Daniel too, even though people call me Tango and that's more my real name than Daniel, same way that for at least the last few years now Sunny's name has been just that, not Daniel. Meanwhile Al is voiding noisily in the toilet. Sorry, but it's true.

'Dinnae open the window, pal, you'll let the budgies out!'

'Sorry,' the Fielding character says, not sounding it, and closes the window again. He glances down at Sunny and Di, still drawing hard on their Camel Lights. Must be one of those real anti-smoking types, I suppose. I do worry about the health of the livestock sometimes. Have I stunted the growth of the hounds by keeping them in a flat where people smoke all the time? Are the budgies going to be more prone for respiratorial diseases in later life? Who can say?

Anyway, it's not cold out and you'd have to say the man does have a point. I make sure the budgies are in their cage, close it and tell the Fielding guy he can open the window again, which he duly does, giving a tight wee smile. Anyway, the smell of his aftershave is honking the place out worse than the fags.

And so to tea. Fielding inspects the insides of his mug quite carefully before accepting any, the cheeky bastard. He's still up at the window, keeping his clear view. The shiny metal briefcase is at his feet. He's wearing jeans with a crease in them, a soft-looking white shirt and an expensive jacket of mustardy leather that looks softer than the shirt. Them shoes with hundreds of holes; brogues? Anyway they're brown. Sunny and Di have switched the TV on and are watching a shopping channel, taking the pish out of the presenters and whatever it is this hour that you canny buy at the shops.

Al comes through – jeans and T-shirt as per usual – and nods at

Fielding and says hello and sits down in the second best easy chair, but no friendly or family hugs or even the shaking of the hands for these two. I'm looking for a resemblance but answer comes their none.

'Sorry,' Al says to Fielding, looking round us all. 'You been introduced?'

'Sunny and Di, this is Fielding,' says I. 'I'm Tango,' I tell him, as I think we might have missed on that nicety. I nod at the good chair. 'Take a seat, pal, make yourself at home.'

'I'm fine,' Fielding says, glancing out the window. He makes a stretching motion. 'Been driving all morning. Good to stand up for a while.'

'Aye, sure,' I say, taking the good seat myself.

'So, what brings you to the Fair City, Fielding?' Al asks. He sounds tired. We've both, over the last fortnight or so, been skelping the arse off the drink and a wide selection of herbal and pharma logical merchandise, all provided by the generosity of Al's last pay packet.

'Well, cuz, I need to talk to you,' the man in the sharp creased jeans says.

Al just smiles, stretches and says, 'Talk away.'

'Well, you know, it's family business.' Your man Fielding looks round at the rest of us, granting us what you might call a sympathetic smile. 'I wouldn't want to bore, ah, your friends with it, you know?'

'I bet they wouldn't be bored,' Al says.

'All the same.' The smiling of the Fielding is a tight affair indeed at this point. 'Plus, I brought some mail,' he says, looking down at the briefcase.

'Fucken wicked case, man, by the way,' Sunny says, seeing the offending article for the first time. He's got one of those high, nasally weejie voices. Di widens her eyes at him and elbows him in the ribs for some reason and they get into a elbowing competition.

'Well, let's have a look at it,' Al says. He starts clearing a space on the coffee table in front of him, redistributing empty cans, ditto bottles, full ashtrays and various remotes onto the mantelpiece and the arms of other seats and the like.

Fielding appears unhappy, looking round us all again. 'Look, ah, man, I'm not sure this is the right place . . .'

'Na, come on,' Al says. 'Here's fine.'

Fielding does not look happy at this idea, but sighs and comes over with the case. Meanwhile I'm helping with the table-clearing, getting a beamer (that means going red in the face, by the by, not anything else) because I hadn't got out of bed in time to do the clearing up in here. Canny get the staff these days, know what I mean? The briefcase is placed on the – being honest – fairly sticky table. The case looks like it's been worn down from a solid ingot of silver at the bottom of a stream for a few hundred years, all sort of worn-polished and curvy-edged and round-cornered. Al is presented with his mail – a big slidey pile of your usual assorted nonsense – and the briefcase is snapped shut again. Fielding looks like he wishes he could handcuff himself to it. Obviously hasn't spotted the stickiness yet. 'Anyway,' he says to Al, 'we still need to talk.'

Al just grunts and starts sorting through the envelope's, throwing most of them unopened onto the tiles of the fireplace, skidding into the base of the electric fire. Fielding stands looking over Al's shoulder for a bit until Al actually opens one of the smaller envelopes and looks up and round at his cousin, who takes his briefcase and goes to stand back at the opened window, checking outside on his wheels again.

'Hey, Tango,' Sunny says, staring at one thumb. 'Where'd you think'd be the worst place to get a paper cut?' Him and Di have desisted from the elbowing of each other and are sitting rubbing their ribs.

'No idea,' I tell him. 'Your eye, maybe?'

'Naw, man,' Sunny says. 'I reckon your cock. Right on the top, along the slit, man; that's goanae hurt like fuck, so it is. Ow! Ya –!'

It's back to the mutual elbowing session again for the young happy couple on the couch. Tea is spilled. Your man Fielding stares out the window with patented disgust.

Al ignores all this and continues through the rest of his mail, discarding most of it, then finally opens one letter, looks at it for a moment and stuffs it into a back pocket in his jeans.

Meanwhile Sunny has jumped away from Di – fare enough, it does look like she has the sharper elbows – and squatted down at the fireplace, looking at Al's mail discard pile. '"Alban",' he says, picking up one junk-mail shrink-wrapped envelope, covered with official-looking stamps and personalised just for Alban like only a big company on the make can. 'Is that really your real first name, big man? Fucken weird yin that.' He grins an already gappy grin at big Al and holds up a bunch of the junk mail. 'Ye finished wi all this, aye, Al?'

'Yeah, take it,' Al says, standing. He looks at his cousin.

There's an alarm going off in the street but it's obviously not coming from Fielding's car because he looks relaxed about it. He puts his mug down on the window ledge. 'Can we talk now?' he asks.

Al sighs. 'Aye, come in to my office.'

Finally he gets the guy out of that scuzzy, smoke-filled living room, down a dim, narrow hallway made even narrower by what looks like a roll of carpet underlay lying on the floor and piles of card-board boxes. The carpet feels sticky, like something from a cheap nightclub. Opposite the kitchen, where a couple of thin, nervous mongrels cower, there's a fist-sized hole in the plasterboard at shoulder height. They enter a small, bare room with a piece of thin material nailed over the window. Al hooks the makeshift curtain up over another nail to let in more light.

No carpets in here and no proper flooring either, not even lamin-ate – just bare floorboards, unpolished and unfinished. Each wall is a different colour. One has what looks like Power Rangers wall-paper, half ripped off, exposing plasterboard. Another has been partially repainted, from green to black. Another looks like it's covered with silver foil, while the last wall is sort of off-white, heavily scuffed. There's a sleeping bag by the wall, a big camouflaged backpack leaning nearby spilling clothes and stuff on to the floor, and a small chrome and fabric seat that looks like it was designed in the Seventies. Al takes some clothes off the seat, dropping them on the floor.

The soft bits of the fragile-looking little chair are covered in brown corduroy. Stained brown corduroy. Stained brown corduroy with little bits of grey stuffing showing round the edges where the stitching has given way.

Al says, 'Take a seat, cuz.'

'Thanks.' Fielding sits down gingerly. The room smells of drink and stale sweat with a hint of what might be air freshener or maybe male grooming product from the more budget end of the range. There's an open screwtop bottle of red wine in one corner. No shade or bulb attached to the ceiling fixture. A dark stain covers a quarter of the ceiling. One shadeless lamp near the wine bottle. Al bunches up the sleeping bag to make a seat, then sits leaning back against the wall and waves one hand.

'So, Fielding, how are you?'

Al looks ruddy, fit – *better quads and abs than me, the fuck*, Fielding thinks – but his hair is a mess, the beard looks like you could hide a flock of starlings in it and there's a sort of crumpled set to his face and a beaten look around his eyes Fielding doesn't remember from before. At least, not as bad. 'I'm fine,' Fielding says, then shakes his head. 'No, I'm not fine. I'm not happy in this situation.'

'What situation?'

'This situation. Look, d'you mind if I close the door?'

Alban shrugs. Fielding closes the door then goes to sit down, then doesn't. He looks about the place, waving. 'I'm not happy here. In this place.' He looks around the room again, wanting to shiver, then shakes his head. 'Alban, tell me this isn't where you live. This isn't your home.'

11

Alban shrugs again. 'I'm just staying here for now,' he says casually. 'It's a roof over my head.'

Fielding looks up at the stained ceiling. On closer inspection, the stained bit looks slightly bulged. 'Yeah, right.'

Another shrug. 'I guess technically I'm of no fixed abode.'

'Wow. What age are you again?'

Alban grins. 'Over twenty-one. You?'

Fielding looks round the place again. 'I don't know, Al, I mean, just look at this. What have you done with—?'

Al gestures at the corduroy seat. 'Fielding, will you sit down? You're making the place look untidy.'

This is one of Gran's phrases. Fielding guesses Alban means it ironically, an attempt at humour.

Fielding says, 'Let me take you for lunch. Please.'

There's some nonsense about taking the dogs for a walk but there's no way Fielding's letting these mangy mutts in the Merc so he pleads an allergy. Then the chav couple with the tobacco habit ask if they'll be going anywhere near the 'middle o' toon'.

'Why?' Fielding asks, in case they're going to ask him to score them some drugs or – worse – bring them back a McDonalds.

'Wur goin' that wiy, boss, ye know?' the male one says. 'Save us the bus fare.'

Fielding's about to piss all over this idea too but then somehow just looking at their pathetic, pasty, thin, proto-junky faces makes him think, *Oh fuck, I'm bigger than this*. The car'll smell of cigarettes for a day or so just from their clothes even if he doesn't let them smoke in it, but what the hell.

Al throws on a grubby-looking green hiking jacket that probably cost a lot when it was new. The Tango guy announces he's got cleaning and stuff to do and waves them off down the echoing, disinfected stairwell. The car is unmolested, the briefcase goes in the boot and Al navigates them out of the scheme towards the centre of the little city. Di and Sunny amuse themselves playing with the buttons that control the rear sun-blinds. Fielding drops them near the Job Centre.

Al suggests he and Fielding take a walk as it's too early for lunch and so they drive on a little further and park by the river in the shadow of some grand Victorian buildings, then walk along the bank, heading downstream with the swirling brown flow of the waters. It's a mild, half-sunlit day beneath a sky of small white clouds that makes Fielding think of the title sequence of *The Simpsons*. The air smells good here by the water, though there's traffic buzzing on both sides of the river.

'Kind of you to pick up the mail, Fielding,' Al says.

'Well, I was in the area.'

Alban looks at the other man, grinning. 'What, in Llangurig?' He sounds amused.

Llangurig is a small town in mid-Wales, near the Hafren Forest, where Al was working for the first half of the year. 'Well, not so much passing through or anything,' Fielding admits, 'as scouring the length and the breadth of the land for your absconded arse.'

Alban makes a noise that might be a cough or a laugh or something in between. 'You were looking for me?'

'Yes. And now I've found you.'

'Kind of guessing you weren't doing all this just to facilitate my re-subscription to *Foresters' Anonymous* and *What Chainsaw?*' Al says.

Fielding looks at him and Alban catches the glance, holds up his left hand, the one with only half a little finger. 'Kidding. Made them up.'

Another attempt at humour, then. Fielding had taken a look at the envelopes his cousin's mail had arrived in and there had been nothing obviously from any such publications, but you never know.

'Well, exactly,' Fielding says. 'As I said, I was looking for you. And you are *not* an easy man to find.'

'Amn't I? Sorry.'

He doesn't sound it. Fielding turns to him, takes one sleeve of

13

his jacket, making him turn towards him, so they stop walking. 'Al, why are you like this?'

Fielding wasn't losing his temper or anything at this point – he'd decided from the start to be calm and reasonable with the guy – but he really would just like to know why Al's gone like this, become like this, even though he realises Alban probably wouldn't tell him even if he could, even if he knew himself. Maybe they're just too far apart; too different these days, family or not.

'Like what?' Alban looks genuinely puzzled.

'Like a man who's trying to lose himself, like a man who's trying to abandon his family or get them to abandon him; I don't know. Why? I mean, your own parents don't know whether you're alive or dead.'

'I sent them a Christmas card,' Alban says. Plaintively, Fielding thought.

'That was – what? Eight? Nine months ago? And they only knew you were still in the country because it had a UK stamp on it. Nobody seems to know where you are. Jesus, Alban, I was on the brink of hiring a fucking private detective to find you when I heard you'd been working in Wales. Even then it was sheer luck I bumped into one of your forester chums who knew you'd started a job round here and *eventually* remembered the firm's name after a curry and about eighteen pints of Stella.'

'Sounds like Hughey,' Al says, and starts walking again. To Fielding, it looks more like wandering off. He falls into step with his cousin, frustrated. 'How was Hughey?' Alban asks.

'Al, I'm sorry, I don't care about Hughey. Why don't you ask how any of the family are?'

'Hughey's a pal. Seriously, how was he?'

'Drunk and well fed when I last saw him. Why do you care more about people like him than about your family?'

'You choose your friends, Fielding,' Alban says, sounding tired.

'Al, Jesus, man, what *is* this?' Fielding asks, controlling his voice. 'What the hell has the family ever *done* to you to make you like this? I know you've had some tough breaks, but we gave you—'

Alban stops and spins round, and just for a second Fielding thinks he's going to shout or at least poke a finger in his chest or maybe just point at him or, if nothing else, express himself with a bit of passion. But the look on his face fades almost before Fielding can be sure it's really there and he shrugs and turns and starts walking again, along the broad sand-coloured pavement, between the twin streams of water and cars. 'It's all a long story. A long, boring story. Mostly I just got fed up with . . .' His voice trails off. One more shrug.

After a dozen or so steps, he asks, 'How's Lydcombe? You been there recently? They keeping the gardens tidy?'

'I was there last month. It all looked fine to me.' Fielding leaves a gap. 'Aunt Clara, everybody else, they're all well. Same with my parents. Thanks for asking.'

Alban just grunts.

Forget the draughty castle and thousands of windswept barren acres the family owns – for now, anyway – in the Highlands. Lydcombe, in Somerset, was the first serious out-of-town property purchase Great-Grandfather Henry made when he started to rake in his millions. Quite a beautiful setting, on the north edge of Exmoor National Park. Bit quiet, and a long way from London, but a good place for family holidays unless you want guaranteed sun. Only forty acres or so, but it's lush and green and sunny and the grounds go rolling down to the coast of the Bristol Channel.

Fielding was brought up in a few different places round the world, but as a kid he probably spent more holiday time there than anywhere else, in the big, rambling house overlooking the terraced lawns, close by the walled garden and the ruins of the old abbey. The main building is listed and, of course, it's all part of the National Park so there are various planning restrictions if you wanted to do anything radical with the place.

Alban knows Lydcombe better than Fielding. It was his home for most of his childhood, then he spent a couple of summers there as a teenager, discovering what green fingers he had. And thereby, of course, hangs the tale.

Fielding's moby chooses to go at this point, inside his jacket pocket. He's left it on vibrate since he made the turn into Skye Crescent and probably missed a couple of calls – otherwise it's been amazingly quiet. Fielding gets a weird, tight, unpleasant feeling in his guts when he's out of touch for this long, like there's vitally important stuff happening that he really needs to know about and there are people on the other end desperate for him to answer . . . Though of course he knows it'll probably be nothing, or more likely just somebody asking a question they wouldn't need to ask if they were seriously intent on actually doing their job rather than always passing the most trivial problem upstairs to cover their miserable asses. Even so – though his hand is itching to grab the fucker – he's not going to answer. He ignores the vibrations, keeps up with Alban.

This is all so annoying! He's a good manager, a good person-manager and he has certificates to prove it, not to mention the respect of his peers and subordinates. He's good at selling, good at persuading. Why is he finding it so hard to get through to this one guy he should feel closer to than most?

'Look, Alban, okay, I can understand . . . Actually, no, I can't understand' (about tearing his hair out here!) 'but I guess I just have to accept you feel the way you do about the family and the firm, but that's part of what I need to talk to you about.'

Alban turns to him. 'Maybe we should get a drink.'

'Whatever. Yeah, okay.'

They find a bar nearby, the lounge of a small hotel in the compressed-feeling town centre. Alban insists on paying and has a pint of IPA while Fielding takes a mineral water. It's still before noon and the place is quiet and dim and smells of last night's cigarettes and spilled beer.

Alban swallows about a quarter of the pint in one series of gulps, then smacks his lips. 'So why are you looking for me, Fielding?' he asks. 'Specifically.'

'Well, frankly, I was asked to.'

'Who by?'

'Gran.'

'Good God, is the old harridan alive and compos mentis?' Al shakes his head and takes another drink.

'Al, please.'

Gran – Grandmother Winifred – is the Wopuld materfamilias, the head of the family and one of its eldest surviving members. She's also, in terms of voting rights, the most powerful person on the board of the family firm. She's not perfect – at nearly eighty, who is? – and she can be prickly and fussy and sometimes even wrong, but she's seen the firm and the family through tough times and good times and a lot of people still have a real soft spot for her, Fielding included. And she is very old and of course everybody feels protective of her, no matter how spirited and feisty she might seem, so it's not good to hear somebody in the family dissing her. Fielding tries to let the hurt he feels show on his face.

Al frowns at him. 'You look like you're straining.'

'What?'

'How'd you find out I was in Wales anyway?'

'I talked to your girl . . . your friend, whatever you . . . you know: in Glasgow. What's her—?'

'VG?'

'VD?'

'Vee, Gee. Those are her initials.'

'Right. What was her name again? Foreign, wasn't it?'

'Verushka Graef.'

'Ver-oosh-ka. That's the one.'

'Yes, I know.'

This, frankly, does give Fielding pause for thought. 'You and her really an item?' he asks.

Alban grins without any apparent mirth. 'Fielding, I can see you looking at me with new respect and a degree of incredulity, but no, we're not an "item". We meet up now and again. Occasional lovers. Don't imagine I'm her only one.'

'Oh, I see. Anyway, she told me the last definite address she had for you was in this Llangurig place.'

'That was good of her.'

'Took some persuading.'

'She knows I like my privacy.'

'Well, hurrah for her. Actually, she took some finding herself, too. Had to go through the university. Are you part of some sort of weird cult or something? I mean, renouncing the use of mobile phones. What the hell is that all about?'

'I don't like being at other people's beck and call, Fielding. VG . . . She just doesn't like being disturbed.'

'She for real?'

'What do you mean, like not a robot or something?'

'Fuck off, you know what I mean. Is she really this shit-hot mathematician?'

Al shrugs. 'Think so. Glasgow University Mathematics Department seems to think so. Not to mention what you could justifiably call a plethora of peer-reviewed journals.'

'So, really a professor?'

'Yeah, really. Not that I actually saw her being invested or whatever it is they do when they make you one.'

'She doesn't look like a professor.'

'That'd be the spiky blonde hair.'

'It was black.'

'Again?' Al shakes his head, drinks. 'She's a natural blonde.'

'Is she mad?'

'She's a little eccentric. Once dyed it mousy brown, just to see.'

'Just to see what?'

'I don't know.'

'Right. Anyway.'

'Anyway.'

'So, Gran asked me to find you and talk to you. There's stuff happening. Stuff you need to know. Stuff you might even want to be involved in.' Fielding's mobile is vibrating again but he's ignoring it.

18

'Really?' Al sounds sceptical.

'Yes, and I think you'll agree when you hear it . . .'

'This going to take long?'

'A few minutes.'

'Hold on then. Better take a leak.' Alban stands up, draining his pint as he does so. He starts towards the exit, then pauses, turning back. 'You could get another round in.'

'Okay, okay.'

Alban made his way to the Gents in the Salutation Hotel, sighing and smoothing his hand over his beard. He smiled at a passing waitress, let himself into the toilets, stood looking at the tall porcelain urinals for a moment and then went into a cubicle, closing the door behind him. He didn't need to sit down; he didn't really need to visit the toilet at all. He pulled the letter from his pocket and sat on the seat cover. He read both sides of the closely-written single sheet, squinting in the dim light. He read the letter once straight through, then re-read a couple of sections. After that he just sat there for a while, staring at nothing.

A little later he shook his head as though pulling himself out of a daydream, stood, put the letter back in his pocket and left. For some reason he flushed the toilet as he did so, and then washed his hands.

Fielding, just putting his mobile away, looked relieved and then slightly annoyed when he saw his cousin again, as though he'd been worrying that Al had run off. At least the pint of IPA was sitting there.

'Right, there's a few things,' Fielding tells Al once he's started on his new pint. 'First of all, Gran is thinking of – well, she's decided, it's happening – to sell Garbadale.'

'Uh-huh?'

'Yes. Well, I mean, come on. She's eighty soon and she had a couple of health scares over the last year or so and some of us have been trying to persuade her to move to somewhere near a decent hospital for a while now. It can take a couple of hours to get to, umm, the Inverness hospital—'

'Raigmore.'

'Yeah, that's the place. Anyway, that's far too long, and that's just a one-way trip, somebody driving her there. An ambulance would take twice as long. I mean, they have an air ambulance, but you can't rely on that always being available. I think that last heart thing she had—'

'She had a heart thing?' Al sounds almost interested.

'Fibrillations or something. She kind of fainted. Of course, that was back in March, so you won't have heard, will you?'

'That's right. Was it serious?'

'Serious enough. Anyway, that seems to have convinced her to move out of the middle of nowhere at last. She's only talking about Inverness or maybe Edinburgh or Glasgow, but I think we can convince her she'd be better off in London and near Harley Street.'

'But they haven't, say, given her only a couple of months to live or anything?'

'Oh, God, no. Nothing that bad. She'll live to be a hundred if she takes care of herself, or lets us take care of her.'

'And you really don't find that depressing?' Al asks, looking at his cousin quizzically.

'Al, stop it.' Fielding sips his mineral water. 'Anyway, there's more. The thing – oh, yes. You're invited to Gran's eightieth birthday party next month.' He digs in his other jacket pocket and produces the envelope with Al's invitation in it and hands it to him. Al looks at it like it contains a bomb, or possibly anthrax. He puts it unopened in his grubby hiking jacket. 'The place is going on the market this week,' Fielding tells him, 'though there's no viewing for a couple of days either side of the party. But it will be the last chance for the family to see the place. Well, you know. To stay there.'

'Think I'll pass.' Al drinks. 'Thanks all the same. Pass on my apologies if I forget to RSVP.'

'There's more.'

'Is there now?'

'This is what it's really all about. I didn't track you down over half the UK just to give you a party invite. The point is, the party's more than just a party. I mean, there'll be the party, but there's other stuff over those few days too. That's what I really need to talk to you about.'

'Will it take long? Should I nip to the loo again?'

'Please don't.'

'Just kidding.'

'It's about Spraint Corp.'

'Oh, really? What joy.'

'Basically, they want to buy us out.'

Al's glass is halfway to his lips, but there it stops, for quite a few seconds. At last – some sort of reaction. He looks surprised. Taken aback, Fielding would even go as far as to say. 'Do they now?' Alban says, and drinks, but it's with a forced casualness. *Now* they were getting somewhere.

'One hundred per cent,' Fielding tells him. 'Total buy-out. One or two of us might get to stay on as consultants. Maybe. It'd be for shares and cash. Mostly shares. They'd keep the name, of course. That's a large part of the value.'

Al just sits there nodding for a while, arms folded. He seems to be staring at his boots; chunky yellow things with lots of laces.

He looks at Fielding and shrugs. 'Is that it?'

'Well, that's where the party comes in. The family, the firm, will be holding an Extraordinary General Meeting the day before Gran's birthday, at the castle, at Garbadale House.' Fielding sips his water. 'Pretty much everybody will be there.'

'Mm-hmm,' Al says, and nods. He's still staring at his footwear. His eyes are open quite wide.

'So you might like to be there for that, too, obviously,' Fielding tells him. 'The EGM is on Saturday, October the eighth. Gran's birthday party is the day after.'

'Okay.'

'Like I say, more or less the whole family should be there. They're coming in from all over the world.' Fielding gives it a moment. 'Be a pity if you weren't there, Al. Really.'

Alban nods, looks at his pint, then nearly drains it and stands up, pulling on his jacket. 'You fit?' he asks, nodding at Fielding's mineral water. 'Continue our walk?'

'Sure.'

They walk down the river embankment, to where the traffic on that side disappears and a railway bridge crosses the river. There's a foot-bridge tacked on to the side of the rail bridge; they take the steps up to it and on.

'So, what do you think?' Fielding asks Alban.

'About the party? The Extraordinary Meeting? The takeover? Our one big happy family getting together for a knees-up?'

'All of the above.'

Al strides purposefully on for a bit, then slows and stops, near the centre of the footbridge. He turns and looks down at the water rushing gently past beneath. It's clear brown like smoked glass and sparkles fitfully under the sun. Fielding leans on the parapet beside him.

Alban shakes his head slowly, light brown curls blowing in the breeze. 'I don't know that I want to be part of any of it. Sorry.'

Fielding feels like saying something and normally would, but sometimes you just have to let people fill their own silences.

Al takes a series of deep breaths and looks up to where the river disappears upstream. 'Once upon a time I felt . . . constrained, all tied up by this family. I had this idiot idea that if I could get away for a year and a day, I'd be free of it somehow, or at least able to accept it on . . . On mutually agreeable terms.' He glances at his cousin. 'You know? Like in the days of serfdom? If a serf could

22

escape his master for a year and a day without being caught, he was a free man.'

'I've heard something like that.'

He laughs. 'Stupid idea, anyway. Glorified gap year. But anyway. After I came back, after I took up my supposedly rightful place in the company, and then got fed up with that, that was when I knew I had to get out, and decided – realised – a year and a day wouldn't be enough, that it would never have been enough. Not with this family.' He turns, gives a small smile.

And then, sometimes, people leave you silences you have no real choice but to fill. 'So,' Fielding asks him, 'how long would be long enough?'

A shrug. 'Somewhere between until further notice and for ever, I suppose.'

Fielding leaves it a bit, then says, 'Look, I seem to remember you left because we sold a quarter of the stock to Spraint in the first place.'

No reaction.

'That's certainly become the story,' Fielding tells him. 'That's the family mythology, that you disagreed with the twenty-five-per-cent disposal and jumped ship. Back in ninety-nine. I mean, is that right?'

'That had a lot to do with it,' Al says. 'Well, something to do with it.'

'So, look, if you're still on the anti side, then—' Fielding pulls back. 'Are you?'

'Am I what?' Alban asks. 'Still sworn to renounce the Spraint Corporation of America, Inc., and all its works?'

'Yes.'

Al shakes his head. 'I'm not sure I care any more, Fielding. I'm not sure it matters very much at all. One group of shareholders: another group of shareholders.' He makes a sort of rolling motion with one hand then the other.

'Shit,' Fielding says, leaning back on the metal tube of the parapet.

'I'll be honest, Al. Some of us were kind of hoping you might help organise the opposition to the deal.'

Alban looks round, surprised. 'There *is* opposition?' He pauses, appears to think. 'We're not getting greedy, are we?' He looks away again. 'Why, that would never do.'

'Of course there's opposition,' Fielding tells him, trying not to respond to the obvious sarcasm. 'This is our firm, our family, Al. It's our name on the board. It's what we've done for four generations. It's what we do, it's what we *are*. That's the point, don't you see? I mean, that's what's thundered through to quite a few people in the family, especially since Spraint took their quarter-share. That it's not about money. Sure the money's good, but – Jeez – we've all basically got enough. If we sell up we'll all be richer, but we'll be just like any other family.'

'No, we won't.'

'Well, okay, like any other well-off family.'

'That may not count as demotion.'

'Al, come on! I thought this at least would get you going! Aren't you interested at all? Doesn't any of this matter to you?'

'Not in the ways you might think, cuz.'

'Shit.'

They stand like that for a while, leaning on the edge of the bridge, looking upstream. A passenger train rumbles slowly past, heading into the city, wheels screeching. It looks very tall and heavily metallic, this close up. A kid waves down and Fielding waves back, then turns to lean with Al again. It's one of those silences.

'Are you seriously trying to tell me,' Al says at last, 'there's any possibility of stopping the sale?'

Fielding keeps deadpan, in case Al looks round at him suddenly. 'Yes,' he states.

'How many people . . . no, make that, what are the percentages involved?'

'Hard to say for sure. People are keeping their cards pretty close to their chests. Spraint only needs twenty-six per cent of the remaining family shares to get control—'

'No, they need a third of the remaining—'

'You know what I mean.'

'I suppose. Would they be satisfied with control, or do they want total ownership?'

'They say they might settle for control, but they really want the lot.'

'"*Might* settle for control"?'

'They'd have to think about it. They say they're so confident we'll take their offer they haven't bothered thinking about what to do if we don't.'

Al snorts. 'Yeah, sure. Well, it's this family. There are always going to be some diehards.'

'Guaranteed.'

Al looks thoughtful, strokes his beard. 'Doesn't the ninety-two-per-cent thing apply here?'

'Yeah. They're really looking for a ninety-two-per-cent share, so they can compulsorily purchase the rest.'

'Mm-hmm.' Alban looks round at his cousin. 'So who's going to stop them?' His gaze seems to search Fielding's eyes. 'I seem to recall you were on the for-sale side, six years ago.'

'Yes, I was,' Fielding says smoothly. 'Struck me as the right thing to do then. Probably still would, circumstances being the same. We needed the cash injection. I mean, I understand – understood – your point of view, but there wasn't much argument that we needed more invest-ment. But anyway. That was then. This is now. We don't *need* to sell to Spraint. We could keep going as a – basically – family firm. We could keep Spraint on board as helpful, even enthusiastic partners, we could be happy with them selling the shares to a third party or we could easily organise a bank loan to buy them back.' Fielding expects Al to look round again at this, but he doesn't. 'Seriously,' Fielding tells him. 'That's a possibility. Our credit's good. Very good. Kath's already . . . That's Aunt Kath – she's Finance Officer now. You knew that?'

25

'Yeah, I knew that,' Al says quietly.

'Anyway, she's held informal talks with a couple of banks and they're like totally up for it. Positively encouraging. I think they think we should go for it.'

Fielding lets Alban mull this over for a while.

'So. Look, Al, there's a couple of people in the family who could be wavering on this. They feel tugged both ways. They can see what Spraint are offering is basically a good deal. It would make sound business sense to sell up. That's a given. Okay. On the other hand, this is their life, their family, their name being sold here. They can see value – and I mean something more than monetary – in staying on board, keeping in charge. It all depends on how much we value the family, I guess. How much all of us do.' Fielding thinks he sees his cousin nod. 'So, some of us would like to at least give Spraint a proper fight. And you could help, Al. There are people – Jeez, my dad's one – people who'd listen to you. Beryl? Great-Aunt Beryl? She's always had a soft spot for you, hasn't she? She's another.'

'What about the old girl?'

'Gran?'

'Yes. Where does she stand on this?'

'Well, she sent me. This was her idea. Well, and mine.'

Alban looks at the other man. 'She's against the takeover?'

'Yes,' Fielding tells him.

'She was for the last one, the twenty-five-per-cent sale.'

'I keep telling you, that was different. That was about keeping the company going. *This* is about keeping the company going.'

'That's not different, that's the same.'

'Jesus, Al, you know what I mean. Without Spraint's money we might have gone under, so we took it and the company survived. But now they want to make it all theirs and it'll only be the name that goes on – the company will have gone. It's business – it's all about survival. Look, you can help here. If you want to you can make a difference, you can matter. I'm serious. You could have a real influence. Just come and talk to a few people.'

Fielding leaves a space.

'Why now?' Al asks. He turns round and his eyes have narrowed and Fielding knows he's got him.

'Why now?' Fielding repeats.

'Why are Spraint so keen now? What's changed, what's on the horizon?'

'Ah, well, now, we think it's because the *Empire!* series has been doing so well on the PC and Gamebox, and they're working on a fresh title for their own new machine, the NG. You heard of that?'

'No.'

'NG. Next Generation, taking over from the V-Ex. Out early next year. Kicks kitty-litter sand in the face of the PS2 and the X-box 360. Better, faster processor than top-of-the-line PCs. Processors plural, I should say – it's got *three*, plus the best dedicated graphics card on the market. Eighty gig hard drive minimum, HD ready. Built-in broadband.'

Alban's laughing at his cousin. 'You're in love, I can see.'

Fielding's laughing, too. 'It is one fuck of a machine. It's going to define the console games market for the next five years.'

'Yeah, no doubt.'

'No, this is *true*.'

'They got the software, the games ready?'

'That's what we're talking about. We reckon the *Empire!* titles and derivatives are going to form a major part of the roll-out and their future plans. One of them might even be bundled with the initial release.'

'Might?'

'Yeah, as in maybe.'

'They're obviously keeping you well up to date with developments.'

'Hey, we're partners, not Siamese twins.'

Al turns away again, but he's thinking. 'Ah, hah,' he says softly. There's a surprisingly long pause. 'And you want to stand in the way of this fucking behemoth.'

'And we can do it,' Fielding tells him. 'If people believe. I mean, we need to get to them before the EGM at Garbadale, but there's time. We could do it. We'd need to be there at Garbadale, too, obviously, but there's work to be done beforehand. Just a couple of weeks, max, Alban, that's all. Expenses on me, obviously.' Fielding leaves a gap. He can hear the river gurgling. 'What do you think?'

Alban shakes his head. Says nothing.

'Jeez, Al,' Fielding says, 'is the tree-chopping business so fucking entrancing you can't tear yourself away?'

Alban laughs. 'No,' he says, pushing his fingers through his hair again. 'I've been invalided out, anyway.'

'What?' *Shit*, Fielding thinks, *did I miss something?* Has Al sliced off a finger or some toes or something? He lost the top of one little finger years ago, not long after he first started this forestry crap, but has he lost something else?

'See these fingers?' Al says, holding up the index and middle fingers of each hand.

Fielding nods. 'They all seem to be there.'

Al looks at them, too. 'Yeah, but so's something called white finger.'

'What?'

'You get it from too much vibration. Starts killing off blood vessels or something. The doc explained it all. Handled too many old chain-saws in my time. Shouldn't really have happened so quickly but I must just be especially vulnerable.'

'Shit. Is it sore?'

'No.' He rotates the fingers round in front of his face, inspecting them. 'Lost a bit of sensitivity, and I need to watch they don't get too cold in the winter, but I can live with it.'

'So you're out?'

'Yup.'

'Couldn't they find you a desk job?'

Al grins. 'It was the cutting-down-trees bit I liked. They offered me a driving job, hauling trees or stripping them or stacking or whatever, but I wasn't interested.'

'So . . .' Fielding holds up both arms. 'Why not—?'

He lets his voice fade as Al turns to look upriver again.

The waters run on away beneath them both.

'Look,' Fielding says, 'won't you at least come and see Beryl and Doris? Jesus, man, it's only Glasgow.' Actually, Fielding has himself a kind of horror of meeting the two great-aunts. Not that he's going to mention that, obviously. 'They'd love to see you,' he tells Alban, possibly truthfully. 'We could drive through today.'

Nothing.

Then Al says, 'Maybe. I don't know.'

God, Fielding thinks, *he sounds depressed, defeated*. Well, this is something, he supposes.

After a while Al says, 'You said that pretty much the whole family's going to be there, at Garbadale.'

'They kind of have to be. Gran's got – well, the Trust has got, but that means Gran – proxy voting rights for anybody who isn't. Effectively.'

'Okay,' Al gives a big sigh. 'And from the States?'

'Oh, whole bunch o' folks.'

Al's shoulders shake with what might be another laugh. 'We're both being coy here, Fielding. We both know . . .'

This time it's Al's voice that trails off.

Fielding clears his throat and says, 'I understand Sophie is going to be there. Cousin Sophie. She accepted the party invitation, registered for attendance at the EGM. I guess she'll be there.' A pause. 'Though, obviously . . .'

Fielding is suddenly aware that he might be about to shoot himself in the foot while it's still in his mouth, so he shuts up.

Alban puts his head down into the V of his outstretched arms and his clasped hands, as though studying the river passing immediately beneath.

As though praying.

He looks up and turns, smiling. 'You fit for some lunch?'

'Good idea,' Fielding says.

They walk back towards the city.

*   *   *

'Oh, God, are you all right?'

It took him a while to get the breath to wheeze, 'Not really.' He tried to curl up tighter, while being perfectly aware that this would do no good whatsoever.

The pain was about as bad as anything he'd ever felt. It seemed to radiate out from his groin like some terrible searchlight, forcing its ghastly dark rays of agony into every part of him, from his hair to his toenails. It went beyond pain, into other realms which included an encompassing feeling of cold and nausea and despair. It also seemed to be getting gradually worse. Alban had lived fifteen years and had never experienced anything like it. He hoped he never would again.

'Oh, God, I'm so sorry.' The girl took off her black riding hat and put it down on the brick path. She knelt by him, hesitating, then she put her hand on to his shoulder and squeezed gently. He was making a noise somewhere between a wheeze and a gurgle. She looked around, but there was nobody else in the walled garden. She wondered if she ought to go up to the house and alert somebody. How bad could this be? At first she'd thought he was exaggerating when he'd fallen like a sack of potatoes and curled up like a hedgehog. Now she thought he probably really was in intense pain.

Scrabbles gave a cough and flexed one hind leg again, backing towards the two of them. Oh, God, she might kick him again. Or her. She tutted and rose, chiding the tall chestnut mare and leading her to where she could munch on some carrot leaves, out of harm's way. Then she went back to the boy lying clutched around his pain on the red-brick path. She bit her lip and patted his head softly. He had curly light brown hair.

'That's called a stringhalt,' she said, not knowing what else to say.

He made a noise that might have been a 'What?'

'Sudden spasmodic lifting of a horse's hind leg,' she explained. 'It's called a stringhalt.'

He made a sort of keening noise and seemed to try to straighten out, then gasped and curled up again. 'Thanks,' he said. It sounded like his teeth were clenched. 'That's good to know.' He paused for breath. 'Felt more like a . . . kick.'

'Actually, you're right, it was more like a kick. I'm so sorry. Is it really, really painful, yah?'

He might have nodded. 'Kinda.'

'Scrabbles has never done that before.'

'Sorry?'

'Scrabbles. She's never done that before. Kicked anyone.'

'Really.' Each of his words sounded clipped, bitten off.

'Yah. You're not really supposed to walk that close to the rear legs of a horse, 'specially one you don't know.'

'Uh-huh. Well,' he said, 'you're not really,' he took another shuddering breath, 'meant to bring horses' – one more breath, wheezing – 'into a kitchen garden,' he told her. 'Either.'

'Sorry. Suppose not.'

'And, are you deaf?'

'I'm sorry? Oh, no. No, I was listening to my Walkman.'

'What were you –' he sucked air in raggedly '– listening to?'

'Oh, ah, *Now That's What I Call Music*; one of those.'

'Right.'

She bit her lip again. All she'd been doing was taking a look round the old walled garden at the end of her ride round the estate and along the beach. She'd just got back from Spain and the first thing she'd wanted to do was take Scrabbles out for a hack. She patted the boy's head again. His hair was very soft. She was pretty sure she knew who he was. 'Should I go get help or something? What do you think?'

'Dunno. Ice?' He looked round at her and she saw his face properly for the first time. His face was contorted, right now, obviously, but she suspected it was probably rather nice when it wasn't. He had beautiful brown eyes, the same colour as Scrabbles' coat. She guessed he was a year or so older than her; sixteen, say. He reminded her a bit of Nick Rhodes, from Duran Duran. She felt she'd rather outgrown Duran Duran about a year ago, but she still had a soft

31

spot for Nick. 'Really no idea,' he gasped. 'Might need a doctor at some point. Just to check, you know?'

'Shit, yah.' She squeezed his shoulder again. 'I'll go up to the house.'

'And will you get that animal out of my carrot lines?'

'Yah, no problem. Back in a bit.'

She led the horse back through the tall gate in the west wall, walking quickly.

The pain came and went, like waves on a shore, every particle of sand a tiny raw testicle being rubbed up against every other one. Dear fucking God this was sore. Why did it have to be this sore? He'd taken a tennis ball in the balls once, maybe three or four years ago, and that had been bad, but this was infinitely worse. Were sex and orgasms and reproduction really worth this demented fucking agony? He'd never even got to do it properly yet, just wanking, and now it felt like he never would. Could balls actually burst? Fucking hell. He'd just been thinking lately it might be good to be a dad one day, eventually, but now maybe that was off the menu entirely, all thanks to some Yah-girl and her mad, man-hating, ball-bursting horse from hell. What he really wanted to do was stand up, take down his jeans and boxers and take a look at the damage, but he couldn't, not when the girl might reappear at any moment, with Uncle James or Aunt Clara or his own parents.

Gradually – far too bloody gradually – the pain started to fade. He stopped feeling quite so sick. He pushed himself upright with one hand and sat carefully on the brick path running between the lettuce beds. He dried his eyes. He hadn't really been crying as such, but the pain and the grimace it had forced on to his face had sort of squeezed his tear ducts, he guessed. He took a hanky from his pocket and blew his nose. Even that hurt. He coughed. That hurt as well. He started thinking about standing up, wondering if that would be painful, too. He looked at the black riding hat the girl had left lying on the path. A single long, curled red hair lay coiled around the velvety surface, shining in the sunlight like a vermilion meridian.

32

She was away five or ten minutes, then returned alone, swinging an ice bucket. 'They've all bloody gone!' she said. 'Nobody there. Cars aren't there either.' He wiped away the last of his tears and looked at her. She was small, a good head shorter than he was. He guessed she was about his age. Quite curvy; well developed, was the phrase, he thought. She looked good in her long black boots, stretchy fawn trousers and long black jacket. Her gathered-up red hair glowed like copper in the sun against the shining blue of the summer sky. She sat down beside him on the raised edge of the path. Green eyes. Gently tanned skin, flushed a delicate red on her cheeks. Nice little nose. 'Here. I got the ice.' She plonked the ice bucket down on the path between his booted feet, then dug into her black riding jacket and pulled out a packet of pills. 'Paracetamol. Thought these might help.'

He made a patting motion. 'Thanks. I'll be okay. It's starting to go now. I'll live.' He put his hands on his knees, stared ahead and blew out a deep breath.

His hands looked long and strong and were incredibly dirty; brown with the soil and quite black under the nails. She felt herself shiver.

'Well, yah. Phew, right?' She smiled.

She had, he noticed, braces on her top teeth. She saw him glance at her mouth and closed her lips. It was almost a pout, he thought. She was very pretty. Well, apart from the braces, obviously. Then she stuck her hand out. 'Sophie. You're Alban, my cousin, is that right?'

He took her small hand and shook it carefully. So they were cousins. That was a pity. 'That's me,' he said. 'Pleased to meet you.'

'Actually we have met, apparently, back when we were very young, but, ah, how-do-you-do anyway.'

He nodded. 'Thanks for the ice,' he said, leaning forward and scowling with pain again. 'But I think I'll just get back to the house. Nice cool bath, maybe.'

She stood and helped pull him up until he was standing, then retrieved the ice bucket and nestled herself under his right shoulder

33

after seeing his first few, waddled steps. She stayed like that, supporting him, all the way back to the house. She was more hindrance than help, but it felt nice and she smelled good, cousin or not.

It was the second full summer he'd spent at Lydcombe since he'd grown up. But he already knew the place well. He'd been born in Garbadale, in the far north-west of Scotland. He and his real mum, Irene, and his dad had lived there until he was two, when the thing with his mum had happened. Then he and his dad had moved to Lydcombe. Both estates, with their large houses, were owned by the family trust. Who got to live where was largely a matter of choice but was ultimately in the gift of the family's elder members. In those days, this effectively meant Grandad Bert and Grandma Win.

He couldn't remember anything of his mother, or of Garbadale. Lydcombe was all he knew. They'd lived here and he'd grown up here, in the house when he was very small, but then, as he got bigger and stronger and braver, the place he really grew up within was the garden and the estate itself.

At first he only felt comfortable on the lawns and terraces around the house, usually staying close to his dad as he sat on his little stool before his easel, painting, but after a while he started to make friends with the Victorian walled garden, and later began to play inside the old apple orchard within the ruins of the ancient abbey. The orchard had gone to pasture and was used to help feed the estate's few sheep and goats, which were more pets than anything else. Later still, expanding what he was starting to think of now as his domain, he began venturing out beyond these concentricities of safety and security and familiarity into the further meadows, copses, fields and woods of the estate. Then, one bright day, he rambled as far as the river with its banks strewn with wild flowers and bushes and, on that day of wanton exploratory zeal, even went on and out past that, across the broad, sluggish ford to the dunes and beach beyond, out

34

to the margin of the land where the rollers boomed and the hills of Wales shimmered in the blue distance.

He'd started at Mardon Primary School, near Minehead. He explored the gardens and estate in the evenings and at weekends. Sometimes he would chance upon his dad, painting some distant view or part of the gardens. His dad sold paintings sometimes, though mostly they seemed to slowly fill up the walls of the house. School friends came to stay, and explored the estate with him. He felt he was special, somehow secretly in charge of it all. It was his.

His father married again. Alban was very suspicious of this Leah person at first, and insisted on calling her Aunt Leah, for ages. (A solemn, secret pledge whispered to the ghost of his real mother under the bedclothes one night.) But Leah was nice to him, even when he wasn't nice to her, and his dad seemed happier than Alban could ever remember, and told him off less. His dad would let him sit on his knee and he always kept a small, spare canvas with him – Alban's Painting – which he let the boy scrawl on, encouraging him to spatter paint across the woven, giving surface. His father some-times suggested subjects, or said not to hold the brush so tight, or just to use one hand, or pointed out colours that might be interest-ing, but mostly he just sat there, patiently, smiling, until Alban got bored and jumped down and went off to play again; then his father would set the little canvas aside once more and continue with his own work.

Alban made a slightly shamefaced apology to the memory of his real mother one night, then started to call Leah 'Mum'.

After being frightened of him – and even resenting his presence – he started talking to the old gardener, Mr Sutton, who let him chatter away while he worked, and sometimes let him help.

Cordelia came along. This incredible new, tiny thing; a sister. Amazing. He realised suddenly they were a family. Cory took up a lot of his parents' time, leaving him even more free to continue exploring the garden. Mr Sutton only came to the gardens in the afternoon of some days now, because he was getting on. Alban had started making maps of the garden, naming parts and features, invoking his own lore. They had very nice long, hot holidays abroad, and short, cold ones in Garbadale. Lots of sunshine was all right, for a couple of weeks, but then they had sun, sea and sand at Lydcombe, too, and the plants and gardens abroad always seemed rather garish and obvious compared to home.

As for the rocky desolation of the steep slopes around the water-logged grounds and rhododendron-choked gardens surrounding the grim grey walls of Garbadale House; that meant little to him and somehow he never felt comfortable there. He did his best to enjoy whatever any given holiday offered (his dad had tried to get him to understand this: appreciate whatever life throws up, make the most of *now*, because all things change, and sometimes not to the good), but most holidays were merely different, not better, compared to life at home. After the first few days of any time away, he always found himself longing for Lydcombe, and whenever they returned from holiday he'd run out into the garden, across the lawns, through the orchard and the echoing abbey ruins, sometimes all the way down to the river and the sea.

Mr Sutton got really, *really* old and went into a Home; two lads from the village both called Dave did some gardening stuff some-times, but they weren't interested in talking to a kid Alban's age. They used to make jokes about the herb garden which he didn't understand, and they didn't seem to care about the garden the way Mr Sutton had, but that just left it more to him, he felt.

Later, he wished he'd stopped just once to think about what a wonderful, privileged, *graced* life he'd been living then.

What happened, when he was eleven and about to go to big school, was that his dad sat him down one day and told him they were leaving Somerset, leaving Lydcombe. His dad was joining the family firm. He would need to work in the company's main office. They would still come back, of course they would, but they were off to the big city now: London! Well, Richmond, which wasn't far away, and had good train connections with the centre. They'd sorted

out a good school nearby where he could be a day pupil and everything.

They'd left Lydcombe. Another lot of people, some aunt and uncle
and their children – he was supposed to know them, but he couldn't
remember meeting them – were going to live there now, now that
his dad was taking up a new post in the family and working in
London.

He felt betrayed, exiled, cast out. Richmond was a strange,
crowded, busy place after Lydcombe. The house was only a little
smaller, apparently, but much more vertical and far more ordered;
fewer eccentric corridors, half-landings, erratic staircases and oddly
shaped rooms. It felt tight and constrained after Lydcombe, as
though the building was forever standing at attention, incapable of
relaxing. The garden was supposed to be huge but this was nonsense;
he paced it out and reckoned it was barely half the size of
Lydcombe's walled garden alone. His dad was out to work most of
the time.

Being taken to films and shows in London made up for some of
this, but not all. School, after a couple of awkward weeks, was actually a comfort. All he had to do was alter his accent a little – though
it had never been especially West Country in the first place – and
take up the challenge of one boy who was older and even bigger
than he was, but slow. They shook hands after the fight, which he
thought was slightly hilarious; very jolly hockey sticks. He enjoyed
learning, enjoyed being one of the lads, enjoyed being taken to
London (especially if it was just him and his dad) and being allowed
to wander the streets and parks of Richmond with his pals, but he
missed Lydcombe more – he realised one terrible night – than he
missed his dead mother.

Now Lydcombe had become the place to go on holiday to, rather
than the place to go on holiday from; a destination, temporary and
somehow conditional. The first time they went back, he noticed
that the half-dozen or so of Andy's paintings that had been left
behind, a present to the house and its new inhabitants, had all been

37

shifted, consigned to bedrooms rather than left in public spaces. If Andy was bothered by this, he didn't say.

He had visited the estate with his mum and dad and sister Cory every year since the great move to Richmond, sometimes stopping for a week or two, sometimes just staying overnight, but he could only barely remember Sophie. He thought they'd each been five the last time they'd met. He had a vague recollection of having made her cry.

Since then their paths had contrived not to cross, even though Lydcombe was her home. Sophie was the child of Uncle James and his first wife, not Uncle James and Aunt Clara, so she was away a lot staying with her birth mother in Spain.

The first time he worked out the implications of this, he thought how weird it must be. Having two mothers wasn't weird – he was used to that – but having two mothers who were each still alive. That *was* bizarre. It was only when he began asking other kids about this sort of thing that he started to realise it wasn't that strange at all. Adults were definitely strange though.

He'd started taking charge of the garden at Richmond almost without noticing, from when he was about twelve. They had a gardener who came in, and he hung around with him a lot, asking questions, helping out and doing some of the spade work and the other heavy-lifting stuff that hurt Mr Reynolds' back. He grew to love the work, love the horti lore, the vast hidden store of knowledge that seemed to exist behind every leaf and blade and petal and sod.

Kew Gardens was not far away. He went there first with his parents, one cool, misty autumn day, in a bad mood for some forgotten reason and really not wanting to be there at all, or anywhere with them (Cory came too, all simpering and sweet for a change, as if sensing his mood and deliberately trying to provide a contrast), but he was reluctantly impressed with the trees and shrubs and the stately, towering confection of the Pagoda looming through the haze. Then came the glasshouses. Those he was quietly stunned by, their smell and heat and pressing humidity containing a whole, fragrant, fabulous world of riotous greenery – plants from everywhere, dreamlike caricatures of plants, some almost night-marish, as though from alien worlds, all flourishing luxuriantly here under a grey English sky. Jets, also from all over the world, roared overhead in the murk every few minutes, on their way into Heathrow. He had to lean over and peer at labels as casually as he could, not wanting to show how deeply impressed he was, how much this was meaning to him. He already knew he'd be coming here a lot.

When he was asked what he wanted to do for his summer holi-days in '84 – he was fourteen and had been invited to come and stay with various outposts of the family, from Garbadale to the States to the Far East – he said he'd like to go to Lydcombe and work in the garden.

By the end of that first summer he'd already almost started to think of the place as his home again. The house itself was all very well, but it was the estate, the gardens, the plants – flowers, shrubs, trees and vegetables, even the differing species of grass on the lawns and meadows, as well as the animal life that they supported – that fascinated him.

An interest in horticulture was a bit naff, as his school pals had taken some satisfaction in telling him, and in a way he knew they were right. But there you were. He just found all this green, supposedly boring stuff utterly spellbinding. God help him, he was a teenager who got a real kick out of growing vegetables.

'So, sitting on a rubber ring are we, Alban?' Uncle James asked. 'Pass the peas.'

'Oh, my poor boy,' Leah said, for perhaps the fifth time, from the other side of the table. There was a comforting smile on her face and a small, sympathetic groan in her voice.

'Muuum,' Alban said, glaring at her. Leah just smiled more widely.

Alban passed the bowl of peas towards the head of the table. 'Actually, it's a cushion, Uncle,' he told Uncle James.

God, this was embarrassing. He was horribly aware he must have sounded like a little child calling Leah 'Mum' like that. Not even just 'Mum', but 'Muuum', the sound all stretched out just as though a little kid had said it. He glanced down the table at Sophie, to see if she was smirking or giggling or anything, but she was just helping herself to more potatoes.

'You poor lad,' Aunt Clara said, brusquely. 'Got to be careful round horses.' Clara was a large, florid lady, prone to wearing smocks and headscarves. Alban didn't think he'd ever seen her with her – sometimes disquietingly orange – hair worn down.

'Doc says there's no permanent damage,' Andy said. Alban's dad had insisted on being present when the doctor had examined him. That had been kind of embarrassing, too, though Andy had been very sympathetic. And it had been a young, female doctor. That had been *excruciatingly* embarrassing.

'Family line secure then, is it?' Uncle James asked Alban's dad. Uncle James was a sort of nouveau fogey. He wore lots of waistcoats, those yellow check shirts real farmers rarely wear, and corduroy trousers, all of which helped bulk out his already slightly oversized frame. He had thick curly black hair, rosy cheeks and a nicely developing paunch.

Andy just smiled. Alban's dad was normal in comparison; thinner, with straightish black hair already going grey. He had a kind-looking face with crinkly bits round his eyes that usually made it look like he'd spent his life smiling, but which occasionally – if you caught him just sitting alone, staring into space the way he did sometimes, and he hadn't noticed you – made him look very sad, until he realised you were there.

'You'll be fine, won't you, darling?' Leah said, still smiling across at Alban. Alban's mum was slight and pale but with the sort of cheerful character people usually associated with somebody twice her size. She had luxuriant quantities of curly blonde hair which she called her crowning glory. Also, as more than one of Alban's school pals had pointed out to his intense discomfiture, she had – for her age – great tits.

'I'll be fine,' he muttered. He bent over his plate and started removing the fat from the edges of the pork chops.

'Hope you weren't doing a Geldof in front of my little girl, Alban,' Uncle James said, slathering apple sauce over his plate.

'Sorry, Uncle?'

'Swearing, like that Geldof guy. It'd only be natural, after getting kicked in the nuts like that; can see that, but I'm just hoping you managed to constrain your profanities from my little girl's ears.'

'James, please,' Sophie said, rolling her eyes.

Sophie's father made a show of turning round in his seat to look behind him at the dining-room door. 'Somebody else come in?' he asked, frowning mightily. 'Somebody called "James"?'

'Dad, Da, Pater, Papa,' Sophie said through tight lips, glaring at him.

'Oh! It's me!' Uncle James said, turning back. 'Sorry, daughter.'

'You'll be glad to hear I didn't have any spare breath to swear, Uncle,' Alban told him. He glanced down the table. 'Your daughter's delicate ears were unpolluted.'

Sophie snorted. ('Dear, really,' her mother said. 'You sound like a horse.')

'I can swear fluently in three different languages,' Sophie said brightly, 'Mother dear, Father darling.'

Uncle James was shaking his head. 'Geldof geezer. Really. What was that group he used to be in? The Boomtown Cats?'

'Rats,' Alban said.

'Oh, quite,' agreed Uncle James. 'Couldn't believe it when he started swearing like that. On television.'

'Dad, it was a *month* ago,' Sophie protested. 'Can't you leave it? Anyway, he did it, it worked; he *got* people to give him their "fookin money". And "fook the address".' She widened her eyes, lowered her voice and made a reasonable impersonation of an Irish accent as she

41

pronounced the last three words. Cory, Alban's minuscule but massively annoying eight-year-old sister, made a shocked peeping noise. Alban, laughing involuntarily, nearly choked on a mouthful of pork.

'Now that's *enough*, young lady,' Uncle James said, suddenly serious and going rather red, pointing his fork at Sophie. 'This is the dinner table.'

'How much did you give to Live Aid, Daddy?' Sophie asked. Alban would have sworn she fluttered her eyelashes.

'That's not really your concern, frankly,' Uncle James told his daughter, and smiled.

'Well,' Sophie said emphatically, 'I gave all the money I'd saved to go skiing last year.'

'You mean all the money that I gave you to go skiing.'

'It doesn't matter where it came from,' Sophie said emphatically, 'what matters is where it went.'

'Well bully for you. Hope the Ethiopians sent you a thank-you note. Now I'd like to get on with my dinner, if that's all right with you.'

Sophie made a growling noise and stared at her plate.

'Sophie, dear. Are you sure you won't try one of the chops?' Aunt Clara asked suddenly.

'Mum,' Sophie said, exasperated, 'I'm a vegetarian!'

'Yes, I know, dear. But they're awfully good.'

Sophie just rolled her eyes. Her gaze caught Alban's, and they shared one of those rueful *parents, eh?* smiles.

Back to Tango's unlocked flat (these people live the US sitcom dream, where friends just wander into your apartment. Ha ha). From the living room, a voice Fielding doesn't recognise is saying,

'Whit are ye talkin' aboot? If ye take aff all yer clothes, of course ye're fuckin' naked.'

'No, but,' Tango says, 'what I'm sayin' is, if ye've got a tattoo, ye canny take *that* off. So you're never totally naked. De ye no' see?'

'Ah see yer aff yer chump, that's – Oh-aye, it's Yakuza. How's it hingin, Yak?'

Al says, 'Afternoon all.'

The new arrival proves to be a fat wee guy with hilariously long dark hair. He's wearing jeans and a black leather waistcoat and looks like a roadie for Black Sabbath circa 1970. Two narrow-set eyes, a large nose and a fat spliff all poke out through the curtains of hair on either side of his face. He looks puzzled when he sees Fielding, then sort of nods. The only other person present is Tango, with whom Al requests a word. They head out of the room. Fielding sits down on the couch, thinking how good it's going to be to get out of here. There's a familiar-looking silvery box sitting by Tango's television, wires joining one to the other and a couple of games controllers lying on the carpet beneath the TV. The wee fat guy sits and looks at Fielding while Fielding looks at him, determined not to be stared down. Fat Boy smokes prodigiously, creating a thick grey screen in front of what little of his face isn't obscured by hair. After a while he grins and holds the joint out. 'Want a toke?'

Fielding nearly does, just because he's expected to say no, but sense prevails. 'No, thanks. Driving.'

The hairy guy nods, sucks another lungful. He holds it, then breathes out. Fielding thinks about opening the window again. He suspects he's getting stoned just sitting in the same room. 'Don't believe we've been introduced,' the hairy guy says at the end of the next exhalation.

'Fielding.'

'Aw aye. Ah'm Burb.'

Fielding smiles perfunctorily and nods. The hairy guy sees Fielding glance at the games machine. 'That's mine,' he says. 'Goanae play a game, me an' Tango.'

'Really.' Fielding spots the DVD lying on the shelf holding the TV, recognises the cover immediately, and grins broadly.

Alban and Tango come back. 'Maybe just a day or two,' Al's saying. Slung over one shoulder is a small backpack, not the scruffy great torso-sized squaddy-issue monster Fielding had seen earlier. *Guess I haven't been quite as persuasive as I'd hoped*, Fielding thinks. Still, one thing at a time.

Al looks at him. 'You fit?'

'Vamanos muchachos,' Fielding says, standing.

'See you later, big man,' Tango says, seeing them to the front door. 'Nice tae meet you, Fielding. Anytime.'

'Too kind. You take care.'

Through in the living room, Fielding can see Burb turning on the Spraint Corp V-Ex games machine. Into the slot is slid the disc that bears the legend *Masters of EMPIRE!*

2

Once, in the middle of the night, in the centre of a great plantation, he'd been drinking with a couple of his co-workers; good guys who'd become pals. They were on Speyside, in what had been a big forest, staying in an old caravan the forestry people had provided. They'd been drinking whisky and cans of beer and playing cards. He'd been making steady money at poker through the evening until a couple of wild bets towards the end of the night when he'd lost most of what he'd accumulated and they all ended up fairly close to where they'd started. They'd had a cup of tea and a biscuit about three o'clock, then collapsed snoring and smelly into their sleeping bags. Tomorrow was supposed to be a full working day but they knew the foreman was away in Inverness until at least noon, and they were ahead of schedule.

He awoke before dawn with a painfully full bladder. He stumbled in the darkness, stepped into his unlaced boots and went out to pee wearing just his briefs.

It was late summer and a clear night. He stood in the bright light of a full moon, a few feet away from the caravan, peeing into the tumble of branches near the side of the road. They'd been clearing the trees, the final cut, bringing down the tall Sitkas, stripping them with machines like giant pencil sharpeners, carting them off on big trucks. What was left – what he could see as far as a ridge a kilometre distant – was a chaos of smashed branches and torn pieces of smaller trees; a pale jumble of fractured wood like something from a volcanic disaster or the first days of a war. He looked up at the stars, then back down at the frozen fury of shattered wood. The pee went on. It had been a very full bladder. He'd better drink some water when he went back in or he'd have a head in the morning.

The fox trotted silently round the corner of the caravan and stopped, head slightly to one side, looking up at him. It was beautiful. Its coat shone in the moonlight: inky black, brilliant white and a red he wasn't sure he could actually make out in the moonlight or was just seeing because he knew it was there. The light was so intense he could see the moon reflected in the creature's eyes. A hint of moisture glistened on its black nose.

He looked back at it and slowly tipped his head to one side, too. The fox took a couple of cautious steps forward, putting its nose near where his urine was landing. He was very tempted to twist his body ever so slightly and direct the piss straight at it – it was, he thought, what most of the guys would have done – but he didn't. The fox took a delicate sniff, then looked up at him again. He was about out now, the stream of pee falling back and breaking up. He smiled at the animal and shrugged. The fox trotted round and past him, head slightly down, giving him one last glance before it disappeared round the other end of the caravan.

He hadn't ever mentioned this to anybody, not even to the guys the next morning. It wasn't all that remarkable, anyway – they saw deer and squirrels all the time and sometimes stoats and wild cats and pine martens – but it was something he wanted to keep to and for himself. He wondered if the fox had lived in the forest and was having to leave because it was all torn up now, or if it was moving in after new opportunities had been opened up for it, or if it didn't – and perhaps couldn't – care. He wondered if the animal had somehow known that men had created this monoculture plantation over the ruins of earlier forests, then created the chaos, and whether it could in any sense blame them.

Alban sat watching the A9 unroll towards the silver snout of the car, the three-pointed star like some indiscriminate gun sight. They were heading away from Perth on the long downward slope towards the plain of the River Earn, a Sitka forest on one side of the car, the view across the flood plain to the northern slopes of the Ochil Hills on the other. A black and red iPod linked into the car's entertainment system was playing old dance music, from Fielding's wild years. Alban could feel the slim bulk of the folded letter in the back pocket of his jeans. He was remembering a conversation from years ago.

'There's a lot you don't know, young man,' Great-Aunt Beryl had told him. 'A lot I can't tell you, at least not now.'

'Then when?' he'd asked.

'I don't know. Perhaps never. Certainly not now.'

'But why not?'

'Sometimes, whether it's a family or . . . any other institution, one has to wait for people to die, or until one knows that things won't matter any more for some reason or other. Though, it has to be said, some things seem never to cease mattering. Or, one has to wait until one knows one is about to die oneself, and so won't care, frankly, when the balloon goes up. You know; when the whatsit hits the fan.'

He'd been silent for a while. 'Then why are you telling me at all?'

Beryl had looked at him with a strange expression. 'Perhaps I'm not entirely sure myself, Alban. Or perhaps it's a way of salving my conscience, even if only partially. Perhaps it's like avoiding telling lies without in any way telling the truth, and so misleading somebody by omission, as it were. Do you understand?'

The music in the car changed from something Alban barely recognised or remembered to the Chemical Brothers' *Block Rockin' Beats.* Fielding whooped and turned up the volume. 'Oh yes!' he said,

47

smiling broadly at Alban. 'Remember this? Remember Singapore? Oh, fuck! That was fucking crazy, man.'

'Yeah,' Alban said. 'I remember.'

'Let's get drunk.'

'Woh! Not like you, cuz. What's the problem? Don't answer that. Good idea. Let me just say that right now. However, I have a counter-proposal. A not mutually exclusive counter-proposal re the above.'

'Fielding, what the hell are you talking about?'

'Let's get wasted as well.'

'Wasted? You have drugs?'

'Most certainly do. Never travel unprepared.'

'You brought drugs to Singapore? Are you fucking insane? Haven't you been paying any attention at all? Do you know what they do to people who import drugs to this place?'

'Alban, get real. I'm not a fucking dealer, just a user. And if I did get caught, so what? I'm rich, I'm white, I'm male, I'm an executive with an internationally respected games company with lawyers to command and, as of the other night, I'm on first-name terms with the British High Ambassador of Commissions or whatever he is.' He laughed, waved his arms. 'What could possibly go wrong?' He laughed louder.

It was 1997. They were in Singapore attending a toys and games trade fair, promoting *Empire!* (unashamedly, in an ex-imperial outpost, Alban had pointed out) and the other products of the Wopuld company to wholesalers. The day's work was done, the trade fair over, their display was being packed away in the exhibition centre and they had a free evening plus a day off to follow so they were in a quiet corner of the main bar of Raffles, drinking Singapore Slings because Fielding had this thing about Geographically Appropriate Alcoholic Beverage Consumption – Manhattans in Manhattan, etc.

'You fucking lunatic. What have you got?'

'E, coke, dope. Some K, but it's rubbish.'

48

'Jesus H. Christ. We'd better take it fast just to get rid of it and remove the evidence.'

'That's more like it.' Fielding raised his own glass and nodded at Alban's. 'Drink up. We'll have a rickshaw race back to the hotel. Loser buys the drinks all night.'

'I am *not* having another fucking rickshaw race. My last guy was four foot tall and a hundred and three. I wanted to get out and take over and tell him to sit in the back and relax while I wheeled him back to whatever old folks' home he'd wandered out of.'

'Well, *I'm* racing. And I'm deeming you to be racing, too, like it or not. If you lose I'm just going to walk out of wherever we end up drinking and you'll either have to pay up or do a runner. Don't think I won't.'

'I might just do the runner. If they catch us, you'll be the one in possession.'

Fielding gasped stagily and picked up his jacket. 'That's not very cousinly of you.'

'Yeah, well, family bonds don't mean what they used to.'

'Ooo!' Fielding camped. 'What's all that about?'

'Nothing. Never mind.'

It's the next day and Alban is seriously fucked up. He seems to have lost a day or a night, and he appears to be living the current waking period in some sort of shuffled order, slabs and tranches of experience and awareness traincrashing into one another in no discernible order whatsoever, just a blurred riffle of sensations and events thrumming past, some of which might be flashbacks – he's not sure.

'History is finished. It's all over! Even Deng said it's glorious to be rich. Capitalist democracy has won and the rest is mopping up. That Jap guy was right.'

'Bullshit. You need to read more science fiction. Nobody who reads SF comes out with this crap about the end of history.'

'Science fucking fiction? Do I look like some sort of fucking anorak?'

'Oh, fuck off.'

'Why have we stopped?'

'Oh my God. We're going to die.'

They were in a cable car that went from this enormous grey building with giant circular windows to a low island just offshore which seemed to be called Semosa or Samosa or Sentosa or Samoa. They couldn't exactly tell because even when they looked right at the signs for the place, the letters seemed to change in front of their eyes. ('Samosa, he was some sort of fascist general or something, wasn't he?' 'Or one of those fried triangles. Don't ask me.') The last time Alban looked at the sign it appeared to say Lampedusa, and that's just totally wrong. He didn't even risk mentioning that one to Fielding.

There doesn't seem to be any good earthly reason for there to be a cable car going from this tall building to this low-lying, just-offshore island, so that's exactly why it seems absolutely necessary to make the trip but now the cable car's come swinging to a stop over the slack brown waters of the strait beneath and they're just hanging there in the baking sunlight, looking out through the haze-crammed sky towards the distant towers of the city centre. They're sharing the car with about a dozen Malays and Chinese and having to mutter, which must look suspicious in itself, only Alban has no reliable idea how loud they're really talking and that's paranoia-inducing all by itself.

'Have we taken all the drugs?'

'Most of them. Will you keep your voice down?'

'What if they've stopped the cable car because they know we're on board and we're carrying?'

'Don't be stupid. Why would they stop the car? What are they going to do? Rappel down from a helicopter?'

'It's suspicious.'

'It's not suspicious, it's just one of those things.'

'Don't trot out bourgeois clichés at me, you—'

'Just try to keep calm.'

'I am calm. This is calm. This is me being calm. See; I am calmness personified.'

'Let go of my shirt.'

But it was the middle of a warm, intensely humid night and they were walking the streets, through the stink of shit and rotting fruit and perfumes and within the echoes of low-rise buildings, stepping over scuttling cockroaches the size of mice that looked the size of rats under the lens of chemical enhancement and passing by sudden courtyards where a tiny, ancient, leathery man is skinning what looks like a monkey on a bloodstained table, smoking as he pulls the furred skin away from the white and pink beneath, and open doorways to temples reveal guys in loincloths and surrounded by fumes and incense and wild bunches of flowers standing chanting, facing barely seen altars; snapped shots of imagery while they pace with jackets over shoulders and their shirts sticking to their bodies and their hair sticking to their scalps because they've just been to a club and they're still hot from dancing and talking to two girls who might not have been real girls and then there was nearly a fight and Alban had to pull Fielding out of it and the only tune they can remember from the club is *Block Rockin' Beats* and it's impossible to cool down because the humidity is like walking around in a wetsuit constantly being topped up from a kettle until they hail a taxi just for the air conditioning and sit listening to the merry chime, chime, chime noise from the device that makes that noise when you go over the Singapore speed limit and Fielding insists on being taken to the zoo because he's heard they have polar bears there in a huge chamber that's kept at the sort of constant, chilly temperature that is acceptable to your average top land predator of the Arctic wastes.

'It's the middle of the fucking night! The zoo'll be closed, you idiot! Look. Look!' Alban holds up his watch. 'It's half past four in the fucking morning!'

'That's not right. Your watch must still be on UK time or something.'

'Then why does the cab's clock say the same?'

'That's not the clock – that's the fare.'

'Believe me, that is not the fare. I'm asking the driver.'

He asks the driver, whose command of English seems mysteriously to have disappeared since he accepted the fare.

'What was that?'

'I don't know.'

'What were you asking him?'

'Whether the zoo would be open at five in the morning.'

'What did he say?'

'He just smiled and talked a lot of . . . I don't know.'

When they get there, the zoo is extremely closed and they nearly lose the cab for the return trip because Fielding wants to negotiate a reduced tariff on account of the fact that the driver should have known the zoo would be closed and was blatantly exploiting their innocent touristic ignorance and he threatens to summon the Tourist Police if there indeed is such an entity and Alban has to calm both him and the taxi driver down and only persuades the latter to take them back to the centre of town again by handing over the whole two-way fare and an arguably extortionate tip in advance, something that even then he only gets away with because Fielding has gone off to shout loudly at – and kick – some nearby chain-link fencing.

Before, or possibly after, with brains totally fried, they're in the World Famous Tiger Balm Gardens, going on all the rides and staring goggle-eyed at the various bizarre and totally twisted tableaux and paintings and dioramas that depict in vibrant, pulsating colour, with little left to the imagination, the suite of utterly grisly tortures that await those who smuggle drugs into Singapore or take drugs while they are there or are in some other way bad. There seems to be some sort of ghoulishly barbaric competition going on between the local belief system's grisly squad of supernatural demons and the jolly japesters of the various Singaporean law enforcement agencies concerning who can be most inventively horrible, and it is profoundly not what you want to see when you're up to your eyelids in a whole unholy cocktail of supremely illegal and remarkably powerful drugs, not all of which are yet safely – ha! – actually inside your body or that of your partner in crime.

They wander around, assaulted by appalling images on all sides, bludgeoned by the screams – happy screams, definitely *happy* screams – of small children and impressionable adults, damp and getting damper as they stroll and stagger through clouds of water vapour being sprayed from path-side sprinklers studded amongst the flowers and shrubs.

Riotous profusions of insanely vivid blooms flourish everywhere; greenery of a thousand shades and wild outburstings of flowers fill every speck of un-concreted, ill-asphalted ground in the gardens. Alban keeps wanting to stop and look at all this fabulously fascinating flora and maybe take notes or something or take photographs with the disposable camera he's bought for the purpose – in fact, with one of the two disposable cameras he now has, because he forgot he'd bought the first one – but Fielding continually hustles him onward, demanding they exhaust the possibilities of the various exciting rides before they start looking at fucking flowers. Throughout the city Alban has sensed this vast, extravagant energy of growth and greenness forever trying to burst out through all the cement and tarmac, clawing at every missed nook and cranny in this fanatically self-controlled city, punching from every vacant patch of ground larger than a postage stamp like a violent reproof.

They get kind of locked into the water slide, which provides a fine view of the harbour and the docks and the ships at the quaysides and anchored offshore and steaming slowly along the nearer shipping lanes, not to mention Sentosa island, they think, which is where they're going next or possibly have already been to. The extra soaking at the bottom of the ride each time makes no difference whatsoever to their clothes and helps keep them cool. Then at the end of one turn, Fielding doesn't get out and Alban realises his cousin is asleep and snoring. In a way this is fine because it means they can go back to their hotel, but in a way it isn't really fine at all because Alban's forgotten which hotel it is they're staying in and has been trying to think of its name for the last two hours or so. He's checked his pockets but can't find a key card and he's looked in Fielding's wallet and pockets too and for the last half-hour or so he's had to contemplate desperate measures like just approaching people at random and asking if they recognise him or Fielding and might remember, say, which hotel bar, reception or restaurant they might have happened to see them in, though he suspects this plan may be a little on the optimistic side.

He's hauling a stumbling, incoherent Fielding along the path to the exit, thinking that maybe by some miracle he'll find a taxi driver in the rank who remembers taking them back to their hotel some time over the last week or so, when a tall tanned white guy in a baseball hat and shorts and a bum bag comes up to them, all smiles, and greets them both by name. *Fuck, we're rumbled; it's the pigs*, Alban has time to think, but he's wrong; it's just friendly cousin Steve – Linda and Percy's eldest – the guy who's never at home because he's always somewhere in the world installing or maintaining or replacing container terminal cranes but whom Alban and Fielding have both met at a couple of family weddings over the last few years. Which is great, though of course cousin Steve has absolutely no idea which is their hotel either.

While Alban is desperately trying to make small talk and remember how people behave when they're straight, Fielding wakes up with a start and stands staring at Steve with a stunned, terrified expression on his face and is unquestionably just about to start gibbering or screaming or throwing punches or running away or possibly all of the above when Alban throws himself on Steve's mercy by claiming they're both suffering mightily from some dodgy prawns consumed a couple of hours ago – the near-hallucinatory effects of which may admittedly have been accentuated by a beer or two – and could do with some help.

Steve's hotel is nearby. He takes them there and they straighten out sufficiently in his room while he's away summoning a doctor to be able to bribe the medic when he arrives so that he accepts and even confirms their story. Fielding wants to score some more drugs off the doc, but that's just going too far.

Somehow they're able to have a couple of beers in the hotel bar with Steve and push down a few morsels of a Vietnamese meal before making their excuses and heading back for the thankfully now remembered hotel and crashing for the next fourteen hours.

The reason he'd wanted to get drunk in the first place – being brutally honest – was because he was feeling sorry for himself. The reason he was feeling sorry for himself was he'd been rejected, again, by Sophie. She worked for the family firm, too, in the US sister company. When he'd started working for Wopuld Games Ltd he'd imagined they'd bump into each other all the time, but they almost never did. She'd been there in Singapore at the trade fair, though.

'You're the love of my life.' (Despairing; a last, pathetic roll of the dice.)

'Well, gee. I'll pass on that privilege.'

She seemed serious. He just stared at her. 'What have you become?' he whispered.

'Wiser.'

'Shit, that was close,' Fielding muttered. There was a beeping noise from somewhere and the big car's nose dipped as it braked sharply. A speed camera zipped past. Fielding was watching the rear-view mirror intently. He flashed Alban a grin. 'Made it!'

Alban had to turn his face away. The exit for Auchterarder and Gleneagles disappeared behind them as the car accelerated again, heading for Glasgow.

He's too young to be there, of course, but he is, all the same. He's with her as she comes down from her room, down the wide, gleaming stair-case under the tall, south-facing window and walks across the creaking parquet of the main hall towards the kitchen, and he's there as she turns into the short corridor that leads past the gunroom and the inside log store and the drying room to the cloakroom, and he watches as she stops and chooses what to wear to go outside.

She's dressed in brown Clark's shoes, a pair of white socks, jeans – her own, but too big, needing to be secured with a thin black belt – a brown blouse and an old white roll-neck jumper. White M&S underwear. No watch or rings or other jewellery; no cash, chequebook, credit cards or any form of identification or written material.

He watches her choose the long dark coat with the poacher's pockets. It's huge and almost black, its original dark green-brown staining weathered and worn and grimed over decades on the estate to something close to the darkness of the brown-black water in a deep loch. Sometimes he watches her go immediately right up to the coat and hoik it off the wooden peg between all the other coats and jackets, and sometimes he sees her stand there for quite a long time, in the gloom and the pervading smell of wax while rain patters off the glass in the shallow, high-set windows (because it was raining lightly, at the time).

The coat is too big for her, drowning her; she has to double back the cuffs of the sleeves twice, and the shoulders droop and the hem reaches to within millimetres of the flagstones. She rubs her hands over the waxy rectangles of the flapped external pockets, and looks inside at the poacher's pockets.

Then she goes through the outside door of the room, into the shining grey of the early afternoon. The door slams shut behind her, leaving him where he's been for some time now, screaming unheard at her; silently and hopelessly, begging her not to leave.

He woke from the doze and the dream – the recurring nightmare, he supposed, if it hadn't become so familiar and if he didn't know the ending so well by now – to find Fielding humming along to the last *Coldplay* album. They were just turning off the M8 where it passes through the centre of Glasgow, about ten minutes or so from Beryl and Doris's house.

Fielding grinned. 'You okay?'

Alban rubbed his face, scratched through his beard and yawned. 'Fine.'

He stood, resting a moment, in the sunken garden, south-west of the house on the far side of the abbey ruins, the rake held at the top in both hands and snugged in under his chin. He breathed deeply, taking in the sharp tang of wild garlic. A strong gust of warm wind moved the branches of the Scots pines along the western edge of the garden, shifting their shaggy, asymmetric tops slowly while the nearby stand of birches swayed together, like dancers. Blackthorns and wild roses rustled in the breeze, white and red blooms bobbing over the long grasses and the herringbone patterns of the brick pathway.

He looked at the wall of the abbey, hanging over the little valley like a grey cliff surmounted by the pointed arches of its empty windows, like a series of giant grey whalebones leaning against the sky. There was some ivy in a few places on the abbey's ruined walls, but last year he'd been to the gardens at Dunster Castle, not far away, just south of Minehead, and seen much more interesting climbers on the walls of the castle; stuff like *Solanum laxum*, *Clianthus puniceus* and *Rosa banksiae* 'Lutea'. They'd look good on the abbey's walls. He knew he'd taken notes at the time of his visit to Dunster but couldn't recall offhand in which direction the wall with the climbers had been facing. Had it been south? This was the abbey's south wall he was looking at. South should be perfect. They weren't the kind of plants that needed a lot of shade. He'd have to see about getting cuttings.

Movement on the path from the house.

Cousin Sophie, in a long white T-shirt and black leggings. Limping. She waved and hobbled down towards him. Looked like she could barely flex her right knee at all.

'What happened to you?' he asked.

'Fell off me 'oss, guv.'

Her gleaming red hair was held back in a ponytail. Her mega

T-shirt said, *Welcome To The Pleasure Dome*. One of his school pals, Plink – Robbie Alford – always seemed to find a double meaning in everything. Alban could just hear him saying something like, You can pleasure my dome any time, love. Alban thought about saying this, then thought perhaps not.

'See,' he said instead. 'Horses. Dangerous animals. Could have told you.'

He meant it lightly and he'd thought he'd been smiling when he'd said it, but she seemed to take it badly, scowling and saying, 'Anyway, how are your balls today, cousin?'

He felt himself rock backwards slightly. 'Ahm, they're, ah, fine, thanks,' he said, thoroughly fazed.

'Super,' she said acidly, nodding at the rake he was holding. 'Well, don't let me keep you.' She turned and started back up the path.

He didn't say anything. He watched her go. When she was almost out of sight, near the corner of the ruined abbey, she stopped, still turned three-quarters away from him, only her upper body visible, and looked down and seemed to nod downwards once, very sharply, as though she was angry or upset. Then she went on, copper hair bobbing slowly away out of sight.

He was annoyed with himself. He should have said something like, Great, actually; had a couple of really painful wanks last night, thanks. That would have got her back. He shook his head and gripped the rake properly, getting back to work. You never thought of the right thing to say at the time.

It was late afternoon of the same day. Alban and Sophie had been given the job of setting the table for a big family dinner that evening, with extra guests invited from amongst the many local friends of Uncle James and Aunt Clara. A couple Andy and Leah had known when Lydcombe had been their home had also been added on.

The table in the dining room was extended to its fullest extent, and had to be polished. The finest silverware was brought out and also had to be polished. It was surprisingly warm work; they opened the dining room's windows, letting in a cooling breeze. Sophie's face shone, little beads of sweat at her temples. She limped upstairs to put her hair up and swap her leggings and baggy T-shirt for shorts and a thin blouse. Later she opened a couple of the buttons, fanning herself.

Alban wondered if she knew how ridiculously, ferally attractive she looked. Was the girl flirting with him? He didn't know. He and his pals had talked about flirting and fancying and how you could tell whether a girl liked you or not and whether she wanted to do it, but for all their boasting and pretended certainty, it was still a madly confusing area. The stuff you saw on films and TV didn't really seem like it was in the real world, and porn was useless. He hadn't seen much porn, but he was damn sure the way to instant sexual success wasn't becoming a plumber or a pool technician. He had no idea. Maybe she was just teasing him because he'd upset her somehow earlier that morning.

Anyway, she was still his cousin. His pals had discussed this, too, after Plink had fallen totally if briefly in lust with one of his cousins, and it wasn't supposed to be illegal or anything, but it was definitely frowned on, discouraged, the stuff of jokes and adults going, *Diddle-ing ding ding ding* ding *ding ding*, which was something called *Duelling Banjos*, from an old film, and seemingly terribly witty.

Once they'd done the cutlery, Sophie announced she was going to the kitchen for a big bucket of water just off the boil, and started hobbling in that direction. He dashed after her and volunteered to do the carrying.

They put the bucket of hot water on the sideboard, on top of some old newspapers. She showed him how to hold the crystal and glasses in the rising steam, before giving them a polish.

'That's a handy tip,' he said. 'Who taught you that?'

'Old waitressing trick.'

'Ah hah.'

'Sorry if I was a bit, you know,' she said, glancing. 'This morning.'

'That's okay,' he said. Probably a bit too quickly, he realised. God it was hard getting this stuff right!

'Just annoyed at myself for falling.'

'That's okay. Sorry you got hurt.'

'Me too. Wasn't my fault, you know.'

'No?'

'No. Scrabbles decided to take a short cut, then changed her mind.'

'Really.'

'Soon as I get this knee working properly . . .' she said.

'Yes?' he asked, grinning, sensing he was being used as a straight man.

'I'm going to kick that bloody horse.'

'Well, give her one for me,' he said, then quickly added, 'Just kidding.'

'Yah,' she said, 'me too.'

They polished some more glasses, presenting them to the silently rising steam until they went cloudy with the moisture, and then smoothing them over with the cotton cloths. Songbirds sounded in the gardens beyond the opened windows, and a magpie gave its sharp, coughy call.

He looked at her. 'Can I ask you something?' he said.

She made a *tsk* noise. 'Does anyone ever say "No" to that sort of question?' she said, shaking her head. The ponytail flicked back and forth. 'Yeah, I suppose.'

'How come your dad got custody of you?'

'Oh, as opposed to my natural mum.' She shrugged. 'I dunno. Just unlucky I guess.'

'No, come on.'

Sophie put her hand to her mouth, rubbing at the little dimple between her top lip and the base of her nose, as though making sure her brace was still in there. She shrugged. 'Well, June – my real mother; you know, biologically – she was a bit wild. That's the family line, anyway. Apparently she ran off with another man. Spanish guy. Madrid. Not Tajo, the one she's with now; another one. Actually Tajo's quite nice. Very good-looking, very Spanish. He's an artist.

60

Very *hairy* though. He's quite a bit younger than her. She calls him "dishy". Honestly.' Sophie tutted and shook her head at such a lack of sophistication. 'Actually they're thinking about getting married.'

'So you've got two mothers as well.'

'Hah?'

'Same as me. I've got my real mother, the one that died, and Leah, Mum.'

Sophie looked thoughtful. 'Hmm. Yah. I suppose.'

They went on with the preparations.

'Young lady, you are *not* sitting down to dinner dressed like that,' Uncle James told his daughter. 'Not in my house.'

Sophie was wearing white heels, sparkly leggings and another T-shirt with a print of Michelangelo's David on the front. She looked down at it. Alban, who'd been out doing a bit of edging round one of the terraces and not realised how late it was getting, was stuck behind Uncle James, who was filling the bottom of the staircase as he looked up at his daughter. Alban really needed to get washed and changed – the house was full of the smell of food and he could hear conversations and smell cigarette smoke coming from the lounge – but he didn't feel he could just brush past Uncle James.

'Oh, sorry, Pops,' Sophie said as she looked back up from the black and white image. She snapped her fingers. 'You wouldn't recognise this. It's called art.'

'It's a full-frontal male nude and I for one refuse to sit looking at *that* at the dinner table,' her father told her. 'Now get changed. That is not suitable, and you know it.'

Sophie looked down at her father, seeming not to see Alban standing behind. 'James,' she said, 'I really hope right now you're secretly thinking, "Oh my God, I'm sounding like my father."'

'Don't tell me what to think, young lady.'

'Oh, that's just one-way traffic, is it?'

'And stop trying to be clever.'

61

She went, 'Ah!' and bent forwards as though hit in the solar plexus. 'Well, so much for that expensive education you're always—'

'Go up to your room and change at once,' he told her.

Sophie looked over his shoulder and smiled. 'Hey, Alban.' She turned on her heel. 'Whatever you say, Father dear.'

Uncle James turned and saw Alban. Uncle James wore a suit and an expression of some frustration. He looked quite red in the face. He smelled of smoke. 'Alban,' he said, standing aside. 'My God, you're filthy! Well, come on, come on. Get a move on. We haven't got all night.'

Alban bounded up the stairs two and then three at a time.

Later, he knew the precise moment when he fell in love with her. It was the day his parents would be departing for Richmond and leaving him behind at Lydcombe for the rest of the summer. A bunch of them – some of Sophie's friends plus Alban – had been down to Lynton, a few miles along the coast in Devon. One of the boys' dads had a speedboat there and took them out a handful at a time for a buzz around the bay, up to Foreland Point or out west to Woody Bay and Highveer Point. He'd been doing this the last few years and always flung the boat about and tried to get everybody soaked and the girls screaming.

Alban had gone out on one of the runs but hadn't really enjoyed it as much as he'd hoped. The guy at the controls was a git, he thought, just showing off in his wraparound sunglasses and his ridiculous stripy T-shirt, trying too hard to get everybody drenched (the sea was calm save for a long, lazy swell and he had to circle and seek out his own wake to find any suitable waves) and not even a very good boat handler, either, Alban suspected, probably putting them all at risk. The guy made everybody else wear life vests, though he didn't wear one himself.

Also, the girls sounded vacuous, the way they screamed so easily. Alban felt sadly disappointed in them, though he didn't really know any of them. He'd noticed that Sophie went back to saying 'yah' a lot when she was around these people. Her dentist had replaced her earlier cemented-in braces with a set she could take out, and she had removed them today.

Alban didn't go on either of the speedboat runs that Sophie took – he stayed in the quayside café, reading *L'Étranger* in French, for next year's class, very slowly, being made occasional fun of, but ignoring it – but he'd have put money on Sophie going all girlie, too, and screaming like a banshee every time the boat slammed off a wave or the least little bit of spray splashed any of them in the face.

The moment hit him as they got back to the house, picked up from Lynton and delivered home by Aunt Clara. His dad was crossing the hall carrying some bags as they came in through the front door, laughing and joking, Sophie leading the way.

'So, Sophie,' Andy asked her, 'did you enjoy the speedboat?'

'Yes I did!'

'Did you get awfully wet?'

'Blimey, Uncle, I didn't enjoy it that much.'

He is collecting her, scooping up the crumbs that fall from her mouth, clutching at them, cradling them, holding them up to look at them, minutely inspecting them, treasuring them, putting them into wildly ornate frames of desire and hope, encapsulating them in precious metal boxes and cabinets studded with jewels like some mouldering flake of bone declared a Catholic relic; something to be venerated, worshipped through its association, its alleged provenance.

The first is not something she said, just something he associates with her. He remembers a line – it's from a play, he thinks, maybe one by Shakespeare, from school (he wishes now he'd paid more attention in that particular lesson). It goes, 'Cuz, cuz, sweet cuz.' That's it. That's all. It's nothing really, just sounds, but it has become like a precious incantation for him, a sort of mantra.

'Cuz, cuz, sweet cuz.' He's been whispering it to himself for the last few nights as he's started to fall for her, lying in bed in the darkness, repeating it over and over, as if it's a spell, as though it might magically bring her to him, cause her to blur and shimmer into existence like she'd been beamed up or something. 'Cuz, cuz, sweet cuz. Cuz, cuz, sweet cuz. Cuz, cuz, sweet cuz . . .'

The rest have accumulated, the rest are all her own. He can still hear her say, 'They've all bloody gone!', still remember, with extraordinary precision, the exact tone and syllabic weighting of her voice when she said, 'Fell off me 'oss, guv', still replay in his head – every subtle nuance of pitch and timing and pronunciation captured as though on the most perfectly faithful recording mechanism ever invented – 'Blimey, Uncle, I didn't enjoy it that much.'

That last one is the jewel of jewels, the star of the cast. The quickness of it, the easy confidence, the sheer unashamed sexuality it revealed! (His dad had looked at her, not getting it for a moment. When he did, Andy had made a single explosive noise halfway between a laugh and an embarrassed cough. Then he'd grinned, gone slightly red and busied himself with packing the car. A couple of Sophie's girlfriends had squealed, one slapping her on the arm. Sophie had just kept on going across the hall, unconcerned, red hair undulating as she skipped to the stairs; la la la.)

He'd got it instantly, might even have been on the brink of saying something himself if she hadn't (the influence of his pal Plink, perhaps, seeing a sexual reference in everything. Or just rampant hormones). He stood and watched her go, her pals streaming around him, a huge smile forming on his face, something between admiration and adoration growing and blossoming inside him.

That night, thinking of her just a couple of rooms away, only three or so walls between them, he replays that phrase in his head time and time again, like a record, like a single you've just fallen in love with and need to listen to again as soon as you get to the end of it, hearing her voice, seeing captured images of her in his head – in the horse-riding outfit, in her shorts and blouse, in her leggings, in her jeans, red hair tumbling. He masturbates three times before he falls asleep, exhausting himself, hurting himself, having to use one cold, damp paper hanky twice, pumping no more than a dribble of thin water the last time before finally slipping into a feverish, troubled sleep where he still hears her silky voice, still sees her walk effortlessly, hips swaying, through the hazy sunlit gardens or swinging in slo-mo across the gleaming, polished wood of the hall.

'Well I don't think they're insipid. In fact, I think they're very sipid indeed.'

He could hear the tone of slightly hurt indignation in her voice, and began to smile so broadly he felt he had to turn away from her in case she was further insulted by his reaction. Then a moment later he realised it might have been deliberate – been wit, in fact, not a childish mistake.

He cleared his throat, turned back, studying Sophie's face. Very hard to tell. 'Sipid?' he asked, trying to sound grown up and knowing and like somebody from a film or something. They'd been talking about what bands they were into, and she liked – predictably, he felt – rather vacuous poppy, singly kind of stuff – just whatever was in the charts, basically. He was more into albums and artists like Bowie and bands like Talking Heads and Prefab Sprout and so on, though he had eclectic tastes; the next album he was going to buy was *Red Roses for Me*, by the Pogues, from last year (apparently their full name was something quite filthy in Gaelic, at least according to Plink). They had a new album out in a month or two, as well. He'd really been into U2 for a while there, but they were starting to look a bit too commercial after Live Aid.

Sophie wore brown hiking boots, black leggings and the Michelangelo David T-shirt Uncle James had objected to a week or so earlier. She'd sewn a little leaf made from some green material over the statue's genitals, which was just the perfect thing to do, because it at once removed the excuse her father had for telling her to take the T-shirt off, while at the same time acting as a constant reminder to him how ridiculous he was being. It had become her favourite piece of clothing, prioritised to the extent that she would

take it out of the just-washed pile and iron it herself – a rare distinction. Alban had noticed that Uncle James's face reliably turned one
to two shades of red darker every time he was confronted with the
article of clothing, which was, of course, often.

'What's wrong with "sipid"?' she asked.

'You sure that's a word?'

'You sure it's not?'

'I'm not claiming it isn't.'

'Then why are you mentioning it?'

'I'm just curious.'

Her eyes narrowed. 'You're just weird.'

He laughed. 'You don't mean that.'

Her eyes went wide. 'So now *you're* telling me what to think!
Thanks a lot.' She looked resentful and sat down on a tumbled piece
of dressed stone half buried in the mossy grass that covered the
inside of the ruined abbey like a green carpet. She'd wandered in
while he'd been de-mossing the grass with a rake. She had a stalk
of straw in her mouth, as though impersonating a yokel. She'd been
fiddling with this while they'd talked and now she replaced it between
her lips.

He shrugged and went back to scraping the moss out of the grass
and depositing it in the wheelbarrow. She watched him work for a
while. He tried to look strong and graceful and purposeful.

'What are you doing?' she asked.

He'd kind of assumed this was obvious. Was she serious? Her
expression was quite solemn, almost resentful, as though she was
still smarting about people ordering her around and telling her what
she thought or what she ought to feel.

'Taking the moss out of the grass,' he said, trying to pitch his
voice just right in case she was being sarcastic, but not making it so
obvious that she'd be further insulted if it had been an honest, innocent enquiry.

'Why?'

'Because otherwise the moss takes over.' He glanced up at the grey remains of the building's high walls. 'It's cos it's quite shaded in here.'

'Can't you just let the moss take over?'

He shrugged again. 'Suppose. It'd always look patchy, though.'

She was silent for a while, seemingly lost in watching him work. 'Dad's talking about getting a swimming pool,' she said.

'Oh.' He supposed the house could do with one.

'Yeah. They went to see some Round Table friends over in Barnstaple the other night – 'member the really hot one?'

'Yeah.'

'They had a pool. Very nice time was had by all, apparently. Well, Mum had to drive back after Dad said he would, but I think she's used to that. Better than him drinking and driving.'

Alban straightened, looked at her. 'Hang on,' he said. 'Where are they thinking of putting the pool? Which bit of the garden?' The more he thought about it, the more he wondered how you could fit one in.

She shrugged, studied the end of the stalk she was chewing. 'I dunno. Somewhere next to the house.'

He tried to think of other places he'd been that had pools. 'Inside? Covered? Or outside? How big?'

She looked at him, tipped her head way to one side so that her long red ponytail hung, swaying heavily in the afternoon sunlight streaming through one of the tall, broken stone arches. 'Underground, twenty-two-point-five metres long. Three wide. Green and purple tiles. Four diving boards and a slide.' She shook her head, eyes widening as she looked away again, chewing on her straw. 'How should I know? Just a pool.'

He stared at the part of the house he could see; a corner of slate roof and one dormer window, side on. They'd have to put this stupid pool on the first terrace, the parterre on the south-west side. Bastards! There were some beautiful flowers and shrubs there. Bastards!

'Huh,' he said. He attacked the moss and the rake dug in, catching soil. He shook it free, altered the angle and pulled at the same patch again, more gently. He tapped the moss into the wheelbarrow, then tugged the reluctant remainders off and threw them in, too.

'How's your knee?' he asked her.

'S'okay.' She was concentrating on smoothing the end of the chewed stalk down, pressing it hard between a thumb and index finger.

'You got a moment?' he asked her. She looked up at him. He shrugged. 'You up for doing a bit of work?'

She raised her dark eyebrows. 'What sort of work?'

'Shifting stuff. Two-man job.'

She gave a taut little smile, as though she wanted to smile more, but was controlling it.

'I'm not a man,' she said quietly to the stalk.

He left a tiny pause. 'Yeah, I'd noticed.' His mouth had gone quite dry all of a sudden.

'Cheers, cousin,' she said archly, rising smoothly from the stone, throwing the straw away and putting her hands on her hips. She looked, he thought, great. 'Okay, what?'

He grinned, mouth not so dry any more. 'Don't worry. Nothing too strenuous.'

'I'm not worried. Come on then.'

He gave her the rake to carry and lifted the wheelbarrow. She followed him.

'What are these?'

'Not entirely sure,' he admitted.

They were standing on a large lawn on the north-east side of the gardens, near the Wilderness and the bog garden, surrounded by azaleas and American Black Walnut trees. The lawn was bisected by a long straight ditch which emerged from beneath the trees on a low bank to the south and disappeared under the azaleas to the north. About three-quarters of the ditch had been partially filled with long wooden posts, covered in places by moss and grass.

'They look a bit like strainer posts or gateposts or something.'

'What's a strainer post?'

'Sort of, umm, heavy-duty post you sink in really deep where a fence changes direction.'

'How interesting. What are they doing here?'

'No idea. Looks like somebody once thought of filling in the rill, but using wood is just mad, it'll—'

'A what? A rill?'

'This is a rill,' he said, indicating the length of the ditch. He squatted and pulled at the grass on the edge of the ditch, lifting up the sod to reveal a flat stone surface. 'A water channel. Artificial; ornamental.'

'Couldn't just call it a water channel.'

'Na, it's a rill.'

'So,' she asked, 'what's the idea? Try not to use any more technical terms.'

'We lift the logs out of the rill and . . .' he looked over at the east edge of the lawn. It was further away than he remembered when he'd first thought of this. 'Roll them over there. That direction.'

She leaned over, looking down. 'They look a bit damp for the fire.'

'It's not for the fire. The idea is to clear the rill, see if we can get it working again.' She didn't look convinced. 'It'd be nice!' he told her. She nodded, looking as though she was humouring him. He spread his arms and smiled encouragingly. 'Anyway. Just getting them out will be a big help. But they're not small. If this looks like too much for you, you know; just, umm, well, you know. It doesn't, I mean, it won't really –'

She was looking down again. 'They're going to be full of insects and worms and stuff, aren't they?'

'Umm, well, yeah, probably,' he had to agree.

She made a show of looking round his rear. 'That a pair of gloves in your back pocket?'

'No, I'm just pleased to, umm, wave you goodbye.'

She looked at him, brows raised, mouth pursed.

He cleared his throat. 'Yeah, that was rubbish. Here; have the gloves.'

The system they worked out was to pull the grass and moss away from each of the semi-decayed logs and dig out the sand and earth surrounding them. Then she stood inside the rill, feet braced against the stone walls of the channel while he leaned over from the side; they slid out one log at a time to make it protrude into the part of the rill that hadn't been filled in so that he could get a good grip underneath it, then they lifted each one together, grunting and staggering, and rolled the log up on to the grass. They'd leave the rolling away bit till later, or another day.

He thought he heard her bite back a squeal the first time they disturbed a big colony of silverbacks, but after that she just seemed to ignore the various insects they uncovered.

'Woh!' she yelled, when they lifted one log and a whole brown swarming family of tiny fieldmice scattered in various directions. She stepped quickly back, then grinned sheepishly at him and took hold of the log again.

The posts were partially waterlogged, heavier than he'd expected. He had the harder job, working from the side and above, but he was still impressed that she worked so hard and uncomplainingly. The day was hot and they both sweated a lot. She rolled her T-shirt sleeves up as high as they would go, not that this made much difference.

When she got a dark brown-green stain on her T-shirt from the end of a log, she said, 'Shit!'

She looked at him, breathing hard. She wiped under her nose with one forearm. She pointed one gloved finger at her T-shirt. 'You won't get any wrong ideas if I take this off, will you?'

Oh, Jesus, he thought. 'Scout's honour,' he said, saluting. He'd been thinking of taking his own shirt off – it was an old one of Uncle James's, frayed at collar and cuffs – but now that might look like, well, like he was getting the wrong idea or something. Maybe he'd just undo one more button and roll his sleeves up a bit further instead.

She took off the gloves then crossed her arms beneath her breasts and pulled her T-shirt up over her head, revealing a lacy white bra.

Oh, fucking hell. This was brilliant; her T-shirt stuck on her head/ponytail and he got a totally free chance to ogle her amazing, completely globular, lightly tanned breasts while she was cursing and struggling before finally pulling the T-shirt off, her face looking red and hot and flustered when it eventually emerged.

'Get a good look?' she asked him, rolling up the T-shirt and lobbing it on to the grass.

Oh, fuck! 'What at?' he asked, missing both convincingly faked sincerity and complicit sarcasm completely and sounding, he was painfully aware, like a total dork; he might as well have leered and gone, *phwoar, yeah!*

She shook her head and looked away, fiddling two-handed behind her head with the band holding her ponytail. This both raised her breasts and made them jiggle. He felt himself getting an erection. *Oh, great.*

The rest of the summer, he could just tell, was going to be about never getting anywhere near this fabulous creature.

'Well, back to work,' she said. 'Tote that log, lift that big lump of wood . . .'

They worked long into the late afternoon, almost wordlessly from the simple effort of it. A light breeze cooled them a little, but it was still hot work. His hair stuck to his scalp and the shirt to his back. They swatted away flies. He caught glimpses of little rivulets of sweat running down between her breasts and within the runnel on her back formed by the muscles on either side of her spine – her body's own miniature rill. He'd kind of hoped to see her panties, maybe, but the leggings rode too high on her hips. The slanting afternoon sun was golden, coating her body in a glowing, honey light.

They finished, and lay on the lawn, one on either side of the revealed rill, each spread-eagled on the cool grass in the shadow of the trees, panting, exhausted. He wondered what would happen if Uncle James, say, discovered them like this. What would he think?

Sophie put her T-shirt back on. They traipsed back to the house, muscles burning.

'We'll be sore tomorrow,' she said.

'Or the day after,' he said as they climbed to the highest terrace just down from the house. The breeze had gone, and the garden seemed stuck in some breathless, timeless moment, only the buzzing of insects indicating any moving life beyond the two of them.

'God,' she said. 'Still hot, isn't it?'

'Yeah,' he agreed, and laughed. 'Be good to have a pool.'

She looked over at him and smiled as they went up the steps and in through the French windows to the smell of a garlicky salad dressing and the sound of a radio.

Suddenly he's kissing her! They're at a party in a big open-sided barn on a farm near Bampton on the edge of the National Park that belongs to the parents of one of Sophie's girlfriends and they've all been drinking cider – gradually lapsing into stupid, growling, absurdly broad West Country accents and probably deeply pissing off any locals present, going 'Oh-arr, Oh-arr!' and 'Oi shall drink moi soyder,' and 'Garr she be lurverly', and all sorts of other rubbish – and dancing madly to a load of bands neither of them has ever heard of – not that they're admitting this, obviously, until he does at one point and she admits the same – and taking little puffs of joints though the smoke barely gets past either of their tonsils, frankly, and they spend a lot of time coughing and having to drink more of the cider to soothe their burning throats.

But he's kissing her! She's letting him! She's kissing him back! They're kissing! He almost can't believe it.

They all watched the sun going down and they turned the music down so that they could go to the farmhouse to phone parents in turn and tell them they were fine. This is meant to be a sort of sleep-over and a lot of the parents think it's the farmer guy and his wife who are in charge of things and making sure everybody behaves themselves, but it's the nephew and his girlfriend who are there instead, giving the older couple a holiday, and the thing is they're into a smoke and a drink and whatever and certainly happy to host an all-night party and they're like totally relaxed about pretty much anything, though the nephew guy does carry a fire extinguisher around with him, even when there's a spliff hanging out of his mouth, because it is a barn after all even though it's mostly empty and there is a fair bit of straw lying around and people are smoking. There's a fairly serious sound system rigged up in the back of the barn and barrels and troughs full of ice or at least cold water to put cans and bottles in. They haven't even needed to bring booze because the nephew guy has bought loads and is selling it almost at cost price and also has this really strong, filthily cloudy cider in a couple of big demijohns which his girl-friend is selling in little white plastic cups – each one strong as a normal pint, she says, and after a couple nobody's disagreeing.

At first Sophie dances with a few other guys and the older nephew who's called Jamie, and Alban just sits and watches people and asks a couple of girls to dance when they look at him, but only one does and she's a bit small and a lot drunk and staggers and soon goes off to throw up and so he doesn't pursue that, while the other girl, it turns out, is with a big fair-haired drunk Young Farmer type who takes considerable exception to this suggested dance and offers to fight Alban, who apologises and holds up both hands and walks away and goes back and sits on one of the straw bales and concen-trates on drinking, until Sophie plonks herself down beside him, breathless from dancing, and moans about how fucking knackered she is because it's only two days after their heroic afternoon's work in the rill.

She's wearing really tight jeans and a sheer black top you can see this black bra through, and she's taken off her boots and is dancing in her bare feet and she really is blaming Alban for making her feel so totally frazzled; it's all his fault, so he offers to dance for her, and so she gets up on his back, head over his shoulder, his arms round her thighs, and he dances like that with a couple of her girlfriends while she waves her arms about and bounces up and down, nearly sending them flying to the ground a couple of times but not quite, and a few other guys do the same thing with their girlfriends. He gets totally exhausted after a couple of songs and has to let her down and stagger dramatically to a wall of bales at the back of the barn; they sit on the ground with their backs to the bales and her leaning alongside him, laughing, until she goes and gets them both cups of the strong, cloudy cider and comes back and sort of slumps against him, still breathless and giggling, then, next thing, while the last of the sunset disappears from the western sky and the barn's lights shine down on them, suddenly – amazingly, unaccountably, without either of them really seeming to start it – they're kissing; just a little sort of dipping/rising mouth-peck at first, then serious, no-exclusion-zone open-mouth tongue-involving action, cider cups set aside/dropped shamelessly on to the ground, turned crushed into each other, arms pulling tighter.

After a few moments she pulls away suddenly, a massive frown on her flushed face. 'How did this happen?' she asks, sounding horri-fied.

He shakes his head. 'I don't know!' he says loudly, waving his arms about. 'Good, though, isn't it?'

The horrified expression dissolves and she laughs and starts to say something but it's smothered as she falls to him again, mouth against mouth against tongue against tongue.

Later, behind the barn, out of sight, while the music thuds on the far side of the corrugated metal wall, they keep kissing and cuddling and fondling and just holding each other. Her hair is the most wonderful thing he has ever smelled. He's been allowed to undo her bra and feel her beautiful, magnificent breasts and rub her between the legs through the jeans but she won't let him undo the jeans at all, though she strokes his cock through his jeans, up and down so that he thinks he's probably about to come a dozen times but never quite does, and his balls ache, like a memory.

'We really shouldn't be doing this,' she says at one point when they're lying there pressed together, panting, giving their mouths a rest.

'It's not illegal,' he points out.

'Yeah, but still.'

'Anyway, we haven't *done* anything yet.'

'What do you mean "yet"? What, you think we're going to? Do you? Huh?'

He hugs her closer, buries his nose in her fabulous hair again. It smells of the outside, of the open air and every beautiful plant and flower and grass in the whole world. 'Well,' he says, 'it's crossed my mind even if it hasn't crossed yours.'

She doesn't say anything to that, but keeps on stroking the small of his back with one hand and the nape of his neck with the other. This goes on for some time. He thinks, *I would never grow bored with this.*

'I'm not really a proper virgin, you know,' she tells him.

He pulls back, looks at her.

'Blame Scrabbles,' she says with a small smile he can just about make out in the darkness. She shrugs. 'Some saddle, anyway.'

'Oh,' he says. It takes him a while to get this. He hadn't known it could work that way. He's always (well, for the last couple of years or so since girls and sex started to become of interest) found this idea that females come sort of factory sealed kind of weird – like nature playing into the hands of religious nutters or something. Oh well. Even when you thought you knew everything about sex, there was always some detail left to learn. 'Well, umm, you know,' he says, feeling a little out of his depth here and suddenly entirely pathetic.

'What about you? Have you done it?' she asks. It sounds to him like she's trying to sound casual. 'Tell the truth.'

He thinks about lying, all the same, but then says, 'Ahm, well, ahm, no. No. 'Fraid not. A virgin too. Totally.'

She goes quiet and still for a while, then says, 'Well, this is just, you know.'

75

He doesn't know. 'What?' he asks.

'Well,' she says. 'Just fun.'

'Yeah. Yeah, it's fun. That's true.'

'I don't think we're going to do anything. I don't think that would be – that would make sense.'

'Yeah, okay.'

In a way he's devastated, because this has all felt like it might be leading up – eventually, even if not tonight – to doing it properly, but on the other hand he fully expected never even to get this far with her, in fact never really thought to get anywhere with her – never to get to kiss her, certainly; not proper kissing, not with semi-serious groping too, so it's all been a bonus in a way . . .

At the same time . . . Oh, hell, she was his cousin. Part of the family. He'd be better off doing it the first time with a civilian. This would have to do for now. This *would* do for now. This was, in the end, great. He wants to throw his head back and laugh out loud, wild and mad and uncaring, howling unhinged into the darkness, but he's worried this would seem a bit weird and alarming, so he doesn't.

She says, 'Let's kiss again.'

They end up crashing out in the barn with about a dozen other sleeping couples, snuggling together under an old tarpaulin, taking cups of water from the stuff in the barrels where the cans and bottles had been stored. A little after dawn, long before anybody stirs, she cuddles up to him, spooning against his back, nestling in, holding him, making tiny, faint, fast asleep noises.

He whispers, 'Cuz, cuz, sweet cuz' to her, to himself, very, very quietly, then drifts off to sleep again, smiling.

Great-Aunts Beryl and Doris live in the upper three-quarters of a fine tall sandstone townhouse cinched within a grand sweep of similar properties forming a terrace in deepest Hillhead. The streets are lined with cars. Amazingly, Fielding finds a parking space almost right outside the place.

He and Alban arrive to a house in turmoil. There are shrieks coming from inside. The front double doors are hanging wide. All the windows are open, curtains billowing from several. What appears to be orange smoke is issuing from one of the windows on the top floor.

A middle-aged man in a boiler suit is standing at the top of the relatively narrow steps rising from the garden flat beneath, holding on to one of the whorls of metal which form the end of the two elegant railings bracketing the broad front steps leading to the main dwelling. He is looking up at the open front door. Halfway between him and the doorway, a large lump of raw red meat is lying in the middle of one step. The meat looks rather squashed and blood is spattered alarmingly around it. The man looks round as Alban and Fielding walk up the steps from the street. 'You the police?' he asks, with what sounds like relief.

'No,' Fielding says firmly, 'we're family.'

3

'Men, Doris! There are men here! We have men!'

'What's that? Have you found it? Say again?'

'*Men*, you cloth-eared old tortoise!' Great-Aunt Beryl bellowed up the stairs to the first floor.

Great-Aunt Beryl was small, thin and ninety but possessed of a surprisingly powerful voice. She was dressed in faded blue overalls with a scarf tied round her head and knotted over her forehead. A few wisps of white hair protruded. She held an old-fashioned broom with a vicious-looking Bowie knife gaffer-taped to the handle. On closer inspection, the turn-ups of her overalls had been gaffer-taped to the rubber of her black Wellington boots.

'Beryl, what's going on?' Alban asked.

'So nice to see you, Alban, and you, Fielding!' the old lady said, the Bowie knife flashing dangerously near to the two men and making them flinch as she reached out to shake their hands. 'Come in, come in! You've arrived at just the right time. We have various escapees. Arm yourselves and come help. Oh, you're men; you won't need to arm yourselves.'

A voice floated down from the floor above. 'Beryl, who is that? To whom are you talking?'

'Beryl—' Alban began.

79

'Men, Doris, men! Nephews!' Great-Aunt Beryl shouted up the stairs. She turned back to Alban. 'What, dear?'

'Who's escaped?'

'Not who, dear; what. About half a dozen mice and, now, Boris.'

'Boris?'

'He's a python. Actually, he's a she, but it was a long time before we found out and Boris rather stuck, d'you know?'

'You have an escaped *snake* in here?' Fielding said, looking worried, his gaze darting about the hallway. 'How big is it?'

'About eight feet in length.'

'Jesus,' Fielding said, drawing his feet together.

'Fielding, language!' Great-Aunt Beryl barked.

Fielding swivelled to look around the hallway again, holding on to his cousin's sleeve as he leaned over and tried to see behind various potted plants and tall vases standing on small tables. The stretch of corridor to the side of the stairs looked suspiciously dark and extensive.

'Beryl, are you talking to tradesmen?'

'No, it's – oh, do listen, dear!'

'There's, ah, a lump of meat lying outside,' Fielding said, gaze flicking this way and that.

'Yes,' Great-Aunt Beryl said. 'We were trying to set a trap but it fell out of the window. Then we remembered we had some indoor fireworks from the Jubilee and thought we might utilise smoke to flush the wildlife into the open, thus far without success. Largely, though, our strategy has consisted of stamping and screaming.'

'Beryl, I demand to know who you're talking to! I can't hold the fort up here myself for ever, you know!'

'Oh, for goodness' sake!' Great-Aunt Beryl said. She thrust the broom with the taped-on Bowie knife at Alban, who started backwards, but took hold. The old lady turned and stamped up the wide wooden stairs. 'First thing tomorrow,' she shouted upwards, 'we call Doctor McLaughlin and make an appointment for another ear-syringing!' She turned halfway up and looked back at the two men.

'If you see any mice,' she told them, 'don't hesitate to skewer the little blighters. Boris prefers them alive, but I reckon if he's hungry enough he'll eat them cold.'

'What about the snake?' Alban asked.

'Oh, for pity's sake, don't skewer Boris. Grab him behind the head. Don't worry if he winds himself around your arm. Though of course if he goes for your neck, dissuade him gently.'

Alban smiled and raised the home-made pike as Great-Aunt Beryl disappeared round the turn in the stairs. 'Righty-ho,' he said. He glanced at Fielding, who was looking at him. He shrugged.

'"Well, you may regard him as you wish," Doris said to me.

'"I shall, too," I said.

'"I still think he's a jolly good egg."

'"Perhaps so," I said, "but his brains are scrambled!"'

Great-Aunt Beryl threw back her head and laughed loudly. Her black wig, topped by a small hat made largely from purple feathers, tipped back alarmingly and threatened to come off, but she snapped her head forward again and it resumed its rightful place. Then she reached over and squeezed Alban's forearm with surprising force. 'More cherry brandy?'

'I'm kind of full up, thanks, Beryl.'

'That's not quite what I meant, dear.'

'I beg your pardon.' Alban reached to the drinks trolley sitting between him and Beryl. 'Allow me.'

'Oh, thank you. Not too – oh never mind, eh?'

Great-Aunt Doris took a moment or two longer to get, or possibly remember, the joke, but then laughed quite loudly, too. Her head didn't go quite so far back. A few little flecks of spittle danced like fireflies under the lights, all of which, like most of the lights and lamps in the house, were covered by thin scarves and gauzy pieces of material. The dining room was tall, bay-windowed and panelled in what Alban was fairly sure was mahogany. Long lilac curtains festooned themselves over the windows and pooled on the teak floor. Only the white cube of a new-looking and fully-plumbed-in Bosch dishwasher, sitting to one side of the attractively tiled fireplace, rather jarred.

Both Alban and Fielding had stared at it when they'd first walked in.

'Saves all that traipsing,' Great-Aunt Beryl had explained.

The two old ladies had dressed in ancient formal evening wear – long, high-necked silky dresses – and opened up their dusty dining room for the occasion, even though the two men had no clothing quite so formal. Fielding had a dark grey business suit, which he duly wore, but the best Alban could do was put on a clean, if unironed, white shirt with his most recently washed jeans.

Dinner itself was a Chinese takeaway, delivered by an amiable young man named Shing who was on first-name terms with Beryl and Doris. The dining table rather outshone the takeaway containers and the ladies confessed that the crockery was only their second best (certain takeaway foods were liable to contain ingredients which might stain the finer plates); however the champagne and wine, selected by Fielding from an old scullery which now served as a wine cellar, had been – save for one lamentably corked bottle of La Mission Haut-Brion 1950 – very good indeed.

'So, Fielding,' said Great-Aunt Doris, addressing Alban.

'It's Alban, dear,' Beryl informed her. She glanced at Alban and shook her head. Fielding wasn't even in the room at that point.

'Of course,' Doris said, waving one hand imperiously. She was a little more robustly made than Beryl – a sparrow to her wren – but still gave an impression of delicacy and even frailty compared to Beryl's aura of air-dried toughness. Doris wore a similar hat to Beryl, though her feathers were crimson and her wig was platinum blonde. She wore alarming horn-rimmed glasses she called her Dame Ednas. 'So, Alban,' she said, 'are you well?'

'Every bit as well as he was fifteen minutes ago, when you last asked, one imagines, dear,' Beryl told her crisply.

'Really?' Doris said, blinking behind her glasses. 'And what did you say then, my love?'

'I said I was well, thanks,' Alban told her, smiling.

'Jolly good,' Doris said. 'Well, perhaps now I've asked you a sufficient number of times, it'll stick, d'you know what I mean? And I shall remember. Ha!'

'Yes, perhaps,' Beryl said.

'I say,' Doris said, looking serious, 'is there any more of that peach schnapps?'

'Here we are,' Alban said, refreshing her glass.

Great-Aunt Doris made little cooing noises as he filled the thin glass, which was somewhere in size between a liqueur shot and a schooner.

'And so,' she said, when the glass was nearly full, 'did you have to get a pink chit from, umm . . . from, umm . . . ?'

'A pink chit?' Alban asked.

'You know – permission to . . .' she waved one thin, vein-ribbed hand around, 'from your other . . . I've forgotten her—'

'Oh. No, I'm not currently with anybody, Doris.' He raised his glass and smiled. 'Not properly.'

'What about that young mathematician girl?' Beryl asked. 'Verushka. She seems jolly nice.'

'She is. But we're not a couple.'

'You aren't?' Beryl said, seemingly surprised.

'No,' he told her. 'That's not really what either of us is looking for.'

Doris tutted. 'A handsome young man like you? You must have the girls falling at your feet, I should say. Wouldn't you say, Beryl?'

'I should say,' Beryl affirmed.

Doris leaned a little closer over the table and lowered her voice. 'Are we still sowing our wild oats?' she asked, and winked.

'While playing the field,' Alban told her.

'Ploughing the field?' Doris looked a little nonplussed. She looked at Beryl. 'Is that rude?'

Beryl ignored her and leaned to Alban. 'And always trying to ensure there's a crop failure, what?' she snorted.

'You're not a gay, are you, dear boy?' Doris asked.

'Oh, Doris, really!' said Beryl.

'Fielding and you aren't—?' Doris went on, now looking thoroughly confused.

'No, Doris. I'm pretty sure neither of us is remotely gay.'

'Oh,' Doris said, frowning. 'Only I'm sure we could have given you a room together.'

Alban laughed. 'I imagine if I find Fielding in my bed tonight, Doris, it'll be because Boris has escaped again.'

'What?' Doris looked alarmed. 'Boris has—?'

'Boris is in his tank, dear,' Beryl said loudly. 'And Alban is not a gay!'

'Oh,' Doris said, looking hardly less bewildered. 'Jolly good. Well, cheers!' She drank from her schnapps glass, then dabbed lightly at her thin lips with her napkin.

Finally everything's ready. He'd thought this was all going to go horribly wrong when he'd found the nearest socket and it was round pin – round pin! – but either the house had two separate circuits or the old sockets had been left in place when the building had been rewired, because there's a normal double socket along the wall a bit.

'Ladies and gentleman,' Fielding says, clapping his hands as he opens the dining-room door, 'presentation is served!'

'Presentation?' Alban asks as they escort the two old bats through to the drawing room. This all takes a while, as Beryl and Doris flutter and fuss and dither one way then the other, collecting shawls and handbags and pillboxes, glasses cases and whatever the hell else and wittering on about God knows what all the time, but finally – holding on to the arms of the men like children – they are led through to the drawing room, where Fielding has chairs set up and the laptop plus projector sitting on the table facing a white sheet slung across the window alcove.

Al looks at Fielding as they get the girls seated. 'You're doing a presentation?' he asks, like it's funny or something.

'Well, *duh*,' Fielding tells him.

'Power Point.'

'What else?'

'Like, with bullet points?' Al says, a big dumb grin on his face.

'Of *course*!'

'Fielding,' Al says, shaking his head.

'What?' Fielding says, but now Al's fussing about getting a table over so the old girls have somewhere to rest their drinks. Fielding turns off the main light so that the only illumination is coming from a standard lamp in one corner and the empty white light the projector is throwing at the sheet.

'I say, Fielding,' Beryl says, 'what is this thing?' She's pointing at the projector.

'That's a projector, Great-Aunt Beryl. Now.' Fielding claps his hands, standing before them, the projector acting like a soft spotlight on him. He's taken off his jacket, rolled up his shirtsleeves and loosened his tie, so he's looking pretty casual. Friendly, even. 'First of all, I'd like to say thank you to Beryl and Doris for a wonderful meal and enchanting hospitality.' This is a bit shameless, Fielding thinks, considering the embarrassment of having to eat a takeaway Chinese, even though the drink was almost tragically good. Never mind. Flatter to be received. They're wined and dined and their bums are on the seats. 'I don't think it's any secret that the family firm, Wopuld Limited – indeed, the whole Wopuld Group – has been approached—'

'Are we going to see some slides?' Doris asks nobody in particular.

'Yes,' Beryl says. 'I think so, dear.'

'Well, it's a computer presentation, technically,' Fielding tells them, taking his silver laser pointer from his shirt pocket and flourishing it. 'Anyway, as I was saying. The Wopuld Company, Limited. The Wopuld Group. And Spraint. The Spraint

Corporation. The Spraint Corporation of America.' Fielding tightens his mouth, looks down and turns sideways to them, then starts to pace slowly, hands behind his back. Fielding thinks of this as his Ladies and Gentlemen of the Jury dynamic. 'I remember when I was—'

'So, is there a computer?' Beryl asks, looking under the table.

'Yes, that's the computer there, Great-Aunt.'

'What, this?'

'Yes, that.'

'Ah. So this is a portable type of computer?'

'Notebook laptop, Great-Aunt. Now—'

'So, shouldn't we be facing it, then? I mean, I can't see the tube, the screen thing. Can you, Doris?'

'What's that, dear?'

'See the screen. On this thing.'

'I . . . well, it's there.'

'Yes, but can you see it?'

'Well, sort of.'

'But not properly?'

What the hell are they talking about? 'I'm sorry, I don't . . .' Fielding starts to say, then realises. 'Oh, I see what you mean! No, that's the idea, you see. The computer tells the projector what to put on the big screen, here. The sheet, see? You don't have to look at the screen on the computer. And I control it with this little remote. All very clever, but that's just the tech.'

'A remote control?' Beryl says, squinting at the device Fielding has just produced from his back pocket.

'Are we going to watch television?' Doris asks.

'Look, ladies, these are just the tools, you know? Not really the point of the whole exercise.' Fielding glances at Alban but he's not being any help at all, just sitting with legs and arms folded, grinning at his cousin.

'I do hope that's not off my bed!' Doris says, staring at the sheet. 'Ha ha ha!'

This, Fielding thinks, *is ridiculous*. 'Look, I'll show you.' He steps to the side and clicks up the company logo opening shot, showing a kind of stylised *Empire!* board with lots of pieces and cards scattered about, the camera swooping down on to the playing surface, banking and swerving around the pieces and over the various territories.

'Oh, my!'

'Good heavens!'

Fielding smiles. That's got their attention. This is just a glorified screen saver really, but it shows how the system works.

'I say, that is clever!' Beryl says.

'Is this a film?' Doris looks confused again. 'Are we going to watch a film?' She leans over to Beryl. 'I shall need to go, you know, if we're going to watch a whole film.'

Fielding clicks on to an ancient sepia photo of Great-Grandfather, company founder Henry Wopuld, looking very grand and Victorian in his whiskers.

'I remember when I was—' Fielding begins again.

'Look, Doris!' Beryl exclaims. 'It's old Henry.'

'Oh, it is slides,' Doris says. 'So what was that other thing?'

'Is this all inside the projector what-do-you-call-it?' Beryl asks.

'No, it's all in the computer,' Fielding tells her, keeping calm. 'The projector just puts what's in the computer on to the screen. Do you understand? And I control it with my remote. It's just the usual . . . It's just the means to the end.' Fielding clicks back to the company screen-saver sequence. 'See?'

'There it is again!' Doris exclaims. She leans over to Al. 'Alban – whatever is going on?'

'Technical wizardry, Doris,' he tells her.

'And are you doing this?' she asks.

'No, Fielding is. I'm just the sidekick.'

'You're psychic?'

'Sidekick, Doris,' he says more loudly, laughing. 'I'm just the assistant.'

Not – in Fielding's considered opinion – that Al's assisting with anything whatso-fucking-ever, the smug asshole. He's just sitting grinning. Meanwhile, Fielding is getting hot under the collar. 'Look, everyone,' he says, 'I realise all this technology might seem quite—'

'So, what else do you have in here?' Beryl is asking, leaning over to look at the computer. She reaches out to touch the machine.

'Beryl! Please don't—!' Fielding starts to say. She doesn't touch it, but he must have clicked the remote because the movie of the game board clicks back to old Henry, then on to some shots of famous people playing *Empire!* as a board game – here's Bing Crosby and Bob Hope looking slightly startled, playing the US version, here's the famous still from that old TV film about the Royal Family with the game in the background at Balmoral, here's another still from when they were playing it in *EastEnders* (they couldn't name it but, again, you could just about make out the board, and one of the characters kept talking about 'this game of world domination'). Then there's a few seconds of action from the latest version of the electronic version, followed by an animated graph of past sales, with projected future sales zooming away into the top right. Basically this is ruining Fielding's presentation. 'Sorry, sorry.' Fielding lets go a sigh and clicks back through the images to old Henry.

'Henry again!' Doris says. 'I think I've seen this bit.'

'I think this is where we came in, dear,' Beryl tells her. She smiles at Fielding, just as he makes the mistake of checking that the laser pointer's working by shining it at the palm of his hand. 'Oo! And what is that thing for? What does that do?' she asks.

'It's a laser pointer,' Fielding tells her, resigned. He points it at the corner of the sheet/screen.

'What's that?' Doris asks.

From this point on Fielding kind of loses them. They're far more interested in the pointer, the remote, and the idea that the laptop is pushing images through the connecting cable to the projector than they are about Spraint Corp's takeover bid and Fielding's carefully worked-up history of, and tribute to, the family's long and successful struggle to bring high-quality board and electronic gaming to a waiting world.

Somehow they end up playing a game of the medieval action version of *Empire!*, hacking and slashing through vast battles and towering sieges and dodging cannonballs the size of basket balls, though without the proper controllers, just using the laptop's configured buttons, it's pretty messy. Being drunk probably doesn't help, either. Doris and Beryl take turns using the laser pointer as either a pretend weapon or to highlight the crotches and codpieces of the various characters. Beryl in particular seems to love the gore, and shrieks regularly and loudly. Doris goes off to make coffee, refuses any help and reappears with tea. Irish tea, if there is such a thing – she's put whisky in it. It tastes hideous.

Beryl advances to the rank of Margrave. Alban laughs a lot. Doris falls asleep. A mouse skitters across the floor from under the screen, heading for the door. They all chase it.

Alban lay in bed for a little while, drinking water and thinking back to the phone call he'd made earlier. He'd asked to use the phone shortly after they'd rounded up most of the mice and discovered Boris wrapped around the hot-water tank in the upstairs airing cupboard. He drank his water, and smiled into the darkness of the room. It was good to be in a proper bed again, a bed with sheets and pillows. This one was an ancient brass double bed, creaky and somewhat sagging, but comfortable enough. He had every hope of not being in this bed tomorrow night. He drank more water, grinning into the darkness, remembering.

'Graef.'

'Hello there.'

'Ah, Mr McGill.'

'How are you?'

'Very well. And you?'

'Well.'

'Where are you?'

'Glasgow.'

'That's good. Shall we meet?'

'Tomorrow?'

'Would be perfect. Though I could become free tonight.'

'Won't pretend I'm not tempted.'

'As you should be.' He could hear her smile. 'And flattered. I'd never risk appearing this eager for anybody else.'

'Wish I could. But there's family stuff to be done.'

'Your aunts? Beryl and Doris?'

'Yes, them. And a cousin.'

'Tomorrow, then. Say hello to the girls from me.'

'Will do. Where do we meet?'

'Come to the office. Any time after seven. I've been away conferencing so there's piles of backlog.'

He's not really there. He knows this but it makes no difference. He knows this but it is no help.

He is not there, firstly, because he knows this is not happening. He's not there, secondly, because there was nobody there – that's known, that's a fact. And he's not there, thirdly, because when it happened he was barely two, and in the dream he is a few years older, maybe five or so, able to understand something of what is going on and to talk and plead with her (even though she never listens, even though she cannot hear, even though she doesn't see him). In the dream he is able to walk fast enough to keep up with her as she walks through the house and into the cloakroom where she chooses the long dark coat with the poacher's pockets, the coat that had been her father's and – sometimes, as now, like this time – he's able to follow her out of the gloom of the house into the light of the day and trail after her as she walks down the dark, dank path under the alders and rowan to the burn-side walk leading towards the gatehouse and the main road and the sea.

* * *

The dream was interrupted when the door of his bedroom opened, light spilled in briefly and somebody stepped into the room, closing the door.

'Alban?' a voice said in the darkness. At first, he wasn't sure whether he was really awake or not, and just for an instant he thought it might be his mother, finally replying. He struggled to wake up properly. It didn't feel like he'd been asleep long. 'Beryl?' he said.

'Put the light on,' Great-Aunt Beryl told him. 'Don't want to bark a shin. One takes for ever to heal at this age.'

He felt for the bedside lamp, found it and switched it on. Great-Aunt Beryl was dressed in a long white nightgown and a warm-looking tartan dressing gown. Her hair – her real hair – was very white and wispy and sparse.

'Is there something wrong?' he asked.

'No,' she said. 'Well, yes, but there's no emergency.'

'Boris still in his tank?'

'As far as I know.' She walked up to his bed and started unmaking the corner of the bed at its foot. 'Shift over, nephew, and pass me a pillow.' Beryl got the sheets at the bottom of the bed undone, accepted the passed pillow and climbed in, putting the pillow behind her so that she could sit up facing him. She fixed him with a disarmingly bright gaze. He pulled the sheets up a little to cover his nipples, bemused at himself for feeling so self-conscious. His great-aunt took a deep breath. 'Now, Alban.'

'Yes, Beryl.'

'Did you get my letter?'

'Yes, I did. Though only today. Fielding brought it from Wales.'

'And you've read it.'

'Yes.' He reached for his water glass. 'Would you like some water?'

'Yes, please. Thank you.'

'You're welcome.'

'So,' she said, clasping her hands. 'Unfortunately, since I wrote that letter, matters have rather come to a head, medically.'

'Oh, Beryl, I'm so sorry,' he said. The letter had just said that she was unwell and undergoing tests. As he'd never known Beryl complain about – or even mention anything regarding – her health, he'd guessed this was something out of the ordinary, something she considered important.

'Oh, I'm ninety – a good innings and blah blah.' Beryl waved away any sympathy. 'However, it would seem that I am highly likely to die within the next year or so. Ha! As though, at this age, that was ever other than true. Annoyingly, though, they have found one of those unpleasant things that end in -oma inside me and apparently that makes the outcome pretty much inevitable, rather than giving one a sporting chance. I ought to have six months though, and possibly a year. The only good thing about getting cancer at this age is it spreads very slowly; the cancer cells are as decrepit and sluggish as every other part of one's body, and take their time multiplying.'

'Oh, Beryl—'

'Do stop it, please,' she said, blinking furiously. 'I take some comfort in people's sympathy, but only so much. We all have to go; in a way I'm lucky to have the notice.'

'If there's anything I can do—?' he began.

'There is,' she said brightly.

'What?'

'Be quiet and listen.'

'Okay.'

'Now, I may, in due course, as my illness progresses and my condition deteriorates, have to take matters into my own hands, because I have no intention of dying in any great pain, if there is no hope of recovery. That is something I feel I have to tell you, Alban, you understand, but you must be assured it is simply a practical means of escaping an unpleasant experience, that is all. Normally, obviously, one doesn't really approve of that sort of thing – bit of an easy way out, always best to just soldier on, you never know what might be around the next corner, that sort of thing – however it is

92

something that has to be faced, and I particularly want you to be prepared. It has also struck me that for some people, the unpleasant experience they are trying to escape through suicide is the rest of their lives. If they see that life as being filled with nothing but emotional pain until they die of old age, well, one can understand that would in itself be unbearable, and the younger you are, the worse. That's the kind of thing one thinks about when one finds oneself in this sort of pickle. So, for what it might be worth, I pass that on.' She paused. 'Yes?' She could see he wanted to say something.

He drew in a breath but eventually just nodded and said, 'Okay. Thank you.'

'Now, the other matter I alluded to in my letter. Which we spoke about once, some years ago.'

There was a pause, then Alban said, 'Ah ha,' for want of anything better.

'I don't know how much you know about the circumstances surrounding your birth.'

Alban looked away, seeming to search the dark corners of the room, lost in the shade.

He shrugged. 'I was born in Garbadale House on September the third, nineteen-sixty-nine. My parents had been married two days earlier, also at the house. They'd been living in London before that. They were students at the LSE; that's where they met. They stayed on at Garbadale and Dad became, well, it was never a formal post, but sort of trainee estate manager. Think that's where he started painting. Winifred and Bert were there, too, most of the time. Mum – Irene – looked after me, though apparently she wasn't very well herself. Some of it might have been postnatal depression. We stayed at Garbadale until . . . Until I was two. Until Irene died.' He shrugged again.

Beryl looked thoughtful, her already small eyes reduced to puckered slits. 'Hmm. I see. All well and good. What I wanted to tell you was from just before you were born, from the end of August that year.'

93

He nodded, folded his arms high over his chest.

'Did you know your mother had been knocked down in the street, by a bus, in London, a couple of weeks before you were born?'

'Yes, I did. That was one reason for her to go to Garbadale, for them both to go; she was recuperating.'

'Hmm. Though undertaking a five-hundred-mile journey, even on the sleeper train and in a big comfy car, does seem a little strange when one's been that knocked about. She had a lot of bruising, and head injuries.'

'So I heard.'

'If it had been a car that knocked her down,' Beryl said, 'she'd probably have had two broken legs.'

'If you say so,' he said. 'But she can't have been that badly injured; they let her out a day or two later.'

'Yes,' Beryl said, sounding thoughtful.

The truth was he didn't like talking about any of this. He didn't like to think about any of this. For most of his life he'd avoided going back to the great gloomy house and the damp, dark garden with the huge, desolate estate of rain-slicked rock and gale-hammered heather surrounding it. There had been those few long weekend visits to Garbadale House in his childhood to see Grandma Winifred and Grandad Bert, and once – shortly after his sister Cory had been born – they had stayed for a week, but he hadn't liked the place and, looking back, was pretty sure his dad had hated it, too. You could hardly blame him. The first time Alban had chosen to go back of his own volition had been to dispose of something that had profoundly needed disposing of. Since then he'd been back a few times, determined not to let the place and the legacy it held intimidate him, but it was always, in effect, with gritted teeth.

'You see, the thing is,' Great-Aunt Beryl said, 'I was in London when your mother had her accident.'

'Oh,' Alban said. Beryl had been a nurse, first in the Wrens, then in the NHS, in Manchester, then in Saudi and Dubai, then – for the last few years before her retirement – in Glasgow.

'She was knocked down in Loake Street, close to a clinic,' Beryl said. 'Private place; surgical. What they'd call elective surgery nowadays. It was one of their doctors who was first on the scene. I visited her in Bart's, the day after the accident. She was quite heavily sedated; couldn't get much sense out of her. Tried talking to her for a bit, but then I was sent packing. Very furious Sister. Explained I was a relative and a senior nurse but she wasn't having any of it. Rather bad form, I remember thinking at the time.' Beryl frowned, as though this thirty-five-year-old incident still annoyed her. 'Thing is, I was only down in the big smoke to visit an old girlfriend from the war. Pure chance I happened to be round for tea with Win and Bert in their flat in South Ken when the rozzers came to say Irene had been knocked down. I'd only just arrived, in fact; barely had time to dunk a biscuit before the door went. It was Win and Bert who dashed off as soon as they heard and left me to man the fort and stand by the telephone and so on. They didn't get back till very late that night and then said Irene was unconscious and not allowed any visitors, though, as I say, I went next day anyway, just to make sure they were looking after her properly. Had to head off for the Gulf the following day, so it was my last chance, really.' She went silent for a bit. 'Never did see her again.'

'Well, you went to see her; that was good of you.'

'Something she said,' Beryl said suddenly. 'While she was lying there. I mean to say, she was semi-lucid at best, poor girl, but she sounded coherent when she said it.'

'What?'

'That he hadn't wanted her to have it, and that was why.'

Alban thought about this for a moment. 'Ah, I'm sorry?'

Beryl said, very clearly: 'He hadn't wanted her to have it, and that was why.'

'Oh, Christ,' he said, eyes widening, 'the "it" here is me, isn't it?'

'Typical man,' Beryl sighed. 'Yes, obviously, the "it" was you. The point is, though, who was this "he"? And did this mean she'd walked out in front of that bus on purpose?'

95

'Fu—' Alban began. 'Jeez, Beryl,' he breathed.

'Before I left for points east I found your father and talked to him.' She paused. 'Alban, has your father ever shown any aptitude for acting, or any sign of being especially good at lying?'

Alban was already shaking his head. Andy was a down-the-line kind of guy. Fairly quiet, arguably a bit boring; just a self-contained, buttoned-up kind of man. He'd been a good, caring father, and – as far as Alban knew – had never told a lie in his life. Jeez, he'd casually told Alban Father Christmas wasn't real the first time he'd been asked directly. Even now, Alban could remember feeling horrified, and wishing his dad could have gone along with the story like everybody else's.

'Acting? Lying? No,' he told her.

'Hmm. Didn't think so. I thought at the time that either your father had missed his vocation as an actor or he was telling the truth. Don't think Andrew was the "he" she was talking about.'

'She was only semiconscious, Beryl, maybe it was . . .'

'Maybe it was all nonsense,' Beryl stated.

'Well, yes.'

'Perhaps,' Beryl said.

They were silent for a moment, then he said, 'Who else could it have been? This "he". Grandad?'

'Or one of your uncles? Blake, James, Kennard, Graeme? I had no idea, frankly. I'm sorry to say I still don't. Thing is, they all doted on you after you were born; Bert especially. If any of them didn't want her to have it, they certainly changed their tune once you were on the scene.'

'Anyway. This was nineteen-sixty-nine, not nineteen-forty-nine,' Alban said. 'It wasn't *that* big a deal, being single and pregnant. Was it?'

'The stigma was much reduced from my day,' Beryl said. Something in her voice made Alban look at her closely. 'Oh,' she waved a hand. 'Not me, but a couple of friends.'

'I'm sorry.'

'Not as sorry as they were.'

'Did you mention this to anyone?' Alban asked her.

Beryl frowned again. 'Only to Winifred. I don't know if she told anybody else.'

'She never told me.'

'No,' Beryl said. She twisted some bedclothes into a knot in front of her. Then she allowed the sheets to unknot, and her hands to fall apart. 'Perhaps I'm just a silly old woman, Alban. It was a long time ago and . . .' She looked down, and Alban thought how suddenly infinitely frail and vulnerable she looked. Her voice died away.

Then she pulled herself up, cleared her throat and said, 'Perhaps you ought to ignore me. Perhaps I shouldn't have said anything.' She smiled; a thin, wavering smile beneath rheumy eyes and a thin, skull-betraying face, yellow with age and marked by prominent blue veins. 'Too late now, of course. Oh well. Put it down to this deck-clearing instinct, eh? One becomes frailer as one ages, in all sorts of ways. The burden of memories and . . . and secrets, suspicions . . . They all start to seem heavier.' She fixed him with a very specific look and said, 'They all start to tell, after a while.'

Then she yawned widely, putting one thin hand up to her narrow mouth. 'I'd best get back to my own bed. Sorry to have disturbed you.'

'That's all right,' he said. He watched her push back the bedclothes. 'Beryl?'

'Yes, dear?'

'Are you telling anybody else about your health problems?'

'Strictly need-to-know basis, dear. Tell people if you feel you have to, otherwise –' she double-tapped the side of her nose '– shtum.'

Beryl slipped out from beneath the sheets.

As tiny and thin as a child, he thought.

She tucked the sheets back in efficiently.

She turned to go, then looked back. 'What was all that nonsense about the company and shares and so on, this evening? What was Fielding on about?'

'Spraint want to take over the whole company. Fielding's trying to organise the opposition, allegedly with Gran's backing.'

'Oh. Is that it?' She looked thoughtful. 'I think I've only got about two or three per cent. Doris has nothing, of course.'

'I'm sure Fielding would tell you it all adds up.'

'Well, I'd never vote to sell out.' Great-Aunt Beryl made her way to the door. 'Might have just asked,' she muttered. At the door she stopped, hand on the handle. 'Oh, tomorrow?'

'Yes, Beryl?'

'You're taking us to Ayr races, apparently. Hope you don't mind.'

'I'm sure it'll be our pleasure.' He smiled.

She started to open the door, then, frowning, said, 'It's not that big a favour, you know. We were going anyway; just means we can cancel the limo.'

Finally Fielding gets the chance to make his pitch, over breakfast the next morning. Al and he have to head out early to find the relevant supplies, and seem to be expected to make it (Alban volunteers, thankfully – Fielding's cooking skills lie more in the appreciation rather than in the practice). The old girls seem horribly perky considering the amount of cherry brandy and peach schnapps they were pouring down their necks last night. Fielding is feeling a little the worse for wear, though hiding it well, and Al looks a bit tired (though at least, Fielding thinks, he's trimmed the beard. It looks almost tidy. Seeing Mathgirl tonight apparently – must be love). Supposedly, last night Fielding agreed to take them all to some race meeting, though frankly he's suspicious. Anyway, he'll just have to think of it as entertaining clients, treat them like prospective customers, and keep up the patter. Soften them up over a fry-up and work on them over lunch.

The girls seem quite receptive. Later, though, while Alban and Fielding are clearing up and the old dears are upstairs getting ready for their day out, Al says, 'You know, Fielding, I'm along here for the ride so far, but I'm not really here – and I won't be going anywhere else – to mount some propaganda campaign against selling out. If I can talk to people, find out what they think, maybe help them think through what it is they really want, fine. But—'

'Cuz, you either believe in this sale or not. Come on – get off the fence.'

He just smiles. 'Yes, but trying to get people to do what they don't want to do is generally stupid and self-defeating.'

Fielding is incredulous. How can anybody be so naïve? 'Trying to get people to do what they don't want to do,' he tells his cousin, 'is what advertising and marketing are all *about*.'

The races are actually okay. Fielding doesn't place any bets, which the girls think is bad form; even Alban has a flutter (loses), but Fielding likes his bets with better odds. He does enjoy risk – that's what business is all about – but the chances of success have to be greater, and more malleable, frankly. More open to being massaged and cajoled and controlled and all that stuff.

It's an enjoyable, breezy day out, the course looks very jolly in a rather old-fashioned, white-painted-wood kind of way and you certainly see a few characters – all the trilby hats in Scotland and northern England seem to have come here, possibly to mate or something – plus they have a pleasant lunch. The girls get tipsy on G&Ts and white wine, and listen with obvious interest to Fielding's pitch about not selling out to Spraint Corp. He's thinking he's almost done here. Mission accomplished.

Al has a couple of drinks but then switches to water. He is indeed seeing Mathgirl this evening and doesn't want to arrive wrecked. Still, Fielding is pretty sure he catches him taking a swig of Beryl's hipflask, after their one win of the day. Fielding, of course, is driving, which was okay on the way down but hellish getting away, trying to leave the car park.

'I hate this,' he says, as they wait their turn to exit, behind God knows how many hundred other cars. You should be able to pay for a quick-getaway car park, he believes; it would be worth it. Why aren't the Gaga Girls VIPs? Alban, in the front passenger seat, doesn't say anything. Beryl and Doris are in the back and have already made alarming noises about needing a loo before too long. They also look sleepy, though. This could either be a lucky break or very bad for Fielding's upholstery.

'I hate this feeling of being stuck,' he says, slumped over the steering wheel. 'I hate being in queues, I hate being shepherded and corralled and controlled and treated like one of the herd. I hate this feeling of . . . inertia.'

'What's that, dear?' Beryl says over the sounds. Fielding is playing some piano-ey classic stuff he keeps to impress clients, hoping it'll take the old girls' minds off their bladders.

'I hate this feeling of inertia,' Fielding says, more loudly. He hits the horn, just for the sheer hell of it.

'Hmm? Eh? Say again?' Doris says, sounding half asleep. At least slurred. 'Hates what?'

'Inertia,' Beryl tells her.

'Yes, dear. I know we are.'

Al looks round at her, then starts laughing. Beryl cackles, too. Fielding shakes his head. Hipflask, obviously.

'Questions and answers are not like the poles of magnets; one does not imply the other. There are a lot of questions without answers.' So saying, she takes his right hand and studies it carefully in the late-evening light spilling from the window above the bed. She strokes each fingertip in turn with her thumb. 'Can you feel this?' she asks.

'Just about.'

She kisses each finger delicately, making a tiny noise. 'That?'

'Mm-hmm. Kissing them better?'

'In case I have any magical healing powers,' she explains. She shrugs, pale breasts wobbling fractionally. 'What is to lose?'

Verushka Graef is half Czech and, very occasionally, he thinks he can hear this in the way she puts words together. He can sense that 'What is to lose?' is going to join a short list of phrases he keeps, tiny talismans of difference, of adoration.

He'd done the same thing with Sophie, of course. He still does, forgetting – it sometimes seems to him – nothing, no matter how much he might wish he could.

Verushka Graef is long and blonde, with black dyed hair now growing out, fair roots showing. Her face is broad, eyes wide-set above a strong nose with curved, flared nostrils and – when her cornflower blue eyes are open – she is rarely without what appears to be an expression of constantly bemused surprise.

Just visible on the lightly tanned skin of her left flank Alban can see a tracery of narrow, shallow pink scars, altogether about a hand wide. Extending across her back, these have been caused by her being dragged seaward over a coral outcrop just off the coast of Takua Pa, an island north of Phuket, Thailand, and constitute a slowly fading souvenir of the Boxing Day tsunami.

When she moves, sometimes, there is a gawky, loose-limbed quality about her and unless she is concentrating on some physical activity she can appear awkward in her tall frame, like a still-growing teenager, unfamiliar in themselves.

'Anyway, doesn't it all depend on the sort of question?' he asks.

'Whether it has an answer?' Her eyes are still closed. 'Of course.' She pauses. A tiny frown creases the space between her pale brows, the sole line on an unmarked face. 'Though to define the question sufficiently precisely, you might have, in effect, to answer it. Which is not so helpful.'

'It's my family. Things are rarely helpful.'

'You have an interesting family. I've liked the ones I've met.'

'You've liked the ones I've felt safe letting you meet.'

'You're protecting them! How sweet.' She opens her eyes and looks at him, grinning. She thinks of herself as fierce.

101

'Of course,' he says. 'What was I thinking of? Of all the people to cosset.'

'I am always available for cosseting.'

She is thirty-eight; two years older than he is. He remembers being surprised when she first told him this, a few days after they met in a hotel which could have been anywhere but was in fact in China. He also remembers being surprised that this age-difference disturbed him slightly, that he felt he should always be older than any girlfriend. What was that about? Why did he feel that?

He still has not ceased to be surprised that they are lovers, and not just because he feels like a Clydesdale to her thoroughbred. She is tall and blonde (well, usually blonde, and certainly she was when he first met her, in Shanghai) and slim – small breasts, narrow hips – when he had a thing for red hair – or rich brown hair – and curvaceous, voluptuous women. She has absolutely no intention of ever having children, while he still harbours a half-secret wish that one day he'll be a father, part of a family. She is a mathematician, an academic, a sportswoman with no interest in gardening or plants – there isn't a single green growing thing in this ascetically clean, sparsely furnished flat – and they even fell out and almost split up over the fucking Iraq war; he'd been reluctantly, suspiciously pro-war (and so now is even more disillusioned and cynical than before) while she had been anti-war from the start – in fact she'd been anti-war since 9/11, guessing that one atrocity would be used as an excuse to commit a still greater one.

At the time he'd thought this was over-cynical: he hoped now that was the last illusion he'd ever lose.

She lives on the top floor of a sandstone tenement in Partick, a building still stained with the soot of century-old smoke from the hearths of long dead fires, yet to be blasted clean, back to its natural pale red. The building is just fifteen minutes' walk from Beryl and Doris's house and only a little further from the university. The flat has a chunked, restricted view of the river and the low hills beyond Paisley. It is a bare place, sparsely dotted with furniture, without a television or a phone. There is one radio, and a dainty CD player beside a small bookcase full of Bach, Mozart, Beethoven and the collected works of Led Zeppelin. There are no curtains or blinds on any of the windows; she likes to wake with the dawn for most of the year and keeps an Air France sleep mask for the height of summer, when the dawn comes in the wee small hours.

This is all in odd contrast to her room in the Maths building, which is wildly untidy and contains three different computers, five screens from bulging cathode ray antiquity to wide-screen cutting edge LCD modernity, two TVs, an overhead projector and a square bookcase filled with a dozen identical red-and-silver lava lamps shaped like spaceships. There are even plants: a small yucca, two busy Lizzies and a dwarf cactus like a booby-trapped golf-ball. These were all gifts and she rarely remembers to water them; colleagues do. The only similarity to the flat is that she never closes the blinds. She claims her job involves a lot of staring out of windows, thinking, and curtains and blinds just get in the way, wherever she might be.

She had been raised in Glasgow, gone to university in Trier, completed a post-doc at Cambridge and her speciality was geometries; tilings, though she was prone – sometimes, after reading papers from other branches of the great growing tree of mathematical knowledge – to shake her head and mutter things like, 'I really should have gone into number theory.'

She sporadically had quite involved and sometimes surprisingly heated email forum discussions with people way outside her field about things like the nature of consciousness and brain-bafflingly obscure questions such as, 'Where are the numbers?' ('Where you left them?' had been Alban's suggestion.) That one was still un-resolved; she was talking about this with a guy from St Andrews who was interested in the philosophy of mathematics – a speciality Alban had never even imagined existing but felt obscurely comforted to know did.

103

He'd opened a deep drawer in the living room once and discovered a collection of about forty glass millefiore paperweights. They were intricate, beautiful, vivid with colour.

'Why don't you display these?' he'd asked, holding one up to the light.

'Dusting,' she'd explained lazily, from the couch. They were playing chess and she'd been considering her next move. He'd beaten her just once in over twenty games, and still half suspected she'd let him win that one.

Her only other extravagance was mostly underfoot; she loved Oriental carpets, the more elaborate in design the better, and the otherwise bare boards of the flat were scattered with Persian, Afghan and Pakistani rugs. The flat had large rooms by modern standards, but only one bedroom and one public room; she had almost run out of floor space for the carpets and had started to hang them on the walls, which made the place, Alban thought, look a little more lived in, less cell-like. The general effect of the flat, though, was still pretty spartan.

Such austerity extended to her clothes. She dressed habitually in a white shirt with black trousers and jacket. She had about thirty almost identical white shirts/blouses, a dozen or so pairs of black trousers plus a few pairs of black jeans and half a dozen black jackets, all of which looked like they formed part of a suit, save for one, which was leather. Her shoes were sensible black lace-ups with minimal heels. She possessed a black coat and two pairs of black gloves for winter, surmounted by a black hiker's ear-flapped hat in the very coldest weather.

She had a long black dress and a short black dress for very special occasions where she really couldn't get away with the usual trousers, shirt and jacket outfit. However, by her own estimate, approximately ninety-nine per cent of the time – when she was not naked or wearing clothes specific to some sport or pastime – she stuck with the monochrome look.

'What about holidays?' he'd asked her.

'Holidays don't count, darling.'

Once – just once – he'd seen her wearing make-up, after a couple of girlfriends had persuaded her to let them apply some for a faculty party. She'd looked breathtaking, he'd thought, but not herself. She'd said that she felt like she was wearing a mask, and that it had been most unsettling at first.

Otherwise she wore no make-up at all and did not possess a comb or hairbrush. Alban had watched her morning routine several times: she splashed her face with water, rubbed vigorously, patted her face dry with a towel, then, with her hands still damp, straked her fingers through her short hair.

That was it.

She showered after sport. She played squash 'like a lethally disjointed cheetah on speed', according to one Eng. Lit. lecturer with a bandaged ear and extensive facial bruising, to whom Alban had spoken at a party. She had a mountain bike that she stashed in the flat's hallway, where it moulted dried mud between excursions. She had played in goal for the university women's football team, was a demon fast bowler in the ladies' cricket team – though what she really wanted to be was a spin bowler – and played golf occasionally with her late father's clubs, each of which was older than she. For a few years she had rowed on the Clyde, but then given up after she'd rowed her scull right over the body of a teenage boy suicide and been thrown into the river with the corpse. She lived for climbing mountains but she had no head for heights. She'd tried rock climbing, specifically to tackle this shaming limitation, persevering beyond sense and expert advice, but the problem was not a fear that could be faced down, and so, eventually, she had accepted this and restricted herself to walking up mountains, with a minimum of don't-look-down scrambling episodes.

She was an enthusiastic if surprisingly graceless dancer.

Alban knew of at least two male colleagues in the Mathematics Department who were hopelessly in love with her.

She had a couple of other sporadic, casual lovers besides himself, he knew – both fellow sporty types.

There had been another, but he'd died in the tsunami.

Her widowed mother also lived in the city. Eudora was a small, lively woman who worked in the Mitchell Library and who dressed and moved with an elegance Alban suspected her daughter had long ago decided never to try to match or even attempt to emulate.

'So, Mr McGill,' the lovely Verushka says, gently releasing his hand and bringing it up to her mouth to kiss the fingers individually once more. 'Your family raises its hydra head again. And what is to be done?'

'Probably nothing,' he says, looking intently at her mouth. She has full, pale pink lips. 'They'll sell out, the family will fall further apart, we'll stop pretending it all really means very much, we'll stop having to decide whether to promote people within the family or bring in people from outside who actually know what they're doing, so it'll all get more efficient and lucrative and slick under the wing of the Spraint Corporation, some of us will sit on the money and retire and resort to hobbies, some will invest in their own businesses or somebody else's and make even more, and some will do the same and go broke. Whatever it is we are, whatever it's supposed to be worth, that'll all . . . disperse.' He stops looking at her mouth and looks at her eyes instead. They are open, now, and crossed. 'What?' he says.

'That is not what I meant at all.'

'You mean Beryl.'

'Yes. What she told you.'

'I was thinking of forgetting it; ignoring everything.'

'You're an idiot.' She places his hand flat on her chest, between her breasts.

'It's probably nothing.'

'So why be afraid of looking into it further?'

'I'm not afraid.'

'Yes you are, Alban,' she says casually, with a smile to take some

106

of the sting out of it. 'You're afraid of lots of things about your family.'

He'd gone to meet her a little after seven at the Maths building where she worked. Hers had been the only office which remained lit and occupied; everybody else was either still on vacation or had better things to do on a Saturday evening, but she was dealing with a backlog of mail and emails after attending a conference in Helsinki. They hadn't seen each other for a couple of months and had come very close to having sex right there, but that, she'd decided, would have been unseemly (she used words like that sometimes). They'd walked smartly back to the flat.

Afterwards, he'd told her about the white finger diagnosis, crashing at the flat in Perth, Fielding's sudden arrival with news about the family firm, and Beryl's bedtime chat, which, for sure, had been a little alarming at first, when he'd wondered, still half asleep, why this ancient, shrivelled old woman was inviting herself into his bed, but had hardly been anything to be genuinely afraid of.

'Well,' he says, defensively, 'they're an alarming family.'

'This you keep telling me. Mum and I have taken the girls for tea and cakes a couple of times when you haven't been present. They were great fun.'

'Tea?'

'Well, drinks and cakes,' she concedes. 'And your parents; they were very nice.' Andy and Leah had been passing through Glasgow a couple of years ago when he'd been staying with her. Verushka had more or less insisted on meeting up, bringing her own mum along. They'd had lunch. He'd been terrified beforehand but it had gone surprisingly well. 'And those two old guys at Garbadale,' she continues, 'when we stopped off there for tea that time after doing Foinaven and Arkle—'

He remembers both mountains, and the insane, über-competitive pace she'd set on each ascent.

He also remembers both of the old guys she's talking about.

'They're staff,' he tells her. 'Servants – not family. And I'd made damn sure Gran wasn't at home.'

'Well, anyway. And Fielding seemed all right.'

'Now, Fielding really is an idiot.'

'He's not so bad. I think he looks up to you.'

'Really?' He is genuinely shocked to hear this. 'Anyway, you still haven't met Gran.'

'Yes, your gran. She sounds interesting.'

'So does chemical and biological warfare.'

'Oh! Shame!' she says, and darts one hand across to tweak his nearest nipple.

He hisses, rubs the offended bulb of flesh.

'She's your grandmother,' she says, vicariously indignant. 'She gave birth to your poor dead mother.'

'And seven other freaks and nutters.'

She hovers her tweaking fingers over his still smarting nipple. He holds her wrist, one-handed, feeling her straining against him. 'How many again?' she asks, looking at the offended nipple with an expression of intense concentration.

'Oh, just stop,' he says. 'Okay, they're not all mad. Some are all right.' He loosens his grip experimentally. She jerks, as though about to attack, and he clutches her wrist tightly again. She's very strong, but he is stronger. He is already wondering how long that will last, now he's stopped working in the forests, unless he too starts getting all sporty. Finally she laughs and withdraws her hand.

'So,' she says. 'Where does your road show go next?'

'Fielding wants to talk to my dad, and his dad. Which means London.'

'So, are you going?'

'Oh, I don't think so. It's probably pointless.'

'Woh,' she says flatly, deliberately monotonic. 'Down, tiger.'

He rubs his face. 'I'm sorry. I just can't summon up much enthusiasm for any of this.'

She is silent for a moment. He can almost hear a carefully marshalled, logically linked series of clearly stated questions being sorted into the most appropriate analytical order inside her head. The bedrock of all these exercises tends to be the same: What are you trying to achieve? What is it you really want?

Answered diligently, each question considered separately, the gulf between the resulting answers is sometimes startling. This technique often works amazingly well, but he still resents it, every time. Sure enough, when she speaks, there is a seminar-room crispness to her delivery that he associates with earlier attempts to force him to sort out his thoughts and feelings. 'Do you care,' she asks, 'that the family firm might be sold to this Corporation?'

He thinks. This is a question he has been asking himself quite a lot lately. 'A bit,' he says, and grimaces, knowing how pathetic this sounds.

'Uh-huh,' she says. He can tell she's having to back-track here, or at least go laterally, still looking for a definitive – or at any rate useful – answer to her first question before any of the subsequent ones can be presented. 'What does "bit" mean in this context?'

'I don't know, I don't *know*!' he says loudly, exasperated not so much by her somehow inappropriate logicality but by his own even more point-defying uncertainty.

There is another silence. 'Anyway,' she says, and her voice lets him know she's abandoned the analytical route for now, 'you should go to this family gathering at Garbadale.'

His heart seems to leap. He feels this, and wonders at it, half hates it. He wants her permission to go to Garbadale even though he has always said he dislikes the place and usually avoids it. He wants – he still wants, even with this beautiful, intelligent, deeply affectionate woman lying in his arms – to see Sophie, to press his suit, to make his case again, to try and redeem all the past hurt by some sort of acceptance, some form of return of feeling, just one degree of acknowledgement.

And, he has to admit to himself, he wants to witness his slightly mad family again, no matter what they decide to do about the takeover offer. He used to have a sort of childish love for them all, for the institution the family as a whole represented, then he came to hate them, hate it . . . Then he tried to be accepted again, and joined the firm and felt that by doing so he was rejoining the family itself, then later still he could stand it all no longer and left them again – the partial sale to Spraint more of an excuse than anything else – but still they fascinate him, attract him, and he knows there is some immature, shameful part of him that profoundly needs their approval, and that included in that – yet beyond that – there is the need to be accepted, somehow, some time, by his girl in the garden, by his lost love, by Sophie.

Verushka is watching him. He looks away from her. 'You know you want to,' she purrs, partly in jest.

'That might be a good reason not to.'

She tuts. 'You should trust your instincts more.'

'My instincts have got me into a lot more trouble than my reasoning ever did.' He's amazed at the sudden bitterness he hears in his own voice as he says this.

'Still, you should go,' she says, either missing – uncharacteristic-ally – or glossing over his tone. 'And ask questions while you're there. Find out what Beryl's talking about. Will she and Doris be there?'

'Probably. Think they've already booked Fielding to drive them there. As a courtesy, they might even have informed Fielding regarding this, but – well – who can say?'

And then, suddenly, she says: 'What about your old love?'

It's asked easily enough.

'Sophie,' he breathes.

He looks up at the window. Verushka had placed the bed under the window specifically to get good light for reading and because she liked the way that you got little cold down-draughts from it on to your face, especially in winter. The bedroom wasn't designed with this in mind and didn't really work properly in that configuration, but she didn't care.

'Yes,' she says gently. 'Sophie.'

'Apparently, yes, she's going to be there. Fielding's said as much. I don't know that I trust him though. I might check with somebody else.'

'And only go if she's there?'

'I don't know.' He shakes his head, honestly not knowing. 'Maybe not go if she is.'

'That would be stupid.' Her voice is very soft. 'You ought to go anyway, in any event.'

He looks at her, feeling himself frown. 'You really think so?'

'Yes, really. Who else might be there?'

'Oh, sounds like they all will.' The thought produces in him a strange amalgam of outright fear and nervous, adolescent anticipation.

'And who might be there that could enlighten you regarding this mysterious "he" Beryl mentioned?'

Alban sighs. 'Gran, obviously.' He makes a sort of 'tchah' noise (Verushka shakes her head). 'Grandad Bert is no longer with us. Uncle James – Sophie's dad – dead too. Blake – he's the eldest of that generation – well, he was caught with his hand in the till thirty years ago and took the FILTH route.'

'The FILTH route? What does that mean?'

'Failed In London; Try Honkers.'

'Honkers?'

'Hong Kong.'

'Ah-ha.'

'He's been out there since God-knows-when. Done all right for himself – multimillionaire – but no real contact with the family any more. He wouldn't be allowed into the EGM; he was disinherited when they found he was on the take. Can't imagine he'd be invited to the birthday party either.'

'But you've met him,' she says, remembering an old conversation, 'haven't you?'

'Sure did. Last saw him back in ninety-nine. Showed me round his skyscraper. The way he talked, he fully expected it was going to get turned into a Red Army barracks as soon as the Chinese had sorted out the paperwork. Big, gloomy, creepy kind of guy. Absolutely no advert for extreme fucking wealth whatsoever.'

'So, who does that leave?'

'Uncle Kennard – Fielding's dad – and Uncle Graeme.'

She is silent for a moment. 'And when is this party-cum-EGM?'

'Gran's birthday party is on October the ninth. EGM's the day before. We're supposed to be there by the Friday to allow for the fact that it is officially the arse-end of nowhere.'

'There you go. Ask me nicely, I might even drive you there.'

'Won't classes be starting about then?'

'I make a dramatic entrance somewhat later in the term, darling. I'd have the time. Don't you want me to take you there?'

She owned some sort of red four-wheel-drive estate thing called a Forester (a coincidence – she'd bought it new and it was older than their relationship). She drove punctiliously, almost primly in town, then like a rally driver on a Special Stage when she hit the open road, especially in the Highlands. He'd been alarmed the first couple of times she'd driven him anywhere at speed, but now felt quite relaxed about it, having decided she was a judicious, quick-witted and extremely fast-reacting driver. It was just that she drove rather quickly, as well – that was all.

'I—' He stops, flops back in the bed. They had promised from the start that they would always be honest with each other. He glances at her. Now she is propped up on one elbow, looking at him. Her right breast, under her, is a long lozenge of loveliness, her left a warm symmetrical scoop of cream. She looks curious, smiling faintly. He waves his hands, lets them fall back. 'Part of me wants you to come with me and stay at the fucking place.'

'This part?' she says, briefly sliding her hand under the duvet to squeeze his cock.

'Mm-hmm. Another part is embarrassed by my family, wants you to have nothing to do with them in case they put you off me. And . . . and another part doesn't want to have to cope with you and Sophie in the same . . . frame of reference.'

'Well, I was only intending to drop you there and then bugger off, frankly; canter up a hill or two, taking the tent or bivvy bag. Bunk-housing in your ghastly Scots Baronial monstrosity wasn't really part of the plan.'

'Oh. Okay. Sorry.'

'Whatever, the offer stands.' She lies back, lifting her hands up in front of her face to inspect her fingers and nails. 'Or Fielding might take you.' She looks over at him. 'And do you still have that ancient smokescreen on two wheels you call a motorbike?'

'Sold it,' he tells her. 'Doc said that wasn't helping the white finger either. Had to go.'

'So: me, Fielding, or just hire a car. No shortage of means. Just go.' She returns to the close inspection of her hands, then reaches over to the bedside table and puts on her glasses, which have black, rectangular frames.

What do I really want? he thinks. This is, of course, an extremely good question. It was just such a pity that, life being as it tended to be, it so rarely came as part of a matched pair, with an extremely good answer.

Well, not being an idiot would be a start. He puts out his hand and strokes Verushka's arm. 'That'd be great if you took me. I'd really appreciate it. Thanks.'

She glances over at him, brows furrowing over the black-framed glasses. 'Are you sure?' she asks. 'The journey could be fraught with safety.'

He grins, traces the line of her full, smiling lips. 'I'm sure.'

Alban and Sophie begin to conduct a sort of secret, technically chaste affair which only goes as far as what they agree is the rather quaint term, heavy petting – the stuff that some swimming pools still have signs saying is banned, along with running by the poolside, jump-bombing from the side, and standing on somebody else's shoulders.

Sometimes she just openly goes with him to help with chores in the garden, sometimes she says she's taking Scrabbles for a hack, then leaves her tethered, cropping nearby grass, sometimes she says she's going for a walk, sometimes she says she's going to the summer-house to read and study. Whatever; it always ends with them hidden by long grass or inside the tent-like space of a big rhododendron bush or in a half-ruined shed on the west edge of the estate or one of half a dozen other secret, private places he knows of.

It's not simple, though. In fact, it's very complicated.

Quite apart from the logistics involved with maintaining the secrecy, there is the ever present problem of, How far do they go? Her breasts have become gloriously familiar territory to him now; he feels he knows each pore and microscopic pucker, each tiny, soft wisp of down, and is convinced that he carries a touch-memory of their weight and giving firmness in his hands. Her nipples are like little brown raspberries, sweet and full and succulent.

A couple of times, when she's worn a dress and his hands aren't filthy, she has let him put one hand inside her panties, and he has found the hot, moist slit, and stroked and slipped his fingertips inside her, but she usually has to stop him before this can go on for very long – gasping, face flushed, heart pounding – because, she confesses, it's just too much, too tempting, too likely to lead to what they can't do because they have no condoms and are both terrified of her getting pregnant and anyway, and anyway . . .

After a week of this, she unzips his jeans and takes his cock out. She's too rough with it at first and he has to show her how to grasp and stroke and gently squeeze it. He comes quickly in her hand and she makes a face.

'Hoo-hoo!' he laughs, looking up at the blue sky above the thick, feathery tops of the breeze-swayed grass.

She says, 'Yeah, well, sorry, but; yuk.'

'We could use a tissue next time,' he suggests. He's aware he's

114

sounding hopelessly eager. He really hopes this hasn't put her off the whole idea.

'Hmm.' She wipes her hand on the beaten-down grass and looks dubiously at his penis, which is still stiff.

Or you could suck it, he wants to say, but doesn't. He cleans up with a paper hanky from his jeans pocket and she lies down beside him on the flattened grass, stroking him.

There is also, at the same time, the larger moral question regarding, What the hell does anything matter when we are forever on the brink of killing ourselves – killing everybody?

This is not a trivial matter. This is 1985, and their parents, the previous generation, they both agree, have managed very successfully to almost completely fuck up the world, and left the solutions – the tidying-up, if any such healing is possible – to the following generation, and their children's children, and their – well, you get the idea. The world still stands on the brink of all-out nuclear war, the superpowers constantly find new excuses to confront each other, half of Africa seems to be starving, hundreds of millions go to bed hungry while the West stuffs its bulging collective face with greasy fries and fat-pumped hamburgers made from diseased meat, and on top of all that this Aids thing looks like making their generation's sex-lives more fraught, limited and dangerous than they ever deserved. It's so unfair. Really unfair; not the sort of unfair kids and teenagers are always complaining about to their parents or teachers or anybody else in authority, but genuinely, manifestly, no-question-about-it unfair.

You always hope and you try to believe that there must be a way forward, because we – humans, the species – are where we are, so we've always found a way forward before, but sometimes hope is a difficult thing to hold on to. Jeez, you just had to watch the news . . .

They talk about this a lot. It matters to them. At the same time, he is aware, being honest with himself, that he's kind of pushing this apocalyptic vision and getting her to talk about the sheer snow-balling awfulness of the world because he does want them to go

115

the whole way, he does – of course he does – want to have proper sex with her, and emphasising the dangers that lie ahead in their future lives, and the possibility that those lives might be horribly, unfairly short thanks to their parents' idiot generation is maybe one way of getting a girl – maybe especially an intelligent, thoughtful kind of girl – to throw inhibition to the winds and – as their American cousins would express it – put out.

It's not something to be proud of, maybe, but it's not like he's telling any lies here.

'I'm thinking about it,' she tells him, the first time he asks her to suck him off, in the old shed on the western limit of the estate, almost in Devon.

She's stroking his cock, kneeling between his legs, his jeans down around his knees, a tissue in her other hand. He'd kind of assumed she'd put the paper hanky over his prick like a sort of soft condom, the way he does when he wanks, but she has discovered that she likes to watch his penis spasm and see the warm white liquid spurt, so she keeps the hanky ready until the last second, then catches his ejaculate on the wadded tissue, smiling as he tenses and gasps and comes.

'Think I'm going to—' he says.

He does, arching his back. 'Maybe next time,' she murmurs.

The question, they agree, is simply, How do we cope sensibly with the present quota of shit left to us by the parental generation without surrendering our souls and just accepting any amount of shit for ever, thus turning sensible acceptance into outright exploitative stupidity and becoming part of the problem, so that we go on to be just as stupid and selfish and thoughtless as the generation before?

Answers on a postcard.

They take turns; he prefers to kiss her while she wanks him; she prefers kneeling over him, watching.

'Do you think our mums and dads did all this sort of thing?' she asks one time, inside a little arbour formed by the tapestry

116

hedge at the side of the south lawn and a curved coppice of sweet chestnut.

She is lying with her head on his chest. 'I suppose so,' he says. 'Dad says every generation thinks it invented sex.'

She is silent for a moment. 'I can imagine your parents doing it.' She shivers. 'Euw! Not mine!'

He's thinking of Uncle James and Aunt Clara. 'No,' he agrees. 'I'd rather not imagine it, either.'

'Maybe they never have,' she says. 'Like, obviously James must have done it with June, cos there's me. And June is quite sexy, I suppose. But maybe they . . .' Her voice trails off. 'No, wait; I think I heard them through a wall once. *That* was horrible.'

They start kissing again. She's wearing jeans and he presses and strokes her between the legs through the jeans for a long time, long enough so that he can feel the heat and the dampness of her through the thick denim and she doesn't stop him, just hugs him very hard and breathes faster and faster, her head buried in his neck until eventually she shudders, her arms grip him even more tightly, she bites his shoulder through his shirt and a strange, cat-like noise is forced from her lips. She gives one final shiver, then goes limp, body heaving against him as she breathes, her breath hot on his neck and cheek.

He says, 'That was you coming, wasn't it?'

She just lies there panting for a moment or two, then, on shaking arms, struggles to raise herself up and look at him. Her face is flushed; a beautiful scent like pine seems to fill the heavy, hanging curtain of her hair. She looks like she's about to say something. Possibly something sarcastic, he suspects, now he thinks about it, but instead she just rolls her eyes, shakes her head and collapses back on top of him.

He grins a huge grin.

Fielding stares at his mobile. He doesn't believe he's hearing this. He knew he should have stayed in Jockland, but there was urgent stuff needing attending to back here in London, and so he had to blast south, leaving Al happily shacked up with Mathgirl. Fielding's been ringing her at her office making a nuisance of himself, asking her to tell Alban to give him a call. Finally this harassment has paid off but now Al's gone all uncooperative.

'Al, I need you here. I can't do this myself. I can try, but I may not succeed. With you, I've got a much better chance. We make a good team. Come on now. I'm serious. I'm kind of relying on you here, man.' Fielding can feel himself making a face as he walks along Wardour Street, on his way for an after-work drink with some Chinese factory owners, in town to pitch units, runs and costs.

'Look, Fielding,' Al says, sounding far too damn calm and casual. 'I've said I'll be at the bash in Garbadale. So I'll be there. But I'm not coming to London to try and browbeat my dad and yours into opposing the sell-off.'

'Don't you want to see your own parents?'

'I'll see them in a couple of weeks anyway.'

'Al, I can't believe you just don't seem to care about this family any more. We're in danger of losing everything and all you can do . . . You're just happy to . . . I mean, I'm happy you're having such a peachy time in Glasgow with Verushka, but this is our *family* at stake here, man. This is our chance to do something, to make a difference.'

'I'm heading back to Perth in a couple of days, anyway,' he says, like he hasn't heard a word.

Perth. Jesus weeping H. Christ. Fielding bites back a whole clip of sarcastic comments about the comparative merits of a rainy sink estate in Perth and the glitzily moneyed buzz that is London, and just says, 'Throwing you out, is she?'

'Yeah,' Al says, obviously not meaning it. 'No, I just feel like I'm taking up too much of her time when I stay with her for longer than a few days. She's a life she needs to lead. I start to feel I'm monopolising her after a while. Makes me uncomfortable.'

'Right.'

Right my fragrant arse, Fielding thinks. He's seen them together.

The woman is totally fucking gorgeous and blatantly worships him. Alban's a fucking idiot. But Fielding's not going to tell him. Some people just seem to spend their misbegotten lives stepping smartly out the way of anything remotely good for them and ignoring any and all good advice well-meaning friends and family might offer. It's a gift. An anti-gift. A curse. Yeah, that's the word, Fielding decides. A curse.

Stupid fuck.

4

I'm in the Volley in the Valley – that's the Volunteer Arms, Valley
Street, for those not fortunate enough to be acquainted with
the more select drinking emporiums of Bonnie Perth – sitting
there quite the thing with Deedee (i.e. D.D., which stands for
Designated Drinker) and Veepil (i.e. V.P.L. which is short for Visible
Panty Liners or something). I've also seen Veepil's name spelt V-
pill; there is a piece of highly fucken derogatory graffiti on a gable
end in Islay Avenue which favours the latter spelling – when in
walks your man Alban.

'All Bran!' Deedee shouts, seeing the prodigal as he comes through
the door and stands looking round. Deedee is waving a suddenly
empty glass. It is well known that the big man is not normally short
of a sheikel or two and some of my more embarrassing friends (just
let me pause while I consider who amongst said bunch would not
qualify for this label, big Al himself excepted . . . well, maybe we'll
come back to that one!!) anyway they sort of exploit him a bit
sometimes, though he never seems to mind. Like I say; embarrassing.

Al waves and comes over. He looks just like he did when he
left, a week ago. Maybe the beard's a bit trimmer. He nods at
Deedee and takes his glass. 'What the fuck happened to the flat,
Tango?' he asks me.

'Fucken D.S. is what happened to the fucken flat, that's what,' I tell him.

He rolls his eyes. 'Oh, for fuck's sake.'

'My feelings exactly, big man.'

'Jesus,' he says. 'Right. First things first. Who wants what?'

In a round is got. Al says his formal hellos and sits beside me, putting his wee backpack on the floor.

'And before you ask,' I tell him, 'yes, they did take your big pack. Heard one of the boys in blue saying what a smart-looking bit of kit it was, too, so I wouldn't hold out great hopes of ever seeing that again.'

'Did they nick anybody?'

'Aye, me!' I poke myself in the chest. 'I had about ten ounces of blow in the place cos Special Kay and Deep Phil were back from Umshter-fucken-dum.'

'Shit. You been charged yet?'

'Aye, fucken possession with intent to supply. No date yet.'

'Ah thought they wur meant tae be no botherin wi blow these days, but,' Veepil says, waving her cig around. This is about the seventh time she's said this over the last couple of hours. Drink has been taken.

'Sorry to hear that, Tango,' Al says. 'You got a legal?'

'Aye, getting aid, and that.'

'Did they leave anything of mine?'

'That'll be right. Maybe some dirty washing.'

'So, are you locked out?'

'Aye. The council took serious fucken exception for some bizarre fucken reason and put me in a fucken B&B on Flowers Street. Fucken shite it is. Sorry, Al; canny put you up now. I had a word, and Sunny D says you can stay at his and Di's if you don't mind sharing a room with the twins.' I hold my hands up, feeling mortified and dead inhospitable, even though this is definitely not my fault. 'Best I can do, big man. I'm really sorry.'

Al pats my shoulder. 'That's okay. Don't worry.'

'Ye'll no be wantin tae go tae Sunny an Di's though, will ye?' Deedee says, giving it serious face.

'No,' Al says. 'I'll pass. Don't worry about me. I'll be fine.'

'Where are you going to go, but?' I ask him.

'Where fate seems to be pushing me,' he says, sighing and staring up at the ceiling. 'Back into the welcoming fucking tentacles of my family.'

Deedee is poking a finger through a handful of small change, mostly copper's. 'Anybody got any dosh fur the fag machine? Ma duty-frees must be back hame.'

Al digs in his pocket.

It begins with a choice. She picks a large coat with the deep, inside pockets that people call poacher's pockets from the variety of coats and jackets and capes in the cloakroom of the house. The coat she selects is an old, shabby one that has been in the family for decades; it has been worn by her father, some of her uncles, perhaps a few of her larger-made female relations over the years, and by most of the males in the present generation of the Wopuld family. She leaves the house by the side door and takes the indirect route towards the main road, heading not down the drive that loops up to the front of the house and through the avenue of tall cedars, but instead walking down to the shadowy path that follows the River Garbh on its way from the inland loch towards the sea.

She picks up the first stone while she's walking through the garden, stooping to pull it from the side of the path. She looks at it, thinking of cleaning some of the damp brown soil from it, but then puts it straight into one of the external pockets of the coat. There's a glove in the pocket. She looks at it as she walks and feels in the other outside pocket, finding the second glove. She puts them on. They're too big, like the coat, but it doesn't really matter.

She walks down the path by the river, listening to the waters roar and shush. Some of the people on the estate call the river a burn. She has always wondered why something full of cold water is associated

123

with a verb denoting fire and heat. There seems to be no adequate explanation for this.

The trees down by the river are what-do-you-call-it; deciduous. They have broad leaves they shed in the autumn. Autumn comes early here, this far north; a month or so early compared to Somerset, compared to Lydcombe. In perhaps as little as a couple of weeks the broadleaf trees here will be starting to turn brown and red and gold and begin to lose their leaves.

The rain has almost ceased now and the sky is going from a dull to a brighter grey. She squats by a stone in the centre of the rough path and tries to prise it out, but it will not come. She takes the gloves off, thinking this may help, but it doesn't. She puts the gloves back on again. She walks down a narrower path to the side of the stream and pulls a rock from the bank, putting that rock into the external pocket on the other side of the coat from the first stone.

She continues down the riverside track, stopping now and again to add stones and rocks to her pockets, beginning to use the deep, inside poacher's pockets. The coat is starting to become heavy, pulling her shoulders down.

Where the road into the estate crosses the river, via an old curved bridge of grey stone, she stays with the path, passing under the road. A car hisses overhead on the still damp tarmac. She hears that, and listens to the tumbling waters echo off the curved surface of arching stone, then she's out from beneath the bridge and walking down the path towards the rocky shore and the dull grey gleaming that is Loch Glencoul, the sea loch. The line of rocks arranged like giant pearls around the shore of the loch are different shades of grey; a rainbow of monochrome. Their colour changes to brown near the water, covered in seaweed. The mountains tower around the loch, their high tops hidden by the uniform blanket of grey cloud.

The coat feels very heavy on her now, weighing her down with the mass of stones she's accumulated, making her shoulders ache. The rocks in the poacher's pockets click and clack as she walks and force her to move with a swaying, halting, slightly unnatural step.

The river shallows and broadens out between banks of rain-bright grass that give way to the rocks and seaweed at ragged, undercut margins of dark, peaty ground where the grey remains of barkless tree trunks and giant branches – element-stripped, time-polished – lie trapped and caught, twisted limbs spread and out-flung in frozen poses of what look to her like agony and despair; a Pompeiian tableau representing the fossilisation of a meaningless end.

There is no discernible path any more. She stumbles down the side of the stream, nearly falling, then stoops to pick up another couple of rocks, adding them to the collections in the poacher's pockets. She thinks she feels something give as she adds the stones to the right pocket, and worries that the material will rip, letting the stones fall out. She recalls a fable about something like that. Aesop, probably. The fable of the woman who tried to carry too many rocks; that would be her. Not that it would ever be written, not that anybody would ever read it. Not that it mattered in the least. Not that anything did.

The rocks on this part of the shore are round and hard to walk over, especially with all the extra weight she is carrying. She had carried less when she had been pregnant with the child, though sometimes it had felt like all the weight in the world. She splashes into the stream as it spreads out still further, leaving behind the grassy banks and forming a rough delta across the rocks, straggled with seaweed and the flayed flotsam branches. Her boots fill with cold water. She stops, takes off the gloves and carefully does up the buttons on the coat, right up to her chin. Then she stoops, plunging her hands through the water rushing around her boots, and picks up a last couple of stones from the bed of the stream. Cradling them in the crook of one arm, she pulls the gloves back on over her wet hands, then holds the stones, one in each hand, rather than risk putting them into the already overloaded pockets of the coat.

She keeps on walking down the stream until the stream becomes the sea, becomes the waters of the loch. By sticking to the stream bed she's walked past the seaweed, avoiding slipping and falling on it. She wonders where the water stops tasting fresh and starts being salty.

The waters of the loch rise around her ankles, calves, knees. The coat's tails float up on the surface of the loch, moving with the small waves, then start to disappear under the surface, weighed down by the stones she has gathered in her pockets. The water is stunningly, sharply, cruelly cold. Already, as the waves chop and surge around her knees, she can hardly feel her feet, and what sensation remains is painful; a bone-chilling ache she remembers from childhood. The coat sinks around her. The water rises to her thighs.

A seagull – wings stretched across the breeze – banks around her, some distance off. Its white head and black bead-eyes swivel once in her direction, then the bird pulls up and flaps slowly away, heading for the shore.

The rain has started again, dampening her hair. She wades further on, each step deeper and draggier than the last, forcing her way out towards the dark centre of the loch as though through a nightmare. The waters reach her groin, then her belly and waist, chilling her utterly, sucking the warmth from her body. Bubbles rise from her clothes. Each step she takes is a little easier now; she feels more sure-footed on the hidden surface of the bed under the brown waters as her body tries to float. She's holding her gloved hands and the two last stones out of the water, hugging them up near her shoulders. Water trickles over her wrists and down her forearms.

Tears fill her eyes and start to roll down her cheeks as she takes each sucking, gasping breath. The cold of the water, gradually transferring itself to her body, seems to be draining the ability to breathe from her chest muscles, putting them into spasm, forcing her to fight for every breath. She wonders if this terrible, wrenching, invasive cold will stop her heart even before she drowns.

She is terrified. She starts to sob, the sobs made sharp and ragged by the penetrating cold of the water and her spasming chest. She had hoped that right now, in these final moments, there might be some sort of peacefulness, that she might find a state of uncaring resignation imposing itself upon her, like a foretaste of the freedom from pain she is looking to oblivion to provide. Instead she is going to her death in a state of dread and cold-flayed agony, blundering across the rocks hidden by the dark brown water beneath her, horror stricken at the thought of what she is doing to those who will survive her, filled with fear at the idea that there might after all be a stupid, vengeful, punitive God, a God ultimately no better than Man, a God who punishes further those so lost to hope they take their own lives in the first place. What if all that nonsense is true? What if the ghastly Christian mumbo-jumbo is based on truth?

Well, let it be. She deserves any punishment, will accept it, embrace it. If this too-humanly formed God really existed, then the afterlife was as vindictive and spiteful as the world, indeed was just a continuation of it, and what she was here she would be there, and so no more deserving of any mercy or relief in that world than she was in this. She knows what she is doing is wrong. The knowing that what she is doing – what she has realised for some time she was committed to doing – will hurt others (one or two deserving, the rest not deserving at all) is itself one of the reasons that she hates herself and her life and what she has become, and so seeks this extinction.

Anyway, it still doesn't matter. Just the chance of not being, not thinking, not suffering, is worth it all. Deep inside, she knows it really is all nonsense, and there is no continuation whatsoever.

Another few steps. She feels lighter still, gasping as the water surrounds her torso like an icily enveloping lover. Her heart is beating very quickly. The coat and the collection of stones keep her down, stopping her from floating. The water comes to her breasts – the obscene, cold lover squeezing like something hungry – and a wave splashes her stone-clutching hands, dribbling water down her wrists towards her elbows. The next wave splashes her face. One more step, then another, sinking deeper. The water is at her chin now. She takes a deep breath, instinctively, then thinks how stupid this is, and lets the air away again, forcing the last of it out as the water ascends to her mouth.

A note. She should have left a note. She thought of this weeks ago, days ago, even last night, but in the end she didn't do it. Perhaps she ought to have left one. It was traditional. Traditional. This thought makes her smile, briefly, tremulously, as the sense-destroying cold-ness of the water splashes up to her nose. No, there was no point leaving a note. What would she have said?

The tears roll down her cheeks and into the slapping waves, taking their own tiny cargo of saltiness with them.

She feels sorry for the child, for Alban.

The gently sloping shelf of the loch bed ends here; she walks off the hidden underwater cliff with a tiny surprised cry, bitten-off, and vanishes immediately under the brown waves, her auburn hair sucked down at last like fine tendrils of seaweed, leaving only a few bubbles which float briefly and then burst and vanish.

Her last breath, taken reflexively the instant before she cried out, held instinctively despite her desire for death, finally surrendered to the crushing pressure of the black water fathoms down, surfaces in a small silvery cluster of larger bubbles about half a minute later.

The gull comes back through the soft veils of grey rain, wing-tipping down, feathers almost touching the surface of the waves over the place where she disappeared, then it curves away once more.

Back on track. He should think so, too.

Alban turns up at the London offices less than a week after Fielding had to leave him in Glasgow. They meet in Reception, Al standing dressed like a tramp in that same grubby-looking hiking jacket and toting his little stained backpack, his dirty jeans and scuffed hiking boots making him look like he's just stepped out of the forests or a workman's van. His beard is looking well trimmed, Fielding thinks, but still. They're surrounded by the prizes, plaques, awards and certificates hanging on the walls, and by the framed newspaper cuttings and photographs of the famous, featuring either a game – usually *Empire!* – or Wopuld family members.

When Fielding walks up to his cousin – nodding and smiling at Suze, the very fit blonde receptionist and switchboard operator – Al's beneath a portrait of their great-grandfather Henry, standing in front of a glass case with one of Henry's original prototype game boards displayed inside, complete with hand-carved pieces.

'Cuz, good to see you,' Fielding tells him, giving him the sincere handshake with added left-hand forearm grip. Fielding steers Al over to Suze. Fielding introduces them – you can see her re-categorising in real time, taking Al out of Shabby Hobo, Possible Thief or Nutter and putting him into Yet Another Eccentric Wopuld Family Member – then Fielding takes Al up to his office. Another portrait of old Henry looks down on them in the elevator as they exchange small talk about Al's journey south.

Dear old great-grandfather.

Henry Wopuld was a clerk with a farming supplies company based in Bristol when he dreamt up *Empire!* in 1880–81. It was the heyday of the British Empire; the map of the world had turned or was turning pink or red or whatever hue map-makers chose to illustrate the holdings of the first Empire in history on which the sun never set, because it encompassed the globe itself. Civilisation, Christianity and trade were being taken to those inhabiting the furthest corners of the world whether they thought they wanted it or not, and in a sense all *Empire!* did was epitomise this, allowing the Victorian middle class – along with the more aspirational denizens of the lower orders – to fight and trade and preach and bluff their way to world domination from the comfort of their own homes. A claimed educational aspect to the game – in the fields of both geography and morality – helped it appeal to all ages and classes, and earn the praise of school boards and parish councils alike.

The game was taken up by a small printing and toys company in London and marketed aggressively, mostly thanks to Henry. He had a partner who owned the original company, but there was some sort of unrelated investment scandal, the partner was bankrupted and Henry bought up the company for a song and never looked back. The family moved to Lydcombe on the proceeds of the fortune Henry made from the original game, but he was already working on new ideas.

The USA, perhaps not surprisingly, proved reluctant to accept *Empire!*; sales were miserable. Henry tried a version of the game based on a map consisting only of the contiguous states of the US, but that did little better. Finally he bought up a small printing firm in Pittsburgh so that the box and board could each bear the legend *Made in the USA*, altered the map of the world on which *Empire!* was based so that the USA was centred – the boundaries of the board cutting through the heart of Asia – renamed the game *Liberty!*, changed nothing else and watched the dollars roll in. He bought the estate of Garbadale in the far north-west of Scotland with the intention of hunting, shooting and fishing there and had the most expensive architects of the day design a grand new lodge in the finest Scotch Baronial style, to be named Garbadale Castle (later House, when tastes in such matters changed).

There were various different editions and versions of the game, and a lot of litigation – or at least the threat of it – as other games suspiciously similar to *Empire!* appeared. Often the easiest way to deal with certain companies threatening the Wopuld firm's position was simply to buy them up and close them down, incorporating whatever of worth there might be in the purchased firm into Wopuld Games Ltd, whether it was company personnel, some minor innovation in the playing of the game, or the manufacture of the product.

Henry died in 1917, leaving a family he hoped was large enough to provide the firm with all the executive officers it might need to carry the Wopuld name onwards, though this was not sufficient to prevent a dip in sales after the Great War.

Mornington Crescent, a game based on the map of the London underground with a complicated double-level board sold well in Britain and modestly abroad. A more purely trade-based game called

High Seas! did reasonable business. Another based on stocks and shares called *Speculate!* was a brief, faddish hit on both sides of the Atlantic, though in the States it was marketed purely as a children's game on the basis that all the adults were feverishly engaged in the real thing, making a game of it superfluous.

The Depression necessitated the sale of the factory in Pittsburgh.

The Thirties saw a partial revival of the family's fortunes. An austerity version of the original game did well for a time during the Second World War, though there was some difficulty over the news that the Germanised version, produced in Leipzig by a now wholly German-owned company, was doing even better. Also, only for a while.

After the war, the rejigged, relaunched, version of *Empire!* – *Commonwealth* (no exclamation mark) – remapped to reflect the changed political realities of the planet, did surprisingly poorly. *Monopoly* (once seen as an upstart, now regarded as the old enemy) outsold the old game for the first time. The company drifted, holding talks with other firms about merging or being taken over, though without serious effect.

The original game staggered on through the Sixties, nearly went under in the Seventies – a very brief-lived game called *Karma!* based on a grotesque mishmash of misunderstood hippy gibberish and cereal-box Buddhism was an unmitigated disaster – and only started to revive in the Eighties. An electronic version of *Empire!* proved popular, then very popular. Then wildly popular. More PC and games-console versions followed, gradually creating a uniquely smooth spectrum of gaming potential to suit virtually all tastes, from those who aspired to the most calm, cerebral, turn-based experience – more akin to chess than anything else – to users who just wanted to wade straight into the most gore-spattered slice- or shoot-them-up, jerking round floors and couches, teeth grinding, eyes wide, face contorted, sweat beading.

The board version became fashionable again on the back of the electronic successes and in 1999 the Spraint Corporation of America,

Inc., making profound noises regarding stuff like vertical integration and OS/platform synergies, bought up a quarter of Wopuld Games Ltd for a significant amount of money and an even more significant quantity of its own forever soaring shares.

Every share-wielding member of the extended Wopuld family suddenly became quite a bit richer.

'Haydn,' Fielding says, calling in at his brother's office on the way to his own. 'Look who's here.'

Good things happen. Sometimes they happen for no particular reason, the way the bad things so often seem to happen.

Once, about seven years ago, less than a year before he left the family firm, and certainly when he was already thinking about doing so, Alban had what may still count as the most exquisite sexual encounter of his life. This all happened about a year after the insanity of the Singapore episode with Fielding and his drugs, about eight or nine months before he met Verushka Graef in a hotel in Shanghai, and about a year before he encountered his sepulchral Uncle Blake for the second time on top of his hulking neon skyscraper in the hazy steam-bath hive that is Hong Kong.

Looking back, his world seemed very Asian, and he supposed they were out there a lot because that was where the factories were these days. It was also where the latest, greatest economic growth happened to be spurting.

The company had come up with a luxury edition of the board game version of *Empire!* The board itself was constructed from semi-precious stones pivoting on titanium hinges, the cards were embossed silver, the dice stacks were formed from mahogany inlaid with mother of pearl and the pieces were carved from jade, ebony, jasper, agate, onyx and porphyry. This cost a cool ten thousand dollars US and they had expected to sell a few dozen to some sheikhs.

Instead – well, as well as – they sold hundreds to what seemed like a whole new breed of the South-East Asian rich. For China and similar cultures, they had what they called the chipped version.

It had been Alban's idea to introduce a gambling element to the old game and they first brought that out as an even more extra-special edition of the luxury version. They also increased the number of potential players to eight, because that was a number with especially good associations in parts of Chinese culture. That too had sold in relatively small but highly profitable and usefully influential numbers. The gambling version of the standard eight-player game subsequently shifted in gratifyingly prodigious quantities, too.

At the time it didn't just seem like Asia. At the time Alban remembers thinking that his life seemed to revolve around initials: HK, KL, LA, NYC . . . The whole world was becoming shorthand, becoming text, becoming txt.

His encounter – his perfect, soul-saving, life-redeeming experience – took place in the deeply civilised, imperially stately and casually cool – if rather less far-flungly exotic – setting of Paris.

He was there to see cousin Haydn, Fielding's elder brother, who worked for the firm as a production wizard, ensuring the snuggest possible fit between supply and demand, and who had had, apparently, some sort of breakdown. Haydn had skipped town a week earlier, leaving the London office in Mayfair and the family home in Knightsbridge to abscond all the way to Paris – specifically, the Ritz – via Eurostar and a grand total of two taxis. Oddly, as well as displaying a singular lack of momentum in his moonlighting, he still seemed to be doing his job, running figures and production quotas off his laptop while staying in the Ritz, tying in – with a hardly reduced degree of exquisite precision – the specific extent to which profoundly need-motivated dextrous-fingered Malaysian, Indonesian and Chinese children should be worked to produce a monetarily measurable quantity of pleasure in buyers from Alaska to Kamchatka. (The long way round, obviously.)

'Oh, Christ. Gran sent you, didn't she?'

Was the first thing Haydn said to Alban when he appeared at

Haydn's usual table in the hotel's main restaurant, lifting over a gilt chair and sitting on it.

'Yes, she did,' Alban said. Somewhere in the near future there could well lie times when he'd have to deceive Haydn, but this was not one of them.

He had, anyway, already decided this was an interesting but probably forlorn excursion. For some reason Winifred – Gran – was treating him as the company's troubleshooter, sending him to do the more off-piste pieces of nonsense that she judged needed to be done for the good of the family and the firm. Oh fuck, he was her secret agent, her man on special assignment, Alban thought all of a sudden as he looked across the napkins, flowers and silver-ware at Haydn's round, shining, fragile face.

Haydn was a fat little guy who insisted on dressing in grey suits about one size too small. It was a perversion, in the sense that it did exactly the opposite of what it was supposed to do; he looked fatter than he really was, not thinner. Haydn had started going bald at about sixteen, which was just a plain cruel thing for an adoles-cent to have to go through as well as all the usual stuff. He had elected ever since for the comb-over option, which was also never going to do him any favours, although – on the plus side – he had yet, at the age of twenty-seven, to suffer from spots.

Since he had ensconced himself here, Haydn had not been answering his suite's telephone, his mobile or his email. He also had most of his meals delivered to his suite, though he did sometimes appear for dinner alone in the main dining room. That was why Alban had had to drag over the shiny chair and plonk himself down across the table from the chap.

'Why are you here?' Haydn asked.

'Well, there's a good question,' Alban said. 'Why are any of us here?' He sat back. 'Are you always this profound over dinner?'

'Stop dicking about, Alban. I just want to know what the hell you think you're doing here.'

Alban couldn't remember hearing Haydn swear before. Paris really was persuading him to let what remained of his hair down. And in a dining room.

'I came to see how you are,' Alban told him.

'Well, you've seen me. How *do* you think I am?'

'I have no idea yet. I've only just found you.'

'Is everything all right here, sir?' the maître d' asked, suddenly table-side.

'Yes, no problem; thanks.' Haydn waved the man away.

'How do *you* think you are?' Alban said.

'Do you mean, how do I feel?' Haydn asked, with what was probably meant to be sarcasm.

'I suppose I do.'

'I'm fine.'

'So why have you decamped,' Alban looked round the high, ornate dining room, 'to here?'

Haydn fiddled with his napkin. 'I needed a break.'

'Gran used the word "breakdown". So did your dad.'

'They would.'

'Well, if it's any comfort, it doesn't look like a breakdown to me.'

'Thanks a lot.'

'Moving a couple of hundred kilometres to a life of abject luxury and keeping doing your day job at the same time doesn't exactly smack of a tortured soul's descent into bedlam.' Alban paused. 'Unless you think you're Napoleon or something.'

'Actually I'm not doing my day job properly,' Haydn said, ignoring this and nodding to the waiter as his consommé was set before him. The slim young waiter turned and walked away. Haydn watched him for a couple of seconds. Haydn was widely assumed within the family to be gay but in denial about it. Haydn looked at Alban. 'I'm only half doing it.' He looked after the waiter again. 'Actually, about a third doing it, or an even smaller fraction. Usually I spend three hours in the morning and three hours in the afternoon working. An hour or two extra on a busy day. Here, I'm doing two one-hour stints.'

135

Alban thought about this. 'Is that it?'

Haydn frowned, dipped his spoon into his soup and let the watery brown liquid dribble away back into the bowl again. 'I'm missing nuances. Going more broad brush,' he said. 'Also, I'm not looking very far ahead. Over time there'll be cumulative errors. They'll build up.' He shook his head. 'It's ticking over. More of a game.' He looked darkly at Alban. 'But don't be deceived; I am not still doing my job properly. I've run away and I'm just playing. You can call that a breakdown if you like.'

He carefully rearranged his napkin, holding it up to alter it from a triangle to a perfect rectangle, lining the edges up to within a millimetre, then replacing it on his lap.

'Well, okay,' Alban said, watching this. 'But it's a very civilised form of breakdown.'

Haydn busied himself with his soup. After half a dozen spoonfuls he paused to dab at his lips with the napkin. He returned the napkin to his lap, still spotless.

Man, you seriously need to get laid, Alban thought.

'So, what's the problem?' he asked.

'You really want to know?'

'Cuz, I'm here.'

Haydn took a deep breath, studying the blank white tablecloth. He grimaced, looked up. 'I'll tell you later. I need to formulate exactly how to express it linguistically.' He nodded at the table in front of Alban. 'Have you eaten? Will you join me? I don't care to drink alone, but we could have a bottle of something.'

'What a good idea.'

'You see, that's the mistake people make. It's not supply and demand; it's demand and supply.'

'Is that a big difference?'

'It's fundamental! It's a whole new way of thinking, of working, of ordering, and of *ordering*.'

They were sitting in the living room of the suite at the Ritz which

136

Haydn was currently charging to the family firm. The suite was quite big. Alban wondered if the main cause for familial concern here was the room rate impacting on the firm's liquidity.

Alban nodded. 'Right,' he said. He felt he sort of half-got the distinction between ordering and *ordering*. He hoped he did. Either that or cousin Haydn genuinely was cracking up. In which case maybe he should hope he didn't get the distinction.

Maybe he shouldn't have come to Paris.

They were sharing a bottle of champagne. Alban was trying hard to convince Haydn to come out on the town. He hadn't wanted to come to the suite but Haydn had insisted, finally admitting it was because he didn't like using public toilets, even if they were the public toilets of five-star hotels. So they'd come up to the suite. But they needed to go *out*, dammit. They were in Paris, for Christ's sake. It was even spring. In the week he'd been here, Haydn had confessed, he hadn't actually been out at night yet. This was so wrong-headed that Alban actually felt slightly angry. It was like going to the Grand Canyon but keeping your eyes shut, or declaring yourself a fan of Jimi Hendrix, but only for his singing.

Alban wondered if he'd basically been sent here to pimp. He certainly wasn't the only person in the family who thought that what Haydn needed more than anything else was a healthy dose of rumpy-pumpy, whichever gender might be involved. Or maybe Gran thought Haydn fancied *him*; maybe she'd sent Alban to Haydn, one cousin to another (very fucking funny), as a present, as a prize to tempt him back to the bosom of his family and responsibilities. He certainly wouldn't put something like that past the old she-goat.

'This isn't the reason you're here, is it?' Alban asked, genuinely confused. 'This so-called breakdown doesn't resolve into a question about fucking semantics or something, does it?'

'No, no,' Haydn said, staring into his champagne. He was sitting, legs up, on an ornate chaise longue. Alban had opted for a single-occupancy chair.

'What, then?'

Alban was painfully aware he was probably the wrong sort of person to send on a mission like this. He'd never thought of himself as having a great aptitude for getting people to talk, or indeed as having any sort of gift for amateur counselling. He was pretty sure nobody else had thought of him in that way, either. Agreed, he'd provided a shoulder to cry on for a few people of both sexes over the years, some close, some not but just – he guessed – desperate, and had had a few people treat him like some sort of cross between a priest and a psychiatrist, but his only skills in this field, he was sure, consisted of knowing when to shut up, make sympathetic noises, ask the very occasional question and resist the sometimes quite powerful urge to shake the person concerned and tell them loudly just to pull themselves together.

Haydn looked uncomfortable, fidgeting on the chaise, mouth compressed into a tight line. 'Excuse me,' he said, getting up. 'I need to visit the loo.' He disappeared.

Alban drained his champagne, studied the empty glass for a moment, then got up, went to the phone on the desk and ordered a taxi.

He heard the sound of a toilet flushing. 'You fucking *shall* go to the ball, Cinders,' he muttered to himself as he returned to his seat.

He'd had to negotiate. He'd wanted to go straight to a club but Haydn had shown every sign of plunging headlong into outright hysteria at the very idea, so they'd compromised with a coffee and a glass of brandy sitting outside one of the cafés at the west end of the Rue-St-André-des-Arts. This was where seven streets converged and the full mad circus show of Parisian road skills is displayed day and night in all its heart-stopping glory.

Alban had had the taxi drop them at the St-Michel end so they could walk the length of the street. This was one of Alban's favourite places in Paris, in the whole world, and if Haydn didn't at least start to fall in love with the city after this then the fucker had no soul and Alban would personally take him firmly by the collar and belt, march him up the Mazarine and drop the sorry witless wazzock off the Pont des Arts to let him swim home to the fucking Ritz.

'Cheers.'

'Santé.'

'So, what then? What is the problem?'

'You really want to know?'

'Haydn, we've kind of been through this. Stop it.'

'Well, okay. It's . . . it's the impossibility of ever getting an order just right.' He grinned quickly at Alban and drank deeply from his brandy.

'What?'

Haydn coughed and then said, 'I am perfectly serious. Every time I place an order, I feel I'm failing. You either order too much of – well, anything – and stock ends up sitting on shelves or pallets in warehouses – costing money, obviously – or you don't order sufficient and have to reorder, which is inefficient, and also costs extra. Two production runs cost more than one run of the same combined total. Don't you see?' Haydn seemed like he really needed Alban to understand. And also slightly pitiful.

Alban looked at his cousin. Haydn's nervous, tense, slightly flushed face was illuminated by the lights of the café at their back and those of the surrounding restaurants, bars and shops, the nearby streetlights, the red glow of a recently ignited gas heater and the headlights of the closest eccentrically parked hatchback.

'For this you run away from your family, you cause your poor mother no end of worry and run up a hotel bill that would feed a—'

'You're sounding like you're pretending to be Jewish.'

'That was deliberate, Haydn. My final word was going to be "Oy". Thanks for spoiling it.'

Haydn looked alarmed. 'You're not anti-Semitic, are you?'

'No I'm not,' Alban said indignantly. 'I'm positively pro-Semitic. And anyway, the fucking Palestinians are a Semitic people. Now—'

'You're anti-Palestinian?' Haydn yelped.

'Oh, dear God,' Alban moaned, putting his face in his hands. 'No!'

he said loudly. 'Do you want to see my subscription details for Medical Aid for Palestine, or what?'

'Sorry.'

'Will you shut up and let us get back to the point?'

'All right, all right. I'm sorry. Don't shout at me.'

Alban took a deep breath. 'You skedaddled because you, because you . . . You never get orders for bits of games right, not precisely right, not to, to the individual unit? Is that what you're saying?'

'Broadly, yes,' Haydn said, looking relieved to have negotiated the minefield of Middle Eastern sympathies and to be back on the relatively safer ground of his own neuroses.

Alban placed one hand flat on the little metal table and looked away, shaking his head. 'Oy,' he said softly. He looked at Haydn. He shrugged resignedly. 'It's just the right word, dude.'

Haydn continued to prove resistant to the idea of going to a proper club with people and music and dancing and such. Alban knew of at least two which were about fifty-fifty straight/gay – to allow Haydn the choice without seeming to impose it upon him – but the guy just wasn't playing ball at all. Instead they walked a meandering path along the route of the St-Germain, sometimes on the boulevard itself, sometimes on smaller streets leading off it, parallel with it and leading back to it again. They walked slowly; Haydn's bulk and short legs meant he was a natural waddler, and he seemed to get out of breath climbing a kerb.

'I don't care to go to these places,' Haydn tried to explain. 'They're too loud, too crowded.'

'That'd be all the people in them, causing that.'

'Also, they're too smoky.'

'Some of them can be,' Alban conceded. 'Others have these things called air conditioning or just extractor fans.'

'Everybody *smokes*,' Haydn said, glancing at two young men as they passed on the pavement, both talking loudly and gesturing with glowing Gitanes.

'Haydn, this is Paris. It's practically compulsory.'

'I just don't like being in large groups of people I don't know. It's just not me.'

'Oh, jeez, Haydn, you just need to *meet* people. Young attractive people who might want to meet you.'

'I'm not attractive,' Haydn said. 'And please don't try to pretend otherwise. I refuse to indulge in that sort of self-deceit.'

'You're young. That's halfway there.'

'Huh, yeah. Plus I look older than I am.'

'Some people like a wise head on young shoulders,' Alban said, then laughed. 'Or better still, between their legs.'

'Oh, please.'

'Haydn; people far less interesting, who are actively ugly in a serious claw-your-own-eyes-out-now kind of way, rather than just not six-packed buff-gods, get laid every day, sometimes by very good-looking women indeed. And men, for that matter. I'm totally serious. It's just a question of giving yourself the chance, of not being so terrified of rejection you don't ask in the first place, and of having just the tiny, teeny-weeniest little bit of self-confidence.' Alban held up one index finger and thumb, tips barely separated, to help his cousin visualise the exact degree of teeny-weenyness they were talking about here.

'Alban,' Haydn said. 'I don't like being with lots of other people, especially strangers. Don't you understand?'

Alban shook his head, then blew out a breath. 'No. Well, yes. If you don't, you don't. I'm sure we could find, you know, a less crowded environment. Someplace quiet, where there might be—'

'Alban,' Haydn said, stopping on the pavement. Alban turned to face him. They were outside a garden in front of a small church, a little patch of darkness in the commercial glitz of St-Germain. Haydn crossed his arms. 'Do you know what?'

Alban nodded emphatically and said, 'Yes.'

'Eh?' Haydn looked confused. 'What?'

Alban waved one hand regally. 'Sorry. Just fuckin' with you. What?'

'I'll tell you what,' Haydn said. 'I know what you're saying, I know what you're – what you're angling at. What you – where you want to get me, or at least the sort of place you want to get me, and why. I know what you think and what the family thinks and what people say behind my back. I am not fucking stupid. And do you know the truth?'

Alban said nothing. Cousin Haydn actually sounded angry. Alban was determined to treat this as a positive development unless and until it ended with him getting biffed on the nose.

Haydn's eyes opened wide. He leaned fractionally towards Alban. Alban leaned back a slightly smaller fraction, still alive to the nascent nose-biffing possibilities inherent in the current situation. Haydn said, 'I don't particularly like sex.' Having said it, Haydn drew himself upright and raised his chins defiantly.

Alban felt the need to cross his own arms. He kind of wanted to lean back – way back – as well, but thought that would look too much like he was taking the mick, so he contented himself with biting the corner of his mouth and leaning to one side, as though there was a young, thin tree directly in between them and he was trying to look round it.

'Really?' he asked, frowning mightily.

'It's like it's a crime or something,' Haydn said, and Alban had the impression his cousin was about to start crying. 'People treat you as though you're mad, or it's a disease they might catch, or as if it's some sort of criticism of them, of everybody else . . . Some even assume it's just a line, some sort of ridiculous, pathetic tactic to get them to sleep with you. The truth is I've had sex. I've tried it. Tried it several times, in fact, and I just don't see the attraction. It's messy, it's undignified, it's hot and sweaty and, and – animalistic.' Haydn was looking down at the pavement by now, as though he was telling the sidewalk what he thought of it. From the corner of either eye, Alban could see other pedestrians giving them a pretty wide clearance zone. Haydn was still speaking: 'It hardly lasts any time, you make a complete fool of yourself in front of another person and then

142

you have to make embarrassing small talk for ever afterwards and the whole *fucking* world is just completely bloody obsessed with it – it's ridiculous, it's preposterous, it's demeaning, it's just so . . . *ridiculous!*' He looked up at Alban, appearing quite angry, breathing hard, arms still crossed over his heaving chest. He reached up quickly and smoothed some of his comb-over back into place and then crossed his arms defensively again.

'Hmm,' Alban said thoughtfully. This was worse than he'd thought. He cleared his throat. 'You have been doing it with the right, ahm . . .' he scratched behind one ear.

'Sex?' Haydn said, almost spitting. 'Gender? Type of person?'

'Well,' Alban said, actually feeling slightly embarrassed. 'Yeah.'

'Yes,' Haydn said. 'I find women quite attractive in a theoretical sort of way. They're smaller, more efficient, better packaged. I just don't have any overwhelming desire to penetrate them with any part of my own body.'

Alban wasn't sure this was at all the right thing to say, but he was drunk and he knew he was going to say it anyway, so he did. 'You absolutely sure? Haydn, I've seen you looking at waiters and guys in the street. Especially good-looking guys—'

'I look at men like that because I wish that I was them,' Haydn said, suddenly bitter. 'I look at them with longing because I long to be like them. Good-looking and assured and attractive to women.' He shrugged. 'Or men. Just to somebody.' He shook his head, looking frustrated at his own inability to explain himself fully. 'Though, and please believe me in this, most of the time – almost all the time, honestly – I just don't care. I don't miss it, I don't feel deprived or sad about it. In fact, in myself I'm perfectly fine; it's the reactions and the prejudices and the, the *stupidities* of other people that distress me.' He blew out a breath after these words, like punctuation. Specifically, a very full full stop.

Alban thought about all this. He looked up at the under-lit clouds above the city. Traffic roared behind him. He looked back at Haydn. 'Fucking hell,' he said.

'If it's any, oh, I don't know; not consolation,' Haydn said, glancing away for a moment. He started again. 'If it makes you feel better, I have sort of tried with a man. It really is absolutely not any of your bloody business at all, and it had better not go any further, but I have tried it. I tried it as far as kissing, anyway, and – you know – touching; fondling, you might say.' Haydn closed his eyes at the memory. 'That was the single most embarrassing incident in my life,' he said with a shudder. He looked at Alban. 'And you?' he asked.

A bit aggressively, Alban thought.

'Me what?' he asked, confused.

'Are you sure you're doing it with the right gender?'

Alban frowned.

'You have something of a reputation as a ladies' man in the family, don't you, cuz?' Haydn said. 'But how do you know? How can you be sure unless you've tried? Have you tried?'

'Well, bit like you,' Alban admitted, scratching behind one ear again. 'Youthful fumblings.' He laughed. 'Fucking hell, Haydn; I went further than you! I was actually wanked off and I've had another guy's cock in my mouth.' He looked thoughtful. 'Never came.' He sounded wistful. 'Always put that down to drink and lack of technique. Anyway.' He cleared his throat. 'Tried. Just not me. Like you say.'

'Well, there you are then.' Haydn sighed.

Alban made a clicking noise with his mouth. 'I think we need more drink.'

They found a little dive bar – smoky but just about bearable – somewhere near the Invalides, the Eiffel Tower visible above the buildings beyond the gardens, golden-lit, searchlight revolving at its summit. The bar was perfect; almost a cliché. There was even a trio of guys on a small stage in one corner playing jazz. Alban had to stifle a laugh and look around as they got to the bottom of the steps, claiming to be trying to spot hep cats dressed in black polo-necks and wearing berets. 'Only in Paris,' he breathed as they walked

144

to a table. He made sure it was near an air duct, to keep Haydn happy.

She came down the steps ten minutes later, dressed in black; mid-length skirt, blouse, a small jacket like a bullfighter's, glittering with detail. She was medium height, with a figure the svelte side of full, and long hair that was dark, dark red. She looked vaguely Asiatic, but was somehow not immediately placeable even roughly anywhere between Istanbul and Tokyo. And her face was one that even a pessimist might grant could stop wars; exquisite, serene, flawless. Alban immediately tried to fit her into his Top Ten Most Beautiful Women I've Ever Seen With My Own Eyes list. That is, he immediately tried to fit her into his TTMBWIESWMOE list anywhere except number one, because he'd met Kathleen Turner once on a flight to LA with his dad when he'd been sixteen, shortly after he'd seen *The Man with Two Brains*, and he'd sworn to himself the Kathleen he'd met that day would keep the number-one spot for ever, no matter what.

It didn't work.

She went to the bar, ordered a glass of red wine and stood there, perfectly casually poised, watching the jazz group. They returned the favour, as did most of the men in the bar, plus the majority of the women. It took about one minute for the first man to approach her. She smiled a little, held up one hand, shook her head.

Alban tore his gaze away.

Even Haydn was looking at her. 'Fucking hell,' he said, 'what a beautiful woman.'

Alban did a double take, then returned his gaze to the woman at the bar. The first rebuffed guy returned to his seat, rejected but still looking happy, almost blessed. Alban thought about taking a crack himself. Hell, he was currently uncommitted, she was stunningly beautiful, and the fact she'd probably say no was almost irrelevant. Because you never knew. Damn it, it would more or less be rude not to. But he'd be abandoning Haydn, even if only briefly, symbolically. That wouldn't be too polite.

145

Alban leaned over to Haydn, not taking his eyes off the beauty at the bar. 'Would you mind terribly if I—'

'Oh, God,' Haydn said. 'Will you just control yourself? Just because you've admitted you've sucked another man's penis that doesn't mean you have to over-compensate by throwing yourself at the first unobtainable woman who drifts into view.'

Alban glanced. 'You don't know she's unobtainable.'

'Oh, get real,' Haydn breathed. He looked round, sighing. 'Do you think they're actually going to serve us at any point?'

'But you wouldn't mind? I mean, you're right, I'll probably be straight back, but—'

'Can't you just leave her alone? That woman probably spends her entire life batting away guys like you. Completely fed up with it, I'd bet. Give her a break.'

'Oh; there goes another one,' Alban said, as a second man left his table and went up to her. She turned him away gracefully, too. Alban looked at Haydn. 'Look, it's paying her a compliment. And the fact she has to do it all the time just means she has lots of practice; water off a duck's back.'

'Alban, you've said yourself she'll almost certainly turn you down, so why bother?'

Alban was still drinking her in. She was looking round the room, sipping from her glass, face currently turning away from him. Alban adjusted his chair a quarter-turn to get a better look at her without cricking his neck. 'You're missing the point,' he told Haydn. 'Even if the chance is one in a thousand or one in a million, she might say yes. And what have I got to lose?'

'Your dignity?' Haydn suggested. 'You'll be humiliated.'

'It's just a knock-back, Haydn. It's not the end of the fucking world. And do you know what?' He turned back to look at his cousin, who made a resigned, What? kind of face. 'That woman,' Alban said, 'is so beautiful it will still be a positive experience. It'll be a privilege to exchange even just a few words with her; a fucking honour to be knocked back by a creature that stunning.' He nodded for emphasis and tapped on the table with one middle finger just in case there was any remaining shred of doubt regarding the matter. 'I'm perfectly serious.'

'Yes, I'm somewhat gathering that,' Haydn said.

Alban looked back at the woman. Her gaze swept round their end of the room, hesitated on him, producing a brief, uncertain smile, then went on. Whereupon she turned back to watch the jazz band.

Alban felt himself do a kind of internal reality check, assuring himself as well as he could that what seemed to have just happened, actually had.

Then he breathed, 'Did you see that?'

'I think I did,' Haydn said, voice also hushed.

'That *was* directed at me, not you, wasn't it?' Alban said. He glanced behind them. Of course there wasn't anybody else behind them; there was just the brick wall.

'It certainly wasn't directed at me,' Haydn said.

'Well, fuck it; that's that,' Alban said, standing. He made his way to the bar.

'Best of luck,' Haydn whispered.

She was called Kalpana. She was some astounding combination of north Indian, Sri Lankan, Native American and Japanese – a mixture of ethnic cues in the bone structure and surface textures of her face that defied any easy racial stereotyping. Planet beautiful; basically that was where she was from. Her hair was the colour of copper beech, her skin like velvet, a moleskin softness somewhere between pearly grey and the brown of a polished conker. Her eyes were hazel, heavily flecked with green. And she moved like she wasn't made from the ordinary stuff of common-or-garden humanity; she moved like she was made of some exotic matter from a dimension composed exclusively of pure sexual radiance, like she came from another universe, an existence where the usual clunky physical laws that governed movement and the getting of clumps of matter from one

147

place to another simply didn't apply. *Fuck me sideways, she's the luxury edition*, Alban thought, watching her rear as she swivelled and stepped her way between the tables, heading for the one by the wall where Haydn Wopuld was staring goggle-eyed at her.

Alban felt the gaze of a very large proportion of the clientele on him as he escorted her away from the bar. He felt himself blush. This was crazy; he was more embarrassed to have succeeded in gaining her attention than he would have been to have got knocked back like the other two guys, which really had been entirely what he'd been expecting, right up until that hesitating glance and that tiny, slightly confused-looking smile. Hell's teeth; even after it.

'Kalpana, this is my cousin Haydn,' he said, pulling out a seat for her.

'Pleased to meet you,' she said, holding out her hand before she sat down. Her voice was soft and made Haydn think of an otter sleekly slipping without a ripple into a sunny brook. He shut his mouth, blinked and then finally got round to shaking her hand. He didn't quite achieve anything intelligible by way of greeting, but made instead a sort of gagging, gargling noise which would have to suffice.

She sat. If a chair could faint with pleasure, Alban thought, that one would have.

Alban sat, too, looking from Haydn to Kalpana. 'There's an explanation,' he explained.

'There is?' Haydn squeaked.

Alban nodded. 'We know each other.'

'You *do*?' Haydn said, 'and you *forgot*?'

'Your cousin was very drunk,' Kalpana said, smiling. A waiter materialised and took their order. Alban suggested only the best champagne in the place would do, and nobody disagreed.

'Mumbai,' Alban said to Haydn while looking at Kalpana.

'I'm a journalist,' she told Haydn. 'I was writing an article about the politics of games. Alban gave me an interview.'

'Did we prearrange this interview?' Alban asked. 'And I turned up drunk? I'm never normally that unprofessional.'

'We hadn't arranged anything. You rather insisted on giving me the interview. I'd already talked to . . . One of your uncles, I think. It was my belief at the time that I already had what I needed. You begged to differ.'

'Oh dear,' Alban said. 'Sorry.'

'That's quite all right. You were very funny.'

Alban narrowed his eyes. 'Did I in any way try it on with you?'

'Yes, you most certainly did.' She smiled broadly, displaying perfect teeth. 'That was funny, too.'

She had been here for a year, writing about Paris and the French and sometimes covering the European Parliament for a variety of Indian magazines and newspapers. She could write in Japanese, too, with care and a good dictionary, and sometimes sold stuff to Japanese publications. She was leaving Paris in a couple of days, to go back to India to be married. To a very sweet American. They would live near Seattle, looking out over the Sound. She was kind of wandering round the city over these last few days, saying goodbye to places she had good memories of, sometimes with friends, sometimes alone.

The champagne arrived. They toasted her forthcoming marriage.

They dropped off a happy, tipsy Haydn at the Ritz. Alban was staying at the George V. Her apartment was in Belleville; she'd take the cab on to there.

At his hotel, the doorman opened the taxi door for Alban, who turned to Kalpana on the seat beside him and smiled, holding out his hand. 'Kalpana,' he said, 'it's been an absolute pleasure.'

She was staring straight ahead, not looking at him. She seemed to have sucked her lips right into her mouth. She looked down at his offered hand, then out at the waiting doorman.

Finally, she looked into his eyes. She took his hand in both of hers. 'Listen,' she began, then sucked air through her teeth, leaned forward and addressed the doorman. '*Pardon, monsieur.*'

'*Pas de problème, madame,*' Alban heard the man say.

She was still looking into his eyes. He saw her swallow. 'Ah,' she said. She swallowed again. 'This is – that is, I'd never – oh dear. Ah – if, ah . . .' She squeezed his hand.

He lifted his left hand and touched it very gently to her lips. 'Kalpana, whatever it is you're even thinking of suggesting, it's going to be perfect by me.'

She smiled, then looked down and sat back, still smiling. He pulled his hand gently away, took out his wallet and handed a large note to the doorman, who grinned, might even have winked, and shut the taxi door again, giving the roof a quick double slap.

He never saw her again, never even tried to contact her – they'd agreed they never would – and he had always assumed that she went on to marry her nice, unutterably lucky American guy and live happily in Washington State for what he hoped would be the rest of a long and exquisitely happy life, but the next evening, after they'd said goodbye, while he was in the taxi being driven away from her apartment, he thought, *That was probably the best eighteen hours I'll ever spend in my entire life.* This did not in any way make him sad.

He supposed not having to use condoms might have made it even better, but then that was just the way things had to be. Nothing else he could think of could have made the experience any better at all.

He saw Haydn once more before he left Paris; they stood in Notre-Dame soaking up the echoes, rode the Métro and had a wander round Montmartre, a district Alban had always rather dismissed as too touristy but discovered that day he quite liked. They sat on the steps at Sacré Coeur, eating ice creams.

'I bet you're going to find you're just not looking at it the right way,' Alban told Haydn.

'You think so?' Haydn was sitting forward, legs splayed, holding his tie back with one hand so that his ice cream wouldn't stain anything.

Alban lounged, stretched back, watching sunlit girls and licking lasciviously. 'Yeah. I knew this guy once who had the neatest, cleanest office you've ever seen; real place-for-everything fixation. You know those tiny hand-held vacuum gadgets you get for keyboards? He had two – in case one broke down. The thing was, he hated anything being out of place, even momentarily. He wanted his office so neat and tidy he couldn't actually do any work in it; he'd convinced himself he'd brought it to such a peak of perfect tidiness even opening a drawer would spoil it. It was like the place was frozen. He wouldn't even have a litter bin in it because that was like some polluting hole of untidiness in itself.'

Alban looked at Haydn, but he wasn't responding, just frowning at his ice cream.

'But the litter bin was the key. I told him, Have a fucking litter bin; it's the sacrificial anode, the mousetrap; where all the untidiness gets sucked away to. In the bin, it's all chaos and no ordering is needed, in fact any attempt to organise it misunderstands its function.'

Haydn still wasn't replying, but he seemed to be listening.

'It's like a good filing system always has a Miscellaneous section,' Alban said. 'It's not a failure to have some things that can't be filed in exactly the right file, it's just acknowledging something about how things work in the real world. That's what Miscellaneous is for and the alternative isn't more accuracy, it's less, because you end up overstretching definitions or creating a fresh file for every single thing, each unit, and that's not filing, that's naming. Miscellaneous is the definition that makes sense of all the others. In the same way, a litter bin is the heart of tidiness.'

He went back to licking his ice cream. Haydn looked round at him, still keeping his tie pressed close to his chest. 'Did it work?' he asked. 'This incisive piece of analysis. Did your friend see the light and become once again a happy, productive cog in the office machine?'

Alban had to decide quickly – he'd been making the whole thing up – so he did and said, 'Yeah.' He was wearing a pair of dark glasses, and he lifted them over his eyes for a moment to smile out at Haydn. 'Yes, it did. Good, eh?' He put the glasses back again.

Haydn had looked unconvinced, at the time.

A week later, though, he was back in London. Alban got some of the credit for this. Personally he thought the guy had just needed a holiday.

'Hmm. So, Alban, are you still a champagne socialist?' Kennard asks.

They are at dinner in Fielding's parents' place in Malison Street: Kennard and Renée playing host to Alban and Fielding (Haydn's here too, but then he still lives at home). Nina – Fielding's partner – was invited but she has some class she has to attend this evening. Probably Mayan Astrology for Cats or something. She and Fielding live in Islington.

Fielding's got Alban to wear an old suit of his. Al's scrubbed up all right, really, though patently a tie was too much to hope for. This champagne socialist stuff strikes Fielding as a load of crap. Alban, when he worked for the firm, took his yearly bonus and company car. Chopping down trees doesn't make you a leftie, and now he just seems to like playing at being poor.

Al glances at his glass of Aussie Shiraz (trust Dad, Fielding thinks, to ask over the wrong drink).

'I used to be a champagne socialist,' Al says.

'So.' Kennard's eyebrows rise. 'You mean you're not any more?'

'No,' Alban says. 'I'm older now. I'm a vintage champagne socialist.' He raises the glass. 'Cheers.'

Kennard blinks. Haydn smiles.

'So, where are you working at the moment, Alban?' Renée asks. Over the years, Kennard's wife has slowly developed the skills required to cover for her husband's mistakes, gaffes and stumped silences.

'I'm not, Renée,' Alban tells her. 'I'm unemployed.'

'Between jobs,' Kennard says, nodding. 'Hmm.' Kennard is not long turned sixty-two, though he seems somewhat older. He has put on some weight over the last year, lost the remains of his hair and developed impressive if at the same time rather offputting jowls. Remarkably bad teeth. He's company Managing Director, which sounds quite impressive. He is oddly good at talking to small children and politicians.

'Between jobs,' Alban agrees.

'And are you seeing anyone at the moment?' Renée asks Alban. Fielding's mother is quite slight.

'Not really,' he says. He catches Fielding looking at him.

'Ah, hah,' Kennard says.

'Alban's got a very bonnie lassie in Glasgow,' Fielding tells them. 'She's a mathematician. A professor.'

'A what, dear?'

'A professor.'

'Oh. That *was* what you said.'

'She's a professor of mathematics,' Fielding tells her, just so there's no doubt about it.

'*Really?*' Renée says.

'Dark horse,' Kennard tells nobody in particular.

Renée looks impressed. She turns from Fielding to Alban. 'And will you be bringing her to the bash at Garbadale?'

'She might give me a lift there, but she won't be staying,' Alban tells Renée. 'She may go off and climb some mountains.'

'Climb mountains?' Renée looks astonished.

'Oh, yes, Garbadale,' Kennard says, as though just remembering they're all supposed to reconvene there in about ten days' time. Which is not impossible.

'She climbs mountains?' Renée says. 'And she's a professor?' She pauses, then laughs that shrill laugh of hers, hand in front of her face. 'She sounds like a man!' She looks at Haydn. 'Haydn. Don't you think? She sounds like a man!'

'I couldn't possibly say, Mother,' Haydn says, and looks at Al with a tiny shake of the head as though apologising for Renée.

'Climbs mountains, eh?' Kennard says. 'Hmm, there's a thing.'

This torture only lasts another hour or so and then they're free to follow Kennard upstairs to the loft and his train set and get some talking and persuading done.

'Alban thinks, as I do, that we should keep the family and the firm together,' Fielding tells Kennard. He glances over at Al, who is still looking out over the train set. The display is at waist level, mounted on a stout base of two-by-fours. It fills most of the loft, with a central spine of forested hills and alpine-looking mountains made from papier mâché dominating the centre. The mountains are riddled with tunnels and the peaks of the higher ones come within a half-metre of the inverted V of the loft's ceiling. 'That's a fair enough thing to say, isn't it, Alban?'

'If it was up to me alone, I wouldn't sell to Spraint Corp,' Alban agrees.

'Dare say you'd rather have a workers' cooperative, wouldn't you, Alban?' Kennard says. 'Hmm?' He's cleaning the underside of one of the locomotives with a small paintbrush.

'Chance would be a fine thing, Kennard,' Al says. He sees a little switch on the edge of the layout. 'What happens if you flick this?' he says, pointing.

Kennard looks over. 'Try it and see.'

Alban flicks the switch. A little cable car starts to whirr its way from the station at the foot of the layout's central mountain and make its way towards the summit, a good couple of metres higher. 'Ah ha,' he says. He folds his arms, inspects the rest of the layout.

Kennard turns another control and a one-carriage funicular train begins to click its way up a cogged track set at forty-five degrees on an only slightly smaller mountain. Meanwhile a couple of other

154

trains – a TEE and a mixed goods – whirr round and round the whole layout, contra-rotating.

Fielding can remember when Kennard was still building all this. He's never seen his father happier or more energised. The layout has essentially stayed the same for the last fifteen years or more, and is still the one place Kennard seems to be truly at home and relaxed. It was important they were here, in this place, to be able to talk to him like this.

'We both think it would be a terrible waste, and a shame, if we sold up to Spraint,' Fielding tells Kennard. 'After everything that Henry built up, and Bert and Win continued and built upon, it would be an act of vandalism to tear it all down.'

'Wouldn't really be tearing it down, would it?' Kennard asks, holding the loco up to the light on its back, almost tenderly. There are strip lights fastened to the underside of the roof trusses all over the loft.

'It would be tearing us away from our heritage, Daddy,' Fielding tells him. 'Spraint will be able to do what they want with the game and you have to assume having paid good money for our name they'll try to make it all work, but it still might not. These things just don't, not always. What is certain is that we'll be separated from the one thing that's made us who we are as a family for the last century and a quarter. I know this matters to you, Daddy. I don't want us all to sleepwalk into something we'll regret later. I just want you to think about it.' Fielding looks at Alban. 'We both do.'

Almost miraculously, Al plays along. 'It is a crunch point,' he says. 'Once it's done, that's it.'

'So we all need to think,' Fielding says. 'It's not just us – it's every-body, Daddy.'

'I have shares, too,' Haydn says. He's here, though sat in a small chair in one corner, reading a book.

'They all count,' Fielding agrees. He looks at Haydn. 'You're still a Don't Know, aren't you, Haydn?'

'No, I'm a Not Telling You.' Haydn looks up briefly and blinks at them. 'Though Spraint have said they want me to stay on in charge of production, if they do take over.' He looks down to his book again. 'Mind you,' he mutters, 'the word they used was "when".'

'We can't just let them roll over us like this, Daddy,' Fielding tells Kennard.

Kennard puts the loco carefully back on the outermost track, then bends and – using a little jeweller's screwdriver – hooks the engine up to its train of carriages. 'Have to put up a fight, eh?' he says.

'I think we must,' Fielding tells him. He waves at the whole layout. 'Otherwise it's just destroying everything we've spent so long building up.'

'Hmm.'

'So,' Fielding says. 'What do you think, Kennard?'

'Hmm?'

'Which way do you think you might vote, Daddy?' Fielding hasn't dared ask his father so directly before, and Kennard has never volunteered any sign at all. This is a man who abstained in the vote on the 25-per-cent sale to Spraint back in '99. Fielding honestly has no idea what he'll say.

'Hmm.' Kennard squints at the top of the layout's highest mountain, where the tiny cable car has just snicked home into the summit station. 'Think about it,' he says. He looks at Fielding, then at Alban. 'You both say No, hmm?'

'That's right, Daddy.'

Al just nods.

'Hmm.'

'In a way, none of this is real.'

Sophie turned in his arms, looked into his eyes. 'What do you mean?'

He waved his free hand around. 'That cliff face, this soil, these rhodies. None of this belongs here.'

She turned on to her front, put her chin in one hand. 'How come?'

'Old Henry, the great, mythical great-grandfather, our glorious founder, he brought all the rocks and the soil and the plants from Scotland, from Garbadale. You been there?'

'Uh-huh. Just once. Rained a lot.'

'Yeah. Anyway, I've looked it up. It was 1903. He had thousands of tons of rock quarried out of a mountain near the big house there and shipped to Bristol, then smaller boats brought it along the coast to a special pier they had built down by the river, then traction engines hauled it all up to here. That's when the ford in the river at the bottom of the garden dates from.'

'The rock was brought from Scotland?' She was playing with a long lock of her red hair, shining in a stray beam of sunlight finding its way through the enveloping canopy of broad, dark leaves. She wound the hair round her index finger, let it unwind again. 'Why?'

Alban shrugged. 'Because he could. There's rock like this every-where; loads on Exmoor. He just wanted this stuff from Garbadale called Durness limestone, wanted it here. Had it made into that little cliff, right there.'

She turned and looked at the low cliff of great, slabby rocks which was visible beyond the western limit of the giant rhododendron bush they were lying inside. A breeze disturbed the ragged umbrella of leaves around them.

They had been here about ten minutes, kissing and caressing each other, though not yet to any sort of climax. They did that some-times – just pulled away a little, took time off to talk, get their breath back, before they started again and, usually, brought each other to orgasm with their fingers. She had taken him in her mouth once, in a bedroom at a friend's party in Minehead a few days earlier, but he'd thrust too eagerly, making her gag, and she hadn't wanted to repeat the experience.

This would be their last week together; the summer holiday was near its end and they'd both be heading off to school soon, him back in London.

The beam of sunlight striking her hair disappeared as clouds covered the sun, and the broad tent of cover under the spreading branches became a little darker.

They talked a lot, too, about the mess the world was in, about music they loved and hated, about how they'd organise things with their parents so they could see each other again soon and, frequently, about TV programmes and films, about war and famine, about what they expected to do with their lives – careers, ambitions – and about whether they wanted children. Sometimes they both assumed they'd be together for the rest of their lives, and get married, or not, and have lots of children, or at least two. Other times they talked in a way that tacitly acknowledged they would never be more than cousins who'd had an adolescent sort of affair, and would meet up at family events in the future – weddings, funerals, big birthdays – probably each with their own partners and children, sharing a conspiratorial look and a smile across a crowded room and maybe having just one dance together, holding each other, discreetly remembering.

They didn't know. They could not be sure, not even of themselves, and playing it out by talking about it was the only way they had to deal with the uncertainties.

'He brought the soil from Garbadale, too, same way,' Alban told her. She was sitting up now, peering through the green gloom at the convincing-looking cliff. They both wore jeans; his T-shirt was the best they could do for a blanket. She still wore her blouse, though he'd undone the buttons and it was hanging open at the front. He knelt behind her, putting his hands to her breasts and cupping them, then nuzzling his nose through the dark, fragrant mass of her hair and kissing the nape of her neck. She pressed back against him.

'Why bring the soil?' she asked. He bit her neck very gently and she shuddered.

'That made a bit more sense; lots of peat in it – very acidic. Let them grow different types of plants.' He ran his open mouth down to her shoulder, tips of his teeth leaving faint red marks on her skin. He pulled back to get some of her hair out of his mouth. 'Plenty of peat on Exmoor, too, though. Must have—'

'Do that again,' she said.

He did that again.

After a while she rose back up against him and then turned so that they were kneeling face-to-face, and kissed him very deeply for a long time, before pulling away and saying, 'Listen; at Jill's party the other night?'

'Uh-huh?' he said.

'I bought some condoms from her.'

His heart leapt. He stared at her. 'You did?' he said, uncertain. Mouth dry.

She nodded. Her eyes looked very wide and she was still breathing hard. She quickly wiped some hair from her mouth then held his face in both her hands.

'So,' he said, then had to stop to swallow. 'Does that mean you want to?'

She nodded again. 'Suppose it must.' Her gaze searched his eyes. 'You?'

'Oh, fuck,' he said, letting himself go partly limp, as though he was about to faint or something. 'Sorry. Yes. Oh, yes. Come on, you know.'

'I was saving them for our last day,' she explained, talking quickly, urgently, 'when your parents are here, but that's mad; there'll be more people around and anyway it's probably when my period starts.'

'Oh,' he said. 'Right.'

'Only one problem.'

'What?'

'I left them in the house.' She twisted one corner of her mouth, raised both eyebrows. 'Eek.'

He reached for his T-shirt. 'Where are they?'

She put her hand on his. 'Too long to explain. I'll go.'

He helped her do up the buttons on her blouse.

'You sure about this?' he asked her.

'Positive.'

'You're serious?'

'Yup.'

She kissed him quickly, stood. She looked up and around in the half-light, hair swinging to and fro. 'Raining,' she said.

He listened, too. He could hear a pattering noise. 'Oh, yeah.'

'Back soon.' She pushed out of the bush. He heard her running on the brick path.

He lay back, chest heaving. He looked up at the pattern of light and shade produced by the glimpses of grey sky and the dark under-side of the broad leaves. It was finally going to happen. He sat up. Was it? What if she changed her mind? What if somebody at the house told her to do something she couldn't get out of or made her go somewhere, or if someone had found the condoms wher-ever she'd stashed them, or what if it was all just a joke, and she was off to lie in a bath, or sit on a couch in the sunroom, eating chocolates, reading magazines and giggling at how she'd left him?

He got to his feet and paced, ducking his head beneath the great bare looped branches of the bush, stepping over an exposed root. No, she wasn't like that. Some of her friends played practical jokes on each other and teased each other all the time, but one of the things he thought was great about her was she didn't take part in any of that. She might laugh with the others, but she didn't like being cruel. So, she'd be back. She'd be true to her word. Maybe he should have a wank first; when they did it properly he'd prob-ably come really quickly and that would be frustrating for her, wouldn't it? Maybe he'd come as he – or she – put the condom on. That would be embarrassing. And a waste.

He paced back, almost hitting his head on a branch. A few drops of rain got through the canopy of leaves and hit him on the face. It was quite dark outside now.

He glanced at his watch. Maybe she wasn't coming back. How long had she been gone? He ought to have looked at his watch when she'd left, but he hadn't thought. Oh, but it might be going to happen, they might be going to do it!

The rain came on harder.

She wasn't coming. She had never meant to come back. He was fooling himself. She was fooling him. He was a fool.

He sighed and looked up, shaking his head. He listened to the rain, sounding quite loud now, all around. The temperature had dropped a little.

Out of the sound of the rain there came the slap-slapping sound of trainers on a wet brick path. He held his breath. He heard leaves rustle nearby, but she didn't appear.

He was about to stick his head out of the bush, but then saw a shadow appear at the place he'd been going to push the branches aside, and she was there, wet through, hair plastered to her forehead, grinning. 'Wrong bloody rhodie bush!' she said. She was breathing hard. The rain-wet blouse stuck to her breasts.

He stepped forward and took her in his arms.

He did come too quickly. She caught her breath when he first pushed into her, though she still said it hadn't hurt. They weren't even sure the condom was on right because it had been reluctant to unroll, but it seemed to work. No blood, which they both thought was good. He got to see her vagina for the first time, even though everything had become very dark under the canopy of leaves. He kind of wished for a torch. She thought it was ugly but he thought it was the single most beautiful thing he had ever seen in his entire life.

They waited, her stroking his back with her hands, listening to the rain, feeling the odd droplet hit their naked bodies. Twigs and old leaves and bits of soil, all dampened by the raindrops starting to patter through the canopy, began to stick to them. They were both beginning to feel cold. Then they did it again, using a fresh condom.

He wanted to tell her that he loved her, but it was such a corny thing to say, and this was somehow such a corny time to say it, he didn't. It took a bit longer this time. She came a few seconds after he did and this made him want to cry.

They lay pressed together, holding each other in the gloom, listening to the rain.

Two days later his mum and dad appeared for the weekend, to take him back to Richmond. They brought Grandma Win with them, though mercifully they'd left the deeply annoying Cory behind with friends.

'Alban's a prefect at school, aren't you, darling?' Leah said, leaning to take a mouthful of profiteroles.

'Leah, please,' Alban said. He could feel his ears going red. He took a drink of lemonade. His father laughed silently, sipped his coffee.

'At her school,' Aunt Clara said, 'Sophie's a monitor.'

'Really?' Grandma Win asked. 'Isn't that a kind of lizard?'

Sophie's eyes widened as she added some sugar to her coffee, but she didn't say anything.

Uncle James looked confused.

Grandma Win was a tall, thin, sharp-looking lady who had what Alban's dad called Thatcherite hair. She was fifty-nine, which was pretty ancient, obviously. She'd be sixty in a couple of months. She carried herself in a very upright, angular sort of way and always looked a little stiff. She wore large glasses with a graded shade element, even indoors, and often wore mauve dresses and tweed twin sets. Her voice was usually soft but a little throaty, which she excused on the grounds that she still liked the occasional cigarette. It was a very English voice, which always surprised Alban because she'd lived mostly at Garbadale for twenty years now with Grandad Bert, who was much older even than Grandma Win and who'd broken his hip last year and tended to stay there at Garbadale all the time.

'So, Alban,' Grandma Win said, 'do you play *Empire!* on the computer? What do you think of it?'

Alban looked up. He glanced at his dad, then at Grandma Win. 'Ah, no, Gran. Not really.'

'Oh dear,' she said, frowning. She looked at Andy. 'Andrew, don't you let the boy play?'

'We've decided Alban can use my home word processor for writing essays and so on. In the coming academic year.' He glanced at Leah. 'We'd really rather he didn't play computer games.'

Leah nodded.

'Oh, I see,' Gran said. 'Well, I think we have to hope that not all parents feel the same way about their precious little darlings, or we'll be bankrupt.' She emitted a brittle smile and leaned forward towards Alban. 'I bet you *want* to play games like *Empire!*, though, don't you, Alban?'

Alban glanced at his dad, who was watching him with a look of wry amusement.

'They look interesting,' Alban said, hoping this would keep everybody happy. He went to take more lemonade but he'd drained the glass. He pretended to drink anyway, hoping nobody would notice. A last dribble. God, he'd thought that – now that he'd Done It – this sort of embarrassment would stop. He'd felt like he'd become a man two days ago, with Sophie, but nobody else seemed to have noticed any difference; they still treated him like a child. Mind you, he supposed it was for the best nobody had noticed.

In fact, he'd already played the arcade version of *Empire!*, and one of his friends whose dad published a computer magazine had a Nintendo Entertainment System and a Sega Master System, and there was another version on the NES which he'd also tried. The arcade version didn't really work because you couldn't make a territory-capturing game fast enough to keep people coming back with more coins, though the games designers had done their best. The NES version was better and more suited to the character of the game but looked clunky, and the board game was still more satisfying. He hadn't wanted to mention any of this in case Andy and Leah disapproved. Looking at Grandma Win, though, he had the oddest impression that she could tell all this. He'd never sat at the same table as her before, never really talked to her properly. He was starting to think she was quite a scary old woman.

'I don't see what's wrong with rounders,' Uncle James said suddenly. 'Or rugby. Children watch too much telly as it is.'

'Oh, James, please,' Sophie said, over her coffee cup. She shared a brief look with Alban as her father did his intensely funny turning round in his seat thing, pretending to look for this person called 'James' who must just have entered the room.

Sophie and Alban had met up twice more and yesterday they had used up their last two condoms in the tumbledown remains of an old cottage at the southern boundary of the estate. He'd found an old tarpaulin and cleaned it up and brought it to spread over the grass and nettles in the centre of the ruined building, and they'd lain together there. They'd laughed and giggled afterwards, tickling each other and trying to keep quiet, just in case. These dinners, afterwards, have almost become fun. They exchange sly looks, catch each other's eye and have to suppress smiles, and – once, last night, the way they were seated – he felt her stroke his leg with her foot. Meanwhile their parents chatter and natter and clatter their cutlery and talk about all sorts of rubbish, perfectly oblivious.

This was the third little shared moment they've had, this meal.

Alban let the sweet, conspiratorial smile linger just a moment. Then Sophie looked away. He asked for a coffee and, as he accepted it, glanced at Grandma Win, to see a hard, narrow-eyed look disappear, like something swallowed in by her whole face, to be replaced instantly by a thin, glasses-glittering smile.

The next morning, the day before they're to leave, he goes to Barnstaple with Andy and Leah and he just walks into a chemist's and – using money that usually he'd have spent on sweets or a single – buys a packet of condoms. His face is scarlet and he can't look at the assistant, who is young and pretty, but it doesn't matter; it's done. He's done it. He feels intensely proud. When he gets out of

164

the chemist's he wants to jump in the air and shake his arms and *scream*! Instead he just makes sure the packet is firmly lodged in a secure jeans pocket and walks with a grin and a swagger back to where they've all arranged to meet.

'Really? Alban, you're marvellous!' she yells, taking hold of his shoulders then throwing herself against him, hugging him and kissing him.

They're down in the long grass on the far side of the old orchard wall, in the early part of dusk. He's supposed to be doing some final tidying-up before the so-called 'proper' gardeners start again next week. She's meant to be taking a walk down to the river in the last of the light.

She'd thought it would be a sorrowful, frustrating goodbye, but now they have condoms, and, thankfully, her period still hasn't started. (He'd completely forgotten about this, he realises as they start undressing each other – if he'd remembered he probably wouldn't have thought it worth the embarrassment of buying the condoms in the first place.)

'This is getting better every time,' he whispers into her ear, a little after entering her. They're bucking and jerking away at each other, not always in sync, but the actual feeling of being joined like this is becoming something he's learning to enjoy properly. The first time or two it was all so quick and complicated. There seemed to be so much going on there was no time to appreciate it.

'I love you inside me,' she whispers back.

Then he feels her stiffen. 'Ssh!'

'What?' he says. Maybe too loudly.

She slaps a hand over his mouth, forces him to lie still on top of her. He wonders if this is some new sex thing she'd read about – he's read about a lot of stuff in Plink's older brother's porn mags, and even in Leah's *Cosmopolitan* – but then he realises she's heard something. He starts to bring his head further up to look her in the eye, but she pulls it down again.

165

He turns his head a little, smells crushed grass, honeysuckle, hints of magnolia and pine.

Now he can hear something. Steps on brick, then the noise of one or two people walking through long grass. Oh fuck, he thinks. Oh fuck. He hears a murmur, then somebody whispering, 'Over there.'

Sophie hugs him very tight, keeping him as low as possible, as still as possible. She squeezes him from the inside and he feels fear start to belittle him, his erection – so fierce and hard a couple of minutes ago it was painful – beginning to go.

The noise of grass being pushed aside shifts, seems to get louder, then starts to fade, then comes back. It stops. He can't see. He has no idea if this person, these people, are just a metre away or ten.

A woman's voice whispers, 'There.' There's a pause. The same voice – it's Grandma Win, he can tell now – whispers impatiently, 'Now!'

Blinding light.

'You fucking little—!'

'Daddy, no! Daddy, it's—!'

Alban rolls over, out of and off Sophie, covering his eyes with one hand as a powerful torch beam flicks from his face to Sophie's, exposing her long white body as she tries to cover herself. He's feeling for his cock and the condom and at the same time he's trying to curl up to cover himself and struggling to kneel.

'Oh, Christ!' Uncle James shouts. Alban's punched hard on the shoulder and falls back in the grass, still trying to get the condom off and get back up again. 'You filthy little fucker!' His jeans are around his knees and this is making everything impossible.

'Get up! Get up! Come on, get up!'

'Daddy—!'

He's glimpsed Uncle James and Grandma Win. James is carrying the torch. He doesn't know if there's anybody else there. 'Get *up*!' he hears Uncle James say. He's turned away, pulling his jeans up, condom still on.

'James, let me,' he hears Grandma Win say. 'Here.'

Alban zips up and turns round into the glare of the torch. Something whacks into his head and the next thing he knows it's half dark again and he's lying in the grass.

'No, Daddy! No!'

'James!' (Grandma Win, loudly.) '*Never* strike a child on the head.'

'The head? I'll cut his fucking balls off!'

'Daddy, *please*! Oh *please*!'

Wow, that had hurt. Sore cheek. Distinct ringing in head. He really ought to get up. Oh fuck, oh fuck, oh fuck. Up; get up.

'Don't be ridiculous, Alban! Get up! Help him up, James.'

Sophie, crying.

Oh, now he knew what the worst and saddest sound in all the world was.

'Certainly bloody not. You're coming with me, young lady. Thank you, Win. Thank you. Right.'

The torch light wobbled off. The sound of Sophie's sobbing slowly faded.

The sky was the colour of a dark, ripe peach.

He struggled to his feet. Grandma Win stood in front of him in the long grass. Her face looked set and hard. 'You young idiot,' she said.

'It's not illegal!' he said. It was just the first thing that came out. He sounded like a child, even to himself.

'Yes it is. You're both under-age. Get dressed.'

He completed getting dressed. He felt tears welling up in his eyes and tried to force them back.

Grandma Win saw him back to the house.

He wasn't allowed to enter. Uncle James wouldn't have him in the house.

He sat on the front steps, then in Andy's car. The hour or so that followed was a nightmare he couldn't wake from. Andy was quietly furious. Leah – pale, shocked – kept wanting to put an arm round him, but he shrank from her. Aunt Clara was in bed, howling, audible from all over the house in the pauses when James stopped shouting.

Sophie: gone, locked away. Assailed, ears battered, by this awful, unending, screaming shouting.

Eventually, Andy drove them to the Lamb in Lynton, taking the one family room which was all that was left. Alban was awake most of the night, listening to his dad quietly snoring and his mum quietly crying.

He felt himself oscillating wildly from anger, from the absolutely certain feeling that it *still* wasn't illegal and what they'd been doing had been beautiful and *right* and they were all over-reacting absurdly . . . to feeling the utmost, utter shame. It was at these points that he wept, burying his face in his pillow to stifle the noise, feeling he'd destroyed his own life and Sophie's and everybody else's, too.

They left for Richmond in the morning.

5

Decking. They've covered half the fucking garden in decking. Alban has developed a certain low-level hatred of decking. It's become all the rage, it's the flavour of the last few years, it's what you do to bring the outside in or the inside out or create a roofless room or however the hell you want to express it, but he just finds it annoying. He shouldn't hate it the way he does because it has its place; it effectively extends the house or flat it's attached to, it's a lot easier to build decking up to the same level as an internal floor than it is having to cart in tons of earth and hardcore to support a stone or brick patio, plus it fits in with people's modern, money-rich, time-poor lifestyle blah blah blah, reducing the amount of actual garden that you have to deal with – all that messy soil and ground and such – and letting you get away with a few artfully placed plant pots . . . but he still hates the fucking stuff. He hates it because everybody's doing it, thoughtlessly. He hates it because it's become the default solution, and he distrusts default solutions. He takes a certain guilty malicious glee in looking forward to when, across the country, it gradually all starts to rot. Shrieks and spilled G&Ts as legs plunge through sudden holes.

'What do you think?' Leah asks, holding him by one arm, hugging him side-on as they look out over the grey, split-level expanse of wood. 'We had to take out a few bushes and flowers and a couple of small trees, but it's made a huge difference. Do you like it? Cory liked it,' she said. 'I think.' His sister was an industrial designer in LA, married with two children. 'What do you think?'

'Looks great,' he says. He smiles and turns to Leah. She is mid-fifties now, hair still curly and blonde though much shorter and less full than it used to be. She's filled out a little, though she still looks good for her age. She wears a pleated skirt and a pale blouse under a light jersey. She plays a lot of tennis and has taken up golf. Alban wonders if she's had a little work done about her eyes; they'd looked droopier, older, the last time he'd seen her, over a year ago.

'You're happy with it?' he asks her.

'Oh, yes! We're out here all the time now. I mean, not in the winter, obviously. Though the patio heaters make a big difference, too.'

They have three big gas-bottle patio heaters; together with the two teak loungers, table and six chairs and double swing-seat with canopy and the barbecue, there isn't much room left for plant pots. In pride of place, though, at the head of the steps down to the next level, they have two of those carefully sculpted, perfectly round lollipop trees in a couple of giant, expensive-looking terracotta pots.

'We're thinking of getting one of those free-standing canvas canopy things,' Leah adds. 'For when the sun's too strong.'

'Wasn't there a water feature here a couple of years ago?' Alban asks. 'One of those marine-ply-and-mirrors things?'

'Oh, that!' Leah squeezes his arm. 'Nothing but trouble.' She squeezes his arm again. 'Oh, Alban, it's so good to see you again!'

'Yeah,' he says, putting an arm round her waist.

'Mind your backs! Here we go.' Andy arrives at the patio doors behind them with a tray of drinks.

Andy is much as ever, though he's thickened around the middle and about the lower face. He's wearing dark chinos and a worn denim shirt. His hair is still only three-quarters white. He's grown a sort of moustache plus goatee thing – same mixture of colours as his hair – which Alban isn't sure about. He's taken to wearing glasses with thick legs and fashionably angular black frames. He grins at Alban, who grins back – it is good to see Andy and Leah. He supposes he has to accept he has spent too much time away from them.

They walk out on to the decking.

It was like the old days. Andy and he went into town to see a film at the NFT. They took an early train, walked across the river, ate Italian near Covent Garden, walked back across the river and caught *Ran*, the latest in a Kurosawa retrospective and which, coincidentally, neither had seen. Leah said she thought she probably had seen it, but they both suspected it was more likely she was just giving them time together.

'Fielding bring you out of hiding, did he?' Andy asked as they walked along the South Bank, curving back towards Waterloo past the concert halls, the river dark to their right, lights glittering beyond, Big Ben and the London Eye rising ahead.

'Oh, he tracked me down.'

'Did you need much tracking down?'

'Well, it wasn't deliberate, but I'd covered my tracks fairly well.' He glanced at Andy. 'You got my cards all right, yeah?' He'd always sent them Christmas cards and birthday cards.

'We got them.'

'Well, sorry to have been so . . . out of touch.' He puts his arm briefly round Andy's shoulder, just a little awkwardly. 'It's good to see you again.'

Andy smiled at him, nodded. 'Good. You too.'

Alban wasn't sure what to say. He and Andy had always had a fairly calm, measured kind of relationship – Andy was a fairly calm, measured kind of guy, so there wasn't much choice. The worst that had ever passed between them had probably been due to that awful last evening at Lydcombe, and even then it had been more the tight-lipped, silently disappointed you've-let-us-all-down kind of very British reaction. The evening they got back to Richmond after more or less being thrown out of Lydcombe, Andy had delivered a short sermon about responsibility, mutual respect, sexual health, the obligations one had as a guest to one's hosts, and legality, even if the law might sometimes seem like an ass. As a punishment, Alban would work every Saturday for the rest of the year at the charity shop Leah helped out in, and donate the money to Oxfam. Dismissed.

Alban remembered thinking at the time, even as he felt grateful for being treated like an adult rather than a child, that he'd almost have preferred a shrieking spit-flecked bollocking.

That wasn't the worst of what happened because of James and Win finding Sophie and him like that, not by a long, long way, but it was the worst that happened between Andy and him.

'You going to the—?' Alban began, then smacked himself on the forehead. 'You're Company Secretary. I guess you kind of have to be at Garbadale for the EGM. Sorry.'

'Yes,' Andy said with a small smile. 'Don't think Leah's looking forward to it, but she feels she has to be there for Gran's eightieth.'

'How about you?'

'Looking forward to it? Not especially.'

'No, me neither.'

'But you're going.'

'Yes, I'm going.'

Andy looked at him. 'Why?'

Andy had always had the disconcerting ability to ask the most obvious questions that turned out – unless you resorted to an insultingly trivial answer like 'Why not?' – to have answers that required an unanticipated degree of complexity if you were to reply truthfully. Sometimes you even had to think.

Alban frowned and rubbed his beard. 'Chance to see everybody.'

'That's a sudden change of heart. You seem to have spent so long avoiding us all. Even Leah and me.'

Alban glanced at Andy, but he wore his usual kindly, slightly quizzical look. His tone of voice had not sounded bitter.

172

'Well, I'm sorry about that,' Alban said. 'Feeling sorry for myself for a long time there. Not the best frame of mind for, well, social-ising.'

Andy thought about this. 'Well, you know Leah and I are always here. We both understand you can't always be running back to us whenever there's a problem, but . . . As long as you know we're here when you need us.'

'Thanks, Dad.'

'Hey, you're welcome,' Andy said, nudging him and grinning. 'Garbadale,' he said. They walked a few more steps. 'I suppose Sophie'll be there.'

'Yeah, but I'm not—' Alban began, then stopped himself. 'I'm not investing any hope in that.' They looked at each other. 'Honestly.'

Andy waited a few moments before saying, 'Okay.'

'But I suppose I should be there for the EGM and the old girl's party.'

'I'm sure we'll all have lots of fun,' Andy said, deadpan. He glanced at Alban. 'You still have the minimum shares. Which way will you vote?'

Alban shrugged. 'Against. Just on principle. Probably futile, but, hey. And—'

'What principle?'

Alban thought. 'Resisting American cultural imperialism?' They both grinned at that. 'And you?'

'I was thinking of selling,' Andy told him. 'And that would be my advice to anybody who asked for my opinion.'

'The keeping-the-family-together argument doesn't impress?'

'Alban, if it takes a set of shareholdings to keep a family together . . .' Andy shrugged. 'Anyway, who would we be keeping it together for? Your generation?'

'Well, there's Fielding . . .'

'He does seem surprisingly concerned,' Andy said. 'I always got the impression he was on the brink of jumping ship, finding a sexier line of business or starting up on his own. But I know he and Nina have been talking about children, so maybe he wants stability, something to pass on.'

'Oh?' Alban felt bad he'd hardly asked anything about Fielding's partner. Oh well. 'Aunt Kathleen?' he suggested.

'She's my generation, not yours.'

'Oh, yeah. Of course. Haydn?' Alban said.

Andy shook his head. 'Guaranteed a job with Spraint.' Andy looked at Alban. 'He is our one star, you know. I wouldn't say he's been wasted on us, but he could easily handle a lot more. Same job, but with a wider remit, more variables, bigger numbers.' They walked on a few more steps. 'But that's it, really. The rest, they're all away doing other stuff.'

'There's a whole new crop of kids, though,' Alban said.

'Maybe, but it's your generation has to think about them, Alban, not my lot. Fair's fair.'

'Just Fielding and Haydn, then.'

'And Sophie,' Andy said reasonably. He glanced at Alban. 'You wouldn't want to forget her.'

'Oh yes, and Sophie,' Alban agreed, oddly embarrassed. He grinned ruefully. 'And, of course, not me.' He thought he might as well be the one to acknowledge this.

Andy didn't say anything for a while. 'Well, you can't convincingly ask people to keep the firm and the family together when you turned your back on both, Alban.'

Alban snorted. 'Yes, well, I'm back. For now, anyway.'

Andy looked at his watch. 'We'd better walk on if we're going to make that train.'

They turned away from the river.

The worst of it – the worst of it initially, anyway – was not knowing how long it would be before he would see Sophie again. He felt at once bloated and empty, filled with that same mixture of anger and shame while at the same time consumed with a restlessness, an unresolved impatience, because he knew that nothing would really be settled or decided until he'd seen her again, talked to her. Even just talking over the phone would be something; it wouldn't be perfect, it wouldn't be enough, but it would be a start. They just needed to talk.

The trouble was he didn't know how to get in touch with her. He wished he'd got the phone number of even just one of her friends; then they could maybe talk when she went round to their house. He tried to think of somewhere public they'd been together that she might go to again, but there was nowhere. She would be back at school now – did that help? He didn't even know which school she went to, or he might have tried calling there.

He rang Lydcombe a few times over the following week, hoping she might answer, but it was always Clara or Uncle James. He never said anything, just put the phone down.

For all that week, he tried to answer the phone whenever it rang in the house at Richmond, running down the hall, dashing downstairs, grabbing the receiver. He was sure Sophie must be as desperate to talk to him as he was to talk to her, but it was never her.

The frustration of it all made him want to cry sometimes, but he didn't cry; he refused to cry. He had cried that first night, lying in the Lamb Inn in Lynton, because of the suddenness of it, the sheer speed and shock of what had happened and maybe because he could hear Leah crying, but he hadn't cried since even though he had come close, many times. Crying, he decided, would be like he was accepting something, as though he was agreeing with the family's hysterical, punitive view of what had happened. Crying would be making himself complicit with them. Crying would be giving in.

He remembered her face, her body, the feel and smell of her; he heard her voice, repeating and repeating the humble mantras of their summer together. 'They've all bloody gone!', 'Fell off me 'oss, didn' I?', 'Blimey, Unc, I didn't enjoy it that much.'

He kept trying Lydcombe.

The third or fourth time he got James. His uncle started yelling

175

as soon as Alban failed to speak after James recited the number, shouting that he was going to call the police. Alban put the phone down quickly, wondering if James had guessed it was him rather than just some crank caller.

He began to think about going back to Somerset and finding her. That might be the best bet. He had saved up nearly thirty pounds in cash; that would easily buy a return by train to Bridgwater, and then he could get a bus or hitch. Maybe he could play truant, or somehow get enough time off school without Andy and Leah knowing, or get one of his friends to lie about something they just had to go to so that he could be excused a Saturday at the charity shop and escape for long enough.

He tried phoning again the next day from a call box. He got an answering machine.

It didn't matter. He could make the journey. The doing of it, the hardship, the danger of discovery or possible failure would be the proof of how much he loved her. She would know then how he felt about her, but then she probably already did, even though they'd never dare use the word itself. But, almost as importantly, *they* would know: her parents, Grandma Win, Leah and Andy – all of them. They would see how serious he was, how serious they were. They might start to understand.

He would do it. He would go.

That evening, over dinner, his dad mentioned – casually, more to Leah than Alban – that Sophie wasn't at Lydcombe any more. She'd gone to school in Madrid and would probably be there until next summer, spending Christmas in Spain.

Alban spent a long time looking at his plate, unable to move or think.

'Are you all right, darling?' Leah said.

He had to ask to be excused.

Sitting on his bed, breathing hard, hands on his knees, staring at the carpet in his room, he came extremely close indeed to crying – he could feel the tickle behind his nose, and the very start of the tears welling up behind his eyes – but still he refused to let the tears come.

No crying, not even now. There would still be a way.

The year went on. His sixteenth birthday came and went. He was allowed a party at the house, but his parents were there the whole time. School was all right. According to a couple of the other boys, he wasn't the only one who'd popped his cherry over the summer, though he'd listened to the accompanying stories and hadn't found the details convincing. He'd refused to speak about his own experiences. He'd developed a way of just smiling when people asked him about it. Half the boys thought he was trying to bluff, the others thought he must indeed have Done It.

Colder weather came in. He lay awake one night, still trying to think up ways of getting to Sophie, about getting to Spain himself or just finding out how to phone her.

An alarm sounded in the street outside. Car or house, he couldn't tell. He should be trying to get to sleep; it was a busy day at school tomorrow. He thought ahead, reviewing all the stuff he had to do, making up a mental list of the books and pieces of kit he'd need for the whole, complicated school day and checking each item off in his head, knowing they were all already packed or easily to hand and obvious.

The alarm was really annoying, going on and on, same two stupid high-pitched tones warbling away, minute after minute after minute.

He had to get to her. But what could he do? He couldn't go there. It was too far, too foreign; he didn't even have his own passport yet. Had they sent her away to Spain because of what had happened? That was crazy, that was over-reacting, wasn't it? Phoning was the only possibility, or maybe writing her a letter if he could get the address. He'd tried rifling through Leah and Andy's desks (guiltily but determined), searching for a number or address that might help. He'd hoped they might have the address of Sophie's biological mother in Spain, but there was nothing.

The alarm wailed on, relentless, inconsolable.

Would there be anybody else in the family who might know anything? Maybe somebody his own age – Sophie's age – who might understand?

Cousin Haydn? He was just a year younger than him and Sophie. But he was a shy little fat kid – Alban found it hard to believe he'd know anything.

The alarm, or a nightmare, had woken Cory; he could hear her wailing from her room, then the distant sound of Leah getting up to go through to her.

Uncle Graeme and Aunt Lauren's children? Cousin Fabiole? Cousin Lori? Fab was eighteen, so maybe too old to understand. Lori: she was the same age as him, wasn't she?

He didn't think they'd been especially close to Sophie either, but he was prepared to try anything.

The alarm went on and on and on and on and on and on . . .

He turned over in his bed, then turned back again. He'd already wanked, hiding the tissue under his bed. Maybe he should have another go. It would help pass the time; might even let him get to sleep. This fucking alarm was really doing his head in. He tried putting his head under the pillow and cramming the pillow down over his ear, and that sort of helped, but he could still hear the alarm.

'Fuck it,' he muttered. He pushed the pillow away and threw the duvet off, crossed to the window and opened it to the first notch, letting cold air spill in and the alarm sound still louder. Something about attack being the best form of defence. Confront the damned thing, show it you weren't afraid of it. This was nonsense, obviously, but he felt it was important somehow.

He went back to bed and went on thinking about how he might get to Sophie, or get to write to her or phone her; somehow speak to her.

It went round and round in his head while the alarm went on and on outside. It would be all right. It was possible. It looked impossible but it wasn't, it couldn't be. Sophie was probably trying just as hard wherever she was to think of ways of getting to him. He was here and she was in Spain or wherever, but they were still together. They would always be together.

It was getting cold in the room; he could feel it on his face. He got up and closed the window. The alarm continued to sound, but it was as though it had been going on so long now that his brain was somehow cancelling it out. He remembered something similar from biology or physiology, about how the nose could only smell fresh smells – it then sort of got bored with the smell and stopped smelling it even though it was still there.

It would be all right. Somehow, it would work out. He knew it would. He would think of Sophie and go to sleep thinking about her and so dream about her. He kept trying to do this.

The alarm cut off eventually, leaving something more than sudden silence.

He could still hear it.

The alarm had stopped, the noise was no more, but he could still hear it. Whatever part of his brain had cancelled out the sound was now creating precisely the disturbance it had sought to negate.

He lay there and he listened to the ghost sound, hearing with the utmost clarity the thing that simply was not there any more, and that was when he started to cry.

He buried his head in his pillow so nobody else would hear and wept on into the night in terrible, body-spasming sobs; desolate, heartbroken, in mourning for all that was lost.

He meets VG in Shanghai in ninety-nine, in a big hotel which is just one of several attached to a conference centre and mall complex it is bizarrely difficult to get out of. He's there for a games and toys trade fair. She's there for a conference. He's been vaguely aware for the last few days that there are other groups of people wandering around the place who obviously aren't part of the trade fair and don't quite look like normal business people or tourists either. A sign propped in a lobby spells out in gold letters: *Welcome To The 23rd Desitter Mathematical Conference.* Mathematicians, then. A high proportion of them are people one might charitably call Characters.

He's there with Fielding. His cousin has cut back quite severely on his drug-taking in the two years since the fun and games in Singapore, and so, he supposes, has he. They don't have any with them here, anyway. Fielding has talked about getting some locally, but it's probably just bravado.

Alban's up relatively early one morning after a late meal with some overenthusiastic production people from Pudong and an uneasy night's sleep interrupted by indigestion. Awake at five, he never really got back to sleep, so he's had a very early breakfast. Now his rhythms will be all messed up, as though they weren't a bit fucked just because of the jet lag. He's getting heartily fed up with all this travelling and schmoozing and partying and forced sociability. It suits some people down to the ground – Fielding just loves all this networking stuff, treats it as really important and fulfilling – but he's finding it wearing. He's just not cut out for it. It's early 1999, he's not even thirty, yet he feels old and jaded and fed up with what ought to be a great job. There's been a modest reorganisation within the firm and he's officially now responsible for Product Development, though in practice his brief runs a lot wider than that and he can meddle with impunity and indeed matriarchal blessing in almost any area of the firm he wants to. To the delight and pleasure of his peers and colleagues, obviously.

Grandma Winifred is entirely in charge of the firm now. She still stays at Garbadale most of the time, but she visits the London office four or so times per year and has even been known to come on jaunts like this one.

Alban's breakfast was relatively light and he thinks about taking a walk before the first meeting he has scheduled. Only it was raining when he looked out the window when he first got up; a hazy, low-cloud kind of rain he's come to associate mostly with South-East Asia (which he supposes this isn't, but still). He feels he hasn't really

180

been to Shanghai yet, even though he's here. The night of the day they arrived they had a guided bus tour through what's left of the old city and along the Bund and round a couple of very large building sites and past some spectacularly unironic buildings, including the famous Oriental Pearl TV Tower. 'It looks like a spaceship that's just landed,' Fielding said, impressed. 'Or the biggest Van de Graaff generator in all the world,' Alban suggested, craning his neck to take in the great globular lattice.

He's walking through the lobby and then along a promising-looking corridor, searching for an outside window to check on the weather situation, thinking maybe he'll go back to his room, brush teeth etc. and order a cab, but then he discovers another part of the conference centre and another corridor. There's still no outside perspective on the weather, though he thinks he hears pattering noises coming from a series of what certainly look like – unhelpfully opaque – skylights. Then he sees a noticeboard outside a smallish conference room saying somebody's going to be reading a paper on Game Theory here in – he checks his watch – five minutes. It's a Desitter thing; the Maths Conference. Open session – all welcome.

Game Theory. Maybe he should check this out. Hell's teeth, these guys start early though. The room could hold about a hundred. Less than twenty seats are taken, all near the front. The people look fairly normal. Maybe a bit too lively for eight in the morning.

He goes in, staying near the back in case he needs to leave because he gets bored and/or starts to fall asleep. He's also very slightly worried that they might instantly see that he's an interloper and all point and scream at him or something or anyway turf him out, so staying near the exit seems like a good idea. He sits two seats in from the aisle itself, so as not to look too primed for a hair-trigger scarper, but is prepared to move if somebody blocks his getaway route.

The room fills to about half-capacity and starts to smell of coffee as people bring paper cups of the stuff in with them. A girl – no, a woman . . . No, maybe you would call her a girl – anyway, this female with blonde spiky hair and dressed in what looks like a black business suit but with no tie sits down on the very end seat two rows down. He's confused. She does not look like a mathematician. The black-and-white look is perplexing, too. But for the fact he hasn't seen any Caucasian help around, he'd probably assume she was a waitress. Only she doesn't look like a waitress either. Mind you, her shoes are sensible shoes, like somebody would wear who had to stand a lot. She has a broad, vaguely Slavic face and looks a bit bleary-eyed. As though hearing him think, she pulls out some dark glasses and puts them on with the sort of deliberation he's come to associate with either fragility or morning-after drunkenness.

She has a great face. And for some reason, he really likes the way she sits. Which is a weird thing to pick up on, he tells himself. She puts an arm out along the top of the seat next to her – towards him, though he's pretty certain this is a coincidence, because after all she's on the end of the row and there's no chair in the other direction. Her fingers drum slowly on top of the seat. She crosses one foot up on to her opposite knee, the way women don't. Maybe she's a man! Definite breasts, no discernible Adam's apple . . . Not that these things mean much these days . . . No, he can't believe she's not a woman. Not his type, of course – too lean and angular and blonde and not really curvy enough – but interesting; definitely interesting.

She takes out a bulky-looking mobile. It's more of a PDA; or one of these spiffing new BlackBerrys, perhaps – he can't quite see. She pushes her dark glasses up on to her spiky blonde hair, checks messages briefly, presses a few more buttons then returns the machine to an inside jacket pocket and her glasses to their place over her eyes. He wonders if he should say something to her. He has a sudden micro-fantasy of her falling asleep during the thing on Game Theory and him accidentally-on-purpose knocking her seat at the end and her waking up and there'd be some Bottom-like moment when she falls for the first thing or person or whatever she sees when she wakes up, or she'd realise he'd woken her deliberately and be grateful and offer to buy him a coffee to say thank you or something.

All highly fucking likely.

No, they'll never speak, never meet – she may not even speak English, and aside from French he's barely functional – they'll sit here a metre and a bit away from each other for an hour or so and that will be that. They'll go their separate ways, never knowing whether they might have been friends or lovers or business partners or a casual shag for each other, however rubbish or sublime (he still thinks of Paris, of Kalpana, and knows with a strange certainty that will remain his most sublime one-night encounter). There must be hundreds of people you almost meet, perhaps thousands, and you'll just never know what might have happened. You might have been seconds, a metre, a word away from the true love of your life, and you'd never know.

Well, whatever. That was just the way the world worked and you might as well get on with it. No point worrying. Anyway, he already had a love of his life and much good it had ever done him.

A tall, hulking guy who looks like a lumberjack arrives on the little podium at the end of the room and goes up to the lectern. He takes off his watch, sets it on the lectern, shuffles his papers, takes a look out over the people there to listen to him and starts reading without preamble, save for the words, 'Good morning.' Coincidentally, these are pretty much the last two consecutive words Alban understands. He struggles for a minute, comprehending perhaps one word in fifteen, then gives up. He's still trying to decide how long he can give it before decently leaving when he falls asleep.

He's woken by somebody knocking into his seat. He starts, jerks upright and sees everybody leaving. He looks round and sees that the only person near him is the girl with the spiky hair, now moving smartly away from the end of the row of seats he's sitting on. She doesn't look back.

*   *   *

'You want more water?'

'No, thanks, I'll take it as it is. I can drink it too easily with water.'

'I find it numbs, sometimes.' Andy waved vaguely at his face.

'Kind of the idea, isn't it?' Alban smiled.

Andy gave a small laugh. 'I meant the mouth and tongue, but, yeah, I suppose.'

They sat in Andy's study, surrounded by bookcases, filing cabinets and screens. Andy had poured decent measures of Springbank. Leah had gone to bed.

Alban knew there should be one small framed photo of Irene on a narrow stretch of wall between two bookcases, and had duly found it. He stood looking at it, sipping the whisky.

'Do you think about her often?' Andy asked him. He was sitting on the corner of his desk. He couldn't see the picture, but he knew what Alban was looking at.

'To be honest, no,' Alban said. 'Once or twice a week, maybe.' He looked at Andy. He couldn't read the expression on Andy's face. He felt a frown gather on his own. 'I suppose some people would say that is quite often.'

'Some people,' Andy agreed mildly. 'Maybe.'

Alban took a deep breath. 'It's something we've never really talked about, isn't it?'

'Your mother?'

'Yeah.'

'I thought we had,' Andy said. He shrugged. 'While ago, I suppose, back when you were a kid. Up to adolescence. We talked about her quite a lot. You wanted to know all you could about her. Come on, kiddo, you can't have forgotten.'

Alban had only very vague memories of this. When he thought about it, he realised they were some of the most vague memories he had from that period of his life, precisely as though he'd been trying to bury them all this time.

'Yeah, I suppose,' he said, uneasy. 'But it's been a while.'

'There's only so much that can be said, Alban,' Andy told him.

'Sometimes you just end up hurting yourself and others more, going back over old ground.'

He wasn't sure what to say at first, so he said nothing, just sipped his whisky and looked at the old photo of Irene. She was sitting in the sunlight on a low stone wall somewhere high, a light blue sea behind her, pale islands in the distance. She wore a short blue dress and her fair brown hair was gathered up. Her legs were crossed and she was holding a glass, looking just to the side of the camera, mouth open, smiling or laughing. Happy.

'I was talking to old Beryl the other night, before we left Glasgow,' Alban said.

'Oh yes?'

He told Andy what she'd told him.

Andy listened, stood, drank about half his whisky, stood for a bit longer, then walked round the back of his desk, sitting in the leather wing-back chair. He put the glass down on the desk. He looked at Alban, who pulled up a seat in front of the desk.

Andy seemed to be about to say something, then appeared to catch himself and said, 'It's not a brain tumour, is it? Aunt Beryl, I mean. She's pretty old, after all. She's not going—?'

'No,' Alban said. 'If anything it's like she's gained a few marbles.'

Andy looked thoughtful, nodded. 'Well, it certainly wasn't me,' he said. 'I mean, about not wanting her, not wanting Irene, to keep it.' He looked down at the desk, running a thumbnail along the edge of the inset leather surface. 'I did everything I could to make sure she did keep it, keep you, kiddo.' His smile was small and sad.

'Did she – was she thinking of an abortion?'

Andy did a lot of swallowing, then picked up his glass again. He sighed. 'Are you sure you really want to know about all this stuff, Alban?' He shook his head. 'It's all so old, and it's all so painful. Sometimes it's best to let things scab over, to let things heal up.'

'I'd really like to know, Dad.'

'Okay, okay,' Andy said, drinking. He frowned at his nearly empty glass. 'Yes, I think your mother did – well, I know she did – think

185

about getting an abortion.' He patted the desk. 'It wasn't something I thought you needed to know.' He didn't look at Alban, preferring to study his hand on the desk, but he said, 'Please tell me you understand this, Alban. More than anything else, Leah and I wanted you to feel wanted, to feel loved.' He cleared his throat.

'Well, I always did, so—'

'We even delayed trying for a child of our own—'

'I appreciate all that, Dad.'

'Ah, shit,' Andy said, putting his hand to the bridge of his nose, pressing and wiping. He sniffed.

Alban felt oddly calm and nowhere near crying. 'Honestly, Dad. I don't blame you for not mentioning the abortion thing. I'm glad you didn't. You did the right thing. And – look, my problems with this family have always been with the whole family, not you and Leah. I appreciate everything you've done for me.'

'She's been a good mother to you, Alban,' Andy said, looking away to the side, towards the hidden photo of Irene. 'She's been your real mother, the one who's been there throughout, in all the important ways.'

'I know,' Alban said. 'I know. Leah's been great, she's been lovely; she always has. She's been kind and tolerant and loving and that's more than a lot of kids get from their biological mothers.' He smiled, spread his arms. 'And I'm okay. Seriously. I'm enjoying my life. I had a good career in the firm and then I got fed up with it and I had a highly satisfying job working in the forests and now I'm thinking about what happens next, but I'm happy.'

'This white finger thing—'

'Yeah, well, I was getting a bit bored with the sound of buzz saws by then, too. No biggie.'

'Look, I'm sorry, but do you need any money or—?'

'Dad, I sold my shares. Well, except for that block of a hundred, so I can still vote. Anyway, I didn't give them away. The family trust bought them. And I haven't been spending it all on horses or girls or drugs.'

186

'Oh, well. But this thing with your fingers . . .'

'Nothing serious. If I'd kept on working with a chainsaw, it would gradually have got worse. But I'm not, so I'll be okay. Absolutely not debilitating.'

'Do you think you should have a specialist?'

'Dad, please.' He let the words hang for a bit. 'Don't worry about it. It's nothing. Really.'

Andy nodded. He drained his glass. 'Refill?'

'I'll take a top-up.'

Andy crossed to the drinks trolley near the door and poured the whiskies.

'Do you think you and Irene would have married if I hadn't been on the way?' Alban asked him. Andy paused as he palmed the cork back into the neck of the bottle.

'Maybe not,' he said. He handed Alban back his glass. He sat in his big seat again, studied his whisky. 'I would have. I mean, the reluctance, if there was reluctance, wasn't from me.' He looked at Alban. 'I loved her from the first time I saw her, in a lecture theatre. LSE. Well, you know what I mean; I started to fall for her, I wanted to get to know her, I was convinced she was the one for me and I was the one for her. Instantly. Made a nuisance of myself for a year; chased her, basically.'

'Was she seeing anybody else?'

'No – I think she was too busy with her studies and a bunch of girls she hung out with. Then there was the family, of course.'

Andy looked back to his whisky. 'There was always somebody passing through London, staying at Bert and Win's, usually. And James had a flat in Bloomsbury at the time. He and Blake were doing their sort of hippy playboy thing, running around with a bunch of artists who used to stage these Happening things, and the sort of junior aristo who gets sent down from Oxbridge for something unspeakable. Graeme and Kennard were part of the same set.' He snorted, drank. 'There was a degree of Upper Class Twit of the Year to the whole thing, except with velvet jackets and drugs. She never got that involved with them. Anyway. I finally—' he looked at Alban, laughed. 'Irene was still a virgin when we, when we finally ended up in bed together.' He held up one hand, apologetic. 'Stop me if this is grossing you out; I know most children prefer to think their parents never actually had sex.'

'Somehow I'm coping.'

'But,' Andy sighed heavily and looked vaguely in the direction of the photograph, 'I don't think I kidded myself at the time and I don't believe I ever have kidded myself since that she felt as much for me as I felt for her. I loved her with all my heart. She—' He stopped, shrugged, looked down. 'Well, she liked me. She thought I was fun to be with.' He gave a sort of shy laugh and glanced at Alban. 'Anyway, I made her laugh, and we had fun together, and we were boyfriend and girlfriend, going steady – all that – but she never pretended to love me. At least, not as more than a, more than a friend.' He shrugged again. 'But a good friend.' He drank. 'I hope.' He cleared his throat. 'Anyway, I hope you've realised by now – you were a wanted child. I wanted you. I wanted her. She . . . Oh,' Andy said, and it was a long, slightly drunken 'oh'; 'she accepted me. Accepted you. Just couldn't accept herself, accept living in this world.' He shrugged, drank.

'I'm sorry to have brought this up, Dad.'

'Ah . . .' Andy waved one hand.

'How close was she to her own dad?'

'Bert?' Andy said. 'Oh, they were very close. She was more like a first daughter to both of them. Linda and Lizzie were always different; kind of a unit because they were twins, you know what I mean? Practically had their own language until they were teenagers. Anyway, there was a nanny for them; Irene was closer to Bert and Win.'

'Do you think it was Bert, then?' Alban asked. 'Who didn't want her to have the baby,' he added when Andy looked uncertain. Andy's eyes were shining.

'I don't know,' Andy confessed. 'Bit late to ask him.' He gave a

188

bitter laugh. 'Bit late to ask him about ten years before he died, poor old bugger.'

'Well, he might have loved her but he might have been one of these fathers who can't stand the thought of his little girl having sex, let alone having a baby.' Alban sipped his whisky. 'Did you get on okay with him?'

'Mm-hmm,' Andy said. 'Yeah, we were cool. Nice enough old guy. He was in Egypt and the Far East during the war; hair-raising stories. Not a great business brain, but at least he'd had the sense to marry Win, who was. Is.' He shook his head. 'Eight children, and she's been the real hand on the tiller for nearly sixty bloody years.' He shook his head again. 'Hell of a woman.'

'Do you think Bert thought you were good enough for his little girl?'

Andy looked into the distance and rolled his bottom lip. 'I think so. We got on all right. No arguments or anything. I worshipped his daughter, I got a good degree, I was a good fit for the firm – I mean, okay, for a long time I didn't fit in anywhere; I was helping to manage Garbadale for a bit and then doing a bit of painting for the first few years at Lydcombe, but I took the shilling in the end and I've done my best for the business. Can't think they have any complaints. No, no, I liked him. Decent old guy.'

'What about Irene's brothers? Would any of them have disapproved?'

'Of me and her?'

'And her getting pregnant.'

'If they did they kept quiet about it, which wouldn't have been like them.'

'So you got on okay with them? Blake, James, Kennard, Graeme? Were you mates?'

'No, I was never mates with them. They were like officer class. I was the first person in my family to go to Uni. But I met them a few times and they were okay. They were a bit loud, a bit hooray-ish, but we got on all right.'

Alban smiled. 'You get on all right with everybody, Dad.'

'Yes, I know, and I assume everybody's as easy-going as I am. Terrible failing, I've been told. But anyway, bloody hypocrisy if they had objected,' Andy said. 'They were all shagging around all over the place. Well, Kennard wasn't especially, he was always the quiet one. But the rest . . . James – no, it might have been . . . no, it was James . . . anyway, got at least one girl pregnant. Abortion. Posh girl. Became Lady something, later. Anyway, don't know of any illegitimate little Wopulds running around out there. Enough of the blighters born in wedlock, God knows. Oh, I don't know, I shouldn't be—'

'Was it Mum who delayed you two marrying until just before I was born?'

'Hmm? Yes. Yes, it wasn't parental disapproval or anything. Certainly not me. I wanted to marry her as soon as we knew she was pregnant.' He shook his head. 'I don't know. Maybe we did the wrong thing staying at Garbadale. She wanted to be there, she said. And I came to love it. It felt right, and Bert and Win seemed happy we were there – they were still in Knightsbridge at the time, mostly, but they were coming up quite often – but maybe we should have stayed in London. She might have got better medical treatment. They couldn't really do all that much for postnatal depression, but they might have been able to do more.' He shrugged again, drank. 'She'd been prescribed some antidepressant – Valium or whatever they had at the time – but she wouldn't take it. Chemicals.' He held up his glass, looking at it.

Alban said, 'Beryl told me Irene walked in front of a bus after coming out of a clinic in town. That was how she came to be in hospital, when Beryl heard her say this thing about somebody not wanting her to have the baby. She wondered if that was a first attempt at suicide.'

'Did she?' Andy said, over a deep breath. He drank some more. 'Did she now.'

'It is a thought.'

190

'Thoughts. Don't ya love 'em?' Andy said. He downed his whisky then put the empty glass down on the desk with a smack. 'Oops.'

'She never said anything to you about this?' Alban asked.

'We never talked about it,' Andy told him. 'We kind of drew a line below everything that happened before your birth, when we moved to Garbadale. Maybe not the most sensible thing to do, but it's what we did. No counselling or analysis or post-traumatic whatsit, just good old British stiff upper lip not talking about unpleasant-ness and hoping it'll all go away with time. And that's what we did. I swear. We just didn't talk about it.' He pat-patted the desk again. 'Anyway, look, you'll have to excuse me; I am suddenly very drunk all of a sudden and I had best get to me scratcher. Excuse I.' He got to his feet, waving towards the drinks trolley. 'Help yourself. Sorry about this. Party pooper. Disgraceful.'

Alban stood and put his arm briefly round his dad's shoulder as he passed. They wished each other good night again and Alban sat in the study by himself for a while, finishing his whisky.

He keeps thinking about her. She is so not his type, but, over the course of that long Shanghai day, he can't seem to get her out of his head. He duly does the trade fair stuff on the firm's stand, does the glad-handing and sincere smiling and two-handed business card handing-over thing and the evening drinks thing and the dinner at whatever glitzy restaurant with whoever it is to be bought food by or buy food for thing and at the end of it rather than go for more drinks he claims he needs a breath of fresh air and maybe an early night and leaves Fielding quite happily assuming the *chef du parti* role and getting overexcited about the idea of the internet being everything good and wonderful in the world of the future, and actu-ally manufacturing stuff being boring and something he calls Sunset (to a group of Chinese and Korean manufacturers, who look mysti-fied) while Alban heads off but – rather than go to bed – makes for the part of the hotel and conference complex where the mathe-maticians appear to hang out.

A bit of walking and listening and tracing a finger over floor plans brings him to a busy bar where the people might be mathematicians or not, he can't be sure; they look very normal. Drinks and loud talking and a few people smoking. He sees a group of people bent over a low table, one of them sketching something that reminds him of high-school geometry, and he starts to think he's in the right place. He makes his way to the bar, listening, gets a bottle of Tsingtao and starts wandering slowly through the press of people. It is crowded. Somebody mentions something about a packing problem and he wonders if this is a practical.

No sign. He wanders a few corridors, ends up back at the same bar and asks an affable-looking little guy in jeans and a T-shirt covered in what appears to be the first few hundred digits of Pi if there's another bar where the maths people are hanging out because he's looking for somebody.

'Who are you looking for?' the little guy asks.

'I don't know her name. She's kind of . . . Tall and blonde? Sort of sticky-out hair. Saw her at a thing on Game Theory early this morning. Dark business suit, white shirt. Dark –'

'Sounds like Graef. Lecturer. Glasgow.' He looks away, shakes his head. 'Odd choice. Sure Cambridge offered.' He looks back. 'Could try the cocktail bar. Some of the hard-core tiling people seem to have colonised it.'

He's not sure quite what this means, and thinks the better of asking. 'How do you spell that name?' he asks.

The cocktail bar is quiet and dark, with good views over the river, ten floors further up in the hotel. He sees her sitting talking with another, older woman and four men, three young, one about his father's age. She looks at him as he enters the bar, watching him while still talking to one of the younger men. She's wearing glasses with round, clear lenses.

Alban's escorted to a table, taking one near the group of mathematicians rather than by the window.

He chooses something called a Shanghai Surprise because it sounds vaguely familiar and for all he knows may even be a classic cocktail, then recalls as he's waiting for it to arrive that it's the name of yet another crap Madonna movie. It looks and tastes very orange. He's chosen his table and seat well; he can look straight at Ms Graef without it being too obvious. He looks over at her. *Very* interesting face. Wide, high cheekbones, thin, strong-looking nose widening to broad nostrils. Hmm, nice nostrils.

Then he thinks, Suddenly I'm a *nostril* man? Where did that come from? She wears – inhabits – an expression of seemingly continual ironic surprise. He can just about make out her voice. It sounds pleasantly mellifluous; not especially Scottish.

She will look at me, he thinks. Pretty much everybody has this ability to spot via peripheral vision that a face with big, front-facing eyes is looking steadily at them, even from some distance away. The message may take a while to thunder through, but people usually catch on in due course and look back.

Finally she does look his way. He hoists his cocktail glass and smiles broadly, as though they know each other. She frowns.

A few minutes later she puts her hands on the ends of the arms of her seat and nods round the various people in the group, like she's getting ready to get up.

She is getting up. Probably going to leave and go to her room, he thinks. Too much to hope she'll come over to talk to him.

She walks over to him, face to one side, frown there again. Well, he thinks, whadaya know?

'You're the guy who fell asleep at the Game Theory paper this morning, aren't you?'

He nods. 'Guilty.'

'So, should I know you?'

'Yes,' he says emphatically. 'You should.'

She lowers her head and looks at him over the top of her glasses, still with half a frown on that mildly, amusedly surprised face.

He stands, holds out his hand. 'Pleased to meet you. Alban McGill.'

*   *   *

They have a couple of drinks. He tries to tempt her out to a club or something but she's tired from the night before; this drink and then she really must to bed. They get on really well, though. She's heard of *Empire!* and the family firm. He's – well, he's done maths at school. He makes an executive decision regarding which he'll inform Fielding in the morning and asks her out for dinner tomorrow. He only finds out much later that as he's asking this she's making a similar decision – actually even more inconvenient for her than his is for him – that allows her to say yes.

They eat in a floating seafood place looking upriver from near the Yanpu Bridge. Drink is taken. Things from the depths which look as though they ought not to exist on any world, let alone this one, and which most certainly do not look as though they should be allowed anywhere near a kitchen, let alone the human digestive tract, are duly served for their delectation, and consumed. More drink is taken.

They've talked about SETI, the search for extra-terrestrial intelligence and about SETI@home, a program that will let computers – computers that are switched on but not otherwise being used – look for evidence of alien intelligence within the mass of radio signal data SETI has accumulated and which its own computers are going to take for ever to sift through unassisted. From there they get to talking about consoles and online gaming. She wonders if games machines could be used in the same way, to tackle tasks like extending the value of Pi or looking for big primes.

They're sitting back in their little red-lacquer-and-gold-leaf alcove, him drinking brandy, her drinking whisky, watching the lights of the ships pass up and down the river to one side, and the waiters and diners on the other side.

'What you should do,' she tells him, 'is try to create an AI by hooking up all the games consoles in the world. Use the connectivity.'

'AI@home?'

'Good a name as any.'

'Through 56k modems?' he says scornfully.

'Not now; once most people are connected by fibre optic or wireless.'

'Anyway, these things are maxing out their hot little chips filling the screen with gore and flying bullets; they've no time left for creating HAL.'

'Get people to leave them switched on.'

'Yeah. Best of luck.'

'Or while they're being used. You'd need to have them all doing something else for a while.'

'What?'

'I don't know.'

He thinks. 'You could have them downloading updates off the net or showing some screen stuff off their hard disks or a CD. Though there's the small matter of time synching everything throughout the world.'

'Do-able, surely.' Her little round glasses keep sliding down her nose and she keeps popping them back up with her right index finger. He's wondering how she'd take it if he leaned over just before she did this herself and did it for her. 'Anyway,' she says, 'you wouldn't need every single one.'

'And you really think you could keep something like that secret?'

'Good grief, no, you wouldn't want to keep it secret!' She looks horrified. 'Why would you want to do that? No no! Tell people they're part of a really cool experiment to create an AI. Give them an incentive; make them cooperate.'

He screws up his eyes. 'Why are we doing this again?'

'What?' she says brightly, almost jumping in her seat, 'having dinner?'

He laughs. 'Creating this AI.'

She shrugs. 'Hell of it.'

He laughs again.

More drink is taken.

*   *   *

195

'Gee, dude, you sound, like, conflicted.'

'And that is a terrible American accent.'

She sucks air through one side of her mouth. 'I know. I keep trying but it never gets any better.'

'May be time to give up.'

'Nevertheless, I intend to persevere.'

'Please reconsider.'

'Umm,' she stares upwards. 'No.'

He shakes his head.

'Sorry,' she says. 'We're just stubborn.'

'What, mathematicians?'

'No, Graef family. So we return to the issue of family and feelings towards.'

'Anyway, I'm not conflicted.'

'I think you are. You love your family and you hate them at the same time.'

'No, I just hate them. See? No conflict.'

'You're conflicted about not being able to admit you love them.'

He squints at her. 'You sure you're a mathematician?'

More drink has been taken. They're in the taxi going back to the hotel.

'Anyway, I'm probably not going to sleep with you.'

'Probably? *Probably?*' He's appalled. 'You can't say *probably*! That's not right! That's not in the rules! You're not allowed to say that!' He's on the point of appealing to the taxi driver on the matter.

'All right, definitely. Not tonight.'

'*What?* Why not? I thought we were getting on great!'

'So did I,' she says. 'Therefore we must have.'

'So, what is it? You never do on a first date?'

'Oh, God, no. Done that . . . Poh! Many a time and oft.'

'Oh, thanks.'

'But these were casual encounters,' she tells him. 'Basically physical. Like sport, really.' She looks pleased with this comparison.

'Whereas we're getting on so well, this is maybe too important to risk just jumping into bed at the first opportunity.'

'We've got on too *well* so you're saying no?' He's genuinely aghast. 'That's girl logic! You're a mathematician; you should be immune to that!'

'Ha,' she laughs. 'Proof against it. Hee hee.'

'Look,' he says, deciding to change tack, 'just supposing we do.'

'Supposing?'

'Will you still respect me in the morning?'

– Not what he meant to say at the start of this but he's always wanted to say that line.

She frowns theatrically. '"Still"?'

Back at the hotel, they have the lift to themselves. He leans against one mirrored wall, hands in trouser pockets, back slightly bent. She leans against the opposite wall of mirror, one leg up behind her, arms crossed. She's smiling at him. He's shaking his head at her.

It's her floor first. There's a delicate *ching* and the doors separate. She steps up to him, pecks him on the cheek, then swivels to the doors, looks back. 'So, Mr McGill, coming?'

'What?' he says, leaning further forward. Thoroughly confused now.

The doors start to close but she blocks them with one sensibly shod foot and a straight-armed hand.

'Well?' she says, nodding her head to the side to indicate the corridor.

He pushes away from the mirrored wall. 'Did I pass a test or something?'

She's out the door, walking down the corridor, hips swinging. 'No, just changed my mind.'

He has to jump out through the closing doors.

'You don't say.'

'A girl can change her mind, can't she?'

He doesn't know what to say. He shakes his head and starts loosening his tie. She's started whistling.

He began to write poems, and long letters to Sophie which he kept, dated and sealed, just ready to have an address added to the envelopes, so that he could post them to her when he discovered where she lived. He sent one short letter to her at Lydcombe, marked *Private* and *Personal* and *Please Forward* and printed out rather than handwritten so that it wouldn't obviously be from him, asking her very formally to get in touch with him and wishing her well, even though he knew the letter was almost certain to be intercepted by James and Clara.

The poems were packed with dark images of loss and betrayal and long lyrical passages full of references to plants and growth and beauty. The letters were a kind of diary, telling her how he spent his days and weeks (partly to assure her that he wasn't trying to get off with any other girls), and partly memories of their time together at Lydcombe, as well as intense avowals of love and declarations of his determination to see her again and give their love another chance.

There hadn't been much more fallout. He'd overheard talk about sending him to the school counsellor but that died a death. Andy had no more man-to-man talks with him. Leah was, if anything, even more loving and sympathetic towards him than before. That could be embarrassing when they went out. He usually tried to walk a few steps behind her if they had to go into Richmond together.

He tried talking to his cousin Haydn when Andy and Leah had Kennard and Renée round for a dinner party. They sat playing computer games in Alban's bedroom. Haydn was hopeless. He wasn't allowed to play computer games at home and had promised not to play them if he went to friends' houses. Alban wasn't sure which was more mad; making this promise or actually sticking to it. Also, Haydn's younger brother Fielding was there too and was a complete nuisance. He and Haydn were obviously expected to keep the brat

198

amused even though he was so much younger than they were. Ten; just a kid. Really.

Happily, Alban was able to dig out an old Rubik's cube from the back of a toy drawer and get the boy fascinated by that – Fielding had never seen one before – so Alban and Haydn were able to play in peace. Haydn had no idea what he was doing, but he loved playing. There was a desperate enthusiasm to his game-play, as though he was trying to pack in a year's worth of competition into one evening.

'How come you're playing here when you won't play with your friends?' Alban asked Haydn as the younger boy handed him the warm handset.

'I promised I wouldn't play with friends, not relations,' Haydn explained, blinking behind his glasses.

'Hmm,' Alban said, seeing an opening. 'Talking about relations, do you ever see Uncle James and Aunt Clara at all these days?'

'Not since last year. They're down in Somerset, aren't they?' Haydn was watching Alban's hands as they fiddled absently with the controls, his turn waiting.

'Yeah. What about cousin Sophie?'

'What about her?' Haydn frowned, still looking at the controls, unused in Alban's hands.

'Where is she these days?'

'I don't know. Are you going to take your turn? I could take yours if you like.'

'Done it!' Fielding shouted, and came bouncing off the bed to shove between them, flourishing a cube with one completed side, all red.

Alban sighed.

He tried phoning and writing to other cousins, but nobody seemed to know anything. He kept on writing his poems and his letters to Sophie. He copied out some of the better and more romantic and tragic poems and included them with some of the letters.

He wondered aloud over a Sunday brunch about whether they

might go back to Lydcombe for Christmas, but was reminded that they were all going skiing in Austria. Maybe next Easter? They were staying at home, or going to Garbadale. The summer, then? he suggested.

'Bor-ing!' Cory sang, turning over her empty eggshell to do the trick where you pretended it was an uneaten one and you didn't want it – would you like it, Mummy?

Andy closed his *Observer* and looked at Alban over the newspaper. 'Alban, I'm afraid we can forget about going back to Lydcombe for the foreseeable future. Certainly for as long as James and Clara are there.' He looked like he was going to say more, but then just exchanged a look with Leah and opened his newspaper up again.

'I think Austria's going to be wonderful!' Leah said.

Austria. That was nowhere near where Sophie had gone skiing before – and so might go skiing again – in the French Alps.

Alban started thinking again about making his own way back to north Somerset and trying to find some of Sophie's friends.

The next big family bash was the marriage of cousin Steve – the son of Aunt Linda and Uncle Percy – to his girlfriend Tessa, in York, the following February. He knew they'd been invited and had RSVP'd. He made sure to ask about where they were staying, just to check that everything was still proceeding smoothly. They were staying at a hotel; now he was sixteen, Alban was even getting his own single room.

She would have to be there, wouldn't she? It was a wedding. They were important, symbolic. There hadn't been a big family celebration and get-together for a couple of years; everybody had to be there. She'd be there. She'd probably insist.

He didn't ask beforehand whether Sophie would be at the wedding – that would look suspicious, desperate. He kept thinking of her, though; remembering her smile, her laugh, her voice, the smell of her hair and the feel of his hands on her body, hers on his, the memory of being inside her.

Her words, the sayings – all now incorporated into poems – were with him still. 'They've all bleedin' gone!' 'Fell off me 'oss, didn' I, guv?' 'Blimey, Andy, I didn't enjoy it that much.' He has made a private ritual of whispering, 'Cuz, cuz, sweet cuz,' to himself each night before he goes to sleep, like a little prayer.

'You must think me terribly rude.'

'Must I? Very well.'

'No, really, Win; I'm sorry about—'

'Think nothing of it, dear. I'm sure I don't.'

Oh, shit, he must be standing beside Grandma Win. The voices are coming from behind him, and sound close.

'Well, so long as we—'

'Of course, of course. Now . . .'

'Fine, then. I'll see you in a bit.'

'Not if I see you first,' he hears Grandma Win say quietly. He hadn't recognised the other voice.

They're in the big hotel near York, for the buffet reception, to be followed by a wedding dinner in the evening. He'd got fed up being collared by old lady relations telling him how much he'd grown (he had to wipe his cheek after Great-Aunt Beryl kissed him) and so he'd wandered over to the windows, carrying a glass of lemonade because Andy says he's still not allowed even a glass of wine until the evening. There were some chairs and he'd thought he might sit down, but then he'd have looked lost and lonely and like a wallflower, so instead he went to look at the view over the grounds which is why he's looking out over the damp grass and the leafless trees towards the distant grey river, standing within the high alcove of the floor-length windows, some very tall green velvet curtains at his back. He wasn't trying to hide, he was just leaning against the inset's white-painted wood panels, but the curtains must be sort of hiding him and now he's trapped.

He turns as carefully as he can, realising that, shit, yes, he's almost completely hidden by the curtains. A chair scrapes on the parquet flooring and the curtains nudge out towards him at chair-back height. Oh, fuck, she's sat down.

He could be trapped here for hours.

On the other hand, he might hear some useful stuff. Maybe he'll even hear Grandma Win tell somebody where Sophie is – you never know.

It had been a disappointing wedding so far. Sophie isn't here. James and Clara are. He's seen them both; Uncle James spotted him while they were filing into the church but ignored him, just looked right through him. Aunt Clara saw him as he came into the ball-room for the reception a little ahead of Andy and Leah and Cory. She scowled at him before quickly turning away. He's been wondering whether there is any point in going up to either of them, just to say hello, maybe even to apologise for any misunderstanding, but he doesn't really want to have to and is almost relieved that they seem so forbidding. Probably no point.

Now he was trapped here, and if he moved or sneezed or this fucking chair was pushed much further back, he'd be discovered, and of course Grandma Win would assume he was deliberately spying on her. Oh, bugger. This is his dad's fault; Andy stopped him from taking his new Walkman to church or to this reception. If he'd had the damn thing he could have pretended that he'd been standing here listening to it and so been completely, innocently unaware of what was going on behind him.

A muffled voice, then Grandma Win saying, 'Of course, dear. Would you? Oh, just a little bit of everything. And a refill, if you would. Graeme; come and sit here. Where's Kennard? Fabiole, dear, see if you can find Kennard, would you? Lauren, you're an absolute dear, but would you sit over there? I'd like to talk to Kennard, and you know he does talk so softly, and that is my good side. Thank you; bless you, dear.'

He knows he really ought to wait here and see if he hears anything about Sophie, but he doesn't know that he dares. If he's discovered, they're bound to blame him. If he goes now he might get an odd look or two, but he should be okay because they've all only just sat down. If he waits, then it's going to be obvious even though he was here first

202

that he chose to stay to listen to what people are saying. And sooner or later his mum and dad are going to wonder where he is and start looking for him, maybe calling for him. That'll just be too awkward.

He had worried about being treated like some sort of freak or leper because of what had happened with Sophie, but so far everything seems normal. Well, as normal as these family get-togethers ever got. He'd had nightmares about entering a room like this in front of everybody and the whole place going silent as they all looked at him, appalled – he'd assumed – that he'd had the nerve to turn up after the disgraceful under-age deflowering of his cousin. Then he'd look down and realise they were staring at him because he was completely naked. Then he'd wake up.

In the end, though – back in boring reality – nobody seemed to be reacting any differently towards him apart from James and Clara. Maybe it had all been hushed up, like the government did with awkward stuff. He supposed, being honest with himself, that suited all of them, including him.

Anyway, he needs a pee; too much lemonade.

He sort of nudges his behind backwards, against the top of the chair-back through the curtain.

'Oh! Who's that?' Grandma Win says. 'There's somebody there!' he hears her say to the others.

He steps round the curtain. 'Hi, Grandma.' He feels himself going red.

'Alban!' Grandma Win says cheerfully, putting out her hand to him. She is dressed in dark lilac and wears a wide hat the same colour. There's a group of family ranged around her, all nodding, saying hello. 'And what were you doing there, young man?' Grandma Win says, smiling up at him and taking hold of his hand, 'Trying to escape? Eh? Planning a getaway?'

'No, I was just—'

'And how are you, young man? You're looking very well. What a lovely suit. And are you sticking in at school? I hear *very* good reports, academically.'

'I'm fine,' he says, not sure what to answer, or even whether.

'I'm very glad to hear it, Alban,' Grandma Win says, patting the hand she is holding with her free hand. 'Oh, I can see you're going to break a few hearts before you're done! Isn't he, Lauren?'

'Bound to,' Aunt Lauren agrees, lighting up a cigarette.

'Oh, Lauren, please,' Grandma Win says, with a sorrowful smile.

'I'm sorry,' Aunt Lauren says. 'Forgot.' She stubs the cigarette out in a little round ashtray she keeps in her handbag.

'Now, Alban,' Grandma Win says, 'I hope you'll have a dance with your old gran this evening. Will you? That won't be too terrible for you, will it?'

A dance? Is she mad? 'Of course, Grandma,' he says.

'Good lad. I can see you're going to be a very nice young man. Now, I'd better let you go, or people will talk, don't you think?' She giggles like a girl and lets go of his hand. He smiles awkwardly and turns to go. 'Oh, Alban?' she says.

He turns back. 'Yes, Grandma?'

'Fabiole seems to have disappeared. Would you be a darling and bring me a glass of champagne?'

'Of course, Grandma.'

'You are so sweet! And – please – do call me Win.'

'Okay, Win.'

'You're an absolute darling.'

Even in their heels, he realises, he is taller than most of the female relatives he has to dance with after dinner.

Grandma Win insists on her dance. She has changed, wearing a gauzy red dress now. She smells of lilies. Her eyes are about level with his chin.

'And how are you really, Alban?' she asks him.

'Really, Win?'

'You know what I mean.'

'I am,' he begins. 'I'm fine.'

'So, you're over your little pash, are you?'

It takes him a moment to realise what she's talking about. A little *pash*? He feels like stepping on one of the old cow's feet. He hesitates, not sure what to say. He's worried that he might break down and start crying if he talks about Sophie, especially to Grandma Win.

'Alban, dear,' Win says quietly as they dance, 'you have to realise that I always try to do what's best for the family. I don't do things for myself, or even for Bert. It's all for this family. That's been my role. It might seem old-fashioned nowadays, but it's what I believe in. I know you must blame me for what happened at Lydcombe, but – oh dear, there really is no other way of saying this – it is for your own good. Can you see that? Are you mature enough to understand that?' They look into each other's eyes at that point. She seems small and frail, but he feels like he's dancing with a flick knife wrapped in a lace hanky. He wants to shiver. 'No, you must hate me for that too, I dare say,' she says, looking over his shoulder again. 'But never mind. I know I hated being told that sort of thing. Everybody does. And of course it's even more annoying when it's true and it honestly is for your own good. Sometimes you just have no choice but to trust your elders.' They dance on a little further. He prays for the tune to end. 'So, are you all right, Alban?'

Of course he's not all right. How can he ever be all right without Sophie, without even knowing where she is? 'I'll be fine, Win,' he says.

'And are you over it?' Her voice is quite soft.

'I will be fine, please believe me,' he tells her. He means, I'll be fine when I can get back in touch with Sophie, and even more fine when we're together again, for ever this time. He is not going to say more, he is not going to deny Sophie, deny his love for her, or say anything that is actually a lie.

'Good,' Win says. 'Well, please believe *me*, I do hope that you are and you will be.' She stops dancing and takes her hands from his hand and his shoulder. 'And now you'd best see me back to my seat, I think. If you'd be so kind.'

He remembers to thank her for the dance.

He dances with Tessa the bride. She's nineteen; only three years older than he is. She's petite, curvy and blonde and, frankly, he fancies her. He gets an erection when he dances with her, but keeps it out of the way so that she doesn't notice. She's dancing with everybody, and just glows and smiles and seems to be having a great time.

He has to dance with Leah, too, who is tipsy and giggles a lot. It's just embarrassing.

There are some very pretty girls and at least one stunning brides-maid from Tessa's side of the family he wouldn't mind dancing with. There's supposed to be a disco later, with proper records rather than this rubbish band; he'll wait till then to start asking girls to dance. He's had two glasses of wine – Andy knows about one, Leah about the other – but he's not really affected much at all. He feels a little merry, if that's the right word, but nothing special. He thinks he'll try for another glass at the bar in a minute.

He's sitting at a table, taking a rest – his shoes are new and not all that comfortable, so it's worth saving his feet for the disco later – when Aunt Lauren comes to sit with him, asking him how he is and if he's enjoying himself. Aunt Lauren is about Andy's age; a round, cuddly-looking woman with fuzzy brown hair and – usually – a taste for alarmingly stripy tights. This evening she's more conven-tionally attired in a floaty peachy thing.

'Darling,' she says quietly, briefly touching his arm, 'I did hear something about you and young Sophie.' She smiles tremulously.

She did? Who told her?

He says, 'Oh?'

'It must have been difficult for you, Alban. These things always are when you're very young.'

'D'you mind if I ask how did you find out, Aunt Lauren?'

'Don't worry.' Aunt Lauren winks at him. 'Nobody else knows.' She leans in closer. 'And not everybody knows that I know.' She smells of cigarettes and perfume. 'But I thought you should.'

'Right.'

'Were you very serious, the two of you?'

'Yes,' he tells her. He can't help feeling she's going to slap him in a minute, or burst out laughing, but she seems to be serious so he treats her the same way. 'Yes, we were.'

'Was it terribly romantic? Was it?'

'It was—' He feels embarrassed, looks down. 'It was . . . it was beautiful, Aunt Lauren,' he tells her, looking up at her, feeling terribly vulnerable, already preparing to be stoical and unflinching if she does now laugh at him, or tell him not to be so stupid, it's just puppy love, a silly infatuation.

Instead, she catches her breath, puts one hand to her peach-lipsticked mouth. 'You poor, poor things.' She shakes her head, her eyes shine and he worries that she's about to start crying. 'You loved her,' she says, nodding.

'Yes, of course.' He keeps his voice calm, level.

She gives a trembly smile and reaches out, ruffling his hair. He manages not to flinch. 'Oh! You're so young! You poor things! Our own little Romeo and Juliet! You're just children, but you grow up so fast nowadays.'

'She's in Spain now, I think,' he says, not knowing what else to say.

Aunt Lauren takes her hand out of his hair. That's a relief. 'I know,' she says. 'Madrid. I know.'

She does, does she? He says, 'Do you know whereabouts she is? I'd like to write to her but James and Clara won't forward—'

'Now, Alban, I've had to promise not to tell you where she is, I'm sorry. But she's fine, I know I can tell you that.'

'All I want to do is write to her, Aunt Lauren.'

'I know, dear, I know. But I can't give you her address. Actually, I don't know her address. Not properly. I know where she is, but not its address.' (He makes a mental note of that 'its'.) She looks thoughtful. 'I suppose it wouldn't be difficult to find out. That should be possible. I suppose.' She bites on the nail of her left small finger.

'Could you do that?' he asks.

This could be the way!

207

'Well,' she says, sounding uncertain.

'Could you maybe forward my letters to her?' he asks urgently, turning to her and leaning forward, keeping his voice down. There doesn't seem to be anybody near enough to overhear. Most of them are up dancing. The music is quite loud, drowning out any other conversations and keeping theirs unheard by others. 'That's all I need, just to be able to write to her. Could you? Please? Please, Aunt Lauren.'

Aunt Lauren takes a breath and draws herself upright. 'Yes. I could do that for you, Alban,' she says. She nods. 'I would love to do that for you. Yes, I would.'

'Oh, Aunt—'

'No, wait. You'd have to promise me you wouldn't be trying to get her to do something her parents wouldn't want. I mean like running off together or something equally silly. I couldn't be party to something like that. You'd have to promise me that.'

'All I want is to talk to her, to see her again.'

'Well, that might happen one day, but you have to promise.'

'I promise I won't ask her to run off with me.'

'Well, if you promise, all right.'

'Thank you, Aunt Lauren. This means a lot to me.'

'That's quite all right. Now, you've got our address?'

'Yes.' He had the addresses of pretty much all the family; Andy and Leah were strict about thank-you letters.

'Right then. Just send me what you want me to pass on to her. I can't promise she'll write back, of course. You do understand that?'

'Of course, Aunt Lauren. Thank you. Thank you so much.'

'Oh, you poor, lovely boy,' she said, and held his face in both hands. He could smell the sweet perfume and cigarette smoke again. 'Now, will you have one more dance with me?'

'Aunt, I'd love to,' he told her. He stood, grinning, and offered her his arm.

Serves Two: boil a kettle (about four cups of water should be enough). Then in a medium-sized bowl or other container big enough, make

208

a double helping of instant mash. Me myself personally I'd always use proper Smash, so you'd pour the wee nuggety bit's into the bowl first and then add the water, but obviously substitute types of instant are acceptable (usually this means putting the water in first – read the fucken packet). Add lump's of marge, butter if you have it and use some milk to replace some of the water if desired. You can season the mash before-hand if prefered, salt and pepper before adding the water, so the one mixing with the fork does two jobs. Add Wooster sauce and Tomatoe sauce part way through mixing, again to taste, I like quite a lot.

At this point, if I'm in a proper kitchen rather than out camping, I'll be adding the tin of baked beans cold, though you can have them heated up first in a wee pan. Anyway, add them now. Just your usual tin-size tin. Mix a bit. Now take a standard size tin of corned beef, dice and add to mixture. There are different schools of thought regarding whether to scrape the fat that you usually get round the top and corners of the beef off of it, but I advise it's removing. Take care to mash the chunks of corned beef well into the mix with the fork, breaking apart any specially lumpy bits (also, if you happen to spot any bits of vein or artery or whatever those pale chewy bits are you sometimes get, at this point, hoick them out – better than discovering them wedged between your gnashers later. Add more chutney's, pickle's and such like to personal taste, always taking into account the proclivities of your fellow diner. For a festive touch, great some cheese over the top, (or just add a few slices if like me some basterts swiped your grater.) Microwave (only in a proper kitchen, obviously, unless they've invented camping microwaves I've no heard of!!!). Usually a couple of minutes does it.

Serve. One soup or desert spoon each should be all thats required.

Oh, sorry; name of dish: Slurry. So named by your man Alban, taking the pish as per usual.

Enjoy!

* * *

In the end he took it down the loch, trussed in a brown paper parcel tied with old, scratchy, hairy string. He'd wrapped it round a big boulder and had intended to let it sink in the deepest part of the loch, but then he'd changed his mind. He undid the package, took the boulder out and dropped it over the side of the boat into the black-brown water, watching its unsteady paleness disappear towards the cold depths within a couple of seconds.

The mountains stood tall on both sides of the long inland loch, greening with the new spring. The eastern peaks shone with the sinking sunlight, the western slopes were dark. A few high clouds spun slow across the sky, wisping pink as the sunset came gradually on. Moderating, gusting, the west wind brought a tang of ocean with it. He was about halfway down the loch, out of sight of the jetty at its head and the windows of the top floor of Garbadale House, out of sight of any habitation or road.

After he'd got rid of the boulder he tied the parcel back up again, then used the petrol out of the boat's fuel can to soak it, holding the bundle over the side to try and avoid spilling the petrol and oil mixture inside the boat. The tipped boat rocked to and fro beneath him, waves slapping on the hull. Some of the fuel mixture hit the water, spreading almost instantly, producing shimmering rainbow colours across the part-calmed waves in the lee of the boat.

The fuel was cold where it touched his fingers. He washed one hand then the other in the icy waters of the loch, holding the dripping, stinking parcel through a loop of string on the top. Then he threw the package out, lobbing it a metre or so from the boat. He brought out the container of windproof matches. He lit one and threw. The wind caught it and so it missed, fizzing out in the water just shy of the quarter-submerged package. He tried again, allowing for the wind. The match struck the package and bounced off and at first he thought it hadn't worked, and so was preparing to strike another match, when he saw the flame on the top of the parcel suddenly show blue, then yellow.

The flames thickened and spread, quickly engulfing the package.

The wind was pushing the boat closer to the little island of flame he'd created; he lifted an oar and pushed it further away. A lick of flame was left on the blade of the oar; he stuck it in the water, dousing it. Then he started the outboard, pulling on the starting lanyard a couple of times until the little two-stroke puttered into life. He sat down, put the engine into reverse and steered the boat a few more metres away from the burning package, then let the engine idle, out of gear, while he sat and watched the parcel burn.

It burned well, the paper and string blackening and disappearing, letting the fuel-soaked coat inside unfold itself as its constraining packaging flamed away, like a dark, burning flower. The old waxed coat burned ever better; the boat's engine fuel starting it, the wax permeating its fibres keeping it going until the whole brown-green skin of it was burning bright and fierce, reflecting off the peaky little waves and warming his face.

He waited until there was almost nothing left, just a few ash-coloured pieces of material, some still licked by tiny feeble tongues of flame, then he gunned the boat's engine, swung it round and ran right over what was left of the coat that his mother had worn when she killed herself. He didn't know what ghoulishness or thought-lessness had driven them to take the coat off her recovered body and keep it – untouched, never to be worn, a ghost in part-human shape, hanging, haunting – in the cloakroom of the house, but it was not something he could bear. He had seen it last year when he'd been here with his parents and could not believe that it was there. He couldn't believe it was still there when he'd come back by himself this year.

He'd talked to Neil McBride but the estate manager had been unwilling to do anything about it; it was a family matter. He'd mentioned it to Grandma Win, but she insisted the coat had to remain where it was and hinted, round-aboutly, that her late husband Bert had wanted it to stay there. It had been his favourite old coat, then one of the boys', and it was in Bert's memory as well as Irene's that it hung there in the cloakroom.

He hadn't cared. He didn't care. He'd stopped off at Garbadale while on a motorbike tour of the Highlands, he'd taken the coat, wrapped it up around a boulder from the shore, got a boat from the boathouse and come down here, out of sight in the dying, gloaming light and burned the fucking thing. His mother. His choice. If they really were upset, well tough; it was done.

Some sodden, flameless rags remained, barely floating. He ran the boat over them a few more times, until there was almost nothing left to see, then turned the bows of the boat to the north-west and the house, opening the engine up and sitting back, breathing hard, the tears drying on his cheeks in the created breeze of the boat's slipstream.

'All Bran!'

'Yo, big man, feck me, you're lookin smert! Fucken hell, wid ye take a look at yon! Fucken hell!'

'Big Al! How're ye doin?'

'Evening all.'

He's back in Perth, at Tango's old flat, order restored, door renewed after the attentions of the police battering ram, Council apparently mollified, rent and bills being paid off and life largely back to normal.

'Take a seat, Al, go on; take a seat. Shone; shift up ya ignorant bam. There. So, big man, how's it hingin?'

'I'm good. How's everybody?'

Pleasantries are exchanged. The living room is fairly crowded and smoky, the coffee table jammed with cans, bottles, ashtrays and mugs. Alban knows six of the eight people present and recognises the other two, one of whom is a large lady sporting a black eye. He can hear children yelling in another part of the flat. 'I was just thinkin about doin a giant-size Slurry fur the assembled party,' Tango explains. 'Utilising a couple of tins of the mulligatawny donated by your man Burb here. You in?'

Alban grins. 'Tempting as ever, especially with the spicy soup, obviously; however I was thinking of treating us all to a meal and it was a curry I was thinking of.'

212

'You flush, Al?'

'As a freshly planed piece of inlay.'

'Whit?' says Shone.

'Curry it is then.'

A takeaway is decided upon, not everybody wanting to have to go out to eat. A large order is placed by phone. Al helps with some tea-making in the kitchen, stepping over the dogs and two unidentified children conducting a game which seems to consist entirely of being chased and screaming a lot.

'Good tae see ye, Al.'

'You too, Tango.'

'Al, awfy sorry, but I still canny offer ye your room back. It's just big Mifty had a bit of a contretemps with her man and—'

'No problem, Tango; staying at a hotel.' He looks in the fridge. 'Need more milk. I'll nip down to the shop.'

'Shite,' Tango says, nudging a passing child with one knee. 'You been pouring the milk down the toilet again?' Children squeal, disappear.

'Tango,' Alban asks, drying his hands on a towel, 'you said some of my stuff reappeared?'

'Aye, like ah said on the phone; fucken miracle, but it did. Out here. In the cupboard.' The big black plastic bag falls out of the hall cupboard as the door opens. 'No actual pack, of course – tolt you that cop fancied it – but they sent you all this lot back.'

Alban takes a quick look inside. 'Right. I'll just leave it here for now, pick it up before I head back to the hotel.'

'Dinnae forget now.'

'I won't.'

The takeaway is delivered; they eat most of it and some is saved for the next day. Tango makes burgers and chips for the children. Cans are drunk, vodka bottles are opened, joints smoked. Deedee admits that he doesn't actually like Tango's Slurry. Tango is horrified. 'But it's my signature dish!'

A heated debate ensues regarding the relative merits of Smash and Mr Mash, the latter finally coming out on top in a vote – despite Tango's howls of protest – largely due to the shape of the pack making it easier to conceal about one's person whilst departing from your average retail outlet without the monetary side of said purchase technically having been completed. Vodka bottles are emptied, more joints smoked. Alban is relatively abstemious, and gets up to leave about eleven, to a chorus of calls to stay.

Tango sees him out. They retrieve the black plastic bag with his belongings from the hall cupboard.

'This you off, then, Al?' Tango says quietly.

Alban looks at him. There's something in Tango's expression, as though he's seen something in Alban's.

'Aye, might be a while,' he says, twisting the top of the bin liner to get a better grip. 'Through to Glasgow tomorrow, up north for a family gathering in a couple of days. After that, we'll see.'

Tango puts his hand out. 'Well, you take care, man, all right?'

'Course I will. You too. Keep in touch.'

'Aw aye?' Tango grins.

'No, seriously. I'm thinking about getting a mobile; maybe even tomorrow. I'll call you.'

'You do that, big man.'

'Cheers, Tango. Thanks for everything.'

'Via con Dios, Al.'

'Not a fucking chance.'

They hug, then he's out the door, down the stairs and away.

6

They're walking along the bank of the River Kelvin on a cool day in Glasgow when it feels like the year's turned, the city a distant grey loudness away and above them, the dank smell of the river – white tumbling down weirs, slack and dark on the long stretches in between – following them, its sound echoing under the bridges and between the walls and abutments hemming it.

She is dressed as ever, with gloves but no coat. He's in boots and jeans and his old hiking jacket, though he's had it cleaned and reproofed. They're walking slowly. They have their arms round each other's waists, her head sometimes resting lightly on his shoulder.

Finally, she is talking about what happened in the tsunami. She wouldn't, before now. The shallow scars on her flank and back were the only memories she was prepared to reveal. They're almost gone now, slowly fading to nothing. Now she'll talk about what happened.

She was snorkelling over the reef, early morning. She'd left Sam, the guy she'd gone on holiday with – another climber – fast asleep in their beach hut. Another beautiful day; she'd felt energised and elated and had swum far along and far out, just happy to feel the sunlight and warm water on her skin. She'd been swimming, head down, watching a bright shoal of tiny fish far below, heading for a small ridge of reef vaguely visible ahead when she realised the fish had speeded up, and so had she; the rippled scape of sand under the fish was, quite abruptly, moving past much faster than it had been. Tiny puffs of sand, moving and lengthening like microscopic smoke trails, showed that some sort of current was moving the whole mass of water she and the fish were swimming in out to sea. She didn't understand this.

She brought her head out of the water, but everything looked normal; waves everywhere, but with some roughness over the reef ahead that she hadn't noticed before . . .

The water was moving away from the land. She started to realise what it might be as she was pulled over the start of the reef, the waves rising, becoming more turbulent. She felt a sudden chill and was uncertain whether this was a patch or current of cold water or something from inside herself. This meant something. She'd heard of this. This was bad. A warning. She put her head under the water again, trying to see the reef. It was very shallow; she didn't want to hit any coral. You weren't supposed to touch the reef, break any bits off. The water was turning cloudy with sand, filling with air bubbles. What she glimpsed of the reef was very close. She tried to swim towards what looked like a slightly deeper part off to one side. The water was getting wild over the reef, sloughing back from the land all along the coast of the island. She got a glimpse of the golden beach, lush green trees and perfectly blue sky in the distance, all seemingly serene and untroubled, as though nothing was happening.

She was pulled sideways on a curving current. Something slammed into her side and started to turn her over. She yelled, spitting out the snorkel's mouthpiece as she was hauled on her back over the rough fingers and hard ridged surfaces of the coral.

Tsunami. It had to be a tsunami. She'd been to a conference in Japan, some place by the sea she couldn't remember the name of where they had tsunami warning signs everywhere and this was one of the things they told you about, the phenomenon that let you know there was a big wave coming; the sea disappeared, pulling

216

back from the land. When that happened you had to get to high ground, because the sea always came back, in a tsunami.

The sea was rough, no longer sparkling and blue but turning a sandy brown colour where it wasn't frothing dirty white. The reef was behind her now. She tried to swim, keeping her body as close to the surface of the water as she could to avoid being hit by any more bits of reef or rock. She started swimming out to sea through the crashing waves. There was no pattern to the waves now, just chaos; she coughed and spluttered, taking in mouthfuls of gritty water. The mask and snorkel, she realised, had gone, torn off. She remembers thinking, quite calmly, that this was annoying and inconvenient, because the snorkel might have come in handy in all this turbulent water, and the fact she'd lost it meant she might die.

'And I thought of Sam,' she says, now, by the bank of the Kelvin. 'He'd wanted to buy me a mobile at the airport before we left, but I wouldn't let him. I had this little waterproof bag on my bikini bottom with money in it and the money was still there. Sam kept his mobile in his. If I'd had a mobile I could have rung him and warned him.'

'Or that might have got torn off too,' Alban says, tightening his arm around her, pulling her closer. 'Or his might have been turned off. You don't know.'

'Anyway, I kept swimming out, following the water.'

'Not to land?'

'I was too far out. Anyway, it had just taken me.'

The water grew less turbulent, a little colder, as she followed its slow retreat. She thought of turning back, of swimming back to land, of running up the beach and along it back to the hotel and beach huts, warning people, warning Sam. But she didn't know how soon the wave would come, was terrified that if she did swim back the tsunami would catch her while she was still running along the beach.

When the wave came it lifted her like a big breaker on a surf beach, but then didn't drop her back; instead the bevelled, not quite yet breaking slope of water was like the edge of a vast moving slab of ocean, powering its way en masse towards the land. She felt herself accelerated in the direction of the shore, and turned and swam as hard as she could out to sea again, really frightened now, starting to panic, feeling the strength leach out of her as her muscles tired. She was a strong, fast swimmer; she tried to put what was happening out of her mind and just settle into a powerful, rhythmic crawl, imagining herself in a pool, trying for a personal best 100 metres.

She heard the wave hit the land, the thunder of its falling on the exposed reefs and sand, the splintering, crashing sound of it smashing trees. She listened for screams, each time she turned one ear upwards to the air, but didn't think she heard any.

Finally, she was too exhausted to do the crawl. She turned on her back, to use a slightly different set of muscles in the backstroke. She could look back at the land now, seeing far distant trees, and waves almost as high. She couldn't tell if she was still being driven towards the land or not. The trees she could see looked quite far away. She kept on swimming. Her arms and legs felt like jelly, like there was no bone in them, like they were as insubstantial and weak as the flesh of a stranded jellyfish. She felt sick, and retched up salty water, coughing and spluttering as some of it came down her nose and feeling for a moment that she was drowning. She kept on swimming.

Some time later a fishing boat picked her up. She tried to help them pull her into the boat but she had no strength left. It took three of the men to haul her in. She lay gasping on the guts-slicked deck, staring up at the rolling sky beyond a stubby mast, trying to thank them, saying, 'Tsunami, tsunami.' They put an old waterproof jacket round her, though she wasn't cold. She got to her knees, puked over the gunwale, then saw they were heading in, towards land.

'You've got to wait,' she tried to tell them. 'Sometimes there's more than one.' Didn't they know this? She couldn't explain. The

218

men were staring at the land and shouting and pointing and arguing, seemingly unable to work out exactly where they were, or not sure whether to go back in or not. They didn't pay her much attention and she was too weak to stand up and start shouting and waving her arms about and punch shoulders and talk loudly or whatever it would take to get them to listen to her and somehow make them understand.

She lay draped over the gunwale of the fishing boat, her hands dipping into the water, her head lying on the wooden rail, her body slack against the inside of the hull, her lower legs splayed across the deck, and she listened to the drone of the outboard taking them back towards danger and to the sound of the men shouting and arguing, and she started to cry as she realised what she was going to have to do.

She waited as long as she dared while a little strength began to return to her muscles, then levered herself up and slipped over the side of the boat. She'd hoped they might circle back and try to pick her up again, which might at least stop them from going any further in, but the boat ploughed on. She never knew if they'd even noticed her throwing herself back into the water again.

'You had to get back in the *water?*' he says.

'I'd convinced myself there was going to be another wave; maybe more than one. I felt as long as I could stay in the water far enough out I'd be safe. I'm at home in the water, I can tread water, I can swim for hours at the right rhythm. Even tired out I felt I had a better chance than being back on shore, facing another wave.'

'Fucking hell.' He stops and swings into her, taking her in both arms, enfolding her, hugging her to him, putting his nose into her short, black-blonde hair, and feeling her respond and clasp him to her. 'And there was another wave?'

'It was almost as big as the first,' she says into the collar of his jacket. 'Then a smaller one after that. I think I saw the fishing boat upside down in the trees a couple of days later, while we were still waiting to be lifted out. But it might not have been the same one.

I forgot to look for a name or number or anything. Just another white fishing boat with an outboard.'

When she says 'we', she means all the surviving holidaymakers. She doesn't mean her and Sam. They finally found his body half a kilometre inland a week after the tsunami hit.

A few things came to fill her mind as she trod water and swam weakly and discoordinatedly against the slow current. First, she wished she had a hat (she kept flapping water over her head to cool herself as the sun rose, beating down). Second, she remembered that Alban had once called her a tough cookie. At the time she had felt somewhat insulted, but just then, floating there wondering if Sam was dead and whether she was going to die, the phrase took on a kind of almost mystical significance. Yes, she was a tough cookie, and she would survive and she would not easily disintegrate and turn to mush just because she had been dunked in the water for a long time.

Also, third, she tried to quantify how hopelessly, uselessly, pathetically weak she felt. It took a long time – she was a mathematician, after all, not a poet, so images were not normally her strong suit – but eventually she decided on one. It involved a banana. Specifically, the long stringy bits you find between the skin and the flesh of a banana. She felt so weak you could have tied her up with those stringy bits of a banana and she wouldn't have been able to struggle free. That was how weak she felt.

She was so exhausted and delirious with the weight of sunshine slamming down on her blonde, short-haired head all those long lonely hours that when she did finally come up with this image of utter and pathetic weakness she gave herself a croaky little cheer.

She didn't swim back in until some time past noon. When she got to the shore, staggering through the debris washing around the tideline, having to sit on the wave-smoothed sand for a while to get some strength back into her quivering legs, she thought that – despite trying to swim against the current and so keep opposite the same stretch of shore all this time – she must be a kilometre or two down the coast. This stretch was unrecognisable, just a wasteland of flattened trees and drifts of branches, leaves and fronds, studded with more smashed wood and the occasional piece of wreckage recognisable as human stuff: white plastic patio chairs, a piece of material that might have been a sundress, a cheery-looking beach towel with a sunset on it, and a parasol – colourful strips hanging tattered from white, twisted ribs. There were some sort of sand-covered ruins off to one side. She walked inland a little and discovered the remains of the tarmac road, and looked back and realised that the ruins were the hotel they'd been staying beside. She had come ashore almost exactly where their beach hut had been.

She escaped with bruising and cuts to her side and back, dehydration, and sunburn that made her face and shoulders peel.

He doesn't know what to say. He just holds her. He'd been waiting for her to tell him, but had started to think that maybe she wouldn't, ever. All he'd known was that she'd been there with this guy Sam – he'd never met him – and Sam had died and she'd survived because she'd been in the sea at the time. The rest, the details, she hadn't wanted to talk about, until now.

'Did you ever get any counselling for this, VG?'

She shakes her head, takes a deep breath and pulls away from him, still holding his waist with both hands. 'No.'

He tips his head to one side. 'You talked about this to anybody else?'

One quick shake of the head. 'No.' She frowns. 'Well. I did try to tell Sam's family, but they . . . They were understandably . . . They were very upset. The more I said the worse it got, so I shut up.'

'Think maybe you should talk to somebody else?'

'No, I don't.' Her eyes are the colour of old ice, and big and bright and very open, the look of perpetual surprise phased into something injured but defiant. 'I've told you. And that's more for you than for me. Feel free to feel privileged. I don't need to tell anybody else. And I'd appreciate it if you didn't tell other people. Not without checking with me first.'

He shakes his head. *Dear God, you're a hard one, VG. Or at least you think you are.* Who is he kidding? She is.

All the things he can think of saying sound trite and tired and clichéd when he thinks of them, so he doesn't say anything.

He puts one hand up to her cheek. She leans her face very slightly towards his hand. Her eyes close. He lets his hand slip round behind her head to the nape of her neck. It feels soft and warm. He pulls lightly, bringing them slowly towards each other, and kisses her gently on the lips, nose and cheeks, then hugs her carefully to him again.

The year went on. Exams came and went. He grew a little taller, then stopped growing. He was shaving every couple of days now; more often if he was going out. He fancied other girls, danced and kissed and copped the occasional feel, but – even when, a couple of times, he was told he could – he didn't take it any further, because he was trying to stay faithful to Sophie. He still wrote poems, and sent her a letter every week, usually writing a few lines each night before he went to sleep. He sent the letters to Aunt Lauren on her and Graeme's farm in Norfolk. He'd sent a whole package the first time, a kind of edited highlights of all the poems and letters he'd written before Lauren had made her offer. He'd asked Sophie to reply in the covering letter that went with that first bundle as well as in most of the letters in the package, and he repeated the request in his first few letters after this secret postal service had been set up.

About a week after the first bundle had been sent, he allowed himself to start getting excited, waiting for the reply that now, surely, had to come. Their post was usually delivered after he'd gone to school, so he had to wait until he got home each day to see if there were any letters. The second Saturday after he'd had the conversation with Aunt Lauren, he'd hung around near the front door when the postman was due, making sure he was first to the mail, but there was nothing for him. The week became a fortnight, then three weeks, then a month. He wondered if something had come for him but had been intercepted by his parents. But that was paranoid. They weren't like that. Were they?

He told himself it would take time. He imagined her being shut up in some forbidding Spanish boarding school – he'd seen photos of the Escorial, near Madrid, and that was the image he had whenever he thought of the place – and it being, perhaps, difficult for her to get out to a post office. He wondered if his mail was being intercepted before it got to her, if there was some strict housemistress who censored the mail of the girls and would never let anything as passionate and improper get through to one of her charges.

He wrote to Aunt Lauren, checking that she really was sending the letters on. She wrote back saying that she was. In his next letter to Sophie he asked her to write care of Jamie Boyd, his best friend for the last term. Jamie was the sort of pal who'd pass on mail dependably and unopened. Nothing came via Jamie either.

The Easter holidays arrived. He hoped that he'd hear something then, when she might be home and so able to write or phone. But still nothing. He decided she was probably staying with her biological mother, still in Spain. He'd have to be patient, wait until the summer holidays. She'd be bound to come back to the UK then. She'd be at Lydcombe and able to write or phone.

More studying, exams, homework, washing the car and doing housework to justify his pocket money, more snogs at parties.

At one party, at Plink's house, a week before the start of the summer holidays, he got the knickers off a girl and used his fingers to make her come, hugging her to him afterwards.

His fingers smelled just the way they had with Sophie, which was achingly nostalgic and sweet, yet somehow sad at the same time. She was called Julie. He fell out with her the next day when he said he didn't really want to go steady.

Andy, Leah, he and Cory spent the first two weeks of the summer holidays in Antigua. He felt he was practically thrown at the sixteen-year-old daughter of a Manchester couple who were in the bungalow next to theirs; the adults suddenly became fast friends and their offspring seemed to be expected to follow suit. Emma was blonde and leggy and attractive in an ice-maiden kind of way but the only similarity to Sophie was that she had braces. They kissed at a dance in the big hotel. The next day they rode around part of the island in a two-person bike thing with a canopy and he told her something about Sophie and his feelings for her. She understood, seemed almost relieved. They played a lot of tennis and kept in touch for years afterwards until she moved to South Africa.

During the summer he had a work-experience job at Kew; just general digging and lugging and so on, but it was at Kew, which was all that mattered, and he loved it. He started going out with one of the girl trainees, Claire. She was small, dark, chunky and curvaceous. They kissed sometimes but she wouldn't let him go any further than putting his hand between her top and her bra. They went to each other's houses; her parents lived in a semi in Hounslow under the Heathrow flight path. They spent time listening to records and playing games and kissing. He still felt he was being faithful to Sophie. This was, partly, an act; cover.

The summer wore on.

Still nothing from Sophie. Grandma Win had invited him to Garbadale for the last two weeks of the holidays, to do some gardening if he was so inclined – goodness knows, the place could do with all the help it could get – just to relax and amuse himself as best he could if he'd prefer. He hadn't said a definite yes or no yet, but he needed to make up his mind.

There's a small family do at the Richmond house; Kennard and Renée come with Haydn and Fielding and while he and Haydn are playing on the NES – he's got a US version of a new game called *Super Mario Brothers* via his pal with the computer magazine-publishing dad – Haydn mentions being at Lydcombe a couple of weeks ago and seeing cousin Sophie. Alban drops the controls.

224

What?

Sophie had been there for about a month at that point. Off to the States to stay with Aunt, umm, well aunt and uncle somebody – he couldn't remember . . . Haydn looks at his new Casio watch, which has an entire tiny keyboard of buttons, and of which he is inordinately proud, even though his fat little fingers can barely manage the buttons . . . Leaving today, actually. This evening, in fact. Ha! That distant roar could be Sophie's plane leaving now, for all they know. That'd be funny, wouldn't it?

For an instant, as he sinks back against the side of the bed – Fielding is on it, cross-legged, reading a comic he's brought with him – Alban thinks of dashing for the underground station and getting to Heathrow, finding her, maybe catching her right at the departure gate the way they did in films, and persuading her to stay behind, at least getting her to promise to write.

He's getting another roaring in his head, and tunnel vision. Last time this happened he'd been smacked full in the face by a football. He hears Haydn talking about Lydcombe, about Sophie. Met some of her pals. Went on a speedboat ride. She tried to get him on a horse but it was very high up. Her boyfriend was very rude to him and Fielding. She'd said the reason for that was because she was leaving for the States soon for a couple of years and he – her boyfriend – knew she was leaving him probably for ever. If and when she came back he'd most likely be married with a couple of brats via some farm girl, and she'd have a Californian hunk in tow. But, hey – such was life.

Alban excused himself, staggered to the toilet, leaving Haydn blinking after him, asking him, Was he all right?

He sat on the loo seat for a long time with his head in his hands.

He needed to get out. He went down to where the oldies were, still at dinner, and said he needed some fresh air (some curious looks, but that was all), went out into the garden and over the back wall, along the lane, across a couple of roads and into the vast darkness

225

of Richmond Park. He lay on the grass, looking up at the sky; a dirty orange cloudscape of reflection. Off to one side, between the clouds, he saw the navigation lights of the aircraft. Coming in, of course. Usual westerly airstream, so cousin Haydn was wrong; her plane would have taken off heading west, heading for the States, out over the M4 corridor, across Wales and Ireland . . .

Except, no, now he thought about it coldly, the planes went north-west towards Scotland before crossing the Atlantic. They'd flown to New York a couple of years ago, and after the trouble he'd gone to to get the window seat – out-tantrumming Cory, basically, though his trump card had been that she'd sleep most of the way – he'd taken care to keep asking his dad what they could see out of the window every now and again. Scotland, had been the reply a couple of times. They might even be flying over Garbadale right now . . .

Anyway, Haydn had been wrong. They wouldn't have heard Sophie's plane taking off. The distant roaring they could hear from the house was made by planes coming in to land.

He closed his eyes and turned his head away, letting the tears come.

He got up reluctantly a little later, feeling old and tired and worn out by it all, like his life was already over. He didn't really want to move, he wanted to stay here lying on the warm, fragrant grass, listening to the traffic on the road and in the sky and smelling the cool night smells of the great park and mourning his lost love, but he couldn't stay. They were probably already starting to worry about him, maybe calling for him in the garden, out looking for him even.

He went back to the house, relieved to find no teams with torches searching the garden. Not even anybody at the back door, calling him. He stuck his head round the door of the dining room; laughter and the smell of smoke. Yes, good, no problem. Feeling better? Fine. They hadn't realised how long he'd been gone.

Upstairs, Haydn was smugly beating a squirming, bleating Fielding at *Super Mario Brothers*.

*   *   *

'And anyway, what are these classy drugs?'

'Sorry, Beryl?'

'On the news. They keep talking about them.'

'Ah: heroin, cocaine?' Fielding says, uncertainly. He looks over at Alban, who looks over at Verushka, who narrows her eyes and then smiles.

'What are what?' Eudora asks. It is the night before Fielding is due to take Great-Aunt Beryl and Great-Aunt Doris towards Garbadale while Verushka will drive Alban there. A dinner has been arranged, at Rogano, in the city centre. Alban has invited Eudora, Verushka's mother.

'And what is it that makes them classy in the first place?' Beryl asks. 'Is it just the price?'

'When I was young,' Doris announces suddenly, 'one didn't have to travel abroad to discover oneself. One was, rather, simply always there.'

'Drugs, Eudora,' Verushka tells her mother.

'Drugs, really?' Eudora says, her gaze darting around the table as though looking for evidence.

Verushka smiles. 'I think we're talking about class A drugs.'

'Why are we talking about drugs, darling?' Eudora asks. She's a tiny, lively old lady – not that old, Fielding supposes; Mathgirl must be about early thirties, so he'd guess her mum would be mid-fifties. She wears a cream suit and dark blouse. Nicely done hair, sort of grey-blonde. You wouldn't, Fielding thinks, but if you had to, it wouldn't be so bad. Not like if you had to with somebody the age of Doris or Beryl – that kind of thing doesn't bear thinking about. Pretty stylish, really, old Eudora. When she walks she moves in a way that seems to have become a lost art.

Actually, maybe you just would anyway.

'Who's for pudding?' Alban asks, as menus are redistributed. Then he leans over to talk quietly to Beryl.

'I'm not entirely sure,' Verushka says to her mother.

'I was thinking of having a cigarette. Do you think this would be all right?'

Verushka looks pained. 'Oh, Eudora, please don't.'

'Oh, I see!' Beryl says, sitting upright.

'You had a gap year, didn't you?' Doris is saying to Fielding.

'Building toilet blocks in Mozambique,' he tells her. 'Hated it. Only went there because of an old Dylan song.' Fielding shakes his head. 'God, that was a mistake. It was rubbish.'

'So, did I hear that you will be going camping while we're all up at Win's?' Beryl asks Verushka.

'I shall be camping,' Verushka says. She's had a few drinks. Not exactly a bucketful – like Fielding, she's driving tomorrow – but sufficient to loosen her tongue.

'I'm sure you could stay at the house if you liked,' Beryl tells her. This is probably not true, Fielding suspects. Sounded like the place is going to be full up, what with most of the family, some people from Spraint and various lawyers being present.

'The camping's not the point,' Mathgirl tells Beryl. 'The climbing's the thing.'

'Climbing? What, mountains?'

'That's right.'

'And is there a group of you doing this?'

'I think I shall have the cheese,' Doris announces. 'And perhaps a small port.'

'No,' Verushka says, 'just me.'

'Really? Just you? Isn't that rather dangerous?'

'Yes, it is,' Verushka agrees. 'Thanks, I'm fine,' she says, handing the waiter back the menu. She sits back, arms folded. 'Not really supposed to climb by yourself. In theory three's the minimum, so if somebody's injured one stays with the injured party and the other goes for help. But that's not so important nowadays with mobile phones and tiny wee walkie-talkies and strobe lamps and pocket flares and space blankets and GPS and bivvy bags and so on. You can have an emergency in comfort these days. Still not advised, going by yourself, but not completely irresponsible.' She sticks a nail between two teeth, digs around and then rinses with water.

'Darling!' her mother says, frowning.

Verushka grins at her mum, tips her head briefly in what might be an apology. 'Anyway, I'm hoping never to see the inside of a rescue helicopter,' she tells Beryl.

'Well, I think you're awfully brave,' Beryl tells her, 'climbing up mountains all alone.'

'Brave or foolhardy,' Verushka agrees. 'Depends on one's definition. Frankly, I'd admit to selfish.'

'For pudding?' Doris says, horrified, looking at Verushka.

Beryl touches Doris's arm lightly. 'Selfish, dear,' she says.

'Oh. I see.'

'Selfish, dear?'

Verushka shrugs. 'I don't like climbing with other people. I prefer to be by myself. And it's taking a bigger risk because of that. So, selfish. Yes.' She takes up her water glass again.

'So, is that why you haven't married Alban?' Beryl asks Verushka, who is taking a mouthful of water at the time and comes very close to spitting it back out again.

'I beg your pardon, Beryl?' she says, somewhere between a smile and laughter.

'Well, you know,' Eudora says, leaning over conspiratorially to Doris, 'I've asked her the same thing myself.'

'Beryl . . .' Alban says, sounding like he's a headmaster addressing a kid. One of those, *Worst of all, you've let yourself down* voices. It's hard to tell with the fairly dim level of lighting back here, but Fielding strongly suspects Alban is blushing. Verushka is looking a little rosy around the cheeks herself. *Wow*, Fielding thinks, *this is fun!*

'Well, you've always seemed very sweet on each other,' Beryl says, sounding perfectly reasonable. 'I simply wondered.' She looks round the table. 'Oh dear, have I said the wrong thing again?'

'Not in the least, dear,' Eudora tells her.

'I'll have the chocolatey thing and this dessert wine,' Doris tells the waiter, tapping the menu with the leg of her glasses.

'Alban,' Beryl says, putting her clasped hands on the table. 'Why haven't you asked this young woman to marry you?'

Alban closes his eyes, puts his elbow on the table and his hand over his eyes, shaking his head once.

Verushka purses her lips and stares at the table.

'Hmm? What's that?' Doris says to the waiter. 'Different sizes? Oh, well, large, I think, don't you?'

'Oh dear, I'm embarrassing my nephew,' Beryl says. She turns to Verushka. 'Am I embarrassing you, dear?'

'I'm pretty hard to embarrass,' Verushka says. She still looks flushed though.

'Well, what would you do if he did?' Beryl asks. Mathgirl has her gaze fixed firmly on Beryl and does not look at Alban. This undoubtedly means something but Fielding is buggered if he knows what.

'Marriage isn't something that I've ever really contemplated,' Verushka says. She smiles widely. 'I'm very happy with my life. It would be hard to improve it.'

'Yes, but just supposing he did ask you.'

'What, now?'

'Yes, I suppose. Now.'

'I'd ask him why he was asking anybody to marry him when he hadn't yet resolved his feelings for his cousin Sophie,' Verushka says, and looks over at Alban, at last, with a small smile.

'And?' Beryl pursues.

'And then I'd listen to what he said in reply,' Verushka says smoothly.

Alban catches Fielding's eye. 'And it was all going so well,' he sighs.

Fielding shrugs. 'C'est la vie, cuz.'

Doris looks round, seemingly confused. 'Have we had coffee yet?'

Beryl holds Alban's arm as they make their way to the door and the waiting cabs. They're bringing up the rear of the party, walking slowly.

'Did I rather put my foot in it there with all that talk about marriage?' she asks.

'It did feel a bit awkward, Beryl,' Alban admits.

'Sorry. One gets impatient at my age. Desire to see ends tied up before one pops one's clogs, sort of thing. But why don't you ask her?'

'To marry me?'

'Yes.'

'Beryl, I don't think I want to get married.'

'Well, just live together. That's what counts, not the piece of paper.'

'I don't know if I want that either. And even if I did, I'm pretty sure it's not what she wants. You did hear what she said.'

'I've never seen two such clever people be so stupid. But it's your life.' She squeezes his arm as they approach the doors. 'However. Any luck with finding out what was going on with your mother saying what she did to me?'

Alban had got used to old people making these ninety-degree changes in conversational direction. 'Not a lot of luck,' he told her. 'I talked to Andy. He says it wasn't him.'

'Never thought it was.'

'Same here.'

'He had no ideas who might have disapproved so much?'

'None. None he was willing to share, anyway.'

'Oh well.'

'Well, we're going to have the whole family in the one place for the weekend. That'll be the time to ask questions.'

'Jolly good,' Beryl says, and pats his arm as they stop at the cloak-room.

Eudora is saying, 'What a lovely evening!'

'Well, carry on then,' Beryl tells Alban. 'Let me know if I can help.'

'Sorry about that.'

'Beryl?'

'The whole marriage thing.'

'Don't apologise. You didn't do anything.'

'Yes, but they're my family. I feel I have to.'

They've dropped Eudora at her flat in Buccleuch Street and are on their way to Verushka's. She looks at him for a moment. He's staring ahead.

She touches his arm. 'Any more you want to add?' she asks him.

'What do you mean?'

She moves over, snuggles up to him, holding his arm with both her hands, her head on his shoulder. 'You do know how I feel about all this, don't you?'

'I think so.'

'I don't want children. I don't want to get married. I may never even want to settle down.'

'That's pretty much what I thought.'

The cab stops, jerks forward, the driver mutters a curse under his breath then they move on again.

'I love being with you.' She says this quite quietly. 'I miss you. When you're away, and the phone rings, always I hope it's you. Every time. Just in a small way, but always.'

He leans his head over so that it touches hers. He says, 'I suppose I've always treated it like there's only so much fun you can have with somebody. If you're with them for decades then it's spread very thin; watery, diluted and tasteless. But if you only live for a few days every now and again, then it's all intense and concentrated.'

She shakes her head, runs a hand through his curls. 'Oh, my poor love,' she says softly through a sad smile. 'You do talk the most utter nonsense sometimes.'

He reaches up and puts his fingers round the wrist of the hand that is stroking his head. 'Do I now?'

She nods thoughtfully. 'Yes, you do.' She's thinking that the action of gripping her wrist like that – gently and lightly, certainly – and stopping her from stroking his head is as aggressive as he ever gets with her. She suddenly realises that she quite happily slaps his arm,

232

punches his shoulder, and even kicks him – albeit softly, pulling the action – in the calf and thigh and backside, and can recall at least once balling her fists and beating him on the naked chest, play fighting . . . And he never even pretends that he is about to respond. He has never raised a hand towards her.

Probably their most violent actions have involved arm wrestling.

Well, and sex, she supposes. But, even there, it is just the conventional lunge and thrust of perfect normalcy; no slapping or clawing, no bites or even love-biting. She's had her ears re-pierced, nipples bitten so hard she's cried out – not in a good way – and been left with bruises, scratches and grazes from other lovers, and in every case made clear her objections . . . But with him, nothing. In bed or out, he has always been gentle, thoughtful, sweet and even – in some sense that she has to confess confuses her own notions of masculinity and femininity – accepting.

This will, she decides, need some thinking about. He lets go of her wrist. She puts her palm to his cheek, feeling the warmth of him through his neatly trimmed beard.

The cab bounces over some road repairs. 'Anyway, I'm sorry, too,' she tells him.

'What about?'

'What I said about you and Sophie. I didn't need to. I was kind of replying in the same coin and I shouldn't have. So, apologies.'

'Oh.' When he thinks about this, he remembers that, yes, he was hurt at the time, that he felt in some tiny way betrayed, even though he feels he shouldn't have, even though it seems a rather petty thing to have felt, and even though everybody round the table, with the possible exception of Eudora, knew pretty much the whole story anyway. He pats her leg just above the knee. 'That's okay.'

She puts her mouth near his ear. 'We're okay,' she whispers. 'We're still okay, aren't we?'

He turns to look into her eyes in the half-darkness of the cab, the slow strobe of orange streetlights flickering over them like film.

'Of co—' he begins, then stops and smiles and kisses her lightly on the lips. 'Yes, we're okay,' he says.

She whispers, 'I just want to get you home and feel you inside me.' She kisses his ear and he turns to her and puts his arms round her, hugging her. They kiss for a while. They break off, see the cab driver looking at them dubiously, and both draw close again, heads bowing to each other, laughing quietly.

When he's eighteen he has a gap year. Later, he won't remember anybody at the time actually calling it that, but that's what it was. He knew a few people who'd taken a year off between school and university and thought it seemed like a good idea. He's left school with very good A-levels. After a lot of thinking he's decided that when he goes to university – St Andrews or Edinburgh, probably – he'll do Media Studies.

When he tells Andy this, his dad lowers his paper, looks at him over the top of his reading glasses and says, 'In my day if you didn't know what to do at Uni you did Sociology.'

Alban is less hurt by this remark than he might have expected. Anyway, in the end he goes to Bristol and does Business Studies. Though, in his defence, as he points out to people for rather too long a time afterwards, he had the good grace to hate it.

He sees quite a lot of the world in his gap year, though – being, effectively, a Wopuld – he sees much of it filtered through the multi-faceted eye of his family. It is much more difficult for a Wopuld family member, especially a young Wopuld family member, to see the world unassisted and unencumbered than it is for the average traveller. There are simply too many Wopulds, too many members of associated clanlets, too many accomplice families, too many ex- and current business partners and too many individuals still displaying – and in many cases also feeling – a soft spot for the family scattered across the face of the planet for one to be able to avoid them without causing severe offence, or conducting one's travelling in conditions of inappropriate secrecy. When you know no one in a country, you are free, if you wish, to experience the place to the full, on its own terms. When somebody who knows the place and is well-disposed to you takes you under their wing, then you have the place discovered for you.

It could, Alban realises as his own little world tour unfolds, cut both ways. On the one hand, having somebody to show you around and do the talking and point out all the interesting places that the guidebooks didn't always know about, is really handy. Such people will also usually buy you meals and drinks and put you up in their houses and apartments for quite long periods of time without showing any of the obvious signs of wishing you gone or expecting payment. On the other hand, you start to fall into the trap of seeing everywhere as essentially the same because everywhere you go there are these roughly similar, kindly-seeming, certainly helpful people, well-disposed to you for whatever reason, who will smooth your path and grease a few wheels and even palms to make your stay more pleasant on their patch.

Getting out, away from this sort of smotheringly helpful succour, might result in getting dysentery, being beaten up by local surlies, fending off the advances of large sweating men in charge of cement trucks, having your wallet skilfully razored from the bottom of whatever deeply cunning pocket you might have secreted it in while sleeping, missing trains and buses due to ruthlessly exploited Brit diffidence and you mysteriously being the only person present to have entirely assimilated the concept of queuing in an orderly – or indeed any – fashion, wishing – while on the trains and buses that are successfully boarded – that you had missed them because anything would be better than being stuck on this hellish conveyance in hundred-degree heat with iffy bowels, either no toilet at all or a blocked toilet – usually within all-too-easy sniffing distance – while the rear end of the bus or the corners of the train carriage go Right Out Over the Thousand-foot Drop and a local with severe body odour problems in the next seat tries so aggressively to sell you drugs that you're convinced he must be an undercover cop with a grudge against young Westerners and a quota to fill and a hundred other vicissitudes the young and inexperienced traveller is liable to experience before gratefully returning home, but at least you know you've been abroad, at least you know what life is really like, if not for the other billions you share the planet with then at least for the hundreds of thousands of the young and relatively rich who take their lives into their hands by going out amongst them.

There are, also, the chance encounters with places and with people – ultimately, arguably, with yourself – that would never truly happen if you had somebody looking after you, and which might actually give some point to all the shit and suffering involved in travelling and make the whole process, the entire exercise, worthwhile: a gleaming temple glimpsed through mists at dawn; a perfect, deserted beach arrived at at the end of a ghastly journey; an evening round a fire with people you didn't know yesterday and may well never see again after tonight but who, for now, you feel close enough to to want to spend the rest of your life with – a sudden, intense connection with others or with a place that you will never, ever forget.

On his travels, Alban tries to balance the amount of time he spends with Wopulds and allied traders and the intervals of what he has come to regard as proper travelling, when there is the opportunity for adventure and, frankly, uncalled-for unpleasantness that at the very least he will be glad has stopped – and to have lived through – and one day may even look back on with a degree of nostalgia and possibly something resembling gratitude.

When he reaches Hong Kong, he judges it is time for a bit of pampering again, and so takes up the invitation of his Uncle Blake – issued rather vaguely via a Christmas card the year before – to come visit.

He flies in from Darwin after a fun but hot and tiring couple of months sharing a microbus across Australia with a pair of recently qualified electrical engineers from Brisbane. Alex and Jace are great, generous, giggly, eternally optimistic guys – especially about sex, which they get exactly none of during the whole journey, though

236

Alban comes close one evening with a waitress in Kalgoorlie – and the three of them get on really well as a hitch from Sydney to Melbourne turns into an epic journey all the way to Darwin via Alice Springs and Perth, but after nine weeks in the same tiny space and a total of about twenty showers between them, he feels they've undergone the male equivalent of that thing women are supposed to get when they're cooped up together, when their periods – allegedly – synchronise. Alban would swear that Jace, Alex and he now have coordinated sweat and he subsequently shares a sort of genetically averaged smell with the two of them.

They part at Darwin Airport, all grins, with a long, grunty group hug and sincere pledges of eternal friendship. (He will never see either of them again.) He falls asleep shortly after take-off and only wakes up as the plane makes the sort of steep, even violent turn that big jets only make, as a rule, when they're either about to crash or actually in the act of crashing. He looks out of the window at a tall building rushing past about a metre from the wingtip. It's night and he sees a Chinese guy looking at him. The guy is wearing stripy shorts and a grey vest and leaning on the concrete balcony of this appallingly close apartment block; he flicks a lighter and ignites a cigarette. Alban will later swear he could identify the lighter as a Zippo and at the time honestly believes that a crash is exactly what is about to happen. In fact it's just all part of the fun of landing at Kai Tak Airport, situated alarmingly close to the heart of downtown Kowloon.

His uncle has sent a driver to pick him up. Alban's still buzzing from the interrupted deep sleep and the near-death experience and stumbles through the clamorous light of the airport and the gritty night-time haze and muggily enveloping warmth of the city into the icy AC of the leather-scented Bentley without really taking much in. He's delivered to a hulking skyscraper by the harbour and directed – by a Chinese angel in a slit-skirted business suit – to an express lift which hurtles upwards, leaving his stomach somewhere around the mezzanine floor. He stumbles out of the gleaming cube with his backpack and is confronted with a vast, glittering room opening out on to a tree-studded rooftop garden the size of a couple of tennis courts, all of this swarming with sleek-looking people of too many racial types to keep track of, every one in suits or cocktail dresses or perfect white uniforms as appropriate and beyond which and whom lies what looks like every electrical light ever manufactured in the history of the world since Edison, shining madly in inchoate swirls, vast ropes of highways, glowing pools of intersections and stadia and mirroring off both the crystal-surfaced complexity of hundreds of tall buildings and the city-blanketing under-surface of a layer of thick, shining cloud which mirrors the colours of the enormous vertical signs on the towers, slabbed neon edges reflected on the vapour producing an overhanging stratus patched with green, blue, red, purple and gold.

A smiling Chinese gent in a starched white jacket which would grace the captain of the *QE2* relieves him of his backpack and guides him via a tray of large champagne flutes to a tall, grey-haired man who is standing near the railed edge of the roof gesturing grandly out over the city before a small group of Chinese men. The grey-haired man turns round. Alban is introduced to Uncle Blake.

'Alban. Good to see you. Do call me Blake.' Uncle Blake is tall and formidable, with a lengthy nose that looks like it was once broken and a kind of determinedly jowly set to his long features. His skin looks tanned grey. He puts out one big, beefy hand and shakes Alban's. Something of the humid closeness of the night seems to communicate itself through the man's enveloping clasp. Alban says Hi. He's introduced to the various important people Blake is with, all of whom seem to have titles or ranks and short but ineffably Chinese names, not an iota of which he remembers a heartbeat later, and has various features of the city, harbour and distant, twinkling islands pointed out to him until finally, perhaps sensing his befogment, Blake steers Alban away towards the elevators with one big dinner-plate-size palm on his back and suggests he might want to get freshened up before rejoining the party. Another gleaming

238

Chinese servant in a jacket seemingly made of pure starch escorts him in the lift down two floors to an apartment on the swish side of lavish, a corner bedroom with glass walls on two sides and a bathroom the size of a squash court.

He has a shower and lies on the bed in a huge white towelling robe to collect his wits and promptly falls asleep. When he wakes up the room's lights are off and Blake is leaning round the edge of the door.

'Sorry, Alban,' he says, deep voice booming. 'Just wanted to make sure you were all right.' He gives what is probably meant to be a friendly smile that succeeds in appearing remarkably ghoulish. 'Long flight, was it?'

'No, just from Darwin,' Alban says, feeling displaced once again. 'What time is it?'

'About midnight.'

'Oh, God.' He's slept for over two hours. 'I'm sorry. Have I missed the party?'

'No, a lot of people are still here.'

'Oh. Right. I'll get dressed.' He swings off the bed.

He only has a few days before a flight to Peru via Hawaii and a visit to his Aunt Else in Lima. The time in Hong Kong passes in a fast-forward blur of overripe high-rise fragrance, blasts of chill in offices and limousines followed by choking hazy interludes in the smothering blanket of fume-laced kettle steam that passes for the open air of Honkers, a buzzing, smog- and smoke-scented pressure suit that seems at once to percolate him and keep him at a distance from the place.

He mixes with the toffs at the races, is wheeled around the harbour and a couple of the nearby islands on Blake's humungous, gleaming power boat – he's given a chance to steer it when they're clear of most of the other traffic and laughs like a loon when he gets to open the throttle and feel this whole ridiculous machine the size of a substantial house lift its sharky nose and accelerate – and spends a bewildering evening at a small party at the home of some of the

239

hyper-rich up on the Peak, with a hazy view that includes the distant summit of Blake's skyscraper near the harbour. The whole Peak seems to smell of jasmine and bananas. The ultra-opulent people are from Canada (him) and Japan (her) and where they live is more like a palace or a museum, walls lined with art plundered from every continent of the planet save Antarctica. Alban sips a cocktail with flecks of gold in it and feels like a child again.

When Blake drops him at the airport with a new Walkman, a shiny Swiss Army knife with a lockable blade, a fat envelope of used ten- and hundred-dollar bills for emergencies and the advice, 'Remember, Alban; always look out for number one. Be selfish. Every other bugger is,' he feels like he's been spat out by the city, and boards the 747 and turns right for Tourist class with something like relief.

He sleeps through Hawaii.

He spends a month in Lima with Aunt Else, Andy's long-absconded sister and the only non-Wopuld relation he visits during his whole gap-year world trip. She runs a pool bar of deranged seediness on the least fashionable edge of the city.

It is an education.

He takes the train to Machu Picchu, hitches down then back up the coast, in trucks mostly, watching waves spin in hypnotically along the hundreds of miles of unrolled golden beach, then heads north – suddenly realising he's starting to run out of time, that there's only a month to go before he's due home – finally ending up in Los Angeles where, almost by chance, while looking in on cousin Fabiole, who harbours pretensions of becoming a film director, he bumps into Sophie.

Alban has forgotten about his cousin fairly successfully, especially over the last nine months that he's been travelling. Sophie fills fewer and fewer of his thoughts since he discovered she'd been back from Spain for most of the summer after the one they spent together, but had not even tried to get in touch with him.

240

They meet in the middle of the desert. Cousin Fabiole is doing some location scouting and has heard about all these hundreds of aircraft sitting in the sunshine on a playa out on the Mojave, left to – well, not rot, because out there it's very dry and that's kind of the whole point; they won't deteriorate even though they're outside – and he thinks it sounds like a great location and so wants to go have a look and maybe get some inspiration. They pile into his car and head for the desert.

Cousin Fabiole is small, wiry, red-haired and voluble. He's at film school, lives in a small condo in Topanga and spends a lot of time looking at things through a rectangle he makes with both sets of index fingers and thumbs. He wants to make inspirational movies like *Rocky* and has already acquired a convincing southern Californian accent.

'*Rocky?* But it's a classic.' Uncharacteristically, he does not on this occasion use the word *dude*.

'I thought it was awful,' Alban admits, then licks some gummed paper carefully. He has been given the job of building joints on the journey. This is one of the many new skills he has developed over the last year or so, adapting his technique to the grass that Americans favour or the tobacco-and-resin approach he's encountered elsewhere, as required. The main challenge here is making sure the grass doesn't blow away. Fab's car is an old Ford sedan with fading red paint and broken air conditioning so they have to travel with the windows down. Fab likes to drive pretty much as fast as the car will go when he's confident there are no cops around, so this is not a trivial matter.

'Orr-fool,' Fabiole mimics, shaking his head. 'Well, whatever floats your muesli, I guess.'

They arrive at the aircraft park, a flat, dusty, windy place in the middle of bright nowhere. There's some difficulty with the security guys at the gate until a phone call is made to the people on the coast that Fab knows who have set this all up, then they're through, though rather than head straight for the rows of parked aircraft they

241

go to the pale, seemingly never-ending expanse of the only runway and an untidy scatter of small hangars near one end.

'Meeting a photographer I know,' Fab explains. 'He's flying in from San Francisco.' He hands the joint back to Alban, who takes a shallow breath of the smoke. 'Friend of,' Fabiole says, then gulps back the smoke, 'cousin Sophe's.'

Just the mention of her name is enough to make Alban's heart leap. He coughs smoke like he's been punched in the gut. The last he heard of Sophie she was in New York at some art college, staying with some relative of her mother's. New York City was going to be his last port of call on his world tour and he had been hoping to try and see her. 'Oh,' is all he can find to say.

He immediately fantasises that she is on the light plane they're waiting for, but can't think why she should be.

A little Cessna appears out of the blue, comes in one wing down on a partial crosswind and lands on about ten per cent of the vast runway, trundling up to the hangars where Alban and Fab are standing leaning against the hood of the car. There are two people in the plane, and – after a long-seeming delay once the prop has stopped turning – the two people get out and one of them is female, but Alban's heart – having leapt again – sinks when he sees the girl is a willowy blonde, nothing like Sophie after all.

'Yo, Fab!' the man says. He's a tall guy, maybe mid-twenties, with untidy dark hair, a bulky camera bag and Ray-Bans.

'Dan-ee-*yell*!' Fab hollers. They run up to each other and high-five.

The blonde – trainers, cut-off jeans and a Cure T-shirt – stops a few steps short when she sees Alban. She's wearing dark glasses too, and pushes them up into her hair to look at him. 'Alban?' she says.

Jesus, it is Sophie.

Dan and Sophie are seeing each other – he's partly based in NYC – and this is how Fab knows him in the first place.

They drive around in the beaten-up Ford, looking at the hulks and husks of the planes, some intact, most with their engines removed. Dan photographs assiduously. Then they take to the skies in the Cessna, Fab using Dan's camera to take more photos. Both in the car and the plane, Alban and Sophie are in the back seats. Dan turns out to be a great guy; full of stories and wisecracks. Sophie laughs a lot at what he says. She and Alban are awkward with each other, not entirely knowing what to say. In the plane they're kind of pressed up against each other. He can smell her perfume, and thinks he can smell the her beyond the artificial odour, the unique scent that is the girl, her skin; a memory of Lydcombe, three summers ago.

The plane banks, one wing pointed almost straight down at the ground, engine revving up as they circle like a wheeling tin vulture over the carcasses of the abandoned aircraft.

Back on the ground, Dan shouts, 'You ever been to San Fran, Al?' as Fab packs up the camera gear while Dan, up a short stepladder, refuels the plane.

'No,' Alban admits, 'I was thinking I might take a look but I don't know if I've the time now.'

'Well, Alban, shit, you don't have to trust your Brit ass to this maniac on the road back to La-la land; come see a real city.'

'Fuck you, dude!' Fabiole shouts good-naturedly.

'What, now?' Alban asks. He glances at Sophie but her expression is unreadable behind the dark glasses. Staring at her in the hammering sunlight, he still can't believe how blonde and slim she's become. She's grown at least three centimetres, too.

'Sure, now,' Dan says, dribbling a last few drops into the plane's starboard tank then securing the fuel cap. 'Come spend a couple of days at mine. You're about my size; you can borrow stuff of mine or just buy shit. We'll throw you on a bus back to LA on Sunday or Monday. I might even fly you back myself if I'm not busy.'

'Fab?' Alban asks. 'You mind?'

'No,' Fabiole says, grinning. 'You go, dude.'

He goes, sitting in the back of the little aircraft and watching the dry duns and khakis and fawns and browns and strips and stripes and circles and squares and rectangles of serene Californian greenery pass by beneath.

They land at Hayward before dusk, pick up Dan's convertible Saab, take the bridge across the Bay then swing north to the city.

They stop at Dan's apartment looking over Lafayette Park and eat at a Vietnamese restaurant just off Columbus Avenue. Back at Dan's – modest but tasteful apart from rather a lot of chrome – he's just opening a bottle of Napa Merlot when the phone rings and he asks Sophie to turn the TV on. Dan keeps the receiver under his chin, wandering through from the kitchen on one of those long phone leads that only seem to exist in the States, holding the bottle and three glasses. He sets these down on the coffee table in the lounge and clicks through to a news channel and a helicopter shot of a yellow school bus being driven fast along a brightly lit freeway, police cars pursuing. 'Got it,' he says. 'What? The thirty-five? Daly, okay. On my way. Yeah 'bye.' He retreats to the kitchen, hangs the phone up and comes back with arms spread. 'Duty calls. You kids'll just have to amuse yourselves. Sorry.'

He's gone a minute later, dashing from the flat pulling a jacket on and clutching two cameras.

Alban and Sophie look at the bottle of wine.

'Or we could just go to the pub,' Alban says. 'I mean a bar.'

Sophie shakes her head. 'We're three years too young, cuz.'

Alban has a good laugh about this and sits down. 'Oh, yeah.' He digs in one shirt pocket, producing a joint. 'Also, I have some of Fab's finest home-grown.' He looks at the number, then into his shirt pocket, then shrugs. 'Oh well, I'm sure he's got more.'

Sophie sits down across from him. She smiles and pours the wine. 'Well, party time.'

They keep the TV on the same news channel with the sound off – the school bus chase continues, now bannered as School Bus Chase – and listen to albums, drinking wine and smoking. The bus chase ends with the vehicle – Alban has been in the States just long

244

enough to start thinking of it as a vee-hickle – crashed but upright and poised on a fulcrum of concrete barriers in the middle of a highway somewhere, surrounded by police cars and flashing lights. Shots from the bus look like sparks, and police are seen diving for cover behind cars.

'This is great,' Alban says, nodding at the TV and passing Sophie the current joint.

'Welcome to America.'

'How long you been here?' he asks.

So far they haven't said anything about what happened at Lydcombe three years ago.

'In the States? Just since last fall, last autumn.'

'Before that?'

'Madrid. Lydcombe now and again; flying visits mostly. How about you?'

She looks so different and so the same. Her mouth is still the mouth he used to kiss, but her teeth look whiter as well as more regular, and her face is framed in different hair, and carried on a far thinner body. He guesses the way she looked before was due to puppy fat, but he'd liked her like that. He feels like he's found her again but she's still lost to him; another person, another life, another lover. Her accent has changed, become mid-Atlantic, but the tone, the timbre are the same. 'Me? Oh, just, you know, at home,' he says, taking the joint back. 'Richmond, then I've been travelling the last, well, nearly year.'

'You look good,' she tells him. 'You've filled out. Tan suits you.'

He grins. 'I bet you say that to all the boys.'

'Yeah,' she tells him, reaching for the joint again. 'I do. Cheers.'

He laughs some smoke out, lifts his own glass. He's sitting on the floor with his legs under the glass-and-chrome coffee table. She's sitting on the couch behind him so it's easier to pass the numbers to and fro while watching the TV.

This is so different from what he imagined. He'd thought that they would either see one another and instantly rush into each other's arms, maybe never to part again, or, alternatively, have the most horrendous, hurtful fight that would leave them both emotionally scarred for life.

Either way, something momentous. Not this strange, edgy, slightly nervous situation where they both act like they were never lovers, like Lydcombe had never happened.

'I tried to get in touch with you for so long after they split us up,' he tells her.

'Really?' She sounds sceptical.

'Really. Did you ever get any of my letters?'

'Not one,' she says, passing the joint back.

He doesn't know what to say to this. *Wasted, wasted, all of it wasted.* Ah well. He takes a deep breath, clears his throat.

'Tried calling. Even thought about coming down on the train and bus and looking for you at Lydcombe, until I heard you were in Spain.'

'In-a-Shpine. In-a-Shpine,' she says, staring at her glass and sounding thoughtful in a stoned kind of way. It sounds like she's quoting somebody else, from some other time, not making fun of him. 'In-a-Shpine . . .' Then she looks at him. 'Did you really?' she asks. 'Really write all these letters. Seriously?'

'Yep, and lots of poems, too. Hundreds of sheets in the end. Aunt Lauren said she'd send them on to you.' He looks up at her. 'You definitely didn't get anything?'

'Not a flippin' fing.' She gets up to change the record. 'Thought you'd forgotten about me,' she says quietly, back to him.

'Well, I didn't.' He looks round at her but she's taking in Dan's wall of records and books. She had changed into a light, short green dress for the restaurant. She reaches up to a top shelf and he sees the tanned back of her thighs.

'Do you have any CDs?' she asks. 'Dan's got some here, though he says he likes the sound of vinyl better. And he has these things.' Reaching down, she pulls out what looks like an album of music from *Chinatown*. 'Laser discs? Like, for films?'

'Heard of them,' he says.

'Hmm.' She slides the laser disc back into its place on the shelves.

'Did you try to get in touch with me?' he asks, looking away and taking the last of the joints out of his shirt pocket.

'Fuck me, how many of those have you *got*?' she asks.

'Last one. Won't light it if you don't want me to.' He already feels pretty wasted though he's trying hard to keep it together. He looks round but she's studying the record collection again, arms folded.

'Na, na, don't let me stop you.' There's a pause. 'Might open a window though.' She turns and glances back at the TV, then away again.

'Sophie?'

'What?'

'Did you?'

'Do you like Joni Mitchell? Dan's a big fan but I'm not so sure. Must bring some Cure over. Did I what?'

'Try to get in touch with me.'

There's a long pause. 'No, hon, I didn't.' The needle clunks down into the vinyl's lead-in spiral with a near subsonic rumble; a hollow, empty sound pregnant with impendence.

His heart feels like it flows out of him and down the three floors to the street. Hon. Short for honey. That's a new word. Probably Dan calls her that. Probably calls her that in bed. Or maybe she calls him that. Maybe she calls that out when she's coming. When he's making her come. Oh, fuck, what is he doing here?

She sits down on the floor opposite him, at the foot of the other couch, her legs slid under the coffee table, parallel with his.

'Things were made pretty bad for me after you guys left Lydcombe,' she tells him. She looks sad and serious and beautiful, but still disorientatingly different. 'They made me feel pretty bad about myself. About everything that happened. About all that we did.'

He still hasn't lit the last joint. He looks into her eyes, trying to

247

imagine how it must have been for her. In all this time, in all this thinking about her, he never really thought about how she must have felt about it; he just pictured her as the same girl she had always been, but stopped, frozen, paused, something caught in amber or carbonite or something but still staying the same person, ready to resume her life, their life, the instant whatever spell had been cast over them could be broken.

He had never imagined that she might change as a result of all that happened. Even after hearing from Haydn that she'd been back to Lydcombe, that she had a boyfriend, he had somehow written that off, dismissed it. That had been somebody else, or that had been just her turning out to have been a bad person all along but only now being exposed as such. And somehow the image that he held of her had not changed; that strange, frozen icon of her that he possessed had stayed with him and somewhere deep inside he'd felt – even after all the travelling and changing he'd done – that he could still wake them both from their dream if he could only find her and somehow nothing essential would have changed. It was only now he realised he never could do that, that everything had changed; most of all the two of them.

'James and Clara made me feel I'd hurt everybody,' Sophie says quietly. 'Themselves mostly, naturally, but Grandma Win, your parents, the whole family. Even you. We had to . . . I had to draw a line under it all and start again. That was the only way forward, the only way out. Put it down to youthful stupidity and move on. If I could do that, if I could not look back, then we'd all be okay. They'd be happy. I'd be saved. You'd get over me quicker.'

He feels tears prick behind his eyes but fights them back, clenching his jaw to try and bite them down. 'So,' he says, and has to clear his throat again. 'Do you think it was just youthful stupidity?'

She looks at him for a long while. Joni Mitchell sings about Cold Blue Steel and Sweet Fire. Eventually Sophie says, 'You going to light that joint or just fondle it all fucking night?'

They smoke the last joint, passing it back and forth over the table.

On the TV, the School Bus Chase is now being labelled as the School Bus Siege. Dan rings to say he'll be there all night and intends to crash at a pal's nearby in Daly City – apologies. Usually he'd feel threatened leaving her in the apartment with such a handsome guy, but – hey – they're cousins and it's not like they're from the Ozarks or something.

They finish the wine.

She gets up, has to hold on to the end of the couch for a moment, goes 'Woo!' then puts on *This is the Sea* by the Waterboys. 'Do you know this?'

It's a record he remembers from just after they were split up.

'Yes,' he tells her. 'I remember this.'

She stands in front of the hi-fi, between the speakers, swaying, head down, eyes closed, hands clasped above her head.

He twists round, watches her for a while.

She turns and says, 'Do you want to dance?'

'You'll have to go,' she tells him.

'What, now?'

'No, but before Dan gets back.'

'Why?' Though of course he knows. He tries not to let the hurt into his voice.

'Because it's too complicated otherwise. And I'm not so great at lying.'

'But why do I need to go if—?'

'Look, it's not like we're going to be able to do this again, Alban. He'll be here. I'll be *here*.'

It's been the first time they've made love in a bed.

'Well, I know, but—'

'I'll say we had a fight. An argument. Some family thing. I can make that stick. That I can do. But not if you're here.'

He waits a while, bringing her a little closer, stroking her hair, her newly skinny side and flank, cupping one sweet, smalled breast. 'Okay,' he says.

She reaches down, pulls at some of the sheet lying crumpled beneath them. 'And I'd better get this washed, too.' She breathes deeply, glancing at the blinds then pushing away from him. 'Christ, it's dawn. Come on; shift. If I get this down to the laundry now I can have it back on by the time he gets back.'

He helps her strip the sheet, wondering when she became so thoughtful, so adept, so managerial.

They say their goodbyes in the apartment block's basement laundry while pale pink sunshine seeps through a high, grubby, pavement-level window. She doesn't let him kiss her deeply, unpeels his hands from her behind and just shakes her head when he tries to say too much.

She puts her forehead against his and says, 'We probably shouldn't have done this.'

'Yes we should.'

'No. No we shouldn't.'

He finds out much later that Dan guessed they'd fucked anyway, almost as soon as he got back, and threw her out.

Since Lima, he's been keeping at least half a grand of Blake's money inside his sock, curled in a sweaty wad round his ankle. He uses some of this to fund a taxi to the station and then buy a train ticket back to LA.

He starts university a month or so later.

Sophie avoids him subsequently.

The next time he'll see her will be at a trade fair in Singapore. She'll have perfect, shiningly white teeth, her nose will be smaller, she'll be slimmer still and even more blonde.

7

Thursday. Verushka drives him north, out of the city in a grey smir of rain along Great Western Road, staying within a couple of mph of the speed limit until the roads near the Erskine Bridge, slowing again subsequently then opening the Forester up once more after Dumbarton. The traffic thickens along the side of Loch Lomond but she manages some coolly judged overtaking nevertheless.

'This thing feels quicker,' Alban says, frowning.

She flashes him a grin. 'Yeah, I've had it chipped.'

'That makes it go faster?'

'Oh yeah.'

'Bet you didn't tell the insurance company.'

'Bet I did, smart alec.'

The back of the vehicle is mostly full of her kit. He has one newly bought bag but she has a substantial backpack plus all her other hiking gear and a spare tent in case she wants to establish a base camp partway between the road and any given mountain – otherwise she'll sleep in the car or wherever's appropriate on the hill in a bivvy bag.

They make good time after the road opens out past Ardlui, scything through drizzle and darting past other road traffic. She gets flashed at once by an oncoming car, and passed by a growling Evo carrying serious tail. The getting passed, she explains, cancels out the getting flashed at. Especially as the flashing was entirely unjustified.

They reach positively dizzy speeds during an unexpected dry period on the few miles before Bridge of Orchy. They stop for fuel and lunch in Fort William. She's in what she describes as mountaineering mode, and packs away an all-day breakfast of considerable size and fat content. He smiles at her, shaking his head. Just out of town they pass the sign for Inverlochy Castle Hotel where Fielding and the duet of great-aunts will be staying the night, breaking the journey to Garbadale.

They listen to her iPod on random, playing through the car's system via a technically illegal radio transmitter unit, and are treated to rather a lot of Bach, mixed in with Berlioz, Gwen Stefani, Hector Zazou, the Kaiser Chiefs, Jethro Tull, the White Stripes, Belle and Sebastian, Michelle Shocked, Massive Attack, Kate Bush, Primal Scream and the Beatles. They're twenty-one tracks in before a Led Zep song, which apparently is some sort of record (though, as she points out, they all are – haw haw).

The obvious route is via Inverness but Verushka has other ideas so they swing west at Invergarry – he asks to stop and look at some interesting trees but she wants to press on – and take the road for Kyle. The roads to the junction at Auchertyre pass in a dazed sweep of sunlit summits, heavy showers and startled overtakees. More pedal to the metal stuff along the roads either side of Achnasheen as the road dries. Verushka is driving with a broad smile on her face.

'Maxed out?' he asks.

She glances at the speedometer, which appears to have run out of numbers to point at. 'Yup.'

'Tyres up to this sort of speed?'

'Yup.'

North of Ullapool – a fuel top-up and scones with tea – the late afternoon brightens further. She lets the pace drop off a little, though they're still zipping past slower traffic. They're less than an hour from Garbadale.

'Have you sorted out what your –' she hoists one eyebrow '– I'm trying to think of another word instead of agenda, here,' she confesses. 'But anyway, have you? Do you really know what you're going there to do?' She glances over at him.

He watches the road ahead unspool towards them.

'I feel like a UN Observer or something,' he tells her. 'I'm going to watch them tear themselves apart, for money. Or stay shackled together, in some dubious spirit of solidarity. Which we are not, frankly, very good at.'

'But what do you want?'

'I suppose being honest with myself I want Spraint to fuck off and leave us alone, though if we're prepared to sell out to them then we deserve whatever we get. With the possible exception of the money.'

'Okay. How much money?'

'They're valuing the seventy-five per cent of the company they don't already own at a hundred and twenty million US dollars. About seventy million of your Earth quids.'

'That a final offer?'

'They say. But they only started at a hundred, so probably not. If we're greedy we'll hold out for something a lot closer to two hundred mill US.'

'And are you greedy?'

'Of course we are.' He smiles humourlessly.

'So if they raised their bid to that level, you'd still vote no and try to get other people to do the same?'

'Yes.'

'But you're not that bothered if it goes the other way?'

'Correct.'

'And it doesn't mean much to you financially?'

'I've a hundred shares left, specifically so I still get a vote. If I'm forced to sell I'll use the proceeds to buy you a slap-up meal and

253

a bottle of something nice to go with it. But there won't be any change.'

She frowns. '*Can* you be forced to sell?'

'If they get ninety-two per cent of the shares, the law says they can buy the rest compulsorily.'

'Hmm.'

She's quiet for a few moments while a moderately fast-moving Audi saloon is dispatched with a series of deft flicks of the wrists and a blip of throttle.

Alban twists in his seat, looking back. 'I think that was Aunt Kath and Lance,' he says. He gives a small wave, in case it was. The Audi flashes its lights. They haven't been flashed since Glen Coe. Or over-taken since the Evo near Crianlarich, for that matter.

'That count?'

She shakes her head. 'That doesn't count.'

'Anyway,' he says, settling back, 'I don't think I'll have much influence on them. They'll sell. Just a question of how much for.'

She looks over at him. 'And what about your cousin? What about Sophie?'

'Yes, she's supposed to be there. Probably.'

'That's not what I meant. Come on.' She says it gently enough.

He watches the road for a while. 'I don't know,' he says quietly. 'It's like I'm always expecting –' he looks over at Verushka '– at this point I'm looking for an alternative to "closure", but, well . . .'

'What? Every time you see her you realise you still feel something for her?'

'I suppose.' He looks down, brushing imaginary specks off his jeans. 'Something like that.' He reaches up and massages his temples, as though he has a headache. 'I don't know. It's . . .' His voice trails off.

'How *do* you feel about her?' Verushka sounds intrigued, no more. 'Come on, McGill. Be honest.' Another glance. 'With yourself; be honest.'

'Oh, I don't know, VG,' he says, shaking his head as he looks out at the mountains sliding slowly past in the distance. 'Sometimes I think the easiest person to fool is yourself. How do I feel about her? I honestly don't know. I look and look and I can't seem to find anything there. I feel that I'll only know when I see her again, but then that never works out either. And she's – she's changed so much. Changed herself so much.' He shakes his head. 'She looks good – she looks ten years younger than she is – but she's had a lot of work done.'

'Think she'll have had anything else done since?'

'Ha! Fuck knows. Botox, probably. Facelift? Bigger bum? Smaller bum? Boob job, either direction? I don't know; what's the fashion these days?'

Verushka grins. 'Gee, dude, you are like so asking the wrong poisin.'

'And your American accent is still terrible,' he tells her, smiling at her.

'Maybe so, but, one day . . . Anyway.'

'Anyway,' he says, reaching out and putting his hand to the nape of her neck.

'That's nice,' she purrs, pushing her head back a fraction. 'If I start to drool, you will stop, won't you?' Another flashed grin. 'Same if we crash.'

'Deal,' he tells her. 'But shouldn't the question you ought to be asking be how I feel about *you*?'

She shrugs. 'I know how you feel about me.'

'You do? Well, tell me.'

'You think I'm great,' she tells him. 'Which, I mean, I am, obviously.' She has a cheerful smile on her face. 'But, you know I've been free with my favours, I'm unrepentantly selfish, I have no intention of ever getting married and I don't want children. So we're fine unless and until you find somebody you can love who wants the things you want, especially children.'

'Or you do.'

'That's the difference,' she says. 'I pretty much already have what I want.'

'Well lucky old you.'

'Yup, lucky me.' She spares a look for the few high, puffy clouds. 'Actually, no, that's not entirely true.'

'No?'

'I miss you,' she says. Brightly, almost. 'I told you last night. I meant it. I wish you lived in Glasgow, or somewhere nearby. I wish we saw each other more often.' She shrugs.

He wonders what to say to this. 'Well,' he says eventually, 'I guess I have to live somewhere.'

'Steady, now,' she says archly, 'these wild rushes of enthusiasm will be the unmaking of you.'

'I'm sorry,' he says. 'That sounded wrong. I just mean . . . But what about you? Would you move somewhere else?'

'Has to have a university and easy access to mountains,' she says crisply. 'Glasgow, Edinburgh, Dundee, Aberdeen. In Europe, woh, anywhere near the Alps would do. Oslo. In the States: Colorado . . . Oh, loads of places. Why?'

'Just checking.'

'I'm not necessarily asking you to move in, you understand,' she says.

'I realise that.'

'Still, you don't want to lose me, Alban,' she says gently, and looks over at him for long enough that when she looks back to the road she has to make a small adjustment to the steering.

'No,' he says. 'I don't.'

He watches her face, side on, for a moment. He loves this woman, he realises, but he doesn't know how to tell her exactly how much without sounding either mealy-mouthed or just too cold. He has never been head-over-heels in love, not even with Sophie, in a sense. Sophie is so long ago, and what happened between them occurred at such a young, even formative age that she forms this awful, unstable, hopelessly compromised foundation for all his feelings for all the women he's ever felt anything for since.

But no, he does not want to lose Verushka.

'Why?' he asks, keeping his voice even. 'Am I in any danger of losing you?'

'No,' she says. 'Not that I can see. But I don't know what's going to come out the other side of this long weekend, when you see your old girlfriend, your long-lost love, the gal what popped your cherry.' She looks over, an unfunny, even sad smile on her face. 'What's worrying is I don't think you do either.'

'Maybe that's why I feel so nervous,' he confesses.

'Really?' She sounds concerned.

He pats his belly through his shirt. 'Really.'

'Oh, come on,' she chides. 'It'll be all right. You'll probably have a great time. You'll persuade them all to join the Scottish Socialist Party and send the Spraint guys back off to California tarred and feathered and questioning the very laws of capitalism itself. Sophie'll have just the sweetest guy in tow and twins she's been keeping secret for the last year and she'll thank you for introducing her to the mysteries of lurve and say it's time you both moved on and you and her husband will bond amazingly well and, oh, all that shit. Even your granny will be nice.'

'She's often nice. Just never without an ulterior motive.'

'But don't be nervous. It's only family.'

'Don't be nervous,' he mimics, muttering half to himself. 'It's only nuclear.'

They leave the main road at the village of Sloy in the shadow of the mountain called Quinag and take a right, heading over a low rise towards Loch Glencoul and the road round to Loch Beag and the great estate of Garbadale.

They turn in through the grand gateway and past the gatehouse. Alban looks back at the waters of the loch and the humpback bridge carrying the road over both the River Garve and the path that leads from the house down to the loch's head. The Forester crunches up the drive between rows of Western Red cedars.

'And thar she blows,' Verushka says, chin on steering wheel, gaze upwards, diverted by the sight of the house starting to appear over and through the curving avenue of tall trees.

The house is revealed in sunlight. There are a dozen or so cars and a couple of white vans parked outside. They drive into the shadow of the south wing, drive out again. 'Aye, here's oor wee hielin' hame,' Alban says.

'What a fucking monstrous pile,' Verushka breathes. 'Did anybody ever need that many turrets?'

'It's for sale,' he tells her. 'You always wanted a pied-à-terre somewhere up here. Even comes with its own mountains. You should make us an offer.'

'Na,' she says, pulling in between a brace of Range Rovers. 'Thanks all the same but actually I was looking for somewhere a little bigger.'

'Well, it's a disappointment, but I understand.'

'Alban! Hello. *Will* you stop doing that? Please! At least inside?'

'Hi, cuz.' Alban raises one hand. 'Hi, ah, small children.'

They're met in the grand hall by Haydn, who has been drafted in as the family member least likely to make a terrible mess of the accommodation and general hospitality arrangements, even though the house does have a manager who is perfectly used to doing this sort of thing. As they enter, four or five waist-high children of indeterminate gender are in the act of running hollering down the stairs, circuiting a large, sturdy octagonal table in the centre of the hall and then dashing out through the front doors. Alban watches them go, hand still raised in unacknowledged greeting. He shrugs.

Haydn blinks through his glasses at Verushka, who stands on her heels, hands behind her back, smiling at him, bathed in late-afternoon sunlight filtered through the double-height stained glass windows. 'And this must be . . .' Haydn looks down at his clipboard, riffling through pages.

'It's all right, I'm not staying,' Verushka says, stepping up to him

258

and sticking out her hand. 'Verushka Graef. You must be Haydn. How do you do.'

'Yes. Pleased to meet you. So, you're not staying?'

'Just passing through.'

'I'm staying,' Alban says helpfully, watching a couple of workmen move a large plant in a weighty pot to the stairs and then start heaving it upwards, one deliberate step at a time.

'Yes,' Haydn says, looking at his clipboard list again. 'Bad news or good?' he starts to ask Alban, then looks, surprised, at Verushka. 'Passing through?' he asks, incredulous. 'To where?'

'Further north,' she tells him. 'This is only Sutherland, after all.'

'Huh,' Haydn says, unclipping a pen and scoring Alban's name through. 'But it was the Vikings called it that.'

'And Greenland Greenland,' Verushka agrees, staring up at the panelled ceiling with its emblazoned shields and pendulous gilded doodahs like giant pine cones. 'Those wacky Vikings.'

'What was that about bad news, Haydn?' Alban asks, putting his bag down on the parquet.

'Oh, you're sharing with Fielding.'

'Does he know?'

'Not yet.'

'Does he snore?' Verushka asks.

'Not as far as I know,' Haydn says.

She nods her head at Alban, says, 'He does,' and walks off a little way to admire a huge brass dinner gong, flicking it with one blunt fingernail. 'Do you get gong tuners?' she murmurs.

'Do I snore, really?' Alban asks, genuinely surprised.

The workmen get the giant plant to the top of the stairs and start rolling the pot along the gallery.

'Well, that's Fielding's problem,' Haydn says.

Verushka glances back at Alban, waggles one flat hand. 'Very softly. Quite sweet really. Can't imagine you'll wake up because Fielding's trying to smother you with a pillow.' She looks at Haydn, frowning. 'You have any spare ear plugs?'

Alban crosses his arms, looks at her. 'So. Don't let us keep you.'

She gives him her best shit-eating grin. 'You're welcome, it was on my way.'

He smiles and walks up to her, taking her in his arms. 'Yeah, thank you for the lift. Seriously. It was great. Very much appreciated.'

'My pleasure,' she says, and kisses him. He kisses back.

'I'd say get a room,' Haydn tells them, walking past, 'but I can't help.' He sits down heavily on a padded leather chair with corkscrew wooden uprights. He looks through the sheets of paper, shaking his head.

'Problem?' Alban asks.

'Trying to keep the older people on the ground or first,' Haydn says. 'But it's a struggle.'

Alban disengages himself from Verushka and walks over to Haydn. 'We must have a belfry you could allocate to Win, no?' he suggests (Verushka notices he takes a very quick look round the hall, stairs and gallery before saying it). The workmen with the plant have disappeared.

Verushka considers saying something on the lines of, I'm a mathematician; maybe I can help, but decides against it on the grounds that this sort of levity has been taken seriously in the past and led only to embarrassment and disappointment all round.

'Ha, ha,' Haydn says, though he takes a look round, too.

Verushka shakes her head, unseen.

'All the Americans arrive tomorrow,' Haydn says, looking at his last sheet on the clipboard. 'I've tried to give the Spraint people the rooms with the best views.'

'What,' Alban asks, 'to compensate for theirs?'

Haydn frowns, blinks, opens his mouth to speak, but then both men look towards the far side of the main staircase from Verushka as a door creaks open. Two enormous shaggy grey dogs – Irish wolfhounds, Verushka is fairly sure – lope in, heads down, and go snuffling up to Alban and Haydn. Haydn grimaces and holds his clipboard up out of the way. Alban grins and ruffles their ears and coats. One animal sees her and pads across.

'That's Gilbey,' Alban tells Verushka. 'Or Plymouth.' He looks at Haydn. 'Jamieson; he still around?'

Haydn shakes his head. 'Dead.'

'There you are; a spirit now. Anyway,' Alban says, 'they're harmless.'

'Uh-huh.' Verushka pats the giant hound on the head, which is about level with her sternum. She has seen full-grown dogs smaller than this thing's head. Shetland ponies are a couple of hands smaller, if also broader. The first dog raises its nose then goes bounding upstairs. Hers chooses to wander off. It collapses untidily behind the giant gong and starts snoring almost instantly.

'Ah, Lauren,' Haydn says. 'Oh! Win. There you are.'

An oldish woman and a very old woman appear from the same direction as the wolfhounds. Lauren is a reasonably preserved sixty, in slacks and a navy sweater, still with a hint of brown in her hair. Win, the soon-to-be birthday girl, is frail-looking with thin white hair, clad in a loose tweed twin set. She's stooped and clutching a tall wooden walking stick in her right hand.

Lauren leaves Win's side, greets and quickly kisses Alban and then asks, 'Did a plant come through here? And two chaps?'

Alban and Haydn both point. 'Upstairs.'

'Damn.' She shakes her head, and with one hand on the banister rail runs up the stairs. Halfway up, she sees Verushka looking at her through the banisters; she smiles briefly and mouths Hello, then she disappears along the gallery, brogues clumping.

'Alban, Alban,' Gran Win says, straightening a little and accepting a kiss on both cheeks. 'You've come. Thank you so much. Will you be here for my birthday, too?'

'Of course, Gran. That's the main reason.'

'Oh, well, people say that, but . . .' Win catches sight of Verushka, turns her head a fraction more and frowns. 'Yes? Can we help you?'

Verushka walks forward and smiles generously. 'Oh, I doubt it.'

Win looks to Alban.

261

'Win, this is my good friend Verushka Graef. She very kindly drove me all the way here from Glasgow.'

Verushka nods. 'How do you do.'

Win looks uncertain. 'Yes, hello. Haydn, do we—?'

'I'm just passing through, ma'am,' Verushka says, before Haydn can answer. 'Mountains to climb.' Win looks at her in a way that causes her to add, 'Literal rather than metaphorical.'

'Oh. I see,' Win says. 'Well, can you at least stay for dinner?'

Verushka glances at Alban and says, 'Thanks. I kind of have my heart set on a foil pouch of reconstituted chicken curry spooned through a midge net, but . . .'

'Oh, please, do stay for dinner,' Win says, her hand on the stick shaking slightly. She glances at Haydn, who is starting to look worried. 'And I'm sure we can put you up for at least one night . . .'

Alban is smiling at her. Good enough, Verushka decides. 'Well, that's very kind,' she says. 'I'd love to.'

Behind his glasses, Haydn closes his eyes. His jaw clenches tight. Then his eyes flick open. He glances at his clipboard. Verushka is ahead of him.

'Inverlochy,' she tells him.

'Yes, of course! Fielding's not here until tomorrow!' Haydn says. 'Splendid!' He looks up at Verushka, gaze swivelling between her and Alban, worried again. 'How good friends . . . ?'

'Sufficiently,' Verushka assures him, taking Alban's arm.

From the room, high on the fourth, attic floor, where once the house's servants lived, the view extends across the back lawn, over the old walled kitchen garden on its southerly slope to the woods, looking down the glen between the twin lines of hills disappearing to the south-east, the landlocked loch – Loch Garve or Loch Garbh according to which map you chose to consult – unseen throughout the milder months from April to October behind a screen of leaves. In the winter, through the net of bared branches, it glitters sometimes under the slanting low-season light.

To the north is a steep hillside of grass and scree and a slanted line of cliff, hiding the upper ramparts of Beinn Leòid. A stream runs off the edge of the furthest, highest part of the cliff. Today, the waterfall catches the light against the darker rocks beyond. Alban remembers looking at the waterfall once, in spring, half a dozen years ago, in a momentary break of ragged sunlight between crushing falls of pounding rain and sleet with a storm blowing a high wind up the glen and howling around the old house.

The wind caught the waterfall that day, bending it back on itself and forcing the water rearing up in a great wind-supported near-circular wave, dumping it in unsteady, billowing veils and lumps back on to the moor it was attempting to fall from. It was like the most fabulous elemental battle between air, water and gravity and he recalls standing at the window in the drawing room, watching this chaos with a feeling of almost sexual excitement. Part of him wanted to run out into the storm, let the rain soak him and the wind buffet him and be part of it all. A more sober part was deeply glad of the roof over his head, the fire in the broad grate and the ancient bulk of the cast-iron radiators sited under each window, the pipes as thick as his arm, gurgling with water and rust or sand or something in them that made them tinkle and rustle.

Then, the family had been at Garbadale for a similar reason to the one that had brought them here, now.

Then it had been about selling off just part of the company. Should they sell any of it, and if so, how much? At the time he'd been against any sale, but was already starting to question his own commitment to the family and the firm. Leaving – resigning – had been on his mind lately. It was obvious early on that a majority of family members/shareholders were quite gung-ho for selling anything up to a 49.5 per cent share to Spraint Corp, and he had kind of withdrawn from the argument. His last contribution had been to suggest that they didn't sell more than 20 per cent.

Subsequently he'd spent a couple of the discussion sessions and

Spraint presentations away from the house, out on the hill with Neil McBride, the Garbadale estate manager.

'Ah, it's all changing. We can see it here. The salmon and brown trout, they're mostly gone. And we don't get the winters we used to. I've got clothes and winter gear I just never wear – well, maybe a day a year or something – because it's milder all the time. Windier, too, and cloudier, less sunlight. I've spotted that, here; with this. Having a hard time persuading any bugger it's actually happening, but I'm sure it is.'

Neil was a shortish guy with a ruddy, outdoors face and hair – and a flourishing moustache – the colour of old bracken. He was in his late fifties and his face looked it because he'd spent so much of his life outside, though he moved like a man half his age.

'That what this does?' Alban asked.

'Aye. It measures sunlight, basically.'

They'd driven Neil's battered Land Rover up a short track off the road to Sloy to the top of a small rise where the estate's weather station was situated. The sun had just set. The day had been breezy but the evening was becoming calm. Long, soft-looking lines of clouds led off across the dappled scape of mountains and hills and moor and loch, going pink as the sunset swivelled west over the Atlantic.

Neil had been taking the rainfall, barometric pressure, wind and sunlight measurements here since shortly after he started work at Garbadale, twenty-five years earlier. He logged all the data – in a set of old ledgers, at first; more recently on a PC – and sent the results to the Met Office daily.

Alban liked the sunlight-measuring device. It was a post with a spherical metal cage on the top at about chest height. A sphere of glass sat in the centre of the cradle. Behind the orb, situated with its centre near due north, a long strip of special light-sensitive paper lay inside a curved glass cover wrapped around the framework. The glass sphere acted as a lens, concentrating the sunlight that fell upon it and directing it on to the paper so that it burned a brown trace across the time-graphed surface, providing a record of how much clear sun there had been that day.

It was, Alban thought, like something out of a magician's workshop, an ancient instrument that worked to this day, that still did good science and provided reliable data and yet looked like it could have come straight from an alchemist's secret chamber.

'I thought the world was warming?' he asked, studying the instrument carefully as Neil changed the paper.

'It is. Certainly warming here. But there's more cloud, so it's dimming, too. Cloud keeps the heat in, so it's all of a piece.' Neil put the strip of paper for that day into an envelope and stuck that in his ancient waxed jacket. He clipped a new strip of paper into place. 'There.' He looked up and around at the hills and moors. The sea was just visible, off to the north-west beyond the low hills.

'Aye, I remember sitting up . . . There,' Neil said, turning and pointing at a hill a kilometre or so away to the south. 'Summer I first started. Seventy-nine, I suppose. Delighted to be here. Knew I'd stay till I was pensioned off or thrown out or died on the job. Loved the place. Running away from the big bad city I was; never liked cities, crowds. Came here, thought, well, whatever else they might do to concrete over the fields and parks and knock down all the lovely old buildings and cover the cities with smog, at least they'll never touch here. The hills will stay the same as they've always been – I mean, I wasnae daft, I knew they'd been covered in trees once and now they were bare, but I meant the hills themselves wouldn't change – the weather, the climate, the rain and the wind, none of that would change. That gave me heart. That really did. You felt, well, something's secure, something's not going to get changed.' He shook his head, took off his worn-looking cap and rubbed his balding head with one hand before replacing the cap. 'But you wouldnae credit it, the stuff that's changing now. The different birds, the game fish disappearing – that's mostly the fish farms and them being caught out to sea, mind, but all the same – the warmer winters, *wetter* winters,

higher wind speeds. Lot less snow. It's all changing. Even the sky.'
He nodded up. 'We're changing the sky and the weather and the sea.
I'm telling you, we're screwing up the whole bloody planet. We just
don't know our own strength.'

'We certainly don't know our own stupidity,' Alban said.

'Aye, we're too daft to know we're daft.'

'The hills will be the same, though,' Alban said. 'The rock; that
won't change. There might be trees again or different ground cover,
but the shape of the hills themselves, the geology; that won't change.'

'Ah well, that's about the only thing that won't.'

'Might not even be us who's doing it,' Alban suggested. 'There
are natural cycles of climate change. Could just be one of them.'

'Aye, maybe.' Neil sounded sceptical. 'But I keep up wi' all this
stuff, Alban. It's part of the job to look ahead, especially when you're
planting trees that might last for centuries, but I find it interesting
anyway, and I'll tell you; the people who'll tell you the jury's still
out on this stuff are clutching at straws, or they're the kind of people
that just can't stand to admit they've been wrong. Either that or
they're just outright liars, back pockets stuffed with dollars from the
big oil companies.' He gave a snort. 'There's just a tiny wee chance,
getting tinier and weer all the time, that they're right, and if we all
try to cut back hard on greenhouse gases and all that, then we're
going to waste a lot of money for no good reason.' Neil shrugged.
'Aye, well. What a shame. But if they're wrong, we waste the whole
fucking planet – scuse my French – and the way it works, once your
positive feedback kicks in and it all goes runaway, no amount of
money will put it back together again. That's what's so stupid, that's
what's so short-sighted about it. All about the short term. All about
increasing shareholder value. Cannae do anything that goes against
the shareholders, eh?'

'We do tend to panic otherwise.'

Neil let slip a small smile. 'Aye, well, I won't tell you my thoughts
on the shareholders.'

'Ah, go on. Won't go any further. Promise.'

266

'Well, I don't mean people like you, not the family firm and such, but sometimes I think, Fuck the shareholders.' He gave a slight forward nod, as though to say, There you are.

'Fuck the shareholders? Never had you down as a revolutionary Communist, Neil.'

'Aye, well, I'm no' that either. And I'm sure there's much cleverer folk than me who'd explain how shareholders are just the total be-all and end-all of everything and they're the ones who'll make it all all right again, through the market, and all that.'

'I don't doubt there are,' Alban agreed.

'Still think it's probably shite, though.' Neil smiled grimly.

Alban wondered at the regretful anger that Neil seemed to be trying to control. 'Well, you could be right.'

'You don't have any children, that right?'

'None I know of,' Alban said. 'You've got a couple, haven't you?'

'One of each. Grown up now. Kirsty's just made us grandparents again.'

'Oh. Congratulations.'

'Aye, thanks. But they'll be the ones that have to clean up the mess we make.'

'Jeez, Neil. I was thinking of having kids myself one day. You're putting me off here.'

Neil slapped him on the arm. 'Ah, dinnae mind me. Come on; I'll let you buy me a pint at the Sloy Arms.' They got back into the Land Rover.

Verushka slides her arms round his waist as he stands looking up at the thin little waterfall high on the cliff. (Gravity always won, the water always won; the wind only blew the water back up to where it must fall from one way or the other, between gusts or after the storm had abated.)

'You okay?'

'Yeah. You?'

'Exceptionally. Sure you don't mind me staying?'

'Mind?' He turns to her to put his arms round her, hug her. 'Fucking delighted.' He nods at the two single beds in the room. 'Sorry it's a twin.'

'Hey-ho. I suspect we'll manage.'

'Do I really snore?'

'Gently. Melodiously. Charmingly. You reassured yet? I could go on.'

As well as Win and Haydn, Verushka is introduced to Aunt Clara, Uncle Kennard (Managing Director) and his wife Renée, Uncle Graeme and his wife Lauren, cousin Fabiole and his wife Deborah and their children Daniel and Gemma, cousin Lori and her husband Lutz (from Germany) and their children Kyle and Phoebe, Aunt Linda and her husband Perce (Brand Manager), cousin Steve (the container port cranes guy – just flown in for the weekend from Dubai, where he lives and where he works almost all the time now), Aunt Kathleen (Finance Officer) and her husband Lance, their daughter Claire, her partner Chay, cousin Emma, her husband Mark, their children Shona and Bertie, as well as corporate lawyer George Hissop of Messrs Gudell, Futre & Bolk, his legal assistant Gudrun Selves, Neil McBride the estate manager, Neil Durril the house manager and Sandy Lassiter, head cook.

Andy (Company Secretary) and Leah, sis Cory and her husband Dave plus their children Lachlan and Charlotte, Aunt Lizzie (twin of Linda), Fielding with Beryl and Doris plus cousin Rachel with her husband also called Mark and their two children Ruthven and Foin and cousin Louise, plus cousin Steve's wife Tessa, her son Rune, his partner Penning and their baby Hannah, not to mention at least two Spraint high-ups – probably two guys called Feaguing and Fromlax – plus their highly pared-down micro-retinues of two flunkies each are all due to arrive tomorrow.

'Got all that?' Alban asked her, looking up from Haydn's clipboard, grinning.

'Yup.'

He took a step back. 'Really?'

'Course not,' Verushka said, going to slap him on the upper arm but pulling the blow at the last moment. 'You think because I'm a mathematician I've got a photographic memory or something?'

Verushka and Aunt Clara are talking:

'I don't understand. What can that mean, "Where are the numbers?"'

'I think it means, Do they exist as abstract entities – like physical laws, as functions of the nature of the universe; or are they cultural constructs? Do they exist without somebody thinking them?'

'This sounds awfully complicated.' They are sitting together at dinner that evening. The dining room is wood-panelled, quite high-ceilinged, and very long. Verushka thinks it's a little like being in an enormous coffin, but has thought better of actually saying this aloud. '*Awfully* complicated,' Clara says again. 'My husband might have understood this, I doubt I shall.' Clara's husband James had died of a heart attack in 2001 and Clara inherited all his shares.

'I don't know about complicated. Esoteric, maybe.'

'Esoteric,' Graeme Wopuld says. Alban's Uncle Graeme, the Norfolk farmer and husband of Aunt Lauren, has been trying to get Verushka to talk to him for the last twenty minutes, without noticeable success. 'What a wonderful word, don't you think?' Graeme is a craggy-looking fellow with wispy, sandy hair, extensive eyebrows and full lips he feels the need to lick rather a lot.

'Isn't it?' Verushka agrees, glancing at him before turning back to Clara, who says,

'And so, what do you think?'

'About where are the numbers?'

'Yes. What's your answer?'

('What was the question?' Graeme asks.)

'I think I have to put it in the form of another question,' Verushka tells Clara.

'I was somewhat afraid of that.'

'Alban got me thinking about it this way.'

'Alban? Really?'

'Yes. He said, "Where you left them," which is pretty much just flippant, but there's a wee grain of possibility there and so my answer to the question, "Where are the numbers?" is, "Where do you think?" See what I'm doing there?'

'Not really. That sounds flippant too.'

'Well, it sounds it at first, but if you take it out of the context of flippancy and treat it as a new question in its own right, you're asking, Where does your thinking happen?'

'In your brain?'

'Well, yes, so if you use one question as an answer to the first, you're saying that the numbers exist in your head.'

'Mine feels rather tight at the moment. Like it's about to burst with numbers and odd questions.'

'Yeah, I get that a lot. Anyway. It's more interesting than just saying, "The numbers are in your head," because otherwise why put it in the form of a question at all? Why not just say that?'

'You mean, say, "The numbers are in your head"?'

'Yes. Because then it becomes a question about boundaries.'

'Boundaries.'

'When you think about numbers, are you using a little bit of the universe to think about *it*, or is *it* using a little bit of itself to think about itself, or, even, about something – about these entities called numbers – that might be said to exist outside of itself, if one uses one of the less ultimately inclusive definitions of the word "universe"?' Verushka sits back, triumphant. 'See?'

'Not really,' Clara admits. 'And my old head is rather starting to spin.'

'Well, to be fair,' Verushka agrees, 'it's an incomplete answer. But I like the direction it's going in.'

'This all sounds very fascinating,' Graeme says.

'It is, isn't it?' Verushka says brightly before turning back to Clara as she says,

270

'And you do this for a living?'

'Not this part, no; this is just for fun.'

'Good heavens.'

'May I?' Verushka offers to top up Clara's glass of red.

'Oh, thank you.'

'Any left?' Graeme asks, holding out his glass. Verushka hands him the bottle.

'Sophie's your daughter, isn't she?' she says to Clara.

'Yes, she is. Arriving tomorrow, we're told.'

'She and Alban. They were . . . They were fond of each other once, weren't they?'

'Yes. Well, they thought they were. They were far too young of course. And they are first cousins, and, well, there are sound reasons for not breeding that close. I've been breeding Labs since I lost James – my mother did the same – and you learn the pitfalls.'

'You think there was a danger of them breeding?' Verushka says, putting her hand to her mouth and widening her eyes to indicate shock.

'My dear,' Clara says, and pats the other woman's forearm, 'it's all a long time ago and a lot of water's flown under the bridge since then. It's not really a subject I care to talk much about. There's really no point.'

'I see.' Verushka smiles. 'Well, I'm leaving early tomorrow so I probably shan't get to meet Sophie, but you must be looking forward to seeing her again.'

'Oh yes,' Clara nods slowly. Her face is deeply lined, her red hair thinning, scalp visible beneath, though she is not yet in her seventies. 'Though in a way I stopped recognising her a long time ago.'

Verushka hesitates at this, but then leans close to the older woman, gently holding one elbow. 'I'm sure she's looking forward to seeing you again.'

'I do hope so.'

* * *

271

Alban was standing minding his own business in the drawing room after the meal – VG was talking animatedly with Kennard, Haydn and Chay – when Aunt Lauren came up to him.

'Alban?'

He was half in, half out of the curtains shielding one tall window, looking up at the distant, moonlit cliff and the white trace of the waterfall. The forecast wasn't good. The weather hadn't broken yet, though he could see a deep shadow of black cloud spreading slowly from the west. He let the curtains fall back.

'Lauren. Hi.'

'Won't you come and talk to Win? She'd love to see you.'

Win was sitting over by the fire at one end of the room.

'How could I disobey?' he sighed. He followed Lauren, pulled a seat over and sat by Win in her easy chair. Lauren turned to talk to somebody else. Aunt Linda – a vision of florid pink corpulence who always reminded Alban of the late Queen Mother, though her tipple was brandy rather than gin – was sitting in the matching wing-backed easy chair on the other side of the fireplace from Win, but she seemed to have fallen asleep.

'Ah, Alban.' Win held out her almost empty whisky tumbler. 'Would you be an absolute dear and refresh this for me? Indulge an old woman.'

'Of course, Win.'

He returned, presented her with the glass.

'Oh, Alban,' she said, 'are you trying to get me drunk?' She shook her head.

He held his hand back out towards the glass. 'I'll drink some of it for you if it's too much.'

Win tutted. She tested the whisky. 'It might need a little more water,' she said. She held the glass out to him. 'Would you mind –'

'I have some here,' he said, holding out his own glass. He'd switched to water.

'Oh. Well. If you— All right.'

Once she was happy with her drink, had been reassured that her walking stick was to hand, a log had been added to the fire and

272

Alban had removed the brandy *ballon* from Aunt Linda's slack fingers – in case it fell and smashed on the hearth – Win was finally ready to talk.

'Your young lady seems perfectly pleasant,' she said.

'Actually she's a couple of years older than me,' Alban told her.

'Really? Well, one's tastes change over the years, I suppose.'

'And how are you keeping, Win? I didn't really get a chance for a full update on all the latest aches and pains.'

'Now, Alban. You don't really want to hear an old woman complaining about all the things wrong with her.'

He smiled with his mouth. 'Sorry to be giving up the old place?' He looked away to the far end of the room, over most of his family, chattering and drinking.

'I'll miss it,' she said. 'I wish we'd buried Bert somewhere else, now.' Old Bert's grave was on a small circular island at the near end of the loch, just a few metres offshore. Alban remembered that Neil McBride had been unhappy with the choice; he was fairly sure the island had been the site of a Bronze Age crannog and should be left undisturbed until it was properly excavated, but Win had wanted her husband buried there and there hadn't been a lot Neil could do about it. 'Maybe Lydcombe would have been better.' She sighed. 'Still. His tomb will stay here. We'll have some sort of continuing presence, something to show for our ownership. We did build the place after all. I've put it into the conditions of sale that it's never interfered with. The grave, I mean.'

'Any such proviso in the contract with Spraint?'

'None that I know of, dear. Why, do you think there ought to be?'

'Not particularly. They'd baulk.'

'They will be paying us for our name, if the sale goes through. That will go on.'

'For a time, I guess.'

'I am minded to vote against, you know, Alban,' she told him. 'Don't cast me as the wicked witch, dear. I've done what I could to muster support for at least showing a bit of resistance. It's mostly your generation that's showing all the enthusiasm for selling.'

He looked back at the rest of the room. 'I kind of thought you'd be on their side.'

'Did you? Well, I'm glad that even at my advanced age I can still surprise you.'

'You've always been good at that, Win.'

'Have I? I've always tried to be rather predictable and dependable, to tell the truth. I didn't think being surprising was really one of my strengths.'

'The Spraint people, what time are we expecting them tomorrow?'

'I think they're expected about noon. They're arriving by helicopter, apparently. That should be exciting.'

'What about the rest of our lot?'

'Oh, I dare say they'll appear in dribs and drabs over the course of the day. I think everybody's flying to Inverness and then taking cars. Then there's Fielding and the two old girls. Haydn has a better idea of who's arriving when.'

'We are going to have a chance for a private meeting, just the family, the shareholders, before the EGM, aren't we?'

'Do you think we should?'

'Yes, I think we should, or have a formal part of the EGM without the Spraint people present; whatever.'

The Extraordinary General Meeting was scheduled for the Saturday evening before dinner, with the Spraint people present. Alban wanted to be able to get everybody in the family together – certainly all the voting shareholders – so they could discuss the proposed sell-out together before the EGM, without the Spraint guys around. It seemed blindingly obvious to him that they should all have some sort of idea what they felt individually and in groups – pro, anti, undecided, whatever – before it all kicked off in public, just to see what sort of united front it might be possible to present to their potential buyers, but when he'd talked to Haydn about this he'd seemed distracted and vague and suggested taking the matter up with Win.

'Yes, a sort of meeting before the meeting,' Win said. 'I suppose we ought. Yes, I'm sure we can arrange that.'

'And would you say something?'

'What, in front of everybody?'

'Yes.'

'Oh, I don't think so. What do you think I ought to say?'

'Say what you feel, what you think. Say whether you're for or against the sale.'

'I've told you – I'm against it. Well, I think.'

'You kind of have to make your mind up, Win, by tomorrow.'

'Don't rush me, Alban, please. I'm old. I rather want to see how everybody feels. I mean, if they're all going to say yes, what's the point in me jamming a spanner in the works?'

'They're not all going to say yes. I've already talked to a few people.'

'You have? Well, yes, of course you have.'

'It's not a done deal, Win.'

'I suppose not.' Win looked thoughtful.

'If you feel the family should keep the firm, Gran, say so; tell people.'

She turned to him and smiled. She looked old but still bright, her skin wrinkled but soft in the firelight. 'Well, I shall, perhaps, I dare say.'

'Win,' he said, clearing his throat, 'you're sort of the keeper of the family archives and photographs and so on, aren't you?'

'Oh, I suppose so. What about them?'

'I'd like to take a look at some of them.'

'Really? Which ones?'

'From when Irene and Andy first met, when all the brothers were in London and you were there too, back in the late Sixties.'

'Oh,' Win said, and looked up and away for a few moments. 'I think they're all packed up already. I'm so sorry. Perhaps once I'm settled again.'

'Ah,' he said. 'That's a pity.'

275

Win was gesturing to somebody. Aunt Lauren came over and stood, bending, at Win's side. 'Lauren, dear,' Win said. 'I'm ever so tired now. This fire is so hot. I'm sweltering. Do you think you could see me up to my room?'

'Of course, Win,' Lauren said.

'I'm sorry, Alban,' Win said as Lauren helped her from her chair and he presented her with her stick. 'Thanks, dearest,' she said to Lauren.

'Good night, Gran,' he said.

'Night-night, Alban.'

He'd already talked to various of his relations before dinner. After a little thought, he'd deliberately targeted the ones that were least likely to be fully in play following the meal. Now he started doing something he kind of hated, which was working the room. It was a horrible-sounding phrase and it could be a pretty grisly process at the best of times. He wasn't sure if having to do it with your own family – well, with his own family – made it better or worse. During this process he kept bumping into Aunt Lauren, who appeared to be doing something very similar.

He saw Neil McBride and decided to take a break from the family business stuff.

'Neil. How's the sunlight?'

'What's that?' Neil looked merry. He was holding a large whisky. Neil was dressed in his Sunday-best suit, tie still knotted.

'The sunlight. That funny glass thing that tells you—'

'Oh, I was right! Did you no' see the *Horizon* programme? About Global Dimming?'

'Missed it. Sorry. Why, were you on it?'

'No! Dinnae be daft. But I was right. No' the first to spot it – some bloke down in Australia noticed it before I did – but the point is it's accepted now, it's science, no' just some daft punter in a deer-stalker on a Highland estate havering about it. So there you are.'

'They should call it the McBride effect.'

'Aye, that'll be right.' He drank from his glass. 'So, you still foresting away? I've got a few hundred Sitka need chopping if you've brought your chainsaw.'

'I got invalided out, Neil.' He held up a couple of fingers. 'White finger.'

'Christ, you're kidding.'

''Fraid not.'

'I thought it was all done with dirty great machines these days, no?'

'Yeah, a lot is, but not all, and we were the steep slope specialists.'

'Must have had ye on hell of an old gear. I've an old Huskie that vibrates like a bastard – scuse my whatsit – but I've never had any problems.' Neil looked at his own right hand with an exaggeratedly worried expression.

'Aye, but you're not handling one of the things day-in, day-out for months on end. I worked out there was one time in Kielder we were cutting every single day, uninterrupted, for eighty-five days solid; twelve weeks without even a Sunday off.'

'Jesus! Must have been a hell of a bonus at the end of that one.'

'Aye, well. That and we'd all got barred from the only pub within twenty miles on the second night.'

Neil laughed. 'So what're you going to do with yourself now then?'

'Don't know. I was doing chainsaw sculptures and sold a few; that's out the window now.'

'Anyway, Alban, nobody makes a living selling chainsaw sculptures.'

'No, I guess not.'

'Back to the family firm?'

'We're probably going to be selling up to these Spraint people.'

'They might still want you.'

'I doubt that, and anyway I'm not interested. Had my fill of life in a suit.'

'Aye.' Neil nodded. 'I see you couldn't be bothered with a tie this evening.'

'Only comes out for funerals.'

'Think they'll – well, you'll – sell, then, aye?'

'I think it's going to be tighter than some people were expecting, but . . . I wouldn't be surprised. What about you? You staying with the estate?'

'Ah, we'll see. It'll be up to the new owners.'

'You going to be okay? I mean, if they want to bring in somebody else?'

'I'll be fine. Got a great reference from the old girl if I need to relocate, and I've always got the house in Sloy; that's no' tied. Spare room if you ever want to come stay.'

'Cheers. Might well take you up on that. That's very kind. Surprised they haven't asked you to put people up this weekend.'

'Na, no need. You could always just open up the north wing.'

'They're not using that?' He'd thought that even though what felt like half the developed world seemed to be staying at Garbadale this weekend the old place ought to have been big enough to swallow everybody without Haydn having to do any room-juggling. Now he thought about it, he'd never been in the north wing, not even as a child.

'Bit damp,' Neil said, nose wrinkling. 'No central heating. Liable to wake up to the sound of wee scampery things scurrying about during the night. You'd have to start setting traps, and making fires in grates, and then it'd be pot luck which chimneys are blocked by bird nests. You'd have to be pretty desperate. That your bird, by the way?' Neil nodded at Verushka, standing laughing with Aunt Kathleen.

'Close personal friend.'

'Your bird, then,' Neil said.

'Yeah, my bird.'

'She's a cracker. I'd hold on to that one.'

'I bet you would.'

'Haw haw.'

'Anyway, thanks for the advice.'

'Any time.'

'To trade fairs, not fair trade.'

Win raised her champagne flute. It glittered in the light of the circular private dining room. Alban looked around the slick facets of the carved crystal held in his grandmother's hand, gazing out through the tall floor-to-ceiling windows into the warm darkness of the Johannesburg night and the lines of golden light beyond; the startlingly bright clusters of towering sodium vapour masts and curved, swooping highway lines of new development crowding out a distant hillside picked out with tiny scattered lights, all random and dull.

There was a murmur round the circular table and much clinking of glasses. After she'd drunk to her own toast, Win looked at him. 'Alban. You're not drinking?'

'Sometimes I just don't have the stomach for it, Gran. You'll have to excuse me.'

'Have I?' She smiled frostily. 'Well, if you're not feeling well . . .' She nodded and he realised he was being dismissed. He wondered if she thought he meant 'excuse me' in the sense of 'I have to go'. Or if she was getting rid of him for not presenting a united front; for dissent. It didn't matter. He didn't care. He wanted away from this crowd of ghastly boring loud-mouth wanks anyway. Seize the chance.

He patted his belly as he rose, placing his napkin on the table. 'Bit unsettled. Think I will have an early night.' He nodded at their host, a Spraint high-up called Hursch. 'Thank you for dinner.'

The next morning he was summoned to her suite for breakfast. The room looked out over Sandton Square and the spread of clean, sparkling buildings clustered there then – beyond – the view took in distant townships grouped around the highways out of greater Johannesburg, indistinct in the hazy light of a warm new morning.

A couple of hotel staff were quietly setting out breakfast. He took a seat, smiled at the two servants.

Win appeared from her bedroom after the two staff exited. She was dressed in a crisp-looking business suit and a silk blouse, her hair freshly done and her make-up film quality. She stood behind her seat, looking at Alban, who made a noise of apology, got up and held her chair for her. Win sat down, flicking her napkin as though trying to create a sonic boom. Alban resumed his seat.

They looked at each other across gleaming crockery, cutlery and a large central dome of chromed steel.

Eventually, Win said, 'I am, in case you're wondering, rather expecting an apology.'

'Are you? For what?' He could feel anger rising inside him, and a sort of ancient legacy of shame. Part of him wanted to start shouting at her now, while another part, a part he thoroughly despised, wanted to say sorry as quickly as possible and as sincerely as he could this side of abjection, just so that everything would be all right again.

Only everything would never really be all right again. At Garbadale, a few months earlier, he'd lost the argument about selling out to Spraint. The family firm was now 25 per cent owned by the big US software Corp, and whatever connection and commitment and loyalty he'd felt towards the company was all starting to trickle away now. Lately the trickle seemed to be swelling into a flood.

How quickly all that stuff dissipated. And how depressingly little it all seemed to have meant. He could still do the job, though these days he was just going through the motions and didn't really believe in what he was doing any more, but even that was no source of relief. On the contrary, discovering that it was perfectly possible to do his job without really caring about it in the least made him feel disillusioned about all the years he'd spent doing it when it had meant something to him. What did it say about his position in the firm, what did it say about him, when any insincere corporate grin-pedlar could have done it just as well all these years? What had been the point?

He'd been made Brand Manager as well as Head of Product Development, with more money, more shares, bigger potential bonuses and a greater say in the running of the company – partly, he suspected, to compensate him after being on the losing side of the Spraint battle – but even that had felt hollow, like he was being thrown a few disposable scraps; an acknowledgement that none of it really mattered anyway.

He knew in himself it was only a matter of time before he left. He'd already written a series of draft resignation letters, though he'd always deleted them without saving them to disk. Maybe he'd be fired instead. Win was just the girl to do it. It was late 1999 and the last thing he felt like doing was partying.

'For what?' Win quoted back at him, eyes wide. 'For not joining in a toast, for that weaselly smart remark about not having the stomach for it. For your whole attitude throughout the meal. In fact, for your attitude this weekend, and recently in general. I think an apology is required. I'd love to hear your reasons to the contrary, if you'd care to air them.'

At moments like this, Alban thought, Win did not look her seventy-four years. She looked ten, maybe twenty years younger. It was as though anger and indignation energised her, kept her young. He did something he'd been doing with her for the last few years at such moments, stepping back inside himself and looking at her as objectively as he could, ignoring the perfect make-up and the power-dressing suit (a bit Eighties, anyway, he thought, almost slightly *Dallas*, if you were inclined to be particularly critical, which he was). He looked, instead, at the loose, chickeny skin at the foot of her throat, the wrinkled hands and wrists, the slight sag under the eyes (though, annoyingly, if also impressively, the consensus amongst those in the family who knew and cared about such things was that the old girl had never had any cosmetic surgery). And that looked like make-up on the backs of her hands. Maybe Win was disguising liver spots.

Had he been displaying a bad attitude during the weekend at the trade fair? He didn't think he had, any more than he thought he'd been anything other than good company at the dinner, right until he jumped ship after the cruel and unusual toast. The only even vaguely controversial thing he could recall saying earlier was something to the effect that if one was being excruciatingly politically correct one would choose the locally-produced wines to go with dinner from post-apartheid vintages. He hadn't even pitched it as a recommendation, let alone a criticism, just an early observation, mostly to see how the assembled Spraint-ocrats would react and so gauge their position on the political spectrum (they'd looked mystified, so default right wing as well as rather dim).

On the other hand, if anybody was going to notice a lack of conviction in one of her family and/or one of her company underlings, it was Win. This, he was all too painfully aware, went right back to Lydcombe, to the looks he and Sophie had been exchanging over the dinner table, thinking, stupidly as it turned out, that their gran would be as oblivious as James and Clara to what was going on under their noses. They'd been woefully wrong then and you could argue that they'd both been paying for it one way or another ever since. Maybe he hadn't been hiding his disillusion with the job so well after all and Win, predator that she was, had spotted a weakness in the herd. He was the wildebeest she had singled out and was going to try and bring down.

Yes, well. Maybe, he thought, he should have done the Kruger National Park after the trade fair, not before.

Anyway; the dear, vicious old thing was waiting on an apology or reasons for not issuing one. He ought not to disappoint.

He did his best to look and sound reasonable. 'I have to say I thought the toast to trade fairs, not fair trade was uncalled for.' He took a sip of orange juice.

'That is *not* what I said.'

'Oh, I think you'll find it was exactly what you said.'

'I said, To trade fairs, not just fair trade.'

'I don't think you did, Win.'

He lifted the giant chromed bowl to reveal a steaming assort-ment of cooked breakfast material being kept warm by little burners. A slightly sulphurous scent of imperfectly combusted fuel wafted across the table. He set the chromed hemisphere down on the floor. 'Shall I serve?'

'Don't try to distract from what actually matters here,' Win said. 'This is not about a single remark, it's about your whole attitude. You were ungracious, even rude. You'd been making anti-American remarks all evening.'

'No I wasn't. I like America. The country's breathtaking.' Alban took his time inspecting the fare on offer and helped himself to a couple of thick strips of bacon. He didn't really have an appetite, but it had to be done. 'Plus I rather like Americans.' He added some mushrooms and scrambled egg to his plate. 'And if they vote for that nice Mr Gore I fully intend to go on liking them for some time to come.' He waved one hand at the breakfast stuff. 'Sure I can't tempt you?'

Win waited a little, looking at him without obvious expression, before saying, 'You know, you are not remotely as funny as you think you are, Alban.'

'I'm not trying to be funny, Win.' He nodded at the breakfast. 'Seriously. Would you like me to serve you? Otherwise, frankly, mine's getting cold.'

'Bacon, chop, kidneys,' Win said. 'Please,' she added.

Alban obliged, holding his tongue over remarks apologising for the lack of sheep's eyes or gorilla testicles.

Win looked, unimpressed, at the plate he presented her with. 'It's a little dull-looking,' she said. 'Perhaps some tomatoes.'

'Presentation matters,' he agreed, and obliged.

'I worry about you, Alban,' Win said, after they'd both taken a few silent mouthfuls.

'Do you, Win?'

'I always have. And I still do.'

'What is it that you worry about?'

'I can't tell you everything that I worry about in regard to you, Alban.' Win was, Alban decided, in one of her more portentous moods. 'But believe me, I do.'

'Okay,' he said.

'Have you ever really known what you're doing?'

Alban sat back. Well, he thought, now there's a question. 'You mean, more than anybody else?'

Win ignored this and just said, 'Have you?'

He wondered about meeting this head on. What sort of question was that, anyway? How many people could answer with an honest, 'Yes'?

'Win,' he said, putting his knife and fork down and sitting back. 'What are you looking for from me?'

'At the moment, an answer to my question.'

'Then the answer is yes. Yes, I have always known what I was doing. How about you?'

'This is not about me, Alban.'

'It seems to me it's about your attitude to me, Win.'

'And it seems to me it's about your attitude to your job, to the firm, to the family and to your life.'

'Well, that's fairly comprehensive.'

'*Have* you ever known what you're doing?'

'Win, what sort of question *is* that?' he protested. 'I mean, yes, I think I have. I've kind of known what I've been doing since I was at school, since I stuck in and made sure I passed my exams. I chose my Uni course knowing exactly what I was doing and then I joined the firm. I thought I'd done a good job. I still think I've done a good job.'

'I never thought you'd join the firm,' Win told him. She put down her cutlery. She was finished. Somehow she'd eaten everything on her plate apart from the tomatoes.

'Well, I did,' he told her.

'I never imagined you'd do Business Studies, and then when you started that course I was certain you'd chuck it in and do something more artistic.'

'Artistic?'

'You used to write poems, didn't you?'

'I was in my early teens. I thought it was mandatory.'

'Well, you surprised me,' Win admitted. She dabbed at the corners of her still perfectly lipsticked mouth with the edge of one starched napkin. 'I even wondered if you joined the firm because your cousin Sophie did.'

Christ, you fucking old bitch.

He laughed, looking away and making it obvious he was having to stifle the laugh to hide quite how preposterous this obviously was. It was, of course, completely true. That was why there was absolutely no possibility he could ever admit it to anybody, least of all to Win. He cleared his throat and sat up, arms folded. 'Well, no, Win. I was over Sophie some time before I decided what I was going to do with my life.'

'Really.' There was, somehow, no question in Win's voice. Her expression was unreadable, too. 'I thought you still felt something for her for a long time afterwards. Even up until a couple of years ago, which would imply you still might, to this day. If you're going to carry a torch for the girl for a dozen years, why not two more?'

He hated the way Win did this, starting with a supposition at one end of a sentence and ending up with it having become a given by the end, and attached to something you had to tackle. Thing was, how much did the old bat know? Had Sophie said something about the débâcle in Singapore? He'd opened his heart to the girl and admitted he still loved her, told her she was the love of his life – she still was; she always would be – but had she then told Win *that*?

Had he blown it by being drunk? Of course he'd been drunk; he was too terrified of rejection to be able to tell Sophie he still loved her when he was sober. The point was that he'd needed the drink to be able to tell her, to overcome this Brit reserve he'd managed to pick up from his family or school or through the water or his genes or something. The drink hadn't had anything to do with the feeling itself, just with the ability to express it; the feeling was there all the time, drunk or sober, asleep as well as awake. He just couldn't admit it. Not without being out of his head. Of course, the chances were he'd overdone it and come across as pathetic, needy, adolescent and immature.

He'd managed to push the incident to the back of his mind very successfully and very quickly, within a day, by the simple expedient of getting utterly mashed on a cocktail of drink and dubious drugs with Fielding. As a way of forgetting what had happened between him and Sophie, of smearing it into something too vague to be made out in his memory, it had worked almost too well. The incident was so close to the demented swirl of humid day-glo idiocy he and Fielding had indulged in that it seemed, in retrospect, like part of it; not wholly real, and the tatters of what seemed like genuine memories associated with it themselves not completely reliable either.

Had Sophie told Win? Was she that cruel, did she want to humiliate him that much? Or did he mean so little to her that she hadn't even thought about how telling Win what he'd said to her would hurt, even shame him?

Tell a half-truth. They were the easiest lies to defend. 'Win,' he said, smiling, and sounding, he hoped, eminently reasonable, 'Sophie's always going to mean something to me. I mean, she was my first love. Puppy love if you want to call it that, but it still felt intense at the time.'

'Yes, so I saw,' Win said acidly.

He knew they were talking about that last evening at Lydcombe, and Win and James discovering Sophie and him in the grass. That feeling of old shame – and an anger at feeling it – built up in him again. He controlled his breathing, tried to think his heart calm. Jesus, he'd thought this was long since brushed under the carpet; ancient history not worth raking over, by mutual consent.

'Anyway,' he said, puffing out his lower lip, sitting back and gesturing with his hands, spreading them a little before clasping them again. 'Water under the bridge.'

'It's one of those things you're not supposed to say these days, apparently; people just sneer at you or simply laugh, but it really was for your own good.' She raised her head to him a fraction, defiant, as though daring him either to sneer or laugh. 'I knew that then and I know it now. You must have hated me, Alban, I understand that.' A wintry smile. 'I suspect somewhere deep inside, you still hate me.'

Deep inside? Just under the surface, actually. And all the way through. 'Oh, Win, really—' he started.

'It would only be natural. I'm not stupid, Alban.'

No, sadly, you're not, are you?

'But I did it for the good of both of you, no matter what you might think. I'm sorry it seemed so brutal at the time. James overreacted, arguably. On the other hand, that was the worst of it over with.'

Oh no it fucking wasn't. You have no idea.

'Well, it's history now,' he told her.

She arched one eyebrow. 'Yes, as though history doesn't matter.'

'Henry Ford thought it was bunk.'

'Yes, but then that remark has become part of history.' Win shrugged delicately. 'He may not have meant what he appears to have meant, but if he did then he was a fool.' Alban looked appropriately surprised. Win smiled. 'Oh, I've met plenty of rich and successful fools, Alban. You must have encountered one or two yourself. Usually one of the things that shows how stupid they are is that they don't understand how big a part luck played in their success.'

From which I'm meant to take the point that you're no fool. 'History matters,' he agreed. 'But I am over Sophie.' He looked her in the eyes and thought, *I'm lying. I am so not over Sophie. I hate you for getting me right. I hate you for reading me like a fucking poster, you old hag. Are you reading this now? I still hate you. I'll always hate you just as I'll always love her. Call it balance.* He thought it very carefully, articulating the thoughts, the words in his mind, as though daring her to read the truth through his eyes or somehow telepathically intuit what he was thinking.

'Well, perhaps that's the reason, then,' Win said. 'But I can see a change in you, Alban.'

'Well, we're all getting older. Everybody changes.'

'Yes, of course,' Win said, one hand waving dismissively, 'but as well as that.'

Hell's teeth, maybe he should just come clean. Maybe the right thing to do was just to admit it, get it out in the open and say yes, he had changed, he was different, he didn't feel the same any more and he was already thinking about quitting. Maybe he should just say all this and hand in his resignation now, here. He'd probably have to say it some time, why not now?

Because he'd always feel he'd been bounced into it by Win, that was why. He'd never be entirely certain that it had really all been of his own volition. Well, he refused to surrender control to her. She'd taken over that time at Lydcombe, making him feel humiliated, ashamed and powerless, and he wasn't going to let her do it again. He wanted to make the decision himself and go in his own time.

Well, they'd circled round this enough. 'Anyway,' he said, 'I'm sorry if I gave you any . . .' He smiled. 'Just cause to doubt me. That wasn't my intention.' *And that*, he thought, *is as close to an apology as you're going to get, old girl.*

Win looked momentarily very old, he thought. It was just for a second or so – as though some mask of will had slipped briefly from her face, only to be snatched back into place again – then the image of constructed self was back, the calculated, calculating façade all accounted for once more. He wondered if she'd seen something similar happen with him. He wondered if that was what she saw all the time, and if this explained her uncanny – and also deeply canny – ability to read people the way she did.

'Accepted,' she said.

He waved at two silvery pots. 'Tea or coffee?'

He'd decided to do Business Studies fully expecting to change his course. He'd come to the conclusion that he had to compromise with his family and their expectations of him. He'd seem to go along with what they expected and then change tack when they'd been bought off. If he started with Business Studies, gave it a good enough go and then switched to something that actually interested him – English, history, even art – then at least he'd have shown willing. That ought to keep them off his back until he graduated. This seemed like a good plan and a not remotely crazy way of making one of life's more important decisions.

Then, a few months into his course, when he was almost enjoying it and even getting reasonable marks for a couple of essays, just because he knew he wouldn't be doing this for very much longer, he heard that Sophie had changed her mind about her own academic course. She was doing Business Studies, too. She was committed to a commercial career, with the family firm if the right opening was there.

Jeez, he'd thought. Was she doing this just because he was doing something similar? Was this a kind of public yet hidden signal? They hadn't been in touch since the sweet and wonderful but also mildly disastrous time in San Francisco, months earlier. He sat in his room in Bristol, looking out at the unleaved trees of Castle Park and the slow grey swirlings on the broad curve of the Floating Harbour, the river that was barely a river, its surface brown and pewter under a low fleet of clouds dragging long trains of rain under their ragged hems.

He remembered the startling desert brightness of the Mojave, the pore-sapping dryness of the air, the squinting glare of the rows and rows of pale, abandoned jets under the peeled-open sky, the little plane landing, Sophie – albeit an altered, mutated Sophie, a Sophie making a sort of phase change of herself – stepping out of the plane. He remembered Dan's apartment, the crackly noises from the old vinyl records, the feel of her dancing up close to him, the smell and feel of her hair, the sheer naked pleasure of bedding the girl after so many al fresco couplings. He tried to forget about the scene in the laundry, the weak sun and the artificial smell of fabric conditioner.

For a moment or two, in the hazy San Franciscan morning chill, in the taxi heading for the railway station, he'd felt pretty good about it all. He'd seen her again, after all; he'd won at last, eventually surmounting all the obstacles the family had put in his way (even if it had happened by chance – that didn't matter) and finally got to meet her again. And they hadn't fought, they hadn't blamed each other for everything that had gone wrong and the years they'd been forced to spend apart; they'd connected, they'd made love again.

She'd wanted him. It didn't matter that she'd later said it had been a mistake, it didn't matter that she was with another guy; these things happened. She'd wanted him. He hadn't forced himself on her, he hadn't seduced her. It had been mutual. Unpressured. And she had suggested dancing, not him.

Still, she'd more or less thrown him out. He believed her that she wasn't a good liar and it would be easier to deceive Dan if he wasn't there, but all the same. Ejected again; torn apart once more. It wasn't a good pattern.

There was an early train leaving for LA just twenty minutes after he arrived at the station. By the time he'd bought his ticket and found the right train – surprisingly busy, full of suits and families – he was away from the city almost before he knew he'd been there.

Gulls moved over the Floating Harbour, banking and wheeling across the banked-up, cradled waters.

Now and again, just sometimes, if he's really drunk or stoned and feeling nostalgic or soppy or whatever you might want to call it, he still whispers to himself: They've all bloody gone, Fell off me 'oss, didn' I?, Blimey, I didn't enjoy it that much, and – now – Not a flippin' fing.

Cuz, cuz, sweet cuz.

He'd tried getting back in touch with Sophie after meeting her in California, but without much success. He'd got her address in New York from cousin Fabiole, sent her a carefully considered letter – friendly, even loving, but not weird or anything – and received in return a terse note saying that she was very busy and didn't think it was a good idea they stayed in touch. She was sorry if she'd hurt him.

That had been two months ago. Now this news that she was doing Business Studies.

He decided that probably it wasn't a deliberate thing, Sophie taking up the same kind of course as him, but that possibly it indicated a desire that she might not know she had herself to somehow track him, keep parallel with him. That would do, he guessed.

He stuck in. He determined that he'd do his best to enjoy the course he'd embarked upon. He made new friends, had various relationships – never really committing, often talking to his girlfriends about Sophie, his childhood sweetheart (that was how he had started to refer to her) – and spent a year during the four-year degree course working for the family firm on Product Development. He'd kind of hoped that being at Bristol, so close to Lydcombe, he might be invited back – he'd like to see how the gardens were doing, apart from anything else – but he never was.

At the next family gathering – Grandpa Bert's funeral, at Garbadale, in the early spring of 1990 – he'd asked Aunt Lauren about Sophie not receiving his letters. Again, she professed to be as surprised as he was. She had certainly forwarded the letters. She'd suggested that maybe Sophie telling him that she hadn't received them was just her way of trying to protect his feelings.

He'd hoped Sophie would be there for the funeral, but she'd been too busy with her studies in the States and everybody agreed that it was a long way to ask somebody to come just to pay their last respects to an old fellow who'd been little better than a vegetable for the past decade anyway.

'And how was he?' Grandma Win said when he mentioned seeing Blake in Hong Kong. She was dressed all in black and looked, Alban thought, like a crow. She carried a handkerchief balled up in one hand and her eyes looked a little red. She looked hurt, now. He was

291

already starting to regret telling her he'd seen Blake; another painful memory, dragging up the past of a familial black sheep. He'd only done so for something to say. He'd rather not have talked to her at all but his parents had insisted. He was so relieved she didn't ignore him or say something horrible about him and Sophie that he'd relaxed, never imagining he might upset her by telling her he'd paid a visit to her son.

'He was fine,' he told her.

'And what did he want?'

'Nothing. Didn't want anything. I mean, he's really rich. Honest, he was okay, Gran. He showed me around Hong Kong. It was brilliant. And he gave me money.'

'I bet he did,' Win said, sounding unimpressed. 'And? So? What did he have to say for himself?'

Alban had to think. 'Nothing in particular. He just showed me around, introduced me to people. He seems to know everybody. I met the Governor and everything. Uncle Blake's seriously rich, Gran. He's got this skyscraper. I mean, it's really his.'

'Well, bully for him. How much money did he give you?'

'I can't remember,' Alban lied.

'Did he talk about the family?'

'A bit. He was okay, Gran. Honestly. I think he'd like to see, well, everybody –'

'Indeed. Well, I don't want to see him again,' Win told him.

'Oh,' Alban said. 'Okay. I'm sorry.'

'Yes,' Win said, with a tone of finality, and turned away.

'And so I had a look for myself, but of course everything Bunty had said was a complete and utter fib: instead, there the fellow was with a *Playboy* in one hand and his John Thomas, thoroughly engorged, in the other. So I closed the door pronto and turned round to find Sister glowering down at me, saying, "Yes? *And?*" and I naturally didn't have the first idea what to say until suddenly I had a brainwave and said, "Well, Sister, I think he's preparing to discharge himself!" Ha ha ha!'

'Ha ha!' agreed Doris, after a modest delay.

Fielding paused as he poured the last of the dessert wine into Beryl's glass, smiling broadly at first and then joining in the laughter when it showed no particular sign of subsiding especially quickly. He sat back in his seat, sighing mightily and taking a surreptitious glance at his watch as he lifted his water glass to his lips. Still not even eleven. He'd hoped it might be close to midnight.

One of the Inverlochy staff appeared at the table, refilling his glass. Doris and Beryl were slapping each other on the forearm and holding napkins to their mouths as they giggled, glancing round the now nearly empty dining room. Most of the other guests at the hotel had moved through to the lounge or the main hall for coffee.

'Discharge himself! D'you see?' Beryl said in a sort of subdued shriek.

'Yes! Oh yes!' Doris coughed. She drained her Sauternes, then looked at the empty half-bottle sitting on the table. 'My, that was lovely,' she told Fielding. She gazed mournfully at her now empty glass and the equally defunct bottle. 'They are such terribly *small* bottles though, aren't they?'

Fielding smiled the smile of a tired, tired man who can associate every bend and straight on the road between Glasgow and Fort William with some confused phrase or cross-purposed exchange of geriatric garrulity and has come to accept that he is not going to see his bed this side of the witching hour. He signalled to the hovering waiter, raising his eyebrows, and held up the sticky emptiness of the Sauternes bottle.

'What are we all going to do if everybody does sell their shares to these Sprint people?' Great-Aunt Doris asked suddenly, watching the waiter exit, defunct bottle in hand.

'Spraint, dear,' Beryl corrected. She smiled at Fielding, who seemed oblivious, fiddling with his napkin. 'Spend our ill-gotten gains on wine, women and whatever, one imagines,' she told Doris.

Doris looked suddenly alarmed. 'You wouldn't up sticks and

abandon me and move to your own desert island or that sort of thing, would you, old thing?' she asked Beryl, blinking furiously.

Beryl smiled. 'No, dear. If there were any desert islands on the cards, I'd take you with me.' Then the smile faded a little and she looked down at the table, letting a silence descend.

Fielding was trying to do origami with his napkin. 'Some people would use the dosh to do things they'd always wanted to,' he said absently, frowning as he tried to tuck one corner of cloth inside another. 'Fund projects, use as seed capital.' The bits of cloth weren't fitting together quite properly. He wished he had three hands. 'Dreams, really,' he muttered. He glanced up to find both the old girls looking at him. His gaze darted from one to the other. 'Probably,' he added. 'I mean, possibly.' He cleared his throat, shook his napkin flat again. 'Maybe.'

'Is that what you would do with yours, dear?' Doris asked.

Fielding shrugged. 'Well, I don't know. I suppose. I was just talking hypothetically. I mean, I, I personally don't have anything—' The waiter reappeared. 'Ah, more wine!'

'Oh!' Doris said, turning in her seat. 'Did we order more? I suppose we must. Oh well, then.'

Beryl smiled sadly. 'Jolly-D.'

The years passed. He got a 2.1 and took up the post waiting for him in Wopuld Games Ltd. Sophie had already started with Wopuld Games Inc., the company's US subsidiary. He felt that basically he was over her, though she was never far from his thoughts and he still hoped they might meet up now and again, through business if nothing else. Then, well, who knew?

He knew about playing a long game.

In third year he had shared a flat in St Judes with three guys who were really into playing the board version of *Empire!* Because his surname was McGill and he'd never mentioned anything to the guys about the family firm – they were all doing English or art and weren't really interested in his course – they didn't realise he was part of the family who owned the rights, made the games, took the profits.

He knew all there was to know about how to play the game, though that still didn't mean he won all the time. *Empire!* wasn't chess; it depended on luck on occasion, both in the initial set-up and then in the playing. Still, you could get a lot better at playing it with lots of practice, and he'd spent a fair bit of his childhood playing the board version.

One of his flatmates was Chris, whose board it was and who thought himself a pretty damn shit-hot *Empire!* player. Chris, Alban was fairly sure, had assumed that he would be the ace game-player in the flat. He dismissed Alban's first few wins as beginner's luck, which let Alban know that Chris wasn't that clever. They'd agreed at the start of the semester that they'd have a league that ran all that academic year, and as Alban gradually built up a lead over everybody else, Chris started to realise Alban was more than just lucky.

After a while Alban noticed Chris beginning to change his game-playing style. Now, he would always choose to attack Alban when-ever Alban's forces got to a level Chris regarded as being too great, even though they might pose no obvious tactical or strategic threat to Chris's homelands, territories or expeditionary forces. Alban still won sometimes, and Chris improved his record only slightly, while occasionally other people used the opportunity to gang up on Alban, or attack Chris while he was busy trying to whittle down Alban's forces. Initially Alban just accepted this, but, after one game when he was left relatively powerless and two other players tussled it out inelegantly, inexpertly, for a win they were each too crap and stoned actually to accomplish – it ended in a smoky stalemate and an agreed draw – Alban decided to change the way he responded to Chris's policeman role.

Next time Chris attacked him, committing a sizeable but restrained amount of forces to the battle, Alban went after him with all he had. He defeated Chris but left himself hopelessly weakened. They were both taken out of the game in the next round. This time one of their pals actually managed to win the game.

Chris protested during the game and at length afterwards when they sat around drinking and watching telly with the sound down.

'Why did you do that, man? I wasn't trying to put you out the game! I was just trying to reduce your power a bit.'

'Yeah, I know,' Alban told him, opening a couple of cans and passing one to Chris. Chris was a gangly guy with frizzy dark hair and bad skin.

'So why did you go fucking mental, Al?'

'I don't like you doing that.'

'But it's all part of the game, man.'

'I know; so's what I did.'

'Yeah, but it's just to stop you getting too powerful.'

'Oh, yeah, I know why you're doing it. I just want you to stop.'

'Well, I ain't gonna,' Chris told him, laughing. He accepted a joint from one of their flatmates, took a shallow toke and passed it to Alban.

'Well then,' Alban said, shrugging.

'But you lost, Al!' Chris pointed out. 'You got me, but you fucked yourself.'

'Yeah, and I'll keep doing it until you stop attacking me when there's no good reason to, apart from this taking-me-down-a-peg thing.'

'What? You're kidding!'

'No, I'm serious. I'll keep doing it.'

'You'll keep on going after me, after me homelands and everything, just cos I attack one block?'

'Yeah.'

'That's crazy! You'll get me out but you'll put yourself out as well!'

'Yeah, I know. Until you stop doing it.'

'Well, what if I don't?'

Alban shrugged.

'But you *lose the game*, man!' Chris pointed out, struggling to see the logic of this.

Alban clinked cans. 'Cheers.'

Chris attacked him in just the same way for just the same reasons in the next two games, and Alban reacted just as he had before.

Chris told him he was crazy, but in the next game, didn't try the same manoeuvre. Alban explained one drunken night, just in case Chris hadn't got it, that there was the game, and then there was the meta-game. Even without a league lasting all year long, there was always the meta-game, the game beyond the game; you had to think of that, too.

Chris told him he was still fucking crazy.

'You take care.'

'You too.'

'I'm serious. The weather forecast looks pretty shitty for tonight and tomorrow. Don't take any stupid risks. Please. Come back safely.'

'Depend on it.' Verushka, already kitted out, booted and fleeced, goes up on tiptoes to kiss his forehead, then crunches back on to the gravel flat-footed and plants another squarely and long on his lips. 'I'm serious too,' she whispers, hugging him close. 'You take good care. *You* don't take any stupid risks.'

'Promise,' he says.

She pulls back, studies his eyes in turn. 'You don't remember last night, do you?'

He raises his brows, tips his head to one side.

She smiles. 'After that. You were talking about your mother. In your sleep.'

He looks shocked. 'I was? I never do that.'

'Unless there's somebody else called Irene, or Mummy.'

'Jesus,' he breathes, looking away down the drive towards the unseen sea loch. He looks at her. 'Wait a moment. I remember you waking me up.'

'Yeah.' She nods.

297

He looks away again. 'Oh well.'

'Anyway,' she says, with one last kiss. 'See you on Monday morning. You go in and get some breakfast.'

'Hey. Listen,' he says, still holding one hand. 'If you get rained off or just think the better of it, come back. Okay? At any point. We'll decamp to a room at the Inchnadamph if we can't stay here together, or Neil McBride and his wife would put us up.'

She stops, puts her head back, eyebrows raised. 'Not rather be here with your family?'

'Hey, we could just break into the north wing with a few logs and get a fire going,' he tells her. 'But no. You come back if you need to. If you want to. Don't hold off.'

'Deal,' she says, and, grinning, holds her hand up for him to kiss.

She slides into the Forester, fires it up and takes off down the gravel drive, one hand waving from the window. He waves back, watching until the car disappears behind the screen of trees.

He turns and walks back into the great house.

8

'I used to have a hearty dick,' Blake told him. 'Now I've got a dicky heart.'

Alban smiled and tried to look sympathetic at the same time. 'Is it really that bad?'

'Bad enough. Docs say I should lay off the booze.' Blake held up his glass of whisky and soda and stared at it with a look of accusatory sorrow, as though it was a trusted friend who had let him down. 'May need a triple bypass.'

'Well, they're pretty routine these days.'

'Hmm. Maybe so, but I still don't like the sound of it. They cut through your breastbone and prise your ribs apart, did you know that? Big steel clamp things. Grisly.' He shook his head. 'And there's a risk with any operation. Things go wrong. Mistakes get made. Infection.'

'I'm sure you'll be fine, Blake.'

'Huh.' Blake drank some more of his whisky and soda.

Alban hadn't seen Blake since his visit during his gap year. This time, he'd been in Hong Kong to meet with some product development people and factory owners from Shenzen, preparing the ground for a redesign of the *Empire!* board and pieces. Hong Kong was both highly altered and just the same. The new airport had

299

taken the fun/terror out of flying into the place, buildings Alban
was sure had been a block from the sea were now six or seven
blocks away as more land was reclaimed and immediately built
upon and the last of the junks and sampans had long since disappeared from the harbour.

On the other hand, it was still stiflingly hot and humid and
berserkly crowded at ground level, the Chinese still spat everywhere
and were not in the least shy about coughing and sneezing right in
your face, everybody constantly pushed and shoved and jostled everybody else as they walked around – and kicked and elbowed you out
of the way if you stopped in the street for any reason – the tall,
teetering, anorexically narrow wooden trams were still liable to burst
into flames at the drop of a match and the racket of rattling that
issued from mah-jong parlours if you happened to be passing when
the doors opened was exceeded only by the choking super-dense
cloud of cigarette smoke that pulsed out at the same time.

'Anyway,' Blake said, 'it was kind of you to look me up. No one
else in the family ever does.'

'I'm sorry to hear that,' Alban told him.

Blake made a desultory flapping gesture with one hand. He was
as tall and thin as ever. When he'd first greeted Alban he'd been
wearing a large floppy hat that made him look like an Anglepoise
lamp.

They were sitting in the rooftop garden of Blake's skyscraper. This
was still near the harbour; the land immediately offshore hadn't
been reclaimed. Not yet, anyway. They were a hundred and something metres up, shaded by a broad canopy and with a moderately
strong breeze blowing, but it was still uncomfortably hot. Drinking,
reclined, was fine, but just the thought of doing anything more energetic, like getting up and moving around, was enough to bathe you
in sweat all by itself.

Alban wondered whether to try and get Blake to talk more about
the family and the reasons he'd left it. He was, after all, on the brink
of doing something similar himself. It was a month or so after the

300

breakfast telling-off he'd received from Win, and in his heart he was moving closer all the time to just chucking it in. He carried a copy of his letter of resignation around with him in an envelope all the time now, like a suicide pill. Maybe he needed one last push, a final prod to make him take the leap. Would comparing notes with Blake do that? Not that their circumstances were that similar; Blake had been thrown out for embezzlement, whereas he was just thinking about resigning after doing a good, conscientious job for the last few years. It wasn't like he'd be punished or sent into exile by the family. He was looking at the equivalent of an honourable discharge, not a dishonourable one like Blake's.

'Do you ever try to contact other people in the family?' he asked Blake. He sipped on his iced water. He was in shirtsleeves, tie loose, shoes and socks off. Blake was even less formal; barefoot too, baggy shorts and a loose silk shirt. The warm breeze brought the scent of jasmine to them; the roof garden held dozens of the plants.

'Not really,' Blake admitted. 'I'm something they'd rather forget. Your grandmother especially.' He looked briefly at Alban. 'She's top dog now, isn't she?'

'Has been for a while,' Alban agreed. 'Family and firm.'

'No love lost there,' Blake said. He sounded sad. 'Anyway. I have my own life here; always have had. Been a good life, I've done well. No complaints. I—'

Blake's mobile, sitting on the low teak table between them, vibrated. 'Excuse me,' he said to Alban. 'Yes?' He listened for a while, then said, 'No. That's not remotely good enough. Tell him that's positively insulting. We'll go elsewhere.' He listened some more. 'Yes, well so have I, and mine tells his what to do, so inform our friend he's welcome to try.' Blake shifted almost without a pause into what sounded to Alban like convincingly rapid Cantonese and spoke that for a minute or so, sounding fairly animated, then said, 'Do that. Yes, later. Goodbye.' He put the mobile back on the table. 'Sorry – deal about to happen, or not. Can't turn the damn thing off. Do you like mobiles? I have to have one like everybody else

301

and they're very handy sometimes, obviously, but I sometimes feel I absolutely hate them at the same time. Do you know what I mean?'

'Yeah, I do,' Alban said. 'It's being at everybody's beck and call.'

'Quite.' Blake nodded, then sipped his drink.

'You can always turn them off,' Alban pointed out.

'Yes,' Blake said. 'But then you worry you're missing something important.' He looked at the phone. 'Still. Could see the damn things far enough.' He looked out over the hazy city. Slim shapes that were distant jets slid minutely across the sky, descending towards the now far distant airport. 'You're, what, thirty now, aren't you?'

'Near enough,' Alban said.

Blake was silent for a while, then said, 'Do you ever get a sort of feeling of wondering what it's all about?' He looked over at Alban, who looked back, not sure at first whether Blake was being entirely serious, and realising that he was. 'About why we bother?' Blake's expression was positively mournful. He looked away again. 'Maybe it's just an age thing. I don't remember feeling like this when I was younger. Seems to have crept up on me without me noticing, like this heart thing. Do you ever get that?'

'What, suspecting everything's pointless?'

'I suppose that's what it is.'

'Not particularly. Kind of had that more when I was younger. Sort of thing you discuss when you're a student.'

'Maybe just me then,' Blake said glumly, and drank.

'Not just you, Blake. Lots of people feel like that, at least now and again. I suppose it's one of the main reasons so many people turn to religion.'

Blake nodded. 'I've started praying again, but I just feel foolish. I realise I'm just talking to myself.' He shook his head. 'Silly, really.' He glanced at Alban. I thought I'd have all this stuff figured out by now. I feel rather cheated that I don't, that I'm having to start thinking again about things that – as you say – one might have expected to leave behind in one's teens.' He held his glass up to the light. 'I think I am like a lot of people, you know: I've spent my life waiting for my life to start. It's as though one needs permission from somebody – parents, God, a committee of one's peers; I don't bloody know – to finally take responsibility for one's own actions, one's own life. Only the permission never comes, and gradually – well, gradually for me, I can't speak for others; maybe their realisation comes in some sort of sudden revelation and a blinding light or whatever – gradually you realise that it never will come, that the way you've lived your life, stumbling through it, winging it half the time, is all there really is, all there ever was. I feel cheated, because of that. I feel, sometimes, like I've cheated myself though I can't see how I could have done much different. And I have a horrible feeling that even if I had a time machine and could go back to visit my younger self to warn him, or at least advise him about all this, he'd – I'd – have no idea what my future self was talking about. I'd think he was an idiot. I'd ignore him. I'd ignore myself.'

'Blake,' Alban said, trying not to sound too amused, 'you sound like somebody who hasn't achieved anything. I kind of had the impression you'd done pretty well for yourself.'

'Oh,' Blake waved one hand, then ran it through his white hair – it looked longer than the time Alban had been here before – 'I've done very well for myself. I'm not complaining about that for a moment. Though, ha, mind you, the commies could take it all away in a moment, on a whim, if they really wanted to. Well, not every-thing, obviously, but almost all my property is here, in Honkers. Can't stuff a building or a plot of land in an offshore account. But . . . Oh, look, you don't mind me talking about all this, do you?'

'Course I don't mind,' Alban said.

This wasn't strictly true; he was finding Blake's late-onset exist-ential angst a little wearing. The guy was a multi-squillionaire and still he was finding stuff to get all morose about. Alban felt almost puritanical about this sort of thing; of course being rich didn't mean you suddenly no longer had anything to worry about, but you ought at least to have the decency to keep quiet about it. Oh well. He'd chosen to look Blake up. It had seemed the right thing to do then and would seem like the right thing to have done later, when he'd be sitting on the plane back to the UK. Visiting the exile, keeping this one distant offshoot of the Wopuld clan from detaching from the family tree completely. Sometimes, Alban felt like he was the family social worker.

'It's just,' Blake said, waving one hand again, 'even having, you know, made a bit of money and so on, even that doesn't seem like so much. You meet other people who've made even more and you think, Well, this person's clearly an idiot. I mean, I'm not saying one should base one's estimation of oneself or anybody else purely on how much money you've made or they've made, but it's hard not to compare these things sometimes, and you think, Well, what does having made a bit really mean, or say about one, if this pillock can make even more than I've made? D'you see what I mean? It's quite depressing, really. Do you understand?'

Alban sighed. He understood there was nothing worse than the very rich feeling sorry for themselves. 'There's always somebody with more, I guess,' he said, trying to sound more sympathetic than he felt.

'But if it's not about money,' Blake persisted, 'or prestige or your immortal soul or whatever, then what?'

'Some people put a lot of value on children,' Alban said. 'Or just on another person.'

Blake looked at him and snorted. 'Yes, well.' He drank from his glass. 'I never did quite meet the right girl.' He studied his empty glass. 'Actually, that's not true. Arguably I met too many of them.'

'You never married, Blake?' Alban knew Blake wasn't married now, but he didn't know if he ever had been.

'Thought about it a few times,' Blake said. 'Never did.' He nodded at Alban's glass. 'Fancy another?'

Alban too looked at his glass of water, now nearly empty. 'Why not? Might even have a proper drink this time.'

'Good man,' Blake said. He put his fingers to his mouth and produced a disconcertingly piercing whistle. He shrugged at Alban and said, 'Quickest way,' as a barman in a white jacket appeared around the side of some jasmine plants to take their order.

'You could still have children, Blake,' Alban told him. 'Get yourself a young wife, start a family.'

'At my age?' Blake looked pained.

'Blake, you're not short of the money for a nanny. *You* won't have to be the one getting up in the middle of the night to warm the milk.'

Blake shook his head. 'I'm too old,' he said. 'And then what if it didn't work? What if I didn't like the child, or its mother for that matter? What if I realised she only wanted me for my money? What if the whole experience was just another cause for realising the essential futility of everything?'

'Jesus, Blake, in the end, you're sitting in the sunshine with people running after you, on top of forty storeys of hi-tech building occupying some of the most prime real estate in the world. And, yes, there'll be women desperate to throw themselves at you for your money. Well, that's not the worst thing that ever happened, either.'

'I know,' Blake said. 'I have this talk with myself all the time, telling myself exactly that. I should be grateful. I should feel lucky, I should feel blessed. I should feel . . . I should feel good about my life.' He looked across the rooftop garden. 'I stand over there, some nights,' he said, looking at the glass wall topped with teak which ran around the edge of the roof. 'I look down on all these tiny brown and white dots; little guys in loincloths running around like blue-arsed flies in the middle of the night, busy collating copies of the *South China Post* and pushing and pulling handcarts full of chickens. And I actually envy them. It must be such a simple – Ah.' This last word was directed at the servant bringing them their drinks.

Blake exchanged a few words in Cantonese and an insincere smile with the guy in the white jacket as their drinks were served.

'Well, there's always this stuff,' Alban said. He held up his G&T. Better this than explain to Blake what a dingbat he had to be to envy guys with no economic choice but to run around in loincloths in the wee small hours collating outsize papers or transporting fucking chickens.

Blake looked into his whisky and soda. 'I probably drink too much already. So the docs say, anyway.'

'Drugs?' Alban said, feeling his patience starting to wear thin.

Blake drank, looked at him. 'Do you mean prescription?'

Alban raised his eyebrows. 'Or the other sort.'

Blake looked away. 'I don't think you're being entirely serious, Alban.'

'I guess not,' Alban agreed. They both drank. 'Do you ever think of trying to mend fences with the rest of the family? I mean, making a real effort, trying to woo them back?'

'Yes, I do,' Blake said. 'But it never takes much thought for me to realise that there'd be very little point in doing so.'

'You seem very sure.'

'I am. We parted ways a long time ago.' Blake looked at the sky again. 'Grown too far apart, basically. I have my life here. You lot, well, you have your own lives. I won't pretend I'm not interested in hearing about people, but it all seems slightly unreal. Anyway, even if I did wish to . . . resume relations, I don't think I'd be welcome. Takes two to tango, and all that.'

Alban just nodded. He hadn't even mentioned Blake's name to Win since that time at Bert's funeral, nine years ago now. He hadn't needed to to form the strong impression it wouldn't be a good idea. Blake was still very much the black sheep. 'PNG, dear boy,' Uncle Kennard had said when he'd mentioned this to him. Kennard didn't seem as viscerally opposed to any contact with his brother as Win had, but he still hadn't actually been in touch with him for all these years, either. 'Definitely PNG.'

'What?' Alban had asked, confused. (Papua New Guinea? What the hell did that have to do with anything?)

'PNG – Persona Non Grata,' Kennard had explained. 'Not welcome, in other words. Old Foreign Office phrase,' he'd explained wisely, then somewhat spoiled the effect by adding, 'or something.'

Alban looked at Blake, sitting in the hazy, saturated sunshine of Hong Kong, a couple of years after the handover, not long before the millennium celebrations, and, for the first time, did genuinely feel sorry for the man. 'Well,' he said, 'people might still mellow, over the years.'

Blake looked at him. 'Would you say Winifred has mellowed at all?' he asked.

Alban had to look away for a bit. 'Well, no,' he admitted.

'Keep in touch,' Blake said coolly, looking away at the distant planes again. 'If she ever does, let me know.'

She'll die first, Alban thought, and knew it was true.

He resigned from the firm a week later.

The weather was awful; a strong west wind dragged a lumpen blanket of thick grey cloud over the whole west coast, bringing sheets and squalls of cold, buffeting rain. Alban thought of Verushka, sheltering in her tent, rain drumming on the bright, paper-thin nylon, or – worse – actually out in it, trudging up a hill through the rain and mist, pack heavy on her back. The weather was so bad he told himself it was a good thing; even VG wouldn't stay out in a heaving wet gale like this. The worse it got the more likely she was to come back, so in a way the worse it got the better it was. Unless she was so stubborn or determined or so set on keeping out of his family's way that she had resolved not to come back no matter how bad the weather got, in which case the worse it got, well, the worse it was. Maybe, he told himself, looking out from the drawing room at the cliff and the mist-shrouded waterfall (blown sideways, not back up), she'd give in and go somewhere else rather than come back here. Maybe she'd just bail out to the nearest hotel.

Meanwhile, the Spraint guys had landed at Inverness but their helicopter was grounded while the wind was so strong and the cloud base so low. They might have to hire a car, too.

Alban was still talking to people; over breakfast, then while people were hanging around waiting for the weather to improve or the others to arrive. A morning's fishing on Loch Garve had been arranged, but that too had had to be shelved due to the weather, so everybody was kind of at a loose end. The children were entertaining themselves noisily in the old library/games room, playing pool and table tennis. Those adults who could be bothered were reading the papers Spraint had sent supporting their bid. People mostly gravitated to the drawing room with its multiplicity of seats, chairs and couches and a roaring fire that served as an antidote to the sheets of rain beating against the windows.

Aunt Kathleen was studying her laptop, sitting at one end of the long table in the kitchen with a bacon roll and a mug of tea. Kath was a comfortably upholstered fifty-one, currently wearing a sea-blue blouse and the skirt of her business suit, jacket slung over the seat back. Brown, greying hair in a long ponytail. She was about the only relevant person he hadn't yet spoken to about the proposed sale to the US corporation.

'Aunt Kath, you're not frittering away what may be our last few hours as an independent company doing anything as frivolous as playing a game, are you?' Alban asked, sitting across the corner of the table from her.

'Hi, Alban,' she said. She swivelled the laptop towards him briefly, then back again.

He looked surprised. 'They have games that look like spreadsheets now? Whatever next.'

'Just reviewing the current state of the Wopuld Group's finances,' she explained.

'And how are the dear old books – still in the black?'

'Black as the ace of hearts,' Kathleen said, then smiled thinly over the top of her glasses at him. 'Joking. Accountant's humour.'

'Really? Well, good just to know it exists at all.'

'Anyway, we're still solvent.'

'All the better for Spraint to gobble us up.'

'You're against, then,' Aunt Kath said, peering at the screen rather than looking at him. 'Thought you would be, heard you were.'

'Well, if it was up to me alone, I'd be completely agin it, but as it is I just want people to make the right decision. Eyes open, you know?'

'Well, my eyes are open.' Kath blew on her mug of tea, then sipped it. She took a bite from her bacon roll.

'And you're for the sell-off,' Alban said.

Aunt Kath nodded for a bit until she'd swallowed. 'Yes, though not at the price they're offering right now,' she said. 'And my eleven thousand shares speak rather louder than your . . .' She performed a few key strokes. One eyebrow went up. 'Hundred,' she said. 'Well, that's about as nominal as you can get. Or did you just forget to sell the last few?'

'Sentimental attachment. Those last hundred are like an old Premium Bond.'

'I'm sure. Well, they'll get you into the shareholders' meeting, I suppose. I hear you want a chance to address the troops later.' She ate more of the bacon roll.

'I thought I'd get everybody together,' Alban said, 'before the EGM itself. Make sure we're all rapping from the same rap sheet, you know? I mean, we won't be, obviously, but we should at least establish the differences. And it wouldn't just be me who gets to talk. Anybody can. You could, Kath. You could put the pro-selling argument.'

'I don't have your charisma, Alban,' Aunt Kath said, more or less expressionless.

'Well, somebody has,' he said, 'and I want it back.' Aunt Kath looked at him. He smiled broadly. 'Ex-forester humour.'

'Really.' Aunt Kath went back to her roll and her tea.

Alban stood up. 'Well, I'll leave you to it,' he said. As he turned to go, Aunt Kath looked at her watch. 'Three whole minutes in the kitchen and not a word about cooking the books,' she said. 'Well done.'

He looked back, but could only make as gracious a gesture as he could, and left.

*　　*　　*

Sophie arrived first, driven by taxi all the way from Inverness. Alban, mooching around the hall at that point and taking occasional peeks through the front doors, hoping to see the red Forester coming fast down the drive, was the first out to the taxi, struggling to control an umbrella against the squalling sheets of rain being curled round the jumbled architecture of the house and sent slamming down from a variety of directions. According to Aunt Lauren, some of the older children were supposed to be doing this umbrella-holding, bag-carrying thing, but they'd managed to make themselves scarce in the interim. Alban was so busy trying to prevent the umbrella blowing inside out while opening the taxi door at the same time that he only realised who the passenger was as she was getting out.

'Oh, Sophie. Hi.'

'Hello, Alban.' Sophie was blonde and slim as ever, dressed in jeans and an ivory cashmere sweater over a pink blouse. Her hair looked perfect, her face looked unchanged from the last time he'd seen her, her skin appeared flawless and her eyes were still – thankfully, redeemingly – the same fabulous, sparkling green they always had been. 'Thanks,' she said as he held the umbrella over her. No kiss.

He saw her into the house – Aunt Lauren was there, doing the whole greeting thing – then returned to the taxi to get her bags. He followed Aunt Lauren as she showed Sophie to her room on the first floor.

'Good grief, no, not a thing packed,' Lauren said in reply to a question from Sophie as they walked along the corridor. Then Lauren seemed to stiffen and her head jerked as though she was about to look back at Alban. She said hurriedly, 'Well, actually, no, no, that's not true. A few things have been packed up for the move. Some, ah, old things. Precious, well, family – things of sentimental value, some of those. Ah! Here we are.'

'Right,' Sophie said. She stood on the threshold.

'Bathroom is third on the left,' Lauren told her.

Sophie looked less than impressed that her accommodation was not en suite. Alban put her bags down near the old free-standing wardrobe and turned to go while Aunt Lauren was still blushing and apologising for the weather and saying how much Win was looking forward to seeing her. Sophie had her wallet out. She started to reach into it for something, then collected herself, looked embarrassed and shot a glancing smile at Alban, who just nodded and left.

He spent the rest of the day in a similar role, still in or near the front hall, hoping to see the Forester, greeting people, helping with bags, getting to see everybody as they arrived, which was good, but feeling menial and put-upon and slightly sick all the time, telling himself he was worrying about VG, but knowing it had more to do with the presence of Sophie and the way she had treated him. Every nuance of the few minutes they had spent in each other's company seemed to fill his thoughts, demanding attention and analysis and dissection.

She hadn't even started to kiss him, hadn't even thought about it. She hadn't even shaken hands. She'd nodded to him. She'd said, 'Hello, Alban,' and that was all. And had she really been about to tip him? She'd had her wallet out. Why? She'd already paid the cab. Had she really – just arrived, maybe a little distracted, possibly even a little flustered (by seeing him?) – been on the brink of offering him money to say thank you for helping her with her bags? What did that say about how she felt about him subconsciously?

'Darling! Oh, you're so sweet!' Leah said as he saw her into the house. He put an arm round her shoulder to keep her within the shelter of the umbrella. The wind whipped rain round their legs on the few steps to the porch and the hall.

'Alban,' Andy said, and – already holding a bag – gave him a one-armed hug.

Andy and Leah were followed in quick succession by most of the rest of the family: cousin Steve's wife Tessa, their son Rune, his partner Penning and baby Hannah, sis Cory, her husband Dave and their children Lachlan and Charlotte, cousin Louise, her sister Rachel

311

with her husband Mark and their children Ruthven and Foin, and Aunt Linda's broad, booming twin Lizzie (unexpectedly, amazingly, with a man in tow, a Mr Portman, her companion, who would of course be requiring a room. Alban foresaw problems for Haydn).

Fielding arrived with Beryl and Doris after lunch.

'Alban, dear, are we north of Aberdeen?' was the first thing Beryl said as he helped her from the Mercedes.

'Quite a bit north, and way west,' Alban told her, kissing her and then Doris as he tried to keep them both dry under the same umbrella and shepherd them to the front door.

'But not in the Arctic Circle?' Doris asked.

'Well, no,' Alban said, laughing.

'You see?' Doris said to Beryl. 'I *told* you!'

'I never *said* we were in the Arctic, I said we passed an artic. An articulated lorry. A pantechnicon,' Beryl said, sounding exasperated. 'For goodness' sake, we passed an Iceland lorry; that doesn't mean we're in bloody Iceland.'

'But I did tell you . . .' Doris was saying, oblivious, as Alban handed the old girls over to Lauren, gratefully.

'Thanks, Al,' Fielding said once the bags were out of the car and sitting in the main hall. He handed Alban the keys and turned to hug and kiss Aunt Lauren.

Fielding obviously expected Alban to park the Merc, which he duly did, shaking his head at Fielding and himself and – in his imagination – not parking the car at all but taking it north to look for any signs of red Forester estates or solo female climbers.

The umbrella finally blew inside out and then out of his hands as he exited Fielding's car after parking it behind the outbuildings beyond the north wing. He started to chase the umbrella, then gave up as a powerful gust of wind picked it up – it was already plainly broken, two ribs badly bent – and blew it up and over the old coal store and away towards the trees lining the head of Loch Garve. He gave up on it and trudged back to the house in the rain. The side doors he tried to get back in were all locked and he ended up having

312

to traipse all the way back round to the front door, getting drenched in the process.

Just as he got there, two people-carrier taxis arrived and disgorged a bunch of tall, well-dressed, well-groomed people. He guessed they were the Spraint execs. Aunt Lauren, Aunt Kathleen and her husband Lance, plus Gudrun the legal assistant, were out with umbrellas to meet them.

Alban – wet through, head down, trudging back to head for his shared room and a change of clothes – was hardly spared a second glance.

Dinner was full-scale but not formal; Alex the cook would have the kitchen and waiting staff of the Sloy Hotel to help him produce the dinners for the next two evenings, but for tonight he'd managed a buffet with just a couple of assistants. People chose their own places to sit at a dozen tables scattered through the length of the dining room.

The place was noisy with family members who hadn't talked properly for years provisioning themselves with gossip and news. Alban sat with Andy and Leah, Cory and her family. He'd caught up with Cory – she was working for Apple now, very excited about stuff in the pipeline she couldn't possibly talk about – and chatted with her husband Dave, an industrial chemist and a nice enough guy but with a sadly inexhaustible supply of stories about paints, pigments, volatiles and finishes.

'I didn't say anything to upset you, did I? I mean when we were talking about Irene last week,' Andy said. He raised his glass between him and Alban. 'You know, I probably ought not to say anything when I've a drink in me. I always worry I might have offended people. Bane of my life.'

'Course not,' Alban said. 'Anyway, I raised the subject. I think we both needed a drink before we could face it.'

'Perish the thought a couple of guys can talk about important emotional stuff when they're actually sober enough to make sense

313

of it,' Andy said ruefully. He sighed. 'But I still always worry I've offended people.'

'You worry too much about that sort of stuff, Dad.'

'Hmm.' Andy sounded unconvinced.

'Remember that time after I got back from my world trip? About a week before I went to Uni. We were sitting in the garden. Very hot. Drinking Pimm's, and I mentioned seeing Blake in Hong Kong and how he'd said, Always look out for number one. Be selfish.'

Andy nodded. 'Vaguely.'

'We got to talking about how some people were selfish and some weren't, and the difference between right-wing people and left-wing people. You said it all came down to imagination. Conservative people don't usually have very much, so they find it hard to imagine what life is like for people who aren't just like them. They can only empathise with people just like they are: the same sex, the same age, the same class, the same golf club or nation or race or whatever. Liberals can pretty much empathise with anybody else, no matter how different they are. It's all to do with imagination; empathy and imagination are almost the same thing, and it's why artists, creative people, are almost all liberals, left-leaning. Hard-headed people – business people – didn't have that sort of imagination; it's all directed at seeing business opportunities, identifying gaps in the market, spotting weaknesses in rivals. Blake and Win – and quite a lot of our family – were like that, you said. It was just the way they were.'

'Did I really say all that?' Andy asked, frowning.

'Yes, you did,' Alban told him. 'The point is, it was really useful to me, it made sense of a lot of stuff I'd been puzzling over, but then you spent the next half-hour or so apologising, saying you didn't want to criticise the family. I almost forgot what it was you said in the first place.'

Andy shrugged, grinned. 'Sorry. Sorry for being sorry.'

Alban smiled, shook his head.

'Anyway,' Andy said. 'Getting back to this thing with Beryl. Did you find out anything else?' He drank from his glass.

314

'No,' Alban said. 'No, I didn't.' He looked at the table where Win was sitting with Aunt Kathleen, Uncle Kennard and the two Spraint Corp execs and their assistants. 'I suppose I could ask Gran.'

Andy coughed. 'Excuse me. Yes, I suppose.'

'Well, she was around back then, in London. She might know something.'

'Yes, you should talk to her, I suppose. Other things on her mind this weekend, mind you. As have we all.'

'Yeah, well, we've already had words this weekend. Not about that though.'

'I've brought some flowers,' Andy said quietly, turning ever so slightly away from Leah.

'Flowers?' Alban asked.

'For Irene,' Andy said, almost whispering. 'I thought I'd take them down to where she died, maybe tomorrow morning, scatter them on the water. What do you think? Would you like to come?'

Part of Alban wanted to say, No, I'd rather do anything than come to where she died, with or without you, Andy, because it means too fucking much to me.

What he said, naturally, was, 'Yeah, of course, Andy. Maybe after breakfast?'

'Yeah, good idea,' Andy said gently. 'Good idea.' He patted Alban's arm.

'Well, mister, you'd better *pray* there's no God!'

Alban stared at the guy. '*What?*' he said.

Somehow, in the drawing room after dinner, he'd got into a theological debate with this Anthony K. Fromlax guy, Vice-President, Mergers and Acquisitions, of the Spraint Corporation, Incorporated under the laws of the state of Delaware, United States of America. Even calling it a theological debate was dignifying it a little; basically they were disagreeing about the very existence of God, groups of gods and so-called higher beings in general. Tony Fromlax was a tall, muscular, lithe-looking guy of about Alban's age with wide, enthusiastic eyes. A sharp-looking haircut ascribed a veneer of order to naturally unruly fair hair. He had a degree in physics as well as an MBA and Alban had half hoped, on being introduced to him by Win, that he'd prove to be one of those Americans who hadn't been born again. This had proved – perversely – to be a pious hope.

It wasn't that Alban went looking for this sort of argument, just that he always seemed to get involved in them. People said something that made it obvious they'd fabricated some assumption that was completely wrong either about Alban or about the way he looked at the world and he seemed to be constitutionally incapable of letting these things go, of treating them like something embarrassing just tripped over and best ignored; he always had to turn back and pick it up, inspect it, shake it, worry it, make an issue of it, demand an explanation. In this case it had been Tony wondering aloud about where people would be worshipping come Sunday. From that had spread a whole escalating avalanche of argument, assertion, counter-assertion and nonsense.

'Pray there's no god? Did you hear what you—?'

'I'm sorry for you, Alban, in your pride and your arrogance, that you can't see that Jesus is reaching out to you, that He would be your friend, your saviour, if only you'd listen.' Tony sat forward on his couch, hands splayed in front of him, reaching out. 'There is no way you can be right, but even if there was, think what a terrible place the world would be without the Word of God to guide us. That's what—'

'Now, Tony, how are we here? This looks like it's lively. Talking share price, yeah?' Larry Feaguing, Senior Vice-President, Mergers and Acquisitions, clapped Tony on the shoulder and sat down by him on the couch. Feaguing was a chunky guy, not much shorter than Fromlax, about twenty years his senior, with endearingly black hair. He had a deep, serious tan that Alban already imagined was visibly fading in the mellowing light of a Scottish October. He had a deep, serious voice, too, and used it to good effect. 'How're you guys getting on?' he asked. 'Okay?'

316

'Mr McGill believes we're descended from monkeys and Christians are no better than Muslims,' Fromlax told his boss, who at least had the decency to look pained.

'Or Jews, to be fair,' Alban said reasonably as Fromlax's eyes widened. 'I'm an atheist, Mr Feaguing,' he said, turning to the other man. 'I was trying to explain to Tony here that, from where I stand, Judaism, Christianity and Islam don't even look like separate religions, just different cults within this one big, mad, misogynist religion founded by a schizophrenic who heard voices telling him to kill his son. And I do indeed believe in evolution rather than magic. I take a pretty firm line on lightning not being divine thunderbolts, too.'

'Well, a man's beliefs are his own business, I guess,' Feaguing said, looking at both men in turn. 'The most important thing is being able to talk, come to agreements, where agreements are possible.'

'The most important thing is to live in peace,' Alban said, hoping this in itself sounded like agreement – it wasn't particularly meant to be.

'Tony,' Feaguing said, putting his hand between the junior exec's shoulder blades, 'would you have a word with Mr Percy Wopuld—'

'It's Schofield,' Alban said. 'Uncle Perce married in.'

'Schofield, of course, I beg your pardon,' Feaguing said, nodding and holding up one hand, glancing at Alban and then smiling back at Fromlax. 'Percy's the Brand Manager? Guy with the glasses over there, sat next to the fire with Winifred? He has some questions.' Feaguing patted his junior's back. 'Would you do that?'

'Certainly,' Fromlax said, and – with a last, part dark, part pitying look at Alban – got up, retrieved his laptop from the narrow table behind the couch and went over towards the group of people gathered round the fireplace.

Feaguing watched as Fromlax joined them. 'She's a very special and wonderful lady, your grandmother,' he told Alban.

'Oh, she's something,' Alban said. He decided he was getting rather good at this seeming-to-agree ploy.

'You'll have to excuse Tony,' Feaguing said. 'The guy takes his religion pretty neat.' He grinned broadly. He was dressed in slacks and a shirt and sweater and held a tumbler with whisky and ice. 'You kinda have to make allowances for some of these younger guys, cut them a bit of slack.' He held up one hand. 'Not that he's any younger than you, Mr McGill. But you know what I mean.'

'Of course.'

'Me,' Feaguing said, gesturing at his chest with his whisky glass, 'I'm a devout capitalist.'

'Please, call me Alban; after all, Tony and I were on first-name terms and we were close to blows.'

Feaguing grinned, sat back. 'I understand you've been speaking up for the family firm staying with the family,' he said. He held up one hand as though to forestall something. 'I just want to say, I completely understand. In your position, I'd have mixed feelings myself.'

Alban thought of saying that his feelings weren't mixed, they were totally against the takeover, but this wasn't strictly true, he supposed, so he didn't.

'It's a big decision,' Feaguing said, sitting forward, cradling his glass in both hands, looking thoughtful. He nodded, also thoughtfully. 'And I know and respect what your family has done with the heritage that *Empire!* and the other games represent. It's a record to be proud of. Your family should be proud.'

'There haven't been too many sins this family hasn't indulged to the hilt,' Alban said. 'I doubt we missed pride.'

Feaguing grinned again, flashing very white teeth. 'Now, look, obviously, I'm here to close the deal.' His hands were spread wide. 'But I want to tell you about the corporate attitude at Spraint, about the way we work, about our philosophy. I did say to call me Larry, didn't I?'

'Yes, you did,' Alban told him. 'Larry, you want to buy the family firm because you think you'll make more money owning what we own rather than licensing it. It then becomes a question of how many of us value our holding above whatever your best offer turns out to be. I don't see how philosophy really comes into it.'

Larry looked pained, scratched behind one ear. 'Well, we've kind of made our best offer,' he said. Alban didn't even bother to do anything with his expression. 'But anyway,' Feaguing went on, 'I want you to understand that I'm sincere here, Alban. Don't be over-cynical, please. Different companies do business in different ways. If that wasn't true, your family firm wouldn't have succeeded so well over the last century and more. If it wasn't true then there'd be no winners and losers, just everybody doing pretty much the same, and life is certainly not like that. At Spraint we believe in the long term, we believe in commitment, we believe in shared values. It's not just about money.'

'I thought you had a duty to increase shareholder value.'

'Absolutely. But there are as many ways of doing that, once you include all the variables, as there are, well, say, of becoming better educated. What classes do you want to do? What do you invest in? Both simple-sounding questions, both infinitely complicated answers.'

'But it is still about money.'

'You know,' Larry said, sitting back, frowning, 'this might sound like a strange thing to say, but in a way money is kind of irrelevant.'

Alban widened his eyes. 'Really?'

'What I mean is, it's just how you keep score. Like a ball game. The scoreboard, the numbers on it; they're just things. It's what those numbers buy you, what they get you that matters; not the numbers themselves.'

'I wish I was an economist,' Alban said, 'we could debate this properly.'

'What matters is how people feel,' Feaguing said. 'Do people feel good having a bunch of money in the bank, or in stocks? Do they feel better owning a Harley or a Lexus or a Sunseeker or a Lear Jet? How many of those can you use? Do they feel better being involved with a company that is simply trying to give them the figures to buy the same sort of stuff they could buy with shares in any other company, or – and here's the thing – do they feel better investing in a company that shares the values they hold themselves?

Values of long-term commitment to worthwhile projects, the very real worth of excellence for its own sake, a proven long-term commitment to extensive charitable works, a belief in the future of science and technology allied to a recognition of the basic human need for diversion and game-playing *and* all the life-enhancing lessons that the best scenarios and games are able to teach.'

Alban sat in his seat, looking at Larry Feaguing. Alban had his legs crossed, one elbow on his knee and his chin on his fist. He had the distinct impression he was getting a regurgitated, slightly jumbled version of a more coherent – and doubtless more inspiring – speech Feaguing had once been on the receiving end of. Alban shook his head. 'Well, they do say Europe and North America are growing further apart all the time. You have to hope they've left enough slack in all those transatlantic cables.'

Larry sat back and looked pained again. 'Alban, I'm just trying to tell you that companies have characters, like people do, and I feel proud of the character of Spraint Corp. That is not bullshit. Excuse me, but I mean this sincerely. We honour what you've done with *Empire!* and the other games and we think we'll be worthy inheritors of that heritage. Your family has done wonderful things with those games in the past. Together we've done wonderful things with the various properties over the past six years, but it's our belief that there's an even greater potential in the titles that we're confident can only be realised if we are allowed the privilege of taking over their stewardship.'

Alban shrugged. 'I won't argue you're not sincere, Larry. But ultimately of course this is all about money.'

Feaguing shook his head. 'I wish I could make you believe otherwise, Alban, I really do.'

'Maybe we're both getting this the wrong way round,' Alban suggested. 'Perhaps you're right about the character and morals of Spraint Corp, but you're giving the Wopuld clan way too much respect for their beliefs and collective character. Maybe all *we're* interested in is money.'

'Do you really believe that, Alban?' Feaguing asked quietly.

Alban looked around the room at all his many, many relations, this widespread but, for now – briefly – concentrated family, which he had loved and hated and served and exiled himself from and longed for and come to an accommodation with and still half loved and half hated sometimes, and then he looked back at Feaguing with a small smile. 'I don't know,' he said. 'But if I were you I'd treat it as a decent working hypothesis.'

Fielding snored, Alban discovered. It was so bad that he ended up having to pad along to the nearest bathroom and make a couple of little wads of toilet paper to stuff in his ears as plugs. He lay awake for a while after that, thinking of VG, wondering where she was laying her tousled head that night, how she was sleeping. The rain and the wind had barely slackened all day.

A gust – which he heard over Fielding's snoring and through the improvised ear plugs – shook the windows in their frames.

He was struggling to make his way down through the upward stream of water, blown this way and that by the pummelling wind and rain. There was somebody down there, somebody ahead of him, somebody who'd fallen through the rushing stream in front of him. He'd watched her go and then realised he had to save her and so thrown himself in too but then the water hadn't let him, it was rushing back up at him, flowing the wrong way, forcing him upwards so that he had to struggle against it and fight his way down.

'Alban!'

The voice sounded distant, underwater. For a few moments he thought it might be her voice, but it wasn't. It was too deep.

'*Alban!*'

He woke up tangled in damp bedclothes, as though the stream he'd been fighting had suddenly set, coagulating around him into a twistedly solid form.

'You okay?' It was Fielding.

Alban realised he was at Garbadale, in a single bed, sharing a room. He took one of his ear plugs out, cleared his throat and ran a hand over his sweaty face. 'Sorry, yeah.' He kicked at some of the sheets, releasing a trapped leg, sticking it out to cool. 'Sorry about that.'

'Nightmare?' Fielding asked, his voice sounding normal now, not underwater.

'Kind of.' Alban looked around. The room was perfectly dark. He couldn't see a thing. He twisted his head and looked at the little bedside cabinet, just to see the sea-green glow of his watch dial, hovering in the darkness like the face of a tiny, constant ghost.

'Sounded like it,' Fielding said.

'Sorry if I woke you up.'

'Never mind. Try and get back to sleep. No more nightmares.'

'Yeah. Thanks. No more nightmares.'

He lay awake for a while after that, staring at the unseen ceiling, listening to the wind and the rain and trying to recall who it had been he had thought he was trying to rescue.

Breakfast was another straggled, well-spaced affair. Alban spent a couple of hours in the dining room, taking a very long and leisurely breakfast and talking to most of the people he hadn't managed to talk to already. He got the impression that a lot of people were assuming everybody else was all for the sale, while they themselves weren't, but still expected to lose the vote. A surprising number were against the sale at any price, or so they said.

The weather was starting to improve and there was talk of some of the adults forming a shooting party after lunch, to cull a few hinds. Various males were already committed to spending most of the day in front of the big plasma screen in the TV lounge, watching sport. Andy came down late for breakfast, looked at the still falling rain and suggested tomorrow might be a better day for Alban and him to scatter the flowers on the loch. Alban agreed.

A treasure hunt in the gardens had been arranged later in the afternoon for those children who didn't think such childish pursuits beneath them. Alban helped set the treasure hunt up during the hour after his elongated breakfast, hiding prizes and instructions, most of them rain-proofed in plastic kitchenware boxes, amongst the trees and bushes and lawns of the garden, all according to a plan drawn up by Aunt Lauren.

He wandered a little, visiting parts of the gardens the treasure hunt wasn't supposed to reach, taking in the pinetum, the arboretum and the old walled kitchen garden, its long-vanished glasshouses present only in the ghostly form of marks on the walls and the channels of the flues for the fires that had heated the plants in the winter.

The rain had almost ceased now, the wind shifting, blowing in clear from the north-west. He walked under the fine, tall trees he remembered from earlier visits – various pines and firs plus a number of Western Hemlock and Wellingtonia – letting the few fat heavy drops of leaf-filtered rain fall on to his face. Too many places were choked with rhodies, he thought. The place was ideal for them – peaty, acidic soil, lots of rain – but it needed a clear-out.

He was surrounded by the signs of autumn – the leaves were turning, the deciduous trees beginning the process of drawing the goodness inward, leaving the leaves to yellow and redden and brown and fall.

He returned to the house as the last of the rain cleared and blue skies appeared between the mountains to the north-west. The temperature had dropped a couple of degrees, but it still felt mild.

Sophie met him in the cloakroom as he took his jacket off. 'Alban, would you come fishing with me?'

'Fishing?' he said. 'What, on Loch Garve?'

'Yeah. Care to?' she asked. She wore chunky black boots, black jeans, a green blouse that matched her eyes and a grey sweater. She stood, arms folded, leaning back against the wall by the door into the rest of the house, one leg up behind her.

'You're not shooting, then?' he asked.

'Not a great fan of guns,' she told him. 'But I've kinda taken up fishing back home. I asked your pal Neil McBride and he said you knew the loch pretty well and you might take me if I asked you nicely.'

'Well, he's the real expert,' Alban said, hanging up his jacket. 'But I've got a rough idea of the best places; the ones Neil's told me about, anyway. Anybody else coming?'

'Just us.' She smiled. 'That okay?'

'Course it's okay,' he said. He looked at his watch – it was nearly noon. 'Give me half an hour to get everything together. You want to eat before we go or take a packed lunch down the loch?'

'I'll organise some food to take with us. Neil's sorting us a boat.'

'Good man. We'll need to be back about five at the latest, that all right?'

'Sure.'

He scratched the nape of his neck. 'We will be out in this wee boat for several hours; I'd schedule a toilet break before we head off.'

She hoisted one eyebrow. 'Aye-aye, cap'n.'

'Okay then.'

'Okay.'

Neil had the boat started and idling at the jetty for them. 'You've got a full tank,' he told Alban, 'and there's a can of fuel under the bow seat, though you shouldn't need it. Already mixed, but you might want to give it a good slosh around before you pour it in, if you do have to. Funnel's in the wee crate under the back seat there, with the rest of the bits and bobs.'

'Cheers, Neil.' Alban stepped in and started stowing the fishing gear in the little boat. Sophie had one of the rods, a fishing bag and the cool box with the food.

'Forecast is fine,' Neil told them. 'Clear. Wind's to stay the same or freshen a bit. Three to a four.'

'That all?' Alban said. 'Good as dead calm by Loch Garve standards.'

'Want a suggestion?' Neil asked.

'Sure.'

'Try down at Eagle Rock, under Meall an Aonaich. Do you know that bit?'

'Nearly at the head?'

'Aye, about a mile this way. There's a buoy off the bit of shore between the two burns. Tie up there and use fly for brownies. The wash-off from the burns pushes them out that way after heavy rain. If that doesn't work 'cause there's too much chop I've put a couple of wee rods in for spinners.'

'Okay.' Alban turned to Sophie as she handed him the stuff she'd been carrying. 'It's a fair distance to get there, but I guess we'll get a couple of hours in.'

'Fine by me,' she said. Sophie wore a dark blue jacket over what she'd been wearing earlier, with a canvas gilet over that, much pocketed. Neil helped her slip into a slim, self-inflating life-jacket, then she put out one hand and Alban held it while she stepped into the boat, taking a long stride to bring her foot down in the centre of the bottom boards.

'Well, have fun,' Neil told them.

'See you later,' Alban said.

'Thanks again,' Sophie told Neil. 'Hope the shooting goes well.'

'For everybody but the deer, aye,' Neil said, casting them off.

Loch Garve was nearly twenty-six kilometres long and nowhere wider than two. At nearly two hundred metres in places it was deeper than the North Sea; a steep-sided inland loch bordered and hemmed in by tall mountains and shaped 'like a dug's hind leg' according to Neil McBride.

The wind was behind them as they headed south-east in the slim, clinker-built boat, the little four-horsepower two-stroke droning away at their backs. He didn't need it for the temperature, but Alban pulled a thick ski glove over his hand holding the motor's throttle tiller. These old two-strokes were rattly, buzzy old things.

'You want to sit up the front?' he asked Sophie, raising his voice over the noise of the engine. 'Keep us better trimmed. Kind of hard to talk over the sound of this thing anyway.' He patted the motor's tiller. The handle of the starting lanyard was protruding a little; he pushed it fully into the cowling. 'We can gossip all we like once we're moored and the engine's off.'

'Okay,' she said. She moved to the front, keeping low, taking care to avoid stepping on the oars and rods in the bottom of the boat, swinging her legs over the midship seat and taking up her position on the little seat nubbed in across the angle of the bows, looking back once at him – they exchanged smiles – then facing forward, away from him and towards the loch and the mountains ahead.

He'd watched the material of her jeans tighten and stretch over her trim little behind as she made the manoeuvre.

Was this no more than it appeared to be? He didn't know. He was happy to be with her, and she seemed to be genuinely interested in fishing, and maybe this was partly her way of letting him know they were okay now, that they could be friends, even if not especially close ones . . . Still, he'd felt surprised when she'd first suggested this little expedition, and almost instantly suspicious. He had Sophie down as one of the definite Fors, a certain Yes. She was almost certainly going to vote to sell to Spraint, even though she was employed by the US side of the family business and wasn't guaranteed a job with Spraint if they did buy them out.

From what Alban knew, Sophie was good at her job of Retail Liaison Officer, even if he'd never entirely worked out exactly what this job description meant. If he'd been Larry Feaguing he'd have had a word by now and made her a verbal promise she would be found a post within Spraint. Though without, of course, putting anything in writing or necessarily meaning to make good on the promise.

Was she going to try to persuade him not to make his pitch at the meeting before the EGM? Was she going to try to get him to change what she – or whoever might have put her up to this – thought he was going to say? He looked out across the hull-slapping waves of the loch and then up at the distant, darkly towering mass of Ben More Assynt coming into view round the shoulder of a nearer hill, both peaks starting to appear as the mass of clouds lifted. Or, he thought, perhaps he was just being too suspicious.

He thought of VG again, maybe now climbing in the dry at last. He knew exactly what she'd ask. What did he really want? What was he really attempting to achieve?

Oh, how the hell should he know? He wanted to be happy but he didn't even know who he wanted to be happy with, or even if he really needed somebody else around to be happy with. *Why* should he know? Nobody else seemed to know, or if they did, they weren't acting on it in any obviously sensible way. He wanted peace and love and all that shit for the whole fucking world and you'd imagine that sort of stuff would be fairly near the top of every-body's wish list, but it was all going in the other direction, descending into madness and barbarism, reverting to a mind-numbing, morality-sapping set of cruel, mutually intolerant superstitions and authori-tarianisms. Stupidity and viciousness were rewarded, illegality not just tolerated but encouraged, lying profoundly worked, and torture was justified – even lauded. Meanwhile the whole world was warming up, getting ready to drown.

Everybody should know better. Nobody did.

Every fucker was mad, nobody paid any attention whatso-bleeding-ever to whatever was in their best interests, so how the hell was he supposed to be any better or different?

He shifted his position on the thin cushion covering the wooden seat. The little engine revved high, wasting fuel. He turned and adjusted the throttle friction control. He turned back and watched the rear of Sophie's head, her neat, shoulder-length blonde hair barely moving as the boat almost kept pace with the wind at their backs.

What did she want? What was her goal?

Maybe the girl just needed to get some quality time in. Perhaps she wanted to do some fishing and soak up some of the tranquillity of the old family estate before it was all sold off. Maybe it wasn't even anything to do with him – with their history together – at all; perhaps it was just her being sensible, going with somebody who knew the loch rather than taking a boat out herself. On the face of it Loch Garve was no more treacherous or difficult than any other inland loch, but it would be an especially unforgiving place to get into difficulties because there was nowhere except the foot of it – the Garbadale end – to go for help; there was no other house or shelter, and no road or even forestry track on either shore, just a rough path on the north-east side which was more or less passable in a well-driven quad bike or an Argocat. Even that was probably a no-go on a day like today, with multiple fording points blocked by streams and burns in spate after all the recent rain.

After about half an hour they made a shallow turn round the shoulder of Mullach and were out of sight of the house. A minute or two later Sophie came swivelling back towards the stern of the boat, still keeping low. Alban watched the bows rise slightly as the boat adjusted to the weight transferral. The waves had grown a little since they'd left Garbadale, partly because they'd left the lee of the trees and the shallow rise the house was built on, but mostly because of the reach becoming greater; the wind had an increasingly long stretch of water to work on, gradually pushing up fractionally taller waves. They were still going with the wind and the waves, however, and so their progress was almost stately. It would feel a bit choppier coming back, but the waves weren't near breaking and the forecast was good; there shouldn't be any drama.

'Okay?' he asked Sophie as she sat next to him, raising his voice over the sound of the outboard.

'Fine.' She leaned closer, nodded at the insulated box. 'Want some coffee?'

'Good idea.'

They sat together on the transom seat, holding cups of coffee.

'Thanks for coming with me,' she said.

328

'No problem; good idea. I guess we won't be able to do this again once the place is sold. Glad you suggested it.'

She looked back and down, frowning at his hand holding the engine's throttle tiller. 'Why are you wearing just one glove?'

He shrugged. 'I can stick this one in my pocket,' he said, holding up his hand with the coffee cup. Not a lie, he told himself, and it saved a lot of boring explanation. They sat together within the companionable noisiness of the engine's monotone drone for a while.

Now she was staring at his left hand. 'Oh my God, what happened to your little finger?'

'Oh, chainsaw accident,' he said, looking at his half-finger. 'Few years ago.'

'Jeez, Alban.'

'Only a nuisance when I'm trying to get wax out my left ear.'

'Thanks for sharing that,' she said.

'Welcome,' he told her. 'Oh. Should have checked this before we started out, but do you know how to work the engine? Just in case I fall overboard – you know, trying to land a marlin or a great white or something – or lapse into a coffee-induced coma or whatever.'

She looked back at the engine. 'It's a two-stroke. There's no little window so I guess you add the oil to the gas before you put it in the tank.' Then she pointed as she said, 'Starting lanyard, choke, twist throttle, throttle friction whadaya-callit –'

'Okay.' He touched her forearm. 'You've passed.'

They rinsed the cups over the side, then she went back to sit up front. He'd switched hands – and glove – once so far, and was about to do so again when he remembered an old trick.

He took some care to make only the most minute adjustments to the tiller to keep their course straight – substituting small increments and patience for coarse inputs and quick results – and waited until the bearing the bows indicated on the mountains far ahead didn't seem to have changed for a minute or so, then he carefully let go of the tiller and stood up, moving forward towards the widest part of the boat, feet planted as far apart as the inner hull would allow.

329

Sophie felt something change in the attitude of the boat and looked back.

Her eyes widened deliberately. 'You going to test me on what to do if you fall overboard?' she said.

He shook his head. 'If you get the engine set just right,' he said loudly, 'and the wind's behaving itself, you can steer like this.' He leaned to the right, tipping the boat a few degrees. Their heading started to change fractionally to starboard. He gave a big grin. 'See?'

'I see.' She smiled broadly, too. 'You're showing off.'

'Nah, me bum was getting sore,' he said, gesturing.

She nodded. 'Well, if you are going to fall overboard, be sure to give me plenty of warning.'

'Will do.'

She turned to face the wilderness of water, hill and sky that was all that was ahead of them.

They ate their lunch while still under way, to make more time for fishing when they stopped.

Half an hour later they moored at the little sun-bleached, pale orange buoy floating fifty metres or so off the portion of shore between the two burns draining the north-west slope of Meall an Aonaich. The sky was almost clear of cloud, though they were in the shadow of the long western ridge leading to Ben More Assynt, so the air felt cool. The wind had dropped a little here in what was essentially a wide bay between the two mountains. Almost the only sound was of waves slapping against the clinkered planks of the boat.

After he'd shut down the outboard, the silence had rushed in like something more than absence, like some anti-sound that was still somehow as loud as the noise it had suddenly replaced. He remembered the burglar alarm, heard from his bedroom during that summer night in Richmond, twenty years earlier. He recalled it as though it was for the last time, gently pushing it away as if it was something that he could now safely consign to the shadowy depths beneath their little boat.

Alban closed his eyes at one point to concentrate on what he could hear. He heard the sound of Sophie's clothes sliding over each other as she reached back and forth, arm swaying, casting. He heard the faint, rasping sound of the reel. Somewhere a seagull called, sounding plaintive and lonely and lost, unechoing.

He opened his eyes, glanced at Sophie – she didn't seem to have noticed him closing his eyes – and felt – even though there was a hint of sadness in there, too – oddly, almost blissfully happy.

'Bit choppy for fly fishing,' Sophie said after a few casts.

Alban was inclined to agree. They switched to spinners, using the smaller rods, casting differently, further, reeling in smoothly.

'How close do you think this vote's going to be?' Sophie asked him, flicking the rod back and then snapping forward, sending the little spinner up just far enough to rise above the ridge shadow and into the sunlight, making it glitter briefly before plunging first into the shade and then into the deeper darkness of the loch.

'Closer than most people think,' Alban said, reeling in with a slow, measured motion. 'Close enough to make Spraint raise their offer.'

Sophie glanced at him. 'You reckon?'

'If they see the way the wind's blowing they'll raise it before the EGM. If they're as smart as they should be.'

'They have the authority for that?' Her voice was quiet. They were both speaking very softly now with so little other sound around them. Stuck out in the middle of a chopping loch in broad, slightly chilly daylight it gave their conversation an oddly enclosed, even intimate feeling.

'Up to some unspecified point, allegedly,' Alban said. 'Feaguing's senior enough to double their initial offer, I'd guess. Aunt Kath feels the same way, and Win. She insisted they send people who could negotiate on the ground rather than just some ceremonial team with a rubber stamp, a crate of bubbly and some pious words about the proud family tradition being safe in their hands. Above a certain point – which they're not giving away, obviously – they

331

have to phone home, but even if they seem to do that it could be a ploy. You know, like when a car salesman says he has to go and talk with his manager to discuss what you're asking for your trade-in and just goes for a coffee or a dump instead and then comes back shaking his head and saying, sorry, if it was up to him, but, gee, his boss is such a hard-ass.' Alban retrieved his lure, cast it again.

Sophie nodded slowly, gathering her own small silvery spinner back in. 'I think I'm going to vote no,' she said.

Alban looked at her. 'Well, that's a surprise. I was sure you'd be for selling.'

'They've offered me a job,' she told him.

'Spraint.'

'Yeah. Say they'll keep me on, with promotion, more money, stock.'

'You got that in writing?'

'No.' She sounded amused.

'And? What? That made you change your mind? Somehow that offer was counter-productive?'

'No, but it got me thinking.'

'Always dangerous.'

She grinned. 'I realised I like what I'm doing just now. Maybe in five or ten years' time I'd be ready to take on something like what they're offering, but right now I'm happy enough. And in addition I don't know that we have the right to sell out the firm when there's another generation that might criticise us for it.' She glanced at Alban.

'Getting broody?' he asked, making a wild guess.

'It's something I've thought of,' she admitted. 'There's a guy I'm seeing, back home.'

'Ah-ha.' He still got this odd feeling when she said 'home' and meant the US.

'Same guy I've been seeing all this time. Same guy I switched courses for, way back.'

Ah-hah, he thought. 'Wow,' he said. 'You have been patient.' Maybe, he thought, too patient; like me.

'Yeah,' she said ruefully. 'You're not kidding. He's been married, had two kids and divorced again in the meantime, but,' she sighed, 'we're back together again. After all that.'

Dear God, he thought. I knew nothing of this. What a gulf, what an ocean, what an Atlantic between us. If we are so much the sum of what we've done and what's been done to us, I barely know this woman at all. Who – where – is the Sophie you think you know?

'I guess we're pretty serious,' she said. 'We've talked about marriage, kids. I've always been, I don't know; unsure, but, hey,' she glanced at him again, 'just getting to that age, you know? Don't want to leave it too much longer.'

'I'm sure you'd make a wonderful mother,' he told her.

'Gee, thanks.' She said it like she thought he'd meant to be sarcastic.

'Seriously,' he said.

She looked at him again, then lifted the dripping lure from the water, swung it back, clicking the reel and casting again. The spinner headed high and struck sunlight once more, glinting briefly. 'Sorry,' she said. 'Okay. But. So. I think I'll vote against.'

'Me and my pitiful hundred shares will be with you. Much to my surprise.'

'Yeah, I think Win was surprised too.'

'You told her?'

'She just plain asked, dude,' she told him. 'Came right out with it, as though she was confused and thought I'd already told her, which I hadn't. And I'm pretty sure she knew I hadn't. Good acting, though. She's a manipulative old bird, isn't she?'

Alban laughed. 'Yes. Yes she is. I thought I was the only person who felt that way.'

'No, I wouldn't put much past her.'

'Same here.'

'We're sure nobody's done any private deals with Spraint?' Sophie asked.

'Hard to see how they could. The family trust has first refusal on any proposed share sell.'

'Okay.' She was silent for a moment. 'Is it true you and Fielding made up some sort of road show, drumming up support for the Anti cause?'

'Yeah, at Win's suggestion, too, apparently.'

'Uh-huh. I had her down as a seller, too.'

'Not that we had much effect, far as I could see,' Alban said.

'No?'

'Well, not much.' He stopped reeling in, letting his spinner sink a little. 'Though it did occur to me,' he said, 'that what we were really doing was upping the price.'

Sophie glanced at him.

He shrugged. 'Maybe Win does want to sell, but not at the current price. She reckoned we were rolling over for them too low, so she thought she'd try and up the numbers who'd vote against. The idea being that Spraint realise there's more opposition than they were expecting so they have to offer more. Win gets her way. But what she wants is just a higher price, not outright rejection.'

'Hmm.' Sophie did not sound as impressed with this bit of vicarious Machiavellianism as Alban had hoped. 'But you'd think she would be the one person who wanted to keep the family firm together,' she said. 'She's the matriarch, this is her watch. She ought to be the guardian of the family values. And the family valuables.'

'I think Win's secretly – actually, not that secretly – an egomaniac,' Alban said. 'Everything has to revolve around her. Soon she'll be dead, or so infirm she won't be able to control the family and the firm any more, and she hates the thought of somebody else being in charge. Better to sell up, liquidate it all, dissolve it into some big corporation. So she gets to be like a bookend, founding father Henry being the other. A fitting sense of finality for her.'

'Okay,' Sophie said, nodding slowly. She seemed slightly more taken with this piece of analysis. 'Well, I suppose.' She looked at

Alban. 'What if it's worked too well? What if nobody wants to sell now?'

'Well, some people definitely do; Aunt Kath for one. But I've been doing the arithmetic and it's tighter than anybody was expecting.'

'Interesting,' Sophie said.

'Oh,' Alban sighed, reeling in, 'isn't it all?'

They were both standing up, letting their feet take their weight for a change, confident that the boat's gentle rocking wasn't close to tipping them overboard and used enough to the motion by now to be easy with it, casting smoothly without disturbing the boat appreciably. They'd caught a couple of slim, glistening brown trout each. They had been borderline small so they'd thrown them back.

He'd wondered if they'd talk much about the old days, about what they'd meant to each other, but they hadn't. They'd mentioned Lydcombe a couple of times, San Francisco just once:

'I'm not sure I ever apologised to you properly for getting you into trouble with your boyfriend,' he'd said.

'Dan? Yeah, that was a tad embarrassing.' Her eyes had gone wide. She'd shrugged. 'My own fault. I got us both drunk, I'd been thinking about our grass-flattening escapades at Lydcombe. I just felt horny and you were there.' She'd smiled. 'Also, I was kind of doing it for closure, though I somehow neglected to inform you of this at the time. I always worried you were doing it because you wanted us to be together for ever or something.' She made a snorting noise.

I did tell you you were the love of my life, he'd thought. He hadn't said it.

'Scarred me for life,' he'd said instead, in a manner to make light of it. 'Well, up until you told me to get out of your sight that time in Singapore.'

'Yeah,' she'd said, turning to him, eyes big again. 'You were *so* drunk then!'

Yeah, he thought. Just drunk. Not sincere or ruined for other women or still burning for you or anything. Just drunk.

Oh well. The stiffened breeze blew some of his hair into his eyes. He brushed it away again.

Alban checked his watch. 'Want to do the last hour or so trawling? We can keep the engine on idle and start to head back up the loch.'

Sophie nodded. 'Yeah, okay. Want me to cast off?'

'Thanks. If you would.'

He put his rod down in the boat, turned and squatted to face the engine, pumped the bulb on the fuel line, adjusted the choke and then grasped the plastic handle of the starting lanyard and began a strong, smooth pull. 'This old thing usually takes a couple of—' he was saying when the starting lanyard broke and he went flying backwards, staggering, falling across the midships seat and whacking his head on the bottom boards.

He looked up. Sophie was looking down at him, a concerned look on her face; her arms were outstretched as she balanced in the rocking boat. 'You okay?'

The back of his head hurt a bit. He was lying in the bottom of the boat with his legs up over the central seat, as though preparing to give birth. He looked at his right hand, which was still holding the lanyard's handle. He listened; waves slapping hull. No engine sound. Shit.

'I'm okay,' he said, and accepted Sophie's hand, lifting himself back up and turning to sit down on the seat.

'Garbadale we have a problem?' Sophie said, squatting in front of him.

He stared at the lanyard. Looked like it had broken near the engine end. Frayed, worn-looking fibres waved in the breeze when he held them up. He felt like throwing the damn thing overboard, but didn't.

'Will we have to row?' Sophie asked.

'Christ, no,' Alban said. 'I'll just take the top of the engine off and reattach the lanyard.' He turned, hoisted his feet over the seat

336

and knelt on the boards in front of the transom seat. 'There'll be a . . .' His voice trailed off as he looked and felt under the seat. 'A fucking tool-box, which is not here,' he finished. There was a small plastic crate under the seat. He brought it out. It contained the fuel funnel, a little hand-bailer, a small first-aid kit, a reel of floating line and an empty cardboard spark plug carton. Alban sat down on the bottom boards, looking round the boat to see where else the tool kit might be. Not anywhere else, really. He put the lanyard in the crate with the other stuff.

'So now are we going to have to row?' Sophie asked.

Alban looked at his watch. 'It'll take us till fucking midnight to get back.'

Sophie had her phone out. She started pressing buttons, then stopped. 'Ah,' she said.

'You'll be lucky,' Alban said. 'Barely works at the house. Nothing down here at all.' Alban sat up on the seat and turned to the engine. He took the plastic top cover off. There were eight twelve-mill bolts that had to be removed before you could get at the drum that housed the starting lanyard. He tested them, on the highly unlikely off-chance they were only finger tight, but they were solid. He looked at his Swiss Army knife. That wasn't going to be adequate.

They checked beneath the bottom boards, in case the tool kit had got down there somehow; all they found was dirty water. Sophie's fishing paraphernalia had nothing any more hardcore than Alban's knife.

He caught a glimpse of the pale orange buoy, some distance off. They were cast off. He looked up to check their position. They were drifting slowly down the loch, further away from the house all the time, heading for the south-east edge of the wide bay. He checked his watch again. It was quarter past three. The EGM was scheduled for six, with the closed session part a half-hour earlier.

They'd be rowing into a moderately stiff breeze for over twenty kilometres. He hadn't rowed any distance for years and Sophie looked gym fit but was probably less powerful than he was. The only alternative was to go ashore and start hiking. Either way they'd never make it in time; it could easily be dark by the time they got back to the house. Realistically, they'd be relying on somebody raising the alarm and coming to look for them in another boat.

Alban felt a growing, gnawing sensation in his guts, a terrible feeling of powerless anxiety, of failure and inadequacy and help-lessness.

'Well,' he said, doing his best to display a confidence-inspiring smile to Sophie. 'I guess rowing is what it has to be.' He gestured for her to sit on the rear seat. 'I'll start off,' he told her. 'You can spell me for a bit if you like.'

'Sure,' she said. He placed the rowlocks in their holes, put the oars in place and started push-pulling to bring them round almost one-eighty degrees.

'You done much rowing?' he asked.

'Kayaks,' she said, an apologetic expression on her face.

'Better than nothing,' he said. 'Piece of piss, really.' There wasn't even room in the slim boat for them to take an oar each.

When the stern of the boat was starting to point in the direction they'd been drifting, he began rowing. The oars weren't quite matched with the rowlocks and kept jumping out. 'Bit rusty,' he said. 'Soon get into the rhythm.'

Sophie smiled thinly. She checked her life-jacket.

He looked behind him. The wind was already an appreciable force against the boat and once they rounded the headland formed by the base of Assynt they'd be straight into the teeth of it.

This was going to be a long pull.

Sophie was looking at her watch. 'We going to make the EGM?' she asked.

'Umm, probably not as currently scheduled,' he admitted. Alban reckoned they'd require a complete about-turn in the wind and the services of an Olympic oarsman to get back before coffee and petits fours.

'Shit,' she said. 'Anything I can do?'

He thought. 'Come to think of it, you can pull the engine up out of the water. No sense dragging that through the loch.' He felt like an idiot. He'd only been rowing for a minute, but it was something he should have thought of immediately. He wondered what else he might have missed.

Idiot, he told himself. Idiot, idiot, idiot.

'Let me know when you want me to take over,' Sophie said.

'Will do,' he said. 'Shout out if we look like we're about to go aground. Ideally we want to just miss that headland.'

She looked round him at the view ahead, nodded.

He settled into a sort of rhythm, though the feeling that the oars were always about to jump out of the rowlocks was constantly unsettling. There was no purpose-built footboard to brace your feet against when rowing, so you had to use the ribs of the boat, which was okay as it was quite narrow, but he seemed to be just the wrong height, slightly too long in the leg for one set of ribs and too short for the next set sternwards. Plus his hands were already starting to chafe. *Fuck* it; his fingers and palms used to be calloused and hard. He'd been out of work for barely two months and already it felt like he had the hands of Marcel Proust. He'd put the gloves on soon.

He tried to empty his mind and settle to the task, into the simple push and pull of rowing. He did his best to feather the oars with each return stroke, rolling the blades of the oars flat to cut through the oncoming breeze. This was the proper way to row and would make a significant difference heading into the wind over the sort of distance they were looking at, but he'd never managed to incorporate the motions required into what passed for his natural rowing technique and he doubted he'd keep it up.

Oh, fuck, this was going to be hellish.

He smiled at Sophie and she smiled back, but she looked concerned and he felt the same way.

What was to be done? What else was there to do?

The phone? No chance. On the other hand, you never knew. Mobile phone masts could leak signals through unlikely little corridors in the hills. If nothing else, this would give Sophie something to do. 'Keep trying the phone for signal, every few minutes,' he told her. He shrugged. 'Just in case.' An oar jumped out and he rolled his eyes and said, 'Shit.'

He looked round at the headland they were aiming for. It didn't look much closer. It looked darker than it had, though; high clouds were closing in from the north-west, putting the surrounding landscape into shade. It was going to get dark even earlier if the cloud cover kept building up.

He stopped, shipping the oars.

'My turn?' Sophie asked.

'No, just putting these on,' he said, pulling out his gloves. He settled back into the rowing. The gloves made it all feel kind of mushy and distant, but at least they should save his skin.

What are we trying to do? he asked himself. Concentrate; what am I trying to do?

Get back to the house. So. Rowing looked like the only way. It was, wasn't it? Hiking would take at least as long.

Think out of the box. Think the way VG would think if she'd got herself into this pickle. (Would she have? Would she have been paranoid enough to have checked the tool kit was there? Never mind. Work with what you have, just watch out for assumptions.)

What assumptions was he making about hiking? Well, direction, for one.

Maybe there was another way out. Could they head in the other direction and tramp out via the head of the loch? He knew there was a track that, eventually, led down to Benmore Lodge and Glen Oykel, but he couldn't remember how far that was. He could visualise the relevant map only vaguely, and seemed to recall it looked like a pretty long walk. Plus, both while they were rowing to the head of the loch and while they were hiking this unknown path, they'd be heading away from any help that might come from Garbadale.

So, rowing.

Was there any other way to start the engine?

It was a pull-start. No electric starter. You used the lanyard or nothing; that was it.

He thought on. If your car wouldn't start you could jump-start it. Well, that was a non-starter in every sense. The only electrical stuff they had were their watches and Sophie's phone. Not enough power there to turn an engine over, even if you could somehow connect the phone's battery to the spark plug (and you'd probably need to start dismantling the engine to do that, too).

You could push-start a car. Could you tow-start a boat? In theory, he supposed, if you could row at ninety knots or something you could restart the engine by just putting the fucker into gear and dropping it into the wash. In practice that was completely useless as an idea, too.

Think think think.

Oh, VG, he thought, I need you here now.

What they really needed was to get the engine going, the piston going up and down, driving through the simple gearbox to the prop shaft and then the prop itself.

Any other way to get the engine turning? Any other way to get the prop turning?

Both oars popped out of their rowlocks. He nearly lost hold of one.

'You okay?' Sophie asked, looking alarmed.

'I've just had a fucking brilliant idea!' he told her. He frowned. 'I think.'

He rowed them into the nearest stretch of shore, finding a patch of beach composed of pebbles and sand and rowing the boat up on to it.

'What's the idea?' Sophie asked. 'Is there a path? Are we hiking?'

'Wait, wait,' he said, digging in the plastic crate for the broken starting lanyard. 'Might not work.' He held up the lanyard. 'But it might. No idea but it's worth a try.'

'What?' Sophie asked.

'Show you,' he said.

He jumped out into the startlingly cold water, up to his thighs in a deeper bit than he'd been anticipating.

He swung the stern of the boat round so it was at about thirty degrees to the little beach and he could get at the prop. He stopped and thought for a moment, then wound the lanyard clockwise round the propeller.

'Okay, drop the engine,' he told Sophie.

When she'd done that he asked her to check the bulb on the fuel line was full and to set the choke and throttle. Sophie had worked out what he was doing. 'This is safe, isn't it?' she asked. 'You aren't going to get chewed up or anything, are you?'

'Just put it into ahead; I'll be okay.' He watched her pull the gear lever towards herself. 'Okay,' he said, bracing his free hand on to the transom of the boat and trying to find a firm footing on the sand and pebbles beneath his feet while the waves lapped round his thighs and soaked the crotch of his jeans. He looked at Sophie. 'You ready to put it into neutral if it catches?'

'Yeah.'

'It's going to jerk you towards me if it does because it's in gear.'

'I know. I'm ready. Just do it.'

'Here goes.'

He pulled hard on the lanyard, making the prop rotate as the rope unwound from it and forcing it, in turn, to spin the drive shaft and – through the gearbox – set the engine in motion.

The engine seemed to catch, then died again.

'You fucking beauty!' Alban yelled. 'This is going to work! Lift it out again!'

He wound the lanyard round the prop again, Sophie dropped the engine into the water, put it into forward gear and kept hold of the gear lever.

This time the engine caught and held, revving noisily and sending the wash back at his legs in a froth of smoky, bubbly water until Sophie knocked it into neutral and adjusted the throttle. He threw

342

the lanyard into the boat and waded out of the water, pushing the boat out by the stem, stern first into the waves. He leapt in.

Sophie held out one hand to let him sit at the stern, then, as he sat, grinning, taking hold of the throttle tiller, she bowed and applauded. 'Well done,' she said. She stepped up to him and planted a modest kiss on his right cheek.

'Home, Jemima, I rather think,' he said grandly, dropping the engine into gear and gunning it to send them curving out into the bay, heading for the foot of the loch and Garbadale.

They were within sight of the jetty and the grey roofs of the house were appearing over the still green treetops when Sophie looked round at him, then down at the lanyard, lying on the bottom boards where he'd thrown it after the engine had started. She picked it up and inspected the frayed end. Then she placed it back on the boards. The expression on her face had stayed thoughtful and serious while she was doing this. She looked into his eyes. Her eyebrows rose in a question.

He shrugged, keeping his expression neutral.

She gave a wry smile, checked her phone once more, then shook her head and turned away again.

He took the starting lanyard with him when they left the boat tied up at the jetty, stuffing the handle and length of grey rope into a jacket pocket.

They loaded up with the gear they needed to take back to the house.

'Wouldn't be impossible, would it?' Sophie said quietly as they walked up the path through the trees.

'Does seem slightly extreme,' he said.

'Wasn't cut.'

'No, that would be a bit obvious. All the fraying looks very fresh though.'

She glanced at him. 'Should we say anything?'

'Leave it with me.'

'Gladly, cuz.'

They walked on back to the house. Halfway there, they found the wreckage of the umbrella that had blown inside out and then away the day before, hanging from a tree a little way off the track. He climbed up and retrieved it and stuffed it into one of the bins at the back of the kitchens.

Sophie went for a bath before changing for the meeting and then dinner. Alban left his jacket in the cloakroom. He thought about taking the starting lanyard with him, but left it in the jacket pocket. He checked the television lounge, saying hi to the various guys and some of the older children. There was an argument going on about having to stop playing computer games and switching to a TV channel with the football results. Fielding told him the deer-hunting party had phoned to say they'd be back at the house in half an hour. Staff from the Sloy Hotel were helping to prepare the ballroom for the EGM. Alban found Aunt Lauren in the kitchen with cousin Steve and his wife Tessa, who was dandling their granddaughter Hannah on her lap.

'This is something called Ba'Aka honey,' Lauren was telling them as one of the waitresses from the Sloy Hotel enfolded some warm toast in a napkin and added it to a large tray set for tea and holding various little jugs and pots, one of which Lauren was pointing at. 'It's from Northern Congo. Awfully hard to get hold of. Very stimulating. So I'm told.'

'What, you haven't tried it?' Tessa asked.

'Well—' Lauren began.

'Hi, Alban,' Steve said. 'How was the fishing?'

'Didn't catch much,' Alban admitted, smiling at Tessa and making a big-eyed face at the baby so that she gurgled and held out one chubby hand towards him.

'Oh, Alban,' Lauren said, 'we were hoping for enough to make a first course.'

'Sorry,' he said. He nodded at the tray. 'That for Win?'

'Yes,' Lauren said. 'I was just about to take it up to her.'

'Allow me.'

'That's very kind but—' Lauren began, but Alban had already lifted the tray. 'Oh, all right then. I'll come with you.'

'No need,' he said, heading for the door.

'I can open the doors.'

'Whatever.'

'Win, it's—' Lauren began. Alban slid past her, tray over her head, into Win's sitting room. The old girl was sitting on a chair by a low table, dressed in her most exemplary tweeds, reading from a sheaf of papers.

'Me,' Alban said. 'Hi, Win.'

Grandma Win took off her reading glasses and looked at him, then at the tray he held. 'Alban,' she said smoothly, 'that's very kind.'

He'd been hoping for something more dramatic, like a swoon or a dropped glass, or at least a look of surprise. He glanced at the windows of the room. Bugger. He'd forgotten. They faced towards the loch. She might have been able to watch them coming back. Or – of course – it was entirely possible he was just being paranoid about what had happened with the starting lanyard.

'My pleasure,' Alban said.

'Will you stay for a cuppa, dear?' Win said, switching to little old lady mode. Alban put the tray down on the table.

'I'll get another cup, shall I?' Lauren said.

'Actually, Lauren,' Alban said, 'I'd like a word with Win in private.' He glanced down, smiling, at his grandmother. 'That be okay?'

'Well,' Lauren said, looking uncertain.

'That's all right, Lauren,' Win said.

'Oh,' Lauren said. 'Oh, all right then. I'll . . . I'll be in the kitchen, I should think.'

Aunt Lauren let herself out.

'So, Alban,' Win said as he poured their tea. 'Do I detect a note of urgency?'

'We need to talk, Win.'

'Well, do we now?' She squinted at her wrist-watch. 'How long till your little talk before the EGM?'

'About forty minutes.'

'Really? Then I suppose I should feel privileged.'

He handed her a cup. 'What sort of price do you think we should sell the firm for, Win?'

'Would you put some sugar in there, dear? My hands are so shaky.'

'Okay, Win,' he said, taking the cup back. 'Milk?'

'Just a little . . . A spot more. There.'

'There's some toast here,' Alban said pleasantly. 'Would you like some? With some of your special honey?'

'Oh, yes, please, Alban. Thank you so much. Oh! Butter first, dear.'

'So,' he said, 'this price. What do you think?'

'Well, I don't know that we should sell, at all. What do you think?'

'I think it's going to be a close call. I think – unless the Spraint guys have worked some sort of magic on the people who went shooting – they'll know by now their offer of a hundred and twenty isn't going to fly. I think they'll move to one-forty with the implication they might just go to one-fifty if we really press them. Their real ceiling is probably two hundred.'

Win crunched into her toast and honey. 'That is an awful lot of money.'

'Mind if I have some toast?'

'Please do.'

He took some of the honey, too. 'Of course, if they really do value us so highly, the implication is we'd make the same sort of money eventually through royalties and licence fees by just holding on to what we've got. Might be worth pointing that out to those who're determined to think with their wallets.' He bit into the honeyed toast and munched away. 'If,' he said at last, 'one wanted to put that sort of view across.'

346

'Yes, but what do you think, Alban? People – well, some people – seem to be looking to you for guidance. You need to sort out what you're going to say, don't you think?'

He finished his first slice of toast. 'This is really very good. Mind if I have another bit?'

'Oh, please,' Win said. She looked a little less gracious than she sounded. 'What good taste you display, Alban. It is particularly rare and expensive honey.'

'Better not finish it, then, eh?'

Win gave a small, uncertain laugh as Alban spooned the firm, dark honey thickly on to the toast.

'Weren't you fishing with Sophie?' Win asked.

'Yes. Not very successfully.'

'It's so fascinating that you two seem to be getting on better again.'

'Isn't it? Listen, Win, I want to offer you a deal.'

'What?' She sounded almost alarmed.

'Ultimately, I think we're going to sell. If we are, we should get the best price. I'd suggest telling Spraint it's one-eighty. Take it or leave it. The only negotiation should be over the mix of cash and stock. I'm prepared to say that, even though in my heart I'd rather we kept control. But I am prepared to say it. That would be my head talking, not my heart. At the moment, I'm not sure what to say.'

Win sat looking at him, blinking. 'Oh,' she said.

'I think one-eighty's a fair price,' he told her. 'But I want to know something before I recommend it. I mean,' he gestured with his hands, 'I may have less influence than either of us thinks and perhaps in the end it'll make no difference what I say, but, working on the assumption . . .' he let his voice trail off.

Win shook her head. 'Yes, Alban? I'm a little confused . . .'

'Win,' he said, sighing, 'I really don't think you are.'

'Oh, no,' she said. 'I assure you I am.'

He smiled, took a breath. 'Let me tell you a little story.'

He told her about what Aunt Beryl had told him, about Irene

347

and what she had said. Win sipped her tea and took another spoonful of the exotic honey, putting it directly into her mouth and then replacing the spoon in the still half-full honey bowl. She looked more and more troubled and unsure as Alban went on.

'Anyway,' he said, 'I think maybe you know what Irene was talking about.'

'Do you, dear?'

'Yes, Win, I do. And if you do, and you'll tell me, then as a mark of my gratitude I'll deliver whatever sort of speech you'd like me to deliver. As I say, I can see merit in either approach, but if you're prepared to trade, I'll take my lead from you. Because I think you do want to sell, certainly at a price of one-eighty. If I'm wrong, do tell me. Am I wrong?'

Win sat quite upright in her chair, the fingers of one hand tapping on the open palm of the other. 'It would be a good price, I suppose,' she said, sounding distracted.

'But I do need to know whatever you might know about what my mother was talking about.'

Win sat slowly back in her chair, her hands folded on her narrow lap, frail and pale on the dark, autumnal tweed. She looked straight at him for some time.

'First, I have a question I must ask you,' Win said.

'Okay.' He sat back, too.

She took her time, then said, 'What are your feelings now for your cousin Sophie? Please, be completely honest.'

He looked down, thinking. Then he met her gaze and said, 'I still feel a lot for Sophie. In a way I'll always love her, but I know she's never felt the same about me. I've accepted that. We seem, just as of today, funnily enough, to be getting on really well again – at last. Had a bit of a drama, down the loch. Came through it together. So, we seem to be . . . Well, as good as we've ever been, since Lydcombe. Even now, I think I could easily imagine spending my life with her, growing old with her, but I know that's never going to happen. I guess we'll stay distant cousins, occasional friends.'

Win nodded towards the end of this, a small smile describing itself on her lips. She kept nodding after Alban had finished speaking.

'I see,' she said. She looked at the tray on the table. 'Would you mind adding some hot water to the pot and pouring me another cup?' When he had done this and handed her the cup and saucer, she said, 'All I can tell you, Alban, is that your mother was a very . . . Depressed. She was a very depressed kind of person. I have always worried that you might have inherited that trait, but you seem to have escaped it, largely. The treatment for post-natal depression is so much better nowadays. Looking back, I don't think that inviting your mother and father up here was such a good idea after all. This can be a bleak, lonely old place, especially if you are in a state of mind to be receptive to feelings like that.' She sipped her tea, looking at the cup. 'Your mother was very sensitive and easily . . . Not led, perhaps, but prone to moods, influences. She often seemed a little confused, the way sensitive people do sometimes. Confused about her own life, about what she really wanted.' Win sipped her tea again. She shook her head. 'I really can't think of any more that would be of benefit to tell you.'

Alban sat looking at her for a while. He sighed. 'Okay,' he said. He looked at his watch. 'I'd better go.'

He rose from his seat.

'I'm sorry if this hasn't been as helpful as you'd hoped,' Win said. He looked down at her. She went on, 'I'm afraid you must just say as you see fit at the meeting, Alban; tell it like it is, isn't that what they say?'

'Yup, Gran,' he told her. 'That's just what they say. Will you be saying anything?'

'I don't think so, dear.'

'Alban,' Neil said. 'You all right?'

'Fine,' Alban told him. He'd found Neil just as he was locking the gunroom. 'You?'

'Aye, good,' Neil said, checking the lock one last time then placing the key carefully in his pocket.

'How was the shoot?'

'Fine, aye. Couple of hinds.' He tested the handle of the door, giving it a few twists. 'No escapees or bad shots. A success.' He glanced up briefly. 'You and the fishing?'

'Couple of trout. All too small.'

'Uh-huh. That all?' Neil said, making to walk past Alban up the corridor to the hall.

'And a wee bit of drama,' Alban said, not moving to let Neil past. 'Though we coped.'

Neil met his gaze for a moment, then said, 'Good. Scuse me, squire.'

Alban let him past and waited until Neil was half a dozen steps away before he said, not too loudly, 'How badly do you need that reference, Neil?'

Neil stopped mid-stride, making an awkward half-step, his head coming up slightly, then he turned with a smile and said, 'Sorry?'

'Nothing,' Alban said.

9

'This is not intended to be just a diatribe against the US in general and Spraint Corp in particular, though I do feel I have to explain a little of why I feel the way I do about the choice that we're being presented with here today.

'Personally, I believe that when faced with an imperial power – and let's not kid ourselves, that's exactly what the USA is – one ought to do everything non-violent that one can to resist it, just on principle. The USA is a great country full of great people. It's just their propensity as a whole for electing idiots and then conducting a foreign policy of the utmost depravity that I object to. You could argue that Bush junior has never been fairly elected at all, but, in the end, at the last election, faced with a choice between the guy with the purple heart and the guy with the yellow belly, the half of the US electorate that could be bothered to vote appears to have plumped for the latter.

'Now, Spraint are not a direct part of this; they're just another US-based company, halfway to being a multinational. Their record on working practices and unions is actually reasonably good from a human-rights point of view, and their main shareholders do give a lot to charitable causes. Well, good for them. Ultimately, the employees have to do whatever they can to uphold shareholder value, with all that can imply, but then that's just them playing by the rules of capitalism as they're currently written. It's a pity that, the way these rules work, they have the effect of putting the fat boys in charge of the tuck shop, but that, for the moment at least, is what we're stuck with.

'Spraint want to buy the Wopuld Group because they can; they have the cash and the high-value stock to do it without making any great dent in their bottom line. Also, we represent a loose end for them; as long as the Wopuld family own the majority of the firm, they're not in complete control of one of their more profitable assets. That makes them uncomfortable; it's untidy, it's unfinished business. As long as they don't have to pay silly money for the seventy-five per cent they don't yet own, it makes sense for them to have complete control. Of course, the definition of "silly" here can vary. Maybe the urge to be tidy here is itself a symptom of a kind of autocratic hubris, but then that's the kind of whim you can pursue without immediate penalty when you have overweening power.

'Personally, I don't think we should sell. Why do I think we shouldn't sell? Purely because of the politics of it. Resist imperialism, whether it's military or cultural. It has nothing to do with the family. Actually, I think it might be best for us as a family to dispose of the firm that bears our name. Maybe, if and when we do sell the firm, that's when we'll have a chance to be a normal family again. Well, as normal as any family is; the more I've seen of this family and everybody else's, the more I've realised there's no such thing as a normal one. They're all slightly mad.

'But – and this is the real point – at least we'll have the chance to discover what we're really like as a group of people tied together by blood, rather than by blood and money. Maybe we'll discover things about ourselves that we wouldn't have discovered otherwise. Maybe we'll discover things about ourselves that we wouldn't have wanted to discover, but – as a rule – I think it's always better to know the truth.

'Cards on the table: I'll be voting, with my hopelessly puny hundred shares, against a sale at any price. However, if we do sell, and I expect that we shall, I'd suggest putting a price of one hundred and eighty million dollars US on the three-quarters of the firm that we still collectively own and accepting no further negotiation except regarding the mix of cash and stock. And there, I'd suggest no more than fifty per cent in the form of shares. In fact, I'd suggest putting that proposal to the vote here and now, or as soon as the formal EGM comes to order, and presenting that to Mr Feaguing and Mr Fromlax as a take-it-or-leave-it choice. First, though, I believe Aunt Kathleen would like to say a few words as well. Thanks for listening.'

Some polite, restrained applause sounded in the slightly chilly ballroom as Alban resumed his seat beside Great-Aunt Beryl.

'Well, I for one thought that was awfully well said,' she told him, patting his hand.

He smiled. At least it was over.

Aunt Kathleen was rather more businesslike. She mostly just ran through the figures, which she'd printed on to a couple of sheets of A4 she referred to once or twice. She professed pleased surprise at Alban's little speech, which she had decided to treat as basically pro-sale. Her own thoughts were that they ought to ask for two hundred million on a take-it-or-leave-it basis and negotiate down to one-eighty as a last resort only if Spraint absolutely refused to swallow two hundred.

Aunt Kathleen was standing on the small dais at one end of the room by herself. Behind her lay the long table where Win, Kennard, Andy, Haydn, Fielding, Perce and she would sit shortly, when the Extraordinary General Meeting would be formally called to order.

She asked if there were any objections to a show of hands on whether a motion to the effect she had just outlined should be put to the meeting as soon as it began.

Alban abstained. Pretty much everybody else voted yes, though Uncle Kennard voted each way by mistake.

*   *   *

Texan oilmen generally believe that you can tell a lot about a man by his closest friends, so they take particular care only to buy the best. Before being head-hunted to join Spraint Corp, Larry Feaguing had been in the oil industry, based in Texas, and knew the Bush clan reasonably well. The remark about only buying the best friends was one that some drawling Houstonian sophisticate had either made up or repeated as their own to him at some Republican fund-raising event when he had still been relatively wet behind the ears. He recalled being shocked at the implication, and dismissive of the – probably closet Liberal – cynic who had expressed it. Subsequent experience in the state and the industry had only shown how disillusioningly true the epithet actually was.

Until this weekend the Bush family had provided Larry's definition of lucky avariciousness and well-connected guile, but now he was beginning to think the Wopulds might have the edge.

'Did I hear that right?' he said quietly, leaning over to speak into Fromlax's ear.

'Yes, sir. Two hundred million.'

'Jesus H. Christ.'

'Sir, please.'

'Huh? Oh, yeah. Sorry.'

Two hundred was the limit they'd been given authority to go to, depending on the cash/stock mix. Feaguing knew the board was prepared to go as high as two-fifty, at a pinch, though he personally thought that was far too much; at that price it would be a vanity purchase, not good business. Anyway, it didn't matter. Two hundred? He wasn't just going to say yes to that, certainly not without putting up some sort of fight. He didn't want to go back to the States having been taken right up to the limit he'd been given, not unless the only other option was not making the sale at all. It would look bad. He might look weak; gullible, even. It would not do his standing in the firm and on the board any good. Yes, he'd have successfully negotiated the purchase of the Wopuld Group and secured the *Empire!* property, so it wouldn't do him any harm, as such, but if he could

354

come back, in effect, with change, it would look even better. At the very least he was going to make the greedy bastards sweat a bit.

The motion passed as near as dammit unanimously on a show of hands. Feaguing was so annoyed he had to be reminded by Fromlax that he had a vote, too. Shit, he represented the biggest single share-holding by a long way. They'd tot up the shares belonging to each of the people voting, but as no individual owned more than six per cent of the whole, that would make no difference. Motion carried before he'd even had a chance to put his pitch, the devious Brit bastards.

He was offered the opportunity to say a few words, for whatever it was worth after that ultimatum of a vote. He'd had a big speech prepared but there was little point in going through the whole thing now. He left out the spiel where he flattered them and their stupid little company and just told them how great Spraint was and what a good deal one-twenty represented, then added that he was deeply worried they were asking for an unrealistic amount of money, but that, unless they reconsidered, he would communicate the offer back to the main Spraint board this evening; although it was the weekend, all the board members were anxious to hear whether they'd been successful and various weekend leisure activities would have to be disturbed. He only hoped they would consider it at all rather than dismiss it out of hand. He thanked them for their time and sat down to surprisingly warm applause.

Two hundred mill. A fifth of a billion bucks. The greedy fucks.

'Well, Alban, you had your say,' Win said to him after dinner that evening. He'd been wandering round some of the various family members gathered in the drawing room rather than working the room this time, just batting around from little group to little group, talking, accepting both restrained praise and severe criticism for his address before the EGM. He fetched up at the fireplace, Win's usual hangout, and wondered which he'd receive from her.

'Yes,' he agreed. 'I did, didn't I?'

'Was that what you always meant to say?' Win asked. She was

355

sitting holding her tumbler of whisky, surrounded by Kennard, Renée, Haydn, Linda, Perce, Kathleen and Lance.

'Pretty much,' he told her.

'I thought the political stuff was completely unnecessary, I must say,' she said.

'People usually do. It's generally the most important content people are either embarrassed by or can't see is relevant.'

'Still, you got it off your chest.'

'From spleen via chest to cuff,' he agreed.

'You are one for going against the flow, aren't you, Alban?' Uncle Perce said. He was Brand Manager these days, husband of Aunt Linda; a tallish, balding, slightly chubby guy with inordinately thick-lensed glasses which gave him a perpetually goggling look. He had a hoarse, slightly breathless voice.

'I suppose I am,' Alban agreed. He felt tired. He'd been more keyed up than he'd have liked to admit before saying his piece at the meeting and the whole business with the boat trip had been surprisingly tiring, too. He was looking forward to going to bed.

Larry Feaguing had communicated the good/bad news to the rest of the Spraint board before dinner, and some of the family were talking about waiting around into the small hours, hoping to hear something definitive from the US. Alban wasn't going to bother. He felt drained and just wanted to sleep.

'There will always be people who believe in making life diffi-cult for themselves,' Win said to Perce and the others. Alban was treated to a sustained round of tactfully subdued head-nods, muffled noises of agreement and some slightly sozzled knowing looks following this gritty little pearl of wisdom. Win smiled at Alban. He smiled back, then excused himself and went off to talk to some-body – anybody – else.

When Fielding finally came to bed – a bit drunk, stumbling around, apologising – a little after three, Alban was still awake. He asked Fielding if there had been any word from Spraint, but there hadn't.

356

Alban lay awake, listening to Fielding snoring softly, snufflingly, intermittently.

Had he said the right thing to the meeting? He'd tried to say what he felt, what he believed. He'd probably been too political, too self-indulgent, but when else was he going to get a chance to say stuff like that to an audience willing to listen? He'd needed to explain that his reluctance to sell was not about the family, that it was about principle, and he had wanted to make the point that the family might gain more than just money if they chose to sell. He hadn't been sure how that would play, but it seemed to have gone down fairly well. A number of people had come up to him at the dinner or afterwards and said they agreed with him. They'd all been from the younger levels of the family: people like sis Cory and cousins Lori and Claire and Steve. They'd understood; the older generations hadn't, not really.

Well, the ball was in the Spraint court now. Alban expected they'd be left to twist in the wind for a bit. There was no percentage for Spraint in coming back with an immediate yes, not unless there was some other suitor on the horizon, and there'd been no sign of that.

With any luck they'd hear something tomorrow. He still thought they'd settle on one-eighty, though obviously the family would be even happier with two hundred. Academic. Just figures. Feaguing was right in a way. And it affected him personally, materially, only to the most trivial degree.

He still didn't know about the whole thing with the boat and the frayed lanyard. Anyway, they'd got out of the situation so it didn't really matter. He'd probably never trust Neil McBride again, and that was the worst of it (he'd never trusted Win).

His attempt to trade with the old girl hadn't gone the way he'd hoped. He'd thought that maybe she'd be unsettled because he was – unexpectedly, he was sure – back on time from the fishing trip. He'd even hoped that she might have had some sort of attack of conscience that would make her prepared to be generous, but no. Maybe Win had guessed that what he intended to say at the meeting wasn't as against her true interests as she'd initially supposed.

Anyway, it hadn't worked and he had the distinct and nagging impression that more than he'd realised had hung on exactly how he'd answered her question about how he now felt towards Sophie.

Ah yes, then there was Sophie. He still didn't know what to think about her, about his feelings for her. Was he now properly, officially over her? Had it been a cathartic, cleansing experience? Or had the whole boat trip and the little drama of the broken lanyard somehow kept the flame alive, even rekindled it, so that he was still not free of this ancient, immature infatuation? He didn't know, not yet. He felt torn, able to see both ways of looking at the matter. He could make an argument to himself for either point of view and he couldn't easily choose between them on merit.

What did he want to be the case?

He wanted, he supposed, to be free of her. It was a stupid, adolescent fixation, well past its sell-by date. He wanted to be able to go to VG and just say, Whatever you want, however much of me you want, you've got. I'll accept whatever degree of proximity and commitment you want to offer or ask for.

Part of him howled at this. Some sort of old-guard element of his being went into fits of apoplexy at the very idea of abandoning his eternal love for, and obligation to, Sophie. He had promised himself he would always love her, he had made that solemn pledge in his heart, back when he was just starting to become who he was. He had built his world around her, even if it had been done from a distance, even if it was without her knowledge or consent, even if the image that he had of her was based on a 'her' that had changed utterly, that had matured and grown and developed away both from him and from her own earlier self, and even if the whole doomed undertaking had been carried out in the teeth of all common sense and rational self-interest.

It was love. It was romantic, pure and perfect love; it wasn't supposed to make sense or be rational. It was the core of him, this passion, this purity of feeling and commitment. How could he think of abandoning it and her? That pledge had been his foundation for all these years. Could he renounce it now? Should he?

He remembered lying in bed at Lydcombe, pledging himself to his real mother, to Irene, swearing to her memory that he would never call Leah 'Mum' or 'Mother' or anything like that . . . Then he remembered renouncing all that, because Leah was nice, because he couldn't hate her, then couldn't feel indifferent towards her, then admitted he liked her, and sometimes calling her 'Mum' just seemed right. He'd felt guilty and mature and pragmatic and like he was betraying Irene, all at once. So, he had form. He'd done this sort of thing before.

Hard to see how you could do otherwise, if you were stupid enough to go around making childish pledges to yourself.

Apostate, he thought. *Serial betrayer.*

Sophie was his religion, he thought, with a kind of shock. He'd built a temple round her image, her idol, her fixed, unchanging, incorruptible icon. The worship of that symbol had become what mattered, rather than the girl as she actually was or the woman she'd become. She represented his faith in his own trueness of spirit, his ability to keep on believing in something. If he could believe in his love for Sophie, he could believe that he was a good person, a worthwhile person, a decent man. He was an atheist and a secularist, but now he had to confront his own idiot faith, this slightly mad belief system that he'd carried with him all this time, and accept it for the nonsense it was. Maybe it had been a useful nonsense, in a state of relative ignorance, the way conventional religions could be, but it was still a nonsense.

He'd once characterised religions as reason abatement societies. Shit, he hadn't realised with what authority he'd been speaking. Maybe he owed Tony Fromlax an apology.

In his mind, he could feel a particularly non-violent and well-spoken mob politely storming the temple complex that held the graven image of Sophie. He could almost hear the wailing of the priests, the lamentations of the faithful as the great washed, the well-scrubbed crowd of intellectuals – waving scrolls (closely argued, ink still damp) rather than burning torches – defiled the sacred ground with their presence and their doubt and their faithless, argumentative lack of certainty.

The inquisitive, terribly polite mob dragged some of the precious texts out of the dark temple into the cold light of day and reason, the powerless priests wailing and tearing their hair out in their wake.

'They've all bloody gone . . .' 'Fell off me 'oss, didn' I guv?' 'Blimey, Uncle, I didn't enjoy it that much . . .' 'Not a flippin' fing . . .' (Plus, the avariciously faithful aspect of him, the obsessive-compulsive part of his personality that collected these little relics had been going to add 'Aye-aye, cap'n' to the canon, as of just today.) All shown to the sun, all shrivelling in the strength of daylight and being made to look sad and pathetic and risible. How shallow had been the foundations of his faith, he realised now. How inadequate the cornerstones of his custom-built, home-grown personality cult.

'Cuz, cuz, sweet cuz.'

He whispered it, very quietly, to the perfectly dark room as Fielding snored obliviously away.

A kind of valediction.

Of course, the mistake would be simply to replace Sophie with Verushka. He knew there was a danger of that. He could easily worship her, she was already a kind of rival religion in his head; a new, shining, more effective, more earthy and hip cult compared to the ancient adoration of Sophie.

That would be pretty stupid. If she ever found out, VG wouldn't thank him for being venerated like that, and – in the end, he had no doubt – to do so would destroy whatever he and VG had and whatever they might have together.

'Just love her, you idiot,' he said in a normal speaking voice, and was shocked anew. It had sounded so loud in the room. He hadn't meant to say it aloud.

Fielding had suddenly stopped snoring. Alban turned to look at where he knew his cousin was, but could see nothing because the

360

darkness was complete. Then he heard Fielding shift, maybe turning over in bed. Soon he went back to snoring again. Alban looked up once more at the unseen ceiling.

Love her, he told himself. If that's what you feel, if you can start to work out what it is you really feel for her now that you're free of this absurd worship of Sophie – maybe, probably – then just be adult about it, be sensible about it. Take it as it comes. See how things work out with her. Okay, so she doesn't want children, and she'll probably never want to live with you. Just give all you can offer, and be honest. And if somebody else comes along that offers you all the things you want, or think you want, then at least VG should understand. She's said so often enough.

Arguably, nobody ever completely knows themselves, so she could be wrong about that and maybe if it ever comes to it she'll feel more jealous than she expects to feel, but of all the people you've ever known she's the one least likely to be that self-deceptive. In the meantime, make the most of whatever time you have together. And if it's effectively for ever, for the rest of your lives, can you think of anybody else you'd rather spend that time with?

Well, no.

He so hoped that she was all right, that she was well and healthy and looking forward to seeing him . . . Tomorrow, if you counted this as today rather than last night. Tomorrow; he'd see her tomorrow. Fate willing, he told himself. Chance allowing.

Finally, he fell asleep.

He was up before six, fully awake but knowing he'd be tired again by the afternoon. He had breakfast alone, helping himself in the kitchen and packing food for lunch, then – borrowing an old fishing bag from the cloakroom as a day pack and leaving a note on the octagonal table in the front hall describing his intended route – he left the house, feeling oddly relieved and even exultant that he'd got away from the place without anyone seeing him.

He hiked through the gardens and woods in light drizzle from a few small, high clouds which soon disappeared to reveal a sharp, clear blue morning. He made a shallow ascent along the path heading north-west along the shoulder of Beinn Aird da Loch, looking down on the place where his mother had died, watching seagulls wheel and dip over the calm, black waters. He only remembered then that Andy had wanted to scatter some flowers on the loch this morning. He thought about going back, but decided not to.

The path turned the corner after a while, taking the sight of one dark loch away, replacing it with another.

He descended again, towards the head of Loch Glendhu, between tipped, parallel lines of cliffs. He crossed the river by the small bridge just upstream from a small, stony beach and followed the track up the far side of Gleann Dubh, the cliffs and walls of rock creating a gloomy canyon of stone it was a relief to hike up out of, towards the blue richness of the sky above the greens, yellows and browns of the encircling hills.

Free of the steep-sided shade of the narrow glen, he struck off the main path and along the north shore of a small loch he'd have to look at the map to remember the name of, making heavy going over coarse, hummocky ground until – skirting the base of Meill na Leitrach, leg muscles complaining – he met the path from Loch More. He followed it for the remainder of its descent to the side of the burn which fed the small loch he'd passed and then stopped for lunch. He sat on a rock, watching a pair of eagles slide across the sky above Ruigh' a' Chnoic Mhóir like a pair of light aircraft with feathers. He drank water he'd bottled at the house, ate his sandwiches and fruit, then continued up the path to the pass, striking out to the right towards the summit of Beinn Leòid. Throughout, he'd been looking for interesting plants – anything beyond the usual heathers, grasses, ferns and wind-stunted trees – but the most exotic species he'd spotted so far had been a couple of small clumps of autumn gentian.

A cool, strong breeze met him at the trig point, and he stood there with his back against the concrete pillar and the wind, breathing hard after the last push to the top.

He gave a small laugh, remembering VG being scurrilous about an ex-colleague she'd dated a few times and then severely fallen out with. 'Ever been walking in the wind and the rain and come up to a trig point on a big, featureless summit, and you just want to get whatever shelter you can from the gale so you can hunker down and eat your sandwiches? Well, I felt about his cock the way you would about that trig point: you're glad it's there, you're happy you don't have to share it with anybody, but you can't help wishing it was just a bit bigger.'

He'd felt vaguely treacherous laughing at this, and got an internal shiver wondering what she'd say about him to some future lover – perhaps, one day – but then she had never been so defamatory or indiscreet about anybody else; he reckoned the guy had probably deserved it.

He looked out across the revealed tops to the north, bright and sharp in the clear northerly airstream, wondering where she was now. Standing on one of those far summits looking out across that same waste of air towards him? Probably not, but the residual romantic in him would still like to think so.

Just come back safely, VG, he thought. Just come back safely to me.

He ate some chocolate then headed cross-country, down then back up to the nameless top from which he could at last look down on Loch Garve, the estate and the house. The best part of three kilometres away, seven hundred metres down, the great grey house, hardly hidden by the trees from this angle, looked tiny and lost and insignificant from here; a vaguely geometrical, human-created inter-ruption in the burgeoning sweep of landscape formed by the long dark lochs and the rock-broken pelts of the arrayed and jumbled mountains, a cheap charm on a thread of road overhung by the surrounding rocky slopes.

It all looked inviolable and changeless from here, yet that was just wrong. Centuries ago there would have been almost nothing to see but forest; now, as ever, the ground cover reflected the use the

363

land was put to, in this case providing a vast, half-vertical paddock for deer and game birds, all there to be shot at by people of means.

Alban tried to see the place as it might be, as Neil McBride might see it; threatened, on the brink of irreversible change. Suppose that some of the great ice sheets melted; that was supposed to be entirely possible before the end of the century. One scenario the climatologists seemed to find eminently plausible had sea levels rising by seven metres. How would that alter the landscape he was looking at? Well, a hell of a lot less than if he was looking out over a bit of East Anglia, or Holland, or Bangladesh, that was for sure. But even here, amongst these sparsely populated mountains, the change would be severe. Harbours, coastal villages, roads along the shore, much of the best arable land; they'd all go. Garbadale House had been built on the remains of glacial till banked up at the end of the great scoured trench that was Loch Garve. It was about eight or nine metres above sea level; close enough for salt spray to buffet the windows on stormy days if Greenland melted. If the Antarctic ice sheets went the same way, then Loch Garve would be a sea loch and the house would simply disappear under the grey waves. Though that, of course, would be utterly insignificant compared to losing every coastal city in the world, and several entire countries.

He thought of Neil McBride's children and grandchildren and the world they would be bequeathed. It was, arguably, in a bit of a mess. He remembered talking with Sophie, back in the garden at Lydcombe, about how the world their generation was inheriting appeared – at the time – to be in just as big a mess. Sometimes it seemed that all that ever went on was each new generation trying to fix the mistakes and problems caused by the previous one – not to mention those accumulated via still earlier forebears. And this never really seemed to be possible, not as a finished result. It always seemed to be required and it certainly was always worth trying, but if you set your heart on fully achieving such a goal, you were bound to be disappointed.

He recalled Verushka talking about some people seemingly being forever in search of the East Pole. She meant that they had simply misunderstood how things worked. It was as though, having heard of the South Pole and the North Pole, they assumed there must be a West Pole and an East Pole too, and so set off confidently expecting to find one or other of them, never knowing they were inevitably destined to fail.

Some hopes and ambitions were manifest only as a direction, not a destination. Maybe the trick was to realise you were involved in a process, not aiming at a completely achievable end result, and accept that, but travel hopefully anyway.

The trouble was that so many people seemed to feel a need for certainty, for clear paths leading to set objectives with tickable goal-boxes, for the assuredly do-able with guaranteed happiness or fulfil-ment or enlightenment apparently promised as a result. And so many other people were determined to offer them just those things, through schemes or programmes or sets of rules or institutions or tribalistic, other-excluding, difference-fearing cliques, but always through some sort of faith; whether it was faith in the person peddling their patent fix or whether it was faith in a full-blown religion or whatever secular belief system had partially replaced such primitive creeds and was currently in vogue – once Marxism, now the market.

Always flocks, always priests.

He shook his head.

Still: to travel hopefully.

He looked down at the house, waiting for some sort of move-ment there, for the glint of sun on moving glass or just one barely discernible speck millimetring its way across the roads or paths or lawns, but he saw nothing for the perhaps five or ten minutes that he watched. For all the life he knew the place contained, there was no sign of it in this early afternoon, the distance and the scale of things reducing whatever might be happening down there to a cheerful triviality.

He hesitated before the descent. There were two obvious approaches to the house from here. The slow, sensible route was a narrow, occasionally indistinct path describing a series of gentle zigzags down the steep grass slope to his right. The quick way meant a scramble round some car-sized boulders at the side of the cliff beneath him and then a fun but frantic bit of scree-running, following the giant fan of fallen grey stones all the way down to the dark mass of spruce trees making up the south plantation.

Scree-running was exciting but dangerous; there was always the chance of a trip or a sprain or even getting hit by a faster-moving rock dislodged from further up. There was even a degree of guilt involved – you were, after all, helping to wear away the landscape. He'd only ever done it twice. Both occasions had been here, once with his dad about twenty years earlier, once with Neil McBride maybe five years ago. He knew that the prudent course – especially given that he was alone – was to take the shallow, zigzag route, but the sheer rattling, flailing madness of taking the scree approach had its own wild attraction.

Whatever; while he'd been pondering his choice of route, he'd had an idea. An idea that might winkle some sort of truth out of Win, if she had any to surrender. He'd have a nap this afternoon, sleep on it that way, then see what happened at Win's big party in the evening.

He turned away from the shallow path, pulled the strap of the old fishing bag as tight as he could across his shoulder, then rounded the side of the cliff and clambered past the giant boulders. He looked down the steep grey pitch of scree towards the treeline, the gardens and the house, then with a whoop jumped on to the slope, surrendering himself to it, running down, heart-hammering, legs pumping, feet sinking into the loose, tearing grey surface, sliding in a barely controlled, tipped-back stagger, limbs falling into the imposed, shared rhythm of the stones all bustling and tumbling along with him, dropping so fast he could feel his ears pop.

Breathless, laughing, legs quivering, he arrived at the trees in a rattle of stones within a couple of minutes of jumping on to the great grey slope of fractured rock.

*   *   *

'Brig-a-fuckin'-doon, yeah right,' Larry Feaguing said. 'I'm telling you, man, this place is the crock of shit at the brownbow's end.'

'Maybe we should buy the estate, too,' Fromlax suggested. He'd estimated that there was no further point in protesting at his boss's expletives, given that the last time he had, a couple of drinks ago, Feaguing had fixed him with an unsympathetic look and told him to pull at least one of his fingers out of his ass. Larry was displeased that the board had agreed to buy the Wopuld Group for two hundred million.

He'd done a pretty good job of disguising his displeasure at the dinner for the old grandmother's eightieth birthday, when he'd clinked his glass and stood up after the other speeches had been completed and told them the sale had been agreed, subject to some negotiation over the cash/stock mix and the usual lawyerly picking-over, blah-de-blah-de-blah (great had been the cheer, manifold the rejoicing, sincere the praise and shockingly unrestrained the consumption of alcohol thereafter), but Fromlax knew Feaguing was privately annoyed at having failed to secure the purchase for less than the maximum amount he'd been allowed.

There was even a hint that some of the board felt that as Larry had been granted authority to just say yes at that price he had rather been wasting their time coming back to them to double-check. So now Feaguing in turn felt that the board had let *him* down by refusing to play ball and say no, at least initially, to the two hundred mill price, depriving him of any lever with which to prise the price downwards. They were surrendering but he would be the one looking weak.

'What?' Larry asked. 'Buy what?'

'Buy the estate; buy this place,' Fromlax said, leaning close to his boss so that nobody else could hear. Given the amount of talking and laughing going on, and the ceilidh band playing enthusiastically on the dais at one end of the ballroom, this was probably an unnecessary precaution. 'It, uh, is for sale.'

Feaguing looked at him as though he was mad. 'Buy Garbage-dale.

367

Yeah, okay; you suggest that to the board,' he said, turning away and shaking his head. His expression flowed into a professional smile as two of the Wopuld women – aunt whatever and niece blank – came up to ask them to dance something called a Dashing White Sergeant. They had no choice but to agree, though, to Fromlax, all these whirling, prancing, Scottish group dances seemed to have been explicitly designed to make foreigners who were ignorant of the complicated steps and bewilderingly intricate movements look and feel clumsy and stupid. They were swept up into the orderly riot on the dance floor once again.

'What were you guys on, that time in Singapore, remember?' cousin Steve, the container port crane guy, asked Fielding. They were standing at the temporary bar at the far end of the ballroom from the band, sweating after an especially spirited dance. They were both wearing formal Highland gear, each dressed in the full Prince Charlie outfit, kilts and sporrans and everything else – save their jackets, which had been sweatily abandoned after the first energetic dance. Fielding had forgotten how warm this attire could make a person. Not all the Wopuld males had chosen to go down this Caledonian wedding route – about a third were in normal black tie – but the family had purchased a lairdship or something when Henry had bought the estate, they had their own tartan, and the men were therefore entitled to wear heavy, pleated skirts, shoes with girlie laces criss-crossed up their thick white socks – socks that were stocking-length if you rolled them right out, frankly – and sport wee (technical term) knives. Apparently.

'Singapore?' Fielding pretended to have to think about this. He shook his head, went to drink some of his champagne – there was a lot of champagne being drunk tonight, as well as copious amounts of whisky – then stopped and wagged one finger. 'Oh, yes, that.' He drank. He fixed Steve with a look. 'You could tell, could you?'

'Looked like more than just drink and dodgy prawns,' Steve said, nodding.

'You'd have to ask Alban,' Fielding said. 'I can't remember.'

'But you were ripped?'

'Off our tits,' Fielding agreed.

'Where were you today?' Haydn asked Alban, plonking himself down at the table and nearly spilling the flute of champagne he'd brought with him. Haydn was also dressed in full Highland regalia, and had for some time been in the zone of alcohol saturation where he no longer felt in any way self-conscious sporting such dress. Alban wore a kilty outfit too, though it was less formal: sensible shoes, plain leather sporran, a toned-down version of the family's slightly technicolour tartan and one of those pull-on shirts with big droopy sleeves and laces at the collar.

'I was walking,' Alban told Haydn.

'What, on the road?'

'No, in the hills.'

'What, just for fun?'

'That's right.'

'We thought you'd stormed off home in a fuss or something,' Haydn told him. 'There was talk of search parties. Your man Neil Mc-thingy was all set to call Mountain Rescue.'

'I know. Apparently the kids were having a paper plane competition from the gallery across the hall to see who could get a plane to fly outside through the main doors. The note I left got made into a dart or something and was later discovered on the gravel under a Range Rover.'

'Ah-hah.' Haydn looked woozily around the assembly of bouncing, dancing people. 'Everybody seems very happy,' he observed.

'Should think so too,' Alban told him. 'Aren't you?'

'Bloody ecstatic.'

'You going to stay with the firm once it's sold?'

'They want me to,' Haydn said, looking out at the swirling mass of people as though hypnotised. 'Mean moving to the States.'

'Whereabouts?'

369

'Manhattan?' Haydn drank from his flute. 'San Francisco?'

'There are worse places.'

'You bet.' He looked at Alban. 'What would you do? In my situation?'

'Me? Oh, I wouldn't move to the States now any more than I'd have moved to Germany in the mid-Thirties. But that's just me. If I was you, I'd probably go. You're not Muslim, which is the new Jewish, so you'll probably be safe.'

Haydn stared one-eyed at him, then remembered binocular vision. 'Win's right. You really take this stuff to heart, don't you?'

'I know. It's a failing, frankly.'

'And people say you and Win never agree on anything.'

'Are we all going to be horribly rich?' Doris asked Beryl, raising her voice over the noise of the band. They were sitting at the table they shared with Andy and Leah, Alban, and Cory and her husband and children. Not that any of the children had actually sat down or been there much; they all seemed to be playing games in the games room, computer games in the television room or off exploring parts of the house that hadn't been open until tonight, now thrown wide to all and sundry in some excess of celebration.

'What's that, dear?' Beryl asked.

'Are we all going to be horribly rich?' Doris repeated.

'Well, I am, dear,' Beryl said. 'You don't have any shares, old girl.'

'That's rather beastly of you.'

Beryl patted Doris's hand. 'We shall both be rich, my sweet. Though I was not aware of feeling any great lack in our lives as they have been, ah, ah, what's the word? Heretofore. Yes, heretofore.'

Doris nodded slowly. She was thinking, obviously. 'I think,' she said firmly, 'that we ought to buy a racehorse.'

Beryl, paused with her drink raised halfway to her lips, looked moderately startled, then said, 'Do you know? I think that's a jolly good idea.'

*   *   *

There is a pattern to the patterned dances. After every two or three or four, the band plays a slow waltz or foxtrot to let people cool down, sit down or just have a chance to dance as a couple rather than as a company.

Alban danced gentle, delicate waltzes with Beryl and then Doris and later with Win, because it was her birthday after all.

'So, we got an extra twenty million, thanks to Kathleen,' Win pointed out. Held, even at the prim remove dictated by the dance, Win seemed almost unbearably slight and fragile. Alban, sporran on one hip to avoid prodding one's dancing partner in unfortunate places, was very aware of his height and strength compared to this little old woman who was getting littler with every year now, compressing and concentrating like something being reduced on a stove or a fruit air-drying. He had, of course, absolutely no illusions regarding this in any way symbolising Win's grip on life – or on the family – weakening.

'Yes,' he agreed. 'There you are. I'd have had us settling for a paltry one hundred and eighty million US dollars and reducing us all to penury. Thank goodness Aunt Kathleen was there to save us.'

'It's rather more than ten per cent of a difference, Alban. Hardly trivial or worthy of that sarcasm you're obviously so proud of gracing us with.'

Win sounded a little drunk, Alban decided. She rarely let herself achieve this degree of inebriation, in public anyway. Well, he told himself, it was her party, and the whole family had just been handed a gigantic present in return for the family firm. Win was quitting the house and estate and the overseer-ship of the company while still pretty much in possession of all her marbles and – he seriously suspected – on something very close indeed to what her own terms had been all along. Always good to celebrate when one had outlasted all rivals, seen off all challengers and achieved what one had long desired. Who wouldn't be triumphalist and feel justified in having a few sherbets?

'And I'm sure everybody will be rather more than ten per cent happier than they would have been otherwise,' Alban agreed.

'Well, at any rate,' Win said, in a sleepy-sounding, little-old-lady voice that instantly warned Alban something acidic was on its way, 'I'm pleased that you were able to play your part.' Win smiled sweetly.

He didn't doubt he had been meant to feel insulted. 'Happy to have been of service,' he told her.

They danced on. *I think I might try my plan*, he thought.

Alban danced with Gudrun Selves, the legal exec with the cool name and the pretty wonderful body. She had short, blue-black hair, was the same height as him in her heels, wore a little black number and had great legs. She was much in demand and happily uninterested in talking about law.

He danced with Leah, who was dressed in a rather matronly blue gown she wouldn't suit for at least another ten years and who was quite tipsy in a vague, happy-but-slightly-sad-too kind of way, sorry to see the family firm being sold off but pleased that everybody else seemed so elated. She told him they should have insisted that Verushka attend the party; he looked happy when he was with her. He said he was glad to hear that.

He danced with Sophie, resplendent in a silvery sheath dress like a glitter ball stretched over her body. He asked her for a favour.

She pulled back as they danced. 'Maybe we should sit down,' she said.

'Maybe we should,' he agreed. He steered her to a vacant table not far from where Win sat with her little circle of family elders and willing functionaries. He sat so that he could see Win over Sophie's shoulder. She wasn't looking at Sophie and him, but he had the impression they hadn't gone unnoticed.

'First, I'd better give you some background,' he said.

'No,' Sophie told him, leaning towards him with a grin. 'First you should get me some more champagne.'

'Okay.'

He thought she seemed quite merry already but he went to the bar and brought back a couple of glasses. He leaned in and kissed her cheek as he put the glasses down, seeing Win from the corner of his eye.

Sophie's eyes narrowed. He hesitated as he was about to sit down, then extended his free hand and said, 'Actually, let's sit somewhere else.'

'What the hell are you playing at, Alban?' Sophie asked, following him to the far end of the room and another empty table near a corner of the ballroom not far from the band.

Once they were sat down he said, 'Sophie, I want you to give Win the impression you love me.'

She laughed. 'After everything?'

'After everything,' he said. 'Let me give you the background. May I?'

'Background away,' Sophie said, waving one hand and drinking her champagne.

He told her something of Irene's troubling, un- or semi-conscious words in front of Beryl in the hospital, his admittedly half-hearted attempts to find out more, and the way Win had expressed herself the day before when he'd confronted her in her sitting room over tea and toast.

'Yeah,' Sophie said, frowning fractionally. 'I heard about this honey. Is it true it's like cocaine?'

'Sophie, are you listening to what I'm telling you?'

'I'm very sorry about your mother,' she said, suddenly serious again. 'Why do I have to pretend to Win that I love you?'

'Because of what she asked me yesterday,' he explained. 'I got the impression, thinking about it later, that if I'd told her I still thought we had a future together then she might have spilled the beans. Like an idiot, I told the truth and so she clammed up.'

'And what is the truth again?' Sophie asked, leaning one champagne-twiddling arm along the table, brows creased in a pretty frown.

'That you were my first, adolescent, love, that I'll always think fondly of you – always worship you, I told her – but that was all.'

'All? That sounds like quite a lot.' Sophie sounded wary. 'This isn't all just some roundabout way of trying to get back into my,' she cast her gaze ceilingwards and muttered, 'be polite,' then looked into his eyes again and said, 'affections, is it?'

He put his hand on his chest. 'I swear. Nothing like that. It's all about trying to prise some information out of Win.'

'Promise?'

'Promise.'

'Seriously?'

'Seriously.'

'You sure?'

'Absolutely. Trust me; I'm a man.'

When they'd both stopped laughing, Sophie leaned closer and said, 'So, what do I have to do?'

Alban spotted Aunt Lauren drifting past not far away, not looking at them. He leaned in still closer to his cousin. He could smell her perfume, heady and warm and intense. 'Just, at some point, get talking to Win,' he told her. 'Give her the impression you think I'm rather wonderful, you've decided maybe we were wrong to stay apart all these years; you want to see more of me, maybe give us another chance.'

'You know,' Sophie said, frowning, leaning so close to him that they were almost nose to nose – Alban could still just about make out Aunt Lauren in the background – 'if this is a complicated seduction technique,' she whispered, 'it's not working, not going to work, and it's basically doomed.'

'Fully aware of that, cuz.'

'Good,' Sophie said, winking slowly. She pulled back and took up her champagne glass again. She raised her flute. 'To being fully aware.'

'Fully aware,' he said, clinking. They drained their glasses and got up to complete their dance, catching only the end of the waltz, then joined the same group for some up-tempo, insanely energetic Strip the Willow and Gay Gordons floor-bashing before finally having a whole slow dance together, all of this being agreed to help convince Win that what Sophie was seemingly about to let slip was actually plausible.

They parted, he for a pee, she to get a very large glass of water from the bar and then call at the court of Win.

After visiting the loo he went through the main hall and stood outside the front doors for a while, just to get some fresh air. It wasn't very smoky in the ballroom – few people seemed to smoke these days – but it was surprisingly hot for a room with such a high ceiling. He'd been hoping to see stars out here, but the night was dark and a very fine rain was starting to fall. The windows of both wings of the house were fully lit and a couple of floodlights high on the main frontage bathed the various cars and other vehicles in a sharp, hard light the gently falling drizzle did little to soften.

He caught a whiff of tobacco smoke, heard the small crunching noise of a foot on gravel. He saw Tony Fromlax appearing from round the side of one of the Range Rovers. 'Evening,' Alban said.

'Oh, hi,' Fromlax said.

'I remember the old days,' Alban said. 'People used to sneak out for a quick joint. Now it's cigarettes that are socially unacceptable.'

'Yeah, well, my last vice,' Fromlax said, looking decidedly embarrassed.

'Your secret is safe with me.'

Fromlax held up and then holstered a mobile phone. 'Calling my brother, too.'

'Yeah, the reception's not the best here.'

'I call him every day if I can. He's in Iraq.'

'Army?'

'Yeah.'

'I hope he comes home safely.'

'Well, we all do. But there's a job to be done first.'

'You're right. The profits of Halliburton and Bechtel have to be protected.'

Fromlax looked down at the stones on the drive, then back up at Alban. 'Don't you despair sometimes, Mr McGill, being so cynical?'

'Don't you despair? Always getting it wrong?'

'We're avenging what was done to us and we're trying to give these people a chance for a better life. We have the right to do one and the moral obligation to do the other. I don't understand how you can find anything wrong in that.'

'The Iraqi state had nothing to do with nine-eleven, if that's what you mean. Just nothing. And if you want to give "these people" a chance of a better life, get the hell out of their country. Stop interfering.' Alban could see Fromlax was about to reply, but he just kept on talking; warming to his theme if you were being polite, or just having got to a straw/camel's back tipping-point of extreme impatience with naïve Americans if you were being honest. 'Jesus,' he said, 'you're constantly making fresh mistakes to compensate for the mistakes you made before, aren't you? You don't like the left-wing nationalists elected to power in Iran so you stage a coup and put the Shah in charge, then get all upset and surprised when it turns out the Iranians don't like unelected US-supported despots and so the mullahs take over; you turn a blind eye to the barbaric, medieval bastards of Saudi Arabia for decades because they happen to be sitting on a desert full of oil and you don't bother your sweet asses they're using their slice of the profits to promote their dingbat fundamentalist Wahhabiism across the whole Muslim world, then you have the cheek to be stunned with fucking amazement when it's cockpits full of Saudi zealots who fly into your buildings on nine-eleven; you back Saddam Hussein against the mullahs in Iran and can't see how that might go wrong; you back the mujahideen in Afghanistan and you get Bin Laden; you back—'

'Yeah? And who would, who do you—?'

'No, wait a fucking minute,' Alban said, taking a step forward and pointing at Fromlax's chest. 'I'm not finished yet. The point is you're still doing it. Now you're backing Musharraf in Pakistan because he might help you catch Bin Laden. All in the cause of democracy, only Musharraf had to stage a coup to get where he is; he's an unelected despot too, a military dictator except *his* state already has nukes and the opposition is getting even more fundamentalist on his ass specifically because you guys support him.' Alban took a step back, put his weight on his back foot and inspected Fromlax over crossed arms. 'Well, gee, what could possibly fucking go wrong with *that* scenario?'

Fromlax shook his head. He held up both hands, palms flat. 'Mr McGill,' he said, looking at the pebbles in front of Alban's feet, 'I'm here on your territory, your estate, your family home, just trying to negotiate the best deal we can for all of us. I think you're a very aggressive and disturbed individual and I would just like to return inside now and I would ask you not to stand in my way.'

Alban looked at the man for a moment. He shook his head fractionally, then stepped aside, taking another step back to completely clear the doorway.

'Mr Fromlax?' he said, just before the American disappeared into the hall. The other man turned to face him, looking wary. 'I was for the war, too, initially,' Alban told him. 'My girl and I nearly split up because of it. I had my reasons, and I could argue them, but do you know what she said to me? I'll quote: "Trying to justify this war is like trying to justify rape; you can dress your excuses up as fancy as you like, but in the end you should just damn well be ashamed of yourself." I spent a year – in denial, basically – trying to find an answer to that, but I never did. How about you?'

Fromlax stared into his eyes for a moment or two, then shook his head and went back into the house.

It took Alban another five minutes standing in the open air to calm himself, to get his breathing back to normal and let his heart rate subside.

Finally he took a deep breath and went back in.

When he returned to the ballroom – more mad dashing around as whole great gyrating circles of whirling people danced the Eightsome Reel – he was met by Aunt Lauren.

'Lauren,' he said. 'You dancing?'

'Perhaps later,' Lauren said, taking his arm. 'Win would like to speak to you,' she said.

'Excellent,' he said. 'Bring her on.'

'She's in the drawing room,' Lauren told him, and they turned for the doors again. 'Alban, she does seem rather upset.'

'Really?' he said. *Obviously my night for upsetting people*, he thought.

'Yes, it's very . . . She was in such a good mood. Well, of course she should be, shouldn't she?' Lauren said as they walked down the hall to the drawing room.

'Birthday,' Alban agreed. 'Big birthday. And all that money. Did she like my card?'

'I'm sure she did.' They were at the double doors into the drawing room. Lauren opened them. The place was mostly dark, just a couple of small table lamps illuminating one long wall each, and the fire – banked, flameless – producing a red glow at the far end. The room appeared empty of people until Alban made out the small figure taking up less than the whole of one of the winged seats by the fireside. 'There she is,' Lauren whispered. 'I'll be here,' she said quietly, indicating a seat by a table to the side of the doors. Alban left her there and walked to where Win was waiting.

The old woman was staring into the shining spaces in the banked-up blackness of the fire; a tiny landscape of little red and yellow caves puncturing a hill of fine dross. Deep red light reflected from the metal coal scuttle to one side of the hearth and made Win's thin grey hair look rosy, like a pink lace skullcap.

'Win,' he said. 'Hi.' He sat down opposite her.

She took a moment before she deigned to look at him. There was a glass of whisky on the table at her side. She looked into his eyes for some time. Then she glanced up the room to where Lauren was sitting, well out of earshot. She raised her glass and drank a little. 'I understand you and Sophie have rediscovered something we all thought was long gone.'

'You might say that,' he said. He wondered exactly how Sophie had expressed what he'd asked her to put across. He'd have liked to have had a word with her first, but Lauren had intercepted him.

Win put her glass down on the table a little unsteadily, watching her hand do this as though it belonged to somebody else. 'You really think you might have a future together?'

'It might be worth a try,' he said, trying to sound unconcerned, even happy. 'I'll always love her, Win; I told you that. I thought she felt quite differently, but, as you've obviously heard, apparently not. We might have a chance of finding some happiness together. That can't be so terrible, can it?'

'Yes, it can,' Win said, still looking at her own hand, which was holding the glass as though securing it to the table. She looked up at him again. 'It can't happen, Alban. It can't be allowed to happen. I won't let it happen.'

He shook his head. 'I'm sorry, Win, but you can't really stop us.'

She looked at him and he saw, to his astonishment, that she was crying. A couple of tears had filled her eyes, glinting in the firelight. One tear began to flow down the side of her nose. She either somehow hadn't noticed or didn't care because she made no attempt to wipe the tears away.

'Will you, please, just take my word that this can't happen?'

'No,' he said, as softly as he could. Why the hell was she crying? Jesus, he'd dreamed of reducing the old bat to tears for a couple of decades but now that she was actually blubbing in front of him he felt awkward and disturbed and just wanted her to stop. Still, this was what he'd planned, wasn't it? 'No, I'm afraid you can't stop us this time, Win. We're both adults. We'll take this as far as we please and there's not a great deal you can do to get in our way.'

Win nodded. One of the tears had reached the end of her nose and hung there, bobbing as she nodded, a tiny droplet reflecting the firelight. He wanted her to wipe it away, or he wanted to do it himself. Could you get so old and insensitive that you didn't know you were crying and couldn't feel there was a teardrop hanging off your nose?

'The one thing you and Sophie can never do is have children,' Win said quietly.

He frowned. He allowed a small sort of part-laugh into his breath as he said, 'Well, Win, we may be getting a little ahead of ourselves here, but I think we'll be the judges of that.'

He opened his sporran. He had a handkerchief in here. He'd offer it to her; anything to get rid of that damn stupid tear hanging like snot off the old girl's nose. She was probably leaving it there as a prop, as a piece of stage management. A lot of men were completely useless in the face of a woman crying. He wasn't one of them.

'The reason that you can't have children with Sophie is that you two are more closely related than you know, Alban.'

He was still looking in his sporran for the handkerchief. He looked up. 'What?' he asked.

'Your father – Andrew, Andrew McGill – is not your biological father,' Win told him, her voice small and tired-sounding.

He was aware of having frozen. One hand held the sporran open, the other was poised inside. What? What had she just said?

'They've both been good parents to you, Alban, but neither of them is your real parent. Not Leah – you know that. But not Andrew either.'

His hands were shaking. He put them together on his lap, clasped them. 'So who the hell is then?' he asked.

'Blake is,' Win said, her voice going out like a sigh between them. 'Blake. He's your real father, your biological father.'

'*What?*' he exclaimed. '*Blake?*'

'Please keep your voice down,' Win said, seeming to collapse in on herself. She reached for the glass of whisky again but her hand didn't seem to be able to lift it. She looked down at it, seemingly forgetting about him.

'Blake?' he said, sitting forward. 'That's—' he began, then sat back again. Blake? Blake was his fucking *father*? That was insane. He sat forward once more. 'How? But he—are you saying—? So is Irene—?'

380

'Irene was your mother. Blake is your father.' Win sounded infinitely tired. She continued looking at the hand, seemingly trying and failing to lift her whisky glass. 'They were lovers, very briefly, in London, after she'd met Andrew. I wish I could tell you it was rape, which might sound like a terrible thing to say, but . . . Nevertheless. It wasn't, as far as we know. Blake didn't rape his own sister, he seduced her. She was at least partially willing, at the time. Though she did come to regret it.' She looked up into his eyes. 'Well, obviously.'

That bit came out strongly. Her voice found some extra strength for that. He shivered, even in the heat of the fire, head swimming as he suddenly saw his recurring dream again. Gone these last few weeks, not even disturbing his sleep while he'd been staying here at Garbadale – he'd been worried that it would – now it flashbacked through him. Irene taking the coat from the cloakroom and walking out of the house, ignoring his dream-self, leaving him, walking down through the gardens to the dark loch and collecting stones as she went and walking out into the waters and drowning.

'That's crazy,' he heard himself tell her. 'You can't know that.'

'It's the real reason Blake was thrown out of the family and the firm. It's why we exiled him, why he fetched up in Hong Kong. He wasn't embezzling anything, but he was guilty of incest. The money that went missing was the money we gave him to start a new life out there. Our accountants redated the books. They understood.'

'But Andy—' he began, hearing a weird roaring noise in his ears. Jeez, and now he was getting tunnel vision; he might be about to black out. This was madness. This couldn't be true. He just didn't believe it. Apart from anything else, Andy had said Irene was still a virgin when they first went to bed . . . But that didn't mean anything. Win had just said they became lovers after Irene and Andy met. But it still couldn't be true.

'For God's sake, Alban,' Win said, sounding angry now, though her voice was still frail, 'that's why Irene tried to kill herself in London. That's why she walked out in front of that bus.' Win had

381

tipped forwards in her seat and now sat, shaking slightly, her fierce, sharp little gaze directed straight at him. 'Just the shame would be sufficient, you might think, but as though that wasn't enough she was terrified she was carrying some inbred monster. Don't you understand?' Win fell back into the seat. 'Then you were born and at least you were healthy and whole, but the guilt was still there. Andy married her knowing it was – knowing you were – somebody else's. As far as I know she never told him who the real father was. I'd suggest you don't tell him either.'

He sat up in his seat, tried to control his breathing. He was not going to do anything as ridiculous as faint. This was nonsense, impossible, absurd. This was just an evil old woman trying anything to stop him being happy for some sick reason of her own. 'I don't believe you,' he told her.

'Well, you will,' Win said, finally succeeding in grasping her whisky glass and bringing it carefully to her lips. 'You will be prepared to believe a DNA test, I take it?' she said, and drank.

Christ.

'I suppose so. Yes. Yeah, I'll believe it. Just tell me when and where I'll have to—'

'Oh, it's already been done,' Win said, with a kind of tired contempt.

'What the hell are you talking about?'

'You went to see Haydn in Paris that time, remember?'

Paris. Haydn. His special-agent-for-the-firm days, the night out in Paris and the beautiful – oh, fuck.

He stared at her. Something in the fire collapsed and a new cave of fire was revealed, sending sparks flying up into the darkness in an orange curve and causing a few brief flames to lick against the remaining scree slope of crushed coal. His mouth was open. He swallowed, cleared his throat and said, 'Are you –?'

'I don't know what name the girl used,' Win said. 'I do know she was one of the most expensive whores in Paris.' Win put her glass down and smiled thinly. 'If I am going to invade a chap's privacy, at least give me credit for doing my damnedest to spoil him as it's done.' The small smile remained, wavering only slightly while she said, 'A sample was procured from Blake in a similar fashion. It was worth it to know, and the technology had become available.' She looked down at the fire, expression sad again. 'Personally, despite all of what one might call the circumstantial evidence, and two confessions, I always hoped your mother had just got her dates wrong and Andrew really was your father. I suspect he's always hoped that too. I'd even hoped that Irene had been more promiscuous, and there was a third party involved.' She looked up at him again. 'No such luck, I'm afraid. Blake, and his sister, Irene, are your parents. You are very lucky not to show any signs of inbreeding, Alban. But, do you see? The chances of two first cousins producing a child with some sign of inbreeding are about one in four. You're related to Sophie twice – as her first cousin, twice over. So the chances are at least fifty-fifty that any child of yours would be deformed or, well, just inbred in some fashion. And that, my dear,' Win said, with another great, deep sigh, 'is why we reacted the way we did when we discovered you in flagrante in the garden at Lydcombe. As though being first cousins and under-age was not enough.'

He saw. He understood. The world and his life seemed to be spinning away from him, but he was beginning to understand. He swallowed a few times until he felt able to speak.

'Who else knows?' he asked. His voice sounded hollow, even to him.

'Kennard and Kathleen,' Win said. 'They say they haven't told anybody else.'

He glanced towards where Lauren sat, near the doors.

'Not Lauren,' Win said. 'She never needed to know. She does what I ask her because she trusts me.'

He sat looking away into the darkness for a while. He felt like he was going to black out again. He was searching for flaws, running it all through his head, trying to spot something, anything, that didn't fit.

It didn't work. Everything fitted together. Guilt, attempted suicide, actual suicide, the disproportionate hysteria that had greeted him and Sophie having sex, even what had been the sheer unexpected blissfulness of his night with Kalpana – and the fact that she insisted on using condoms, of course – even some of the things Blake had said to him in Hong Kong.

Oh dear fucking God. He so did not want any of this to be true, but it made more sense than anything else he could think of. Oh dear holy shit.

'I'll arrange for the DNA test reports to be sent to you,' Win said. 'Oh; and you can have back all your love-letters and poetry – all the things you sent to Sophie. Lauren was under instructions to send them to me. I'm sorry,' she told him. 'If it's any comfort, I haven't read them. They were never opened.'

'Be careful what you wish for,' he said quietly, more to himself than to her.

'Hmm?' Win said. 'Yes. Well.'

He tried to summon up some hatred for Win, or even feel some resentment towards her. How dare she manipulate his life and Sophie's like this? And yet, she'd done what she thought was the right thing. There might still have been other ways – he'd have to think about this – but once the family had decided to keep the whole thing secret he supposed there hadn't been much choice for her. He couldn't blame her. He felt he ought to, somehow, but he couldn't.

Blake, he thought. *Blake?*

Andy and Leah would always be his parents, always be his mum and dad. But now he had another father as well as an extra mother. Well, he had long been half used to this. It was symmetrical if nothing else.

'Please say you won't . . .' Win began. She stopped and tried again. 'That you and Sophie won't—'

'No-no,' he said quickly. He held up one hand. 'No, don't worry about that. Forget all about that.'

Win let out what sounded like a long-held breath. 'Well,' she said, sighing deeply. 'That's enough from me. I'm tired out. This has been an eventful day. You'll excuse me.'

'Let me,' he said, seeing her reach for her stick, resting against the edge of the fireplace. He helped her up as Lauren came up to them, walking the length of the drawing room.

'Bedtime?' she said brightly.

'I think so,' Win said.

'Thank you, Alban,' Aunt Lauren said, letting Win take one arm. 'Might see you later.'

'Yeah, sure.'

'Don't forget to put the guard on the fire, all right?'

'Okay.'

'Good night for now.'

'Yes,' he said, 'good night.' He stood by the fire and watched the two women go. After a few seconds he said, 'Thank you.'

They both stopped. Win turned a fraction, looked at him for a moment, then just nodded. She and Lauren continued to the doors and exited. He looked down at the table and the glass she'd left. There was some whisky left in it. He picked it up and drank it. He put the fireguard in front of the fire in case it sparked.

He sat down again and stayed for a while by the fire.

He's with her as she comes down from her room, down the wide, gleaming staircase under the tall, south-facing window. She walks across the creaking parquet of the main hall towards the kitchen, and he's there as she turns into the short corridor that leads past the gunroom and the inside log store and the drying room to the cloakroom, and he watches as she stops and chooses what to wear to go outside.

Irene is dressed in brown Clark's shoes, a pair of white socks, jeans, a brown blouse and an old white roll-neck jumper. White M&S underwear. No watch or rings or other jewellery. No cash, chequebook, credit cards or any form of identification or written material.

He watches her choose the long dark coat with the poacher's pockets.

385

It's huge and almost black, its original dark green-brown weathered and worn and grimed over decades on the estate to something close to the darkness of the brown-black water in a deep loch. He stands in the gloom, surrounded by the pervasive smell of wax. Rain patters on the shallow, high-set windows. He watches her go to the coat and take it off the wooden peg.

The coat is too big for her, drowning her; she has to double back the cuffs of the sleeves twice. The shoulders droop and the hem reaches to within millimetres of the flagstones. She rubs her hands over the waxy rectangles of the flapped external pockets and looks inside at the poacher's pockets.

Then she goes through the outside door of the room, into the shining grey of the early afternoon. The door swings shut behind her, leaving him there, silent.

'Alban? Alban?' He's being shaken awake, somebody waggling his right elbow.

He opens his eyes.

He's sitting by the fire in the drawing room at Garbadale, at night. Something had happened, he knew. Something momentous, awful. Then he remembers.

Blake? *Blake?*

'Alban? Alban?' The person shaking his arm is Chay, cousin Claire's partner.

He shakes himself, tries to wake up. 'Sorry. Chay; hi. What?'

'Phone call for you.'

'What? Phone?'

'Yeah. For you.'

Alban looks at his watch. Ten past four in the morning. A phone call for him, here?

Oh no, not – VG.

'Who—?' he starts to say, then coughs. He struggles to his feet, leg muscles complaining.

Oh please no, not VG, not if it was the police, not if it was the

Mountain Rescue people or a hospital. Please, not her, not that, not after what he'd just learned. He couldn't take it. He tries to tell himself it had all been a dream but he knows it wasn't.

Please not VG. Please not.

'Who is it?' he asks Chay at last.

'Dunno. Some guy from Hong Kong.'

He follows Chay down the corridor to the office of Neil Durril, the house manager. They pass the ballroom, where a disco is playing, not especially loudly but with lots of flashing lights. Looks like about half the people are still up, though only a dozen or so are dancing, caught in frozen strobed poses in the walking glimpse he gets.

At least it's not VG, at least it's not about her. Just time difference, that's all.

'Cheers,' he says, sitting down behind Neil D's desk and lifting the receiver resting on the surface. The office is small: filing cabinets, computer, photocopier, box files everywhere. Chay closes the door behind him, leaving Alban alone.

'Hello?'

'Alban?' comes the voice. There is something flat about the way the word is said that sends a shiver down his spine.

'Blake?' he says. He can feel himself starting to choke up. This is so pathetic, but he can't help it. He tries to pull himself together all the same.

'Hello, Alban. I'm told you've . . . You know the truth.'

'Ah, well, yeah, I guess.' He doesn't know what to say. He's assuming that somebody – Lauren? Win herself? – has phoned Blake so they're all working from the same set of assumptions, but he's not sure. How can he be sure?

'I just wanted to say how sorry I am,' Blake says. His voice is reasonably clear, though Alban can tell he's using a mobile.

'That's . . . That's all right. Ah, obviously I'm a bit, well, still in shock, but—'

'I always wanted you to know, and I never wanted you to know, do you understand?'

'Yeah, I guess I do.'

'It's all too late, though, I think. It's a relief that you know, but it is unbearable as well. Don't think badly of me. I've spent all my life since regretting what happened. I'm very glad I met you. You'll – oh, sorry, hold on . . .' his voice disappears and Alban can hear the sort of broken, close-up rubbing noises you hear when people press their phones against their clothes or try to hold their phone tight to their shoulder.

'Still there?'

'Still here,' Alban says.

'The little coolie chaps are all gone. Nearly lunch-time. Lots of people and traffic . . .'

'Look, ah, Blake,' Alban says, 'I suppose – I mean, I think – we ought to meet up. If you like I can—'

'Sorry,' Blake says. Alban can hear his breath, loud against the microphone of the mobile. 'I'm afraid I don't think I could bear that. I'm so sorry.' He makes a strange noise as though he's just hurt himself. There's a noise like a sigh, then the breaking, rubbing noise again. The noise of the sigh begins to sound like the breeze, like the wind.

'Blake?'

'Sorry,' Blake says, loudly. The wind howls across his voice. 'You'll be all right.' The sound of the wind rises to a scream, and perhaps is one.

Alban starts to realise what might be happening. The hair on the back of his neck rises, then that on his scalp.

'Blake?' he shouts.

'—orry, son.'

Then just the noise of the wind.

Then a thud then nothing.

10

Who'd have thought I'd end up with Big Mifty? Life is bizarre to the max sometimes, I'm telling you. The weans still miss their dad a bit (fuck knows why mind you on account of the fact the bastard used to knock seven bells out of them), but they've taken to me and the older one, Moselle, is starting to call me Daddy, which I don't mind telling you is a bit freaky but also gives me the choke, quite frankly, and, seriously, like, I'd do anything for those kids.

So anyway. We've just went to Al's place and come back after a highly convivial evening, thank you very much. Have to say, what a house. Still in Perth like, obviously, but one of those posh one's on the far side of the river from the Inch – you know, the big long green bit like a park – just ten minutes walk from the city centre and posh as feck. Seems we're welcome any time, even the weans. And we can bring pals. House rule's are a wee number's okay but no cunt allowed liable to shoot up on the premises. Bit severe, maybe, in some ways of looking at it, but I suppose the guy has his posh neighbours to think of.

Met the girlfriend. Big Al's, I mean. Highly fucken tasty, and real nice. Big Mifty thought she was a bit up herself at first but it's just she speaks a bit hoity – well, Al does too a bit, to be fair – but they had a chat over a game of snooker and subsequent to this the Big M decided the Verushkoid is actually pretty cool. Uses a lot of big words and talks over your head a bit, but she's not trying to impress, that's just how she speaks. You canny blame a body for that.

Anyway, the blessed Al of Ban obviously has the total dotes for her and it was great seeing the man with a smile on his face, because that's what he has when she's around.

He's away a lot in Glasgow, at hers, and you'd think the way they get on and are always laughing together and touching each other and such like and generally behaving like young lover's dream that they'd do the decent thing and get shacked up the-gether, but apparently not. Quite happy with the current arrangement, we're told. Nothing weird as folk, sure enough.

So, the man's doing well. Relative or two died and left him pots of money (we always kind of knew he was a toff, though a nice one though but).

Plus he's related to those Wopulds that have that computer game 'Empire' which I used to play with Burb before his games machine got wheeched. Big Al even thought of changing his name to Wopuld, I mean like his second name, his sir-name, which would be a bit of a strange thing to do you'd think, good Scotch name, McGill, for goodnes's sake, but that was knocked on the head too and he's stuck with McGill. Think so too, what would his ma and pa have thought? (Met them one time I was out walking the dogs and stopped in for a cup of tea at Alban's place – Nice couple.)

Anyways, the guy is casting around for something to do and hasn't quite found it yet, but I'm sure he'll think of something. Currently talking about getting a place with lots of trees and a loch somewhere a bit west of here but not too far aways to start up one of those Outward Bound type places for disadvantaged city kids or something, which sounds like a heap of trouble to be putting yourself in the way of (and he's trying to rope yours truly in on it as well, which must make me as daft as him as apparently I've said yes – Oh feck).

Anyway, but; we'll see.